D0629336

From the corner of one eye, he could see a vision floating up the steps as if on a cloud. He took off his sunglasses and turned his head for a better look as the vision crossed the deck. She was taller than Mia and had dark hair worn long and free and curly. Her face was small and heart-shaped, her eyes huge and startlingly light blue. She wore a pale pink strapless dress of some sheer fabric that did nothing to hide her curves and all but foamed around her when she moved. He wondered what kind of material could do that—and he wondered who she was.

"Wow. It's true what they say." The pretty woman in the floaty dress walked directly to him and looked up at him through darkly fringed eyes.

"What's that?" he asked, and found his mouth had gone unexpectedly dry.

"All you Shields guys *do* look alike."

Mia laughed. "Grady, I want you to meet Vanessa Keaton, Beck's sister, and a very dear friend of mine. Ness, this is my brother Grady."

He was surprised by her strength. "Nice grip."

"Thanks."

"Ness owns a shop here in St. Dennis," Mia told him. "I'm a frequent and happy patron."

"What do you sell?" he asked.

"Girlie things. Froufrou stuff. Clothes and bags and jewelry." She took a sip from her glass that held some fruity-looking drink, something that looked sweet and syrupy. Grady never understood why anyone would want to drink one of those things.

"Nothing a cowboy would be interested in," Vanessa added.

ALSO BY MARIAH STEWART

Acts of Mercy
Cry Mercy
Mercy Street

Forgotten

Last Breath
Last Words
Last Look

Final Truth
Dark Truth
Hard Truth
Cold Truth

Dead End
Dead Even
Dead Certain
Dead Wrong

Until Dark
The President's Daughter

Coming Home

The Chesapeake Diaries

MARIAH STEWART

BALLANTINE BOOKS • NEW YORK

Copyright © 2010 by Marti Robb
Excerpt from *Home Again* copyright © 2010 by Marti Robb

All rights reserved.

Published in the United States by Ballantine Books, an imprint of The Random House Publishing Group, a division of Random House, Inc., New York.

BALLANTINE and colophon are trademarks of Random House, Inc.

This book contains an excerpt from the forthcoming mass market edition of *Home Again* by Mariah Stewart. This excerpt has been set for this edition only and may not reflect the final content of the forthcoming edition.

ISBN 978-1-61664-301-0

Cover design: Scott Biel

Printed in the United States of America

For my dad and my brother—who both passed on in the last months of 2009, and who are loved and missed every day. And for Elliot, whose birth reminds us that life does indeed go on, and that the chain remains unbroken.

Many thanks to:

Those incredible folks at Ballantine Books for their support, encouragement, and enthusiasm—Linda Marrow, Libby McGuire, Scott Shannon, Kim Hovey—and Kate Collins, my fabulous editor, whose guidance has made every one of my books better; Scott Biel, for coming up with the beautiful covers that are *so right* for these stories; and last but not least—the long-suffering production staff.

The lovely Grace Sinclair, whose winning of a drawing at Country Meadows Retirement Village in Hershey, PA, inspired a character.

Victoria Alexander, who saved me from reinventing the wheel. When I told her I wanted to write a series set in a small town filled with interesting characters on the Chesapeake, she reminded me that I already *had* a little town on the Bay filled with interesting characters (St. Dennis from *Last Words*) and I should set my new series there and write more about the characters I already had. So I did.

And as always, St. Loretta the Divine.

Coming
Home

Diary—

Whatever did we do here in St. Dennis before our little village was "discovered"? I remember a time when the first warm days of spring brought buds and blooms, not tourists and day-trippers, the likes of which we get these days. But no complaints! Thanks to our visitors, St. Dennis has had a rebirth in every sense. From the shops on Charles Street to the Realtors, just about everyone in town has benefited from the "new" St. Dennis. What with the monthly special attractions over the winter to tide us over till the real season begins once again in May, every business in town is faring quite well. Lord knows my little newspaper would have folded long ago if the local merchants hadn't kept advertising twelve months each year. And the Inn has certainly prospered—my son was saying just the other day that he's had to add to his off-season housekeeping and kitchen staff for the first time since he took over from Daniel and me. Good news indeed!

Aren't we lucky to have such a pretty town to show off? And I hear the Chamber of Commerce has been busy organizing even more events for the new season! Lord give me strength to keep up with it all!

—Grace

Chapter 1

At 6:02 p.m. on a Tuesday evening, Vanessa Keaton turned the key in the back door lock of her sweet little boutique on Charles Street and flicked off the lights. Foot traffic had been scarce, and would be, she knew, for another two weeks, at least until the St. Dennis Secret Garden Tour brought the first of the serious visitors to town. And that was just fine with her. Once the tourist season began in earnest, there would be fewer opportunities for dinners with friends or for closing early to enjoy slow walks through the town she had come to call her own.

She turned the dead bolt on the door leading down into the basement, then let herself out through the front and locked that door behind her as well. She paused to take a deep breath of the spring fragrance which she found unique to St. Dennis: salt from the Bay mixed with the scent of the hyacinths, daffodils, and early tulips planted in the wooden barrels— compliments of the garden club—that stood outside each of the shops along Charles Street. The very colors of the flowers said spring to her: purples and pinks, yellows and whites. Just to see them made her smile.

She stepped back to take a good long look at the window she'd spent most of the day designing. Was it too early to display the tennis whites and the pastels that many of the local ladies liked to sport while golfing at the new country club outside of town? Maybe she should move those items to the smaller windows on the side of the shop, and dress her mannequins in something other than sportswear. Maybe those pretty cocktail dresses she got in from New York last week, and maybe a few of those darling evening bags from that designer she found in Cape May over the winter.

The promise of warm weather put a bounce in her step, and as she crossed the street, visions of all the new items she'd recently ordered for Bling danced in her head.

"Step lively there, miss," the driver of the car that had stopped to let her cross called out. "Or I'll have to arrest you for jaywalking."

"Oh, you . . ." Vanessa laughed. "Why aren't you out chasing bank robbers or car thieves?"

"There hasn't been a bank robbed in St. Dennis for as long as I've lived here." Gabriel Beck—chief of police and Vanessa's half brother—pulled his car to the side of the road and activated his flashing lights. "And the last report of a stolen car we received turned out to be Wes Taylor's fifteen-year-old son sneaking out in the middle of the night to see his girlfriend."

"Slow day, eh, Beck?" She walked over to the car and leaned into the open passenger-side window.

"Just another day in paradise." He hastened to add, "Not that there's anything wrong with that."

"Well, wait another few weeks. Once the tourists start pouring into town, you'll be wishing for a day like this, when you can cruise around town in your spiffy new official police-chief car and stop to chat with the locals."

"Only way to stay in touch, kiddo."

"Well, I admit I like the calm before the storm. I like to be able to close up shop at six and have the evenings to myself. I know it won't last—and I'm grateful that my shop does so well. But it's nice to have some quiet days to enjoy this glorious weather before the crowds arrive." She stood to wave to the driver of a passing car. "So where's the fiancée?"

"I dropped her off at BMI early this morning. She's on her way to Montana to see her brother." He glanced at his watch. "Actually, she should be arriving at his place anytime now."

"Is this her brother the hermit?" *The one I like to think of as Mountain Man?*

Beck nodded. "She's hoping to talk him into walking her down the aisle."

"Your wedding's in five weeks." Vanessa frowned. "Isn't she cutting it a bit close?"

"She already asked her other brother, Andy, and he's on board. But she wants them both to give her away, since their dad died last year."

"Well, I wish her luck with that."

"Yeah, me, too. I offered to go with her, but she thought she'd have a better chance on her own. Mia doesn't think he's left his place for any length of time since their dad's funeral. We'll see." He didn't appear optimistic. "So where are you off to now?"

"I'm meeting Steffie for dinner."

"I don't think she's closed up yet. There was a group in town this afternoon for a lecture over at the Historical Society. From the crowd gathered outside Steffie's, I'd say they all stopped at her place for ice cream before getting back on their bus."

"Thanks for the tip. I'll walk on down and see if I can give her a hand."

"You just want ice cream," he teased, and put the car in drive.

"You know what I always say." She stepped back onto the curb. "Eat dessert first."

She waved good-bye as he pulled away, and glanced back at Bling, the front window dressing still on her mind. She mentally slapped herself on the forehead. *Duh.* The display should reflect the upcoming wedding. Pretty dresses and shoes to wear to the event. Flowers— maybe some terra-cotta pots planted with something colorful across the front of the window. Pansies, maybe. Vases of budding flowering cherry in the cor- ners. Lots of white chiffon, puffed like clouds . . .

It was less than a ten-minute walk from Bling to Steffie Wyler's ice-cream shop. Her arms swinging, Vanessa strolled along, marveling, as she always did, at the twists and turns her life had taken since she first arrived in St. Dennis. It was hard to believe that just three short years ago, she'd been destitute and ex- hausted mentally and physically from the stress of re- moving herself from a marriage that had started to go bad even before the petals had begun to drop from the yellow roses she'd carried on her wedding day.

Even now, the mere sight of yellow roses could make her knees go weak.

That was then, she reminded herself sternly. *This is now. No need to go back to that place and time. Keep the focus on all the good things that have happened since I came to St. Dennis.*

Finding that she had a half brother—finding Beck—was probably the best thing that had ever happened to her. That he and his father, Hal Garrity, had welcomed her so warmly, had urged her to stay, and had offered to help her start up a business in a storefront that Hal owned just when St. Dennis was emerging as a tourist attraction . . . well, who could have foreseen all that happening?

Timing is everything, she reminded herself. *Everyone knows that.*

She waved through the window of Lola's Café at Jimmy, one of Lola's geriatric waiters, and passed Petals & Posies, the flower shop next door, where tall galvanized steel containers outside held long branches of blooming forsythia and pussy willow, and the windows held the eye with a rainbow display of cut tulips and daffodils.

Next to Petals & Posies, at the corner, was Cuppachino, where many of the townies gathered first thing in the morning for coffee, the latest gossip, and to watch the news on the big-screen TV that hung on the side wall before heading off to their respective mornings. Through the screened door, propped open to encourage the evening breeze to enter, Vanessa noticed Grace Sinclair, the owner and editor of the local weekly paper, the *St. Dennis Gazette,* at one of the front tables. She was deep in conversation with

Amelia Vandergrift, the president of the garden club. Gathering tidbits for a piece on the upcoming tour, no doubt, to remind everyone to buy tickets to the event. Vanessa considered Grace, a white-haired septuagenarian with unlimited energy who knew everyone and everything, the town's number one cheerleader. Secretly, Vanessa attributed half of what she'd learned about St. Dennis to Hal, and the other half to Grace Sinclair's weekly editorials about the community.

She rounded the corner of Charles and Kelly's Point Road, and moments later, passed the municipal building, with its new wing that housed the police department. She noted that Beck's car had not yet returned to its designated parking space.

Probably out doing what he does best, she mused. *Reassuring the locals that all is just skippy in St. Dennis.*

At the end of the road, right where it T'd into the wooden boardwalk that ran next to the Bay, stood One Scoop or Two, the onetime crabber's shanty Steffie Wyler had turned into a charming ice-cream parlor. Seeing the crowd gathered around the tables out front of the small structure, Vanessa quickened her step. She excused herself to those patrons waiting patiently in line, smiling as she walked around them and between the two freezer cases to grab an apron off the pegs that hung behind the cash register.

"I can help the next person in line," Vanessa announced. She slipped on a pair of thin, clear plastic gloves as a pleasant white-haired gentleman stepped up to place his order.

"I owe you big-time, babe," Steffie whispered in Vanessa's ear on her way to the cash register.

"Yes, you do. And you'll pay up." Vanessa smiled and turned to the customer. "Sir, did you want the blackberry or the chocolate on the bottom?"

Thirty minutes and four dozen customers later, the crowd had been served and the last cone dipped. When the buses departed, Steffie sank into a chair at one of the small tables that stood along the outside wall.

"Got caught shorthanded, eh?" Vanessa scooped a small ball of rum raisin into a paper cup and took the seat opposite Steffie.

"Did I ever," Steffie groaned. "Who knew that the lectures at the Historical Society would be so popular, or that they'd start so early in the season?"

"Maybe you should get a copy of their schedule."

Steffie rolled her eyes. "I can't believe I didn't think of that sooner."

"Well, it's the first year that they've invited groups from other communities to come," Vanessa reminded her. "Who could have guessed they'd have such a turnout? What was the topic, do you know?"

"No. And at this point, I don't care." Steffie pulled a nearby chair closer and rested her feet on the seat. "Any other day of the week and I'd have had Taffy Ellis with me, but she had a meeting with her prom committee after school and wouldn't have gotten here until after five. I didn't bother calling anyone else in because I figured I could handle things for an hour on my own."

"You probably should always have someone else here with you," Vanessa pointed out. "I don't think you should be here alone."

"This from someone whose only regular employee doesn't start until Memorial Day? And that one part-time?"

"I'm up on Charles Street and have shops on both sides and a busy restaurant directly across the street. You're down here with a very dark, large parking lot on one side and the Bay on the other. Who knows who could be lurking around here after dark?"

"Well, thanks a heap for putting that in my head."

"Seriously, haven't you ever stopped to think about how isolated you are down here?"

"Not until now." Steffie glared at her pointedly. "But you're forgetting that our fine police department is just a stone's throw down the lane there, right across from the parking lot."

"Not close enough to hear you scream."

"*Au contraire, mon amie.* I have had occasion to scream, and none other than the chief himself showed up."

"I don't remember that." Vanessa frowned. "When was that? What happened?"

"Before you moved here, while I was first renovating this place. I came in one morning and there were bats flying around."

"That would freak me out, too." Vanessa shuddered at the thought. "So did Beck chase them out?"

"Yeah. He opened the windows and they all took off." Steffie fell silent for a moment. "So I guess he's really getting married."

"He is."

Steffie placed both hands over her heart. "Heavy sigh."

Vanessa laughed. "Stef, you would not have been

happy with Beck. If that was going to work out, it would have while you were dating him. As I recall, neither of you really seemed to look back once you stopped seeing each other."

"True enough. But still . . ." Steffie got up and went behind the counter. "Want something else while I'm back here?"

Vanessa held up her empty ice-cream bowl. "I'll take a dabble of cherry vanilla since you're offering."

"You really are an ice-cream hound, aren't you?" Steffie opened the display case and scooped ice cream into another paper cup and handed it to her friend when she returned to the table.

"Thank you." Vanessa smiled and dug in. "You're not having any?"

Steffie held up a bottle of water. "Bathing-suit season is six weeks away. Less, if we get a hot spell near the end of May. I don't walk as much as you do. You're lucky that you live closer to the center of town. I'm out near the point, and that's too far a walk since I run late just about every day. Plus, let us not forget that I make my own ice cream, which means I have to taste-test it as I go along. Believe it or not—and this goes against everything I've ever been told—calories you ingest as part of your job do count."

Steffie dropped into her chair. "So, Mia asked you to be in the wedding?"

Vanessa nodded. "Bridesmaid."

"Any chance I'm on the invitation list?"

"Why wouldn't you be?"

Steffie made a face. "Hello? Old girlfriend?"

Vanessa waved her hand to dismiss the thought. "You're an old friend. Your brother went to high school with Beck and your dad grew up with Hal. That trumps whatever came after."

"Just thought I'd check. I hadn't seen an invitation."

"They're just going out. Since they decided to move the date from June, they're a few weeks off the normal schedule."

"So who else is in the wedding party?"

"Mia's brother Andy's wife, Dorsey, is the other bridesmaid, and the matron of honor is a friend of Mia's from when she was in the FBI. She wants both of her brothers to walk her down the aisle, since their dad died last year. Andy's on board, but she had to fly to Montana to try to talk the other one into coming. Beck took her to the airport this morning."

"I heard the one in Montana is, like, a recluse or something. Barbara and Nita were talking about it in the coffee shop. And they said that there was another brother who had been in the FBI, too, but he was, like, a really creepy guy, into all kinds of really bad stuff."

Vanessa shrugged. "I don't really know. Mia doesn't talk about him, and I don't ask."

"Nice family your brother's marrying into." Steffie tilted her head back and took a long drink of water.

Vanessa glared.

Steffie shrugged. "I'm just saying."

"I've met most of the others, and they're all really nice."

"What happened to the other brother? The creepy one?"

"Oh. Brendan." Vanessa nodded. "All I know is that he's dead, and everyone's okay with that."

"Maybe the one from Montana's hot." Steffie wiggled her eyebrows. "It could make for an interesting day."

"I've met Andy, and I have to say, he is really cute. Mia said once that all the guys in her family look alike, so Mountain Man probably is pretty cute, too. But I'm thinking he's gotta be strange, living by himself all this time. So thanks, but no thanks."

"So what? You've done strange before."

"That's exactly my point. I've met so many guys with issues that I'm starting to believe there's no other kind. I don't care how hot the hermit is. I'm done with all that." She shook her head. "Uh-uh. Give me boring and normal, if you give me anything at all. No baggage, no issues, no drama."

"Doesn't sound like much fun to me."

"I've had fun enough to last a lifetime. If there is a next guy—and I'm not sure I will ever want another one for any length of time and for anything other than occasional sex—he's going to be excruciatingly bland." She held up her empty ice-cream cup. "Vanilla, not rum raisin. Someone who washes the car in the driveway on Saturday morning and who rakes the leaves in the backyard in the fall and reads the newspaper at the breakfast table. He's going to be one of those guys whose idea of a good time is watching a movie at home with a bowl of popcorn in one hand and me in the other."

Steffie rolled her eyes.

"I can't believe I'm hearing this. You've just described my sister's excruciatingly dull life, and it terrifies me to think that someday I could end up like that. It's my worst nightmare."

"Which nicely explains your commitment phobia."

"Don't knock it, since you obviously haven't tried it."

"That was a low blow, Stef."

"Sorry. Really. Damn. I *am* sorry." Steffie looked contrite. "Give me a minute to remove my feet from my mouth."

"It's okay. It's true. At least, it was true, once upon a time. But two really bad marriages have cured me of all that." She finished the last of the ice cream and licked the spoon clean. "Anyway, like I said, Mountain Man is probably as weird as they come after living like a hermit for a couple of years, so it doesn't matter how hot he is. I'll be my usual sweet and pleasant self at the wedding, because he's Mia's brother, but if what she's said about him being antisocial is true, he'll be on a plane back to Montana before his sister even tosses her bouquet. And that's just skippy with me."

"Well, if he gets bored and lonely while he's in St. Dennis, you can send him my way." Steffie lowered her feet to the floor and wearily pushed herself up from the chair. "Do you mind if we do dinner at Captain Walt's tonight? I'm not really dressed for Lola's and I'm too tired to go home to change."

"Walt's is fine. I love their broiled seafood platter." Vanessa stood and gathered the paper cups, napkins, and plastic spoons and tossed them in the trash near the front door, all thoughts of the potentially hot guy already replaced by visions of a few broiled scallops, a piece of rockfish, and one of Walt's famous jumbo lump crab cakes.

Chapter 2

From the top of the ridge, Grady Shields reined in the chestnut mare and watched an unfamiliar Jeep pull all the way up his driveway and park near the barn. He unsnapped his binoculars from the saddlebag and raised them to his eyes, corrected the focus, then smiled broadly when he recognized his unexpected visitor. He urged the horse down the path, but halfway to the bottom of the hill, he froze in the saddle, his smile fading slowly as he recalled the last time she'd come unannounced.

A knot in his stomach, he followed the path to the bottom of the hill and crossed the field to the paddock area next to the barn.

"Gray!" Mia shouted joyfully. As he swung down from the saddle, she jumped into his arms, startling the horse.

One hand managed to hold on to the spooked animal while the other hugged his sister, in spite of his anxiously pounding heart. If someone had died, would she be so happy?

"Don't you look all Marlboro Man?" she teased. "You've gone totally cowboy."

"Well, when in Rome . . ." He removed the wide-brimmed hat from his head and placed it on hers. It slid down onto her forehead.

"Wow, I almost forgot that you have such a view here." She adjusted the hat and looked past him to the hills beyond. "And you have a horse!"

She stretched a hand out to stroke the animal's neck.

"The view is mine, but the horse is not. I rent out the paddock area to some neighbors. The horse belongs to their son, who's away at school for another two weeks, so Chance here and I keep each other company most afternoons. Right, girl?" He patted the horse affectionately, then asked cautiously, "So. Is everything all right at home? Everyone's okay?"

"Everyone's fine. Everything is better than fine."

"Good." He sighed his relief. "When I saw you, I wondered if maybe . . . at first I was afraid . . ."

He left the thought unfinished.

"Afraid? Why afraid?" Mia paused midsentence. "Oh. You're thinking of when Dad died and Andy and I came to tell you?"

He nodded.

"This time the news is all good." She held up her left hand and wiggled her ring finger. "Gray, I'm getting married."

"You and the cop . . . ?"

"Beck. You met him at Dad's funeral."

"I remember. He seemed like a nice enough guy." He took her hand and turned it to him. "That's a really pretty ring, Mia. Congratulations."

"Thanks, Gray. He's a great guy. The best." Grady couldn't help but see that her face glowed.

"You could have called me, you know. You didn't

have to make the trip all the way out here to tell me you were engaged." He looped the horse's reins over the fence, wondering what was coming next. "Not that I'm not happy to see you."

"I needed to ask you something, and I wanted to ask you in person."

"Uh-oh," he teased. "When your little sister flies three-quarters of the way across the country to ask you something, you know it's something big."

"It *is* big." Mia became very solemn. She followed him to the fence. "I want you to walk me down the aisle at my wedding, you and Andy. I want you both to give me away."

He fell silent and unhooked the saddle's girth.

"Gray?"

"Mia, I . . ." He struggled with his words. How to explain . . . ?

"I know," she said softly. "I know you hate to come back. I know you hate to be away from here. I know that—"

"It's not so much that I *hate* to go back, Mia. It's because I've made a life for myself here." He slid the saddle from the horse's back and went past her through the open barn door.

Mia grabbed the horse's reins and followed behind him, leading the mare.

"I know you feel guilty about Melissa. I know you feel that it's your fault that she died," Mia told him.

He swung the saddle onto a rail and took the horse from her and led it to a stall.

"We all know you stay here because—" She trailed behind him.

"Stop right there." One hand on the stall door, he

looked over his shoulder at her. "You only think you know."

"Okay, then, explain it to me."

"I put the blame for Missy's death squarely where it belongs: on Brendan. I don't feel guilty about her dying because I refuse to take on his guilt for him."

"Well, if it's not guilt that keeps you here," she asked bluntly, "why do you stay here by yourself?"

"Like I said, I've made a life for myself here."

"You have a life back with us. You could come back home."

"Come back to do what?"

"The boss asks about you all the time. He'd love to have you back at the Bureau."

Grady nodded. He'd heard from John Mancini numerous times. "I know. He's been in touch."

"What do you tell him?"

"I tell him that I'm probably done with the FBI. It just doesn't mean what it used to mean, Mia. At least, not to me." He turned back to the horse and guided her into her stall.

This was something else he couldn't explain. The Bureau had been his life before Melissa's murder, but her death was so closely connected to that job and the people there that he couldn't just go back as if nothing had happened.

He walked past Mia to a deep sink inside the door. He grabbed a bucket from under the sink and proceeded to fill it from the tap. When the bucket was filled, he returned to the stall and poured the water into the trough.

"What do you do here that you couldn't do back home?" Mia had followed as far as the stall door.

Without waiting for his answer, she went on: "How do you spend your time if you don't work? You just sit around and watch TV at night?" She paused. "You do get television up here, right?"

"Cute. Since you ask, at night, I read. I watch movies. And yes, sometimes at night I do watch TV." Amused by her assumptions, he tried to keep from smiling. "I do the same thing I'd do if I were anyplace else."

"Except that here, you do it alone."

"Solitude's not all that bad."

"Have you made any friends?"

"I've gotten to know some of the neighbors, sure. And a couple of people in town. I see folks. It's not like I lock myself in the house all day, Mia."

"Don't you get lonely?" she persisted.

"Not so much. Like I said, I have things to do." He removed the horse's bridle and looped it over his shoulder.

He'd finished tending to the mare, so he came out of the stall and closed the half door. He walked out of the barn and toward the house, his sister quickening her steps to keep up. He went directly to the kitchen sink to wash his hands. When he finished, he reached for a towel.

He finished drying his hands, then draped the towel over the dish drainer on the counter. "When is your wedding?"

"It's in five weeks."

"I'll be there."

She hugged him from behind. "Thank you, Gray. Thank you so much. I can't tell you how much this means to me, to have you and Andy there with me."

"I couldn't *not* be there for you, kiddo." He smiled. He never would have let her down. "I'll check the airlines, see when the flights are, and I'll—"

"Oh, I already did all that." Suddenly all business, Mia sat her bag on the kitchen table and opened it. "Here's the itinerary and the schedule for the week."

"The week?" He stared at her as if he hadn't heard correctly. "It's going to take a whole *week* for you to get married?"

"Well, sure. You're going to need to be fitted for your tux." Her eyes twinkled. "Oh, sure, the tux might be at odds with your new rugged Wild West look, but hey, it's my wedding. Maybe you could even shave."

He laughed and fingered the week's growth on his face. "Maybe I could."

"Andy said you're the same size, so he'll order your tux for you, but you're still going to have to go into Annapolis—that's where the men's store is—and make sure the sleeves are right, that sort of thing. The guy in the store said you needed to do that by Monday at the latest in case they need to make any alterations. There's a rehearsal and then a rehearsal dinner on Thursday evening instead of Friday because the minister already committed to something else on Friday night. Oh, and the bachelor party is actually going to be on Tuesday night, because Beck has to work most of that week and the weekend before, so . . ."

Grady glanced down at the schedule. There was something filled in for every day of the week before the wedding.

"What's this on Friday night?" He pointed to the date.

"Oh, Andy said the two of you should do something, so you're having a dinner for the wedding party and the immediate family."

"Well, that's nice of us."

Mia laughed. "I guess if you wanted to bail on Andy, it would serve him right for not asking you first."

"Nah, I'm happy to do it. I'm guessing Andy has made the arrangements, though?"

She nodded. "It's going to be at Lola's. That's a really nice restaurant in St. Dennis."

"I guess it's too late to try to talk you into eloping."

"No way, pal. I've waited forever for the right guy, and I'm going to have one hell of a gorgeous wedding to celebrate."

"You sure, honey?" Grady asked. "You sure he's the right guy?"

"There's no doubt in my mind." Mia looked up at him and even he could not miss the stars in her eyes. "He's just . . . just the best guy I ever met. Andy agrees. I hope you think so, too, after you get to know him a little better."

"If Andy approves, I'm sure I will, too." He folded the paper she'd given him with the schedule and the flight information and placed it on the kitchen table. "I'll be there for whatever whoop-de-do you have planned for the week. Just don't expect me to hang around after the wedding."

"Why not?" Mia took a seat on one of the two oak kitchen chairs and draped her bag over the back. "Why not visit with Andy and Dorsey for a few days? I know they'd love to have you."

When he didn't answer, she didn't press, and he

was grateful. Some things just were too hard to explain, like how you weren't sure where you belonged, because your old life just didn't fit anymore. Besides, there were those *things to do*.

"It's up to you, of course. I'm just so happy that you're going to walk me down the aisle. Everyone will be happy to see you, Gray. We've all missed you."

"I'll be happy to see everyone, too." He glanced at the clock that hung over the door leading in to the dining room. "Almost dinnertime. We can go out for dinner, or I can cook."

Her eyebrows raised almost to her hairline. "I'm sorry, would you repeat that last part? It sounded like you said you could cook."

"That's what I did say."

Mia's eyes narrowed suspiciously. "Who are you and what have you done with my brother?"

He laughed good-naturedly. "When you live alone, you learn how to cook, or you eat out every night. You might have noticed, if you drove through West Priest, that there is only one restaurant there."

"Right. Sullivan's. I saw it."

"Did you stop in?"

She shook her head.

"Everything is hit-or-miss there. One day the soup might be great, but the sandwiches, not so much. Next day, might be the reverse. The guy who runs it has a problem with consistency in his kitchen. Their spotty menu aside, there's the fact that when winter hits, it hits hard and fast. There are times when you can't get into town for weeks. You have to keep supplies on hand and you need to know what to do with them."

"So you learned how to cook."

"It was that or starve. The first year I was here, I bought a freezer and a backup generator to keep things going when the power goes out."

"So what can you make?"

"I make a truly mean mac and cheese."

"Like Mom's?"

He nodded. "Maybe better."

"Let's do it."

Grady went to the refrigerator and took out a large brick of Cheddar cheese. From a cabinet he took a large bowl, a grater, and finally, a glass baking pan.

"What can I do to help?"

"You can make a salad when it gets closer to dinnertime. Meanwhile, how about a glass of wine or a beer?"

"I think I'd rather have something hot. Tea or coffee, whichever you have."

He opened another cabinet and pointed to a shelf that held both. "Take your pick."

"I think I'll go with tea." She rose and took down the box of tea. "Kettle?"

He shook his head. "I have a small pan you can boil water in."

"Good enough."

He handed her the pan and she filled it with water, then set it on the stove while he began to grate cheese.

"Are you chilly?" he asked.

Mia nodded. "A little. It's already warm back home. I didn't stop to think that it would be so much cooler here."

"We'll stay cool for another month or so." He looked up and grinned. "Summer's a short season here."

"I knew that. I just wasn't thinking."

"Let me get you a sweater." He put the grater down into the bowl. "I'll be right back."

He returned in minutes carrying a pale yellow cardigan that obviously wasn't his. He handed it to Mia. "Here you go."

"Thanks." She started to put her arm into the sleeve. "You still have Melissa's things here in the house?"

Grady nodded. "I don't know what to do with them. I can't bring myself to just throw them away."

"There must be something like Goodwill, or the Salvation Army, or a thrift store in the area."

"There is. But I don't know what to say." He picked up the grater and resumed working on the block of cheese. "I mean, do I call and say, 'Hello, my wife was murdered a few years ago and I have all these clothes of hers that I was wondering if you'd want'?"

"That's pretty much it, yeah." Mia finished putting on the sweater and buttoned it halfway up, then rolled up the sleeves. "I'd forgotten how much taller Melissa was than me."

Grady glanced over his shoulder and smiled. "You're a peanut, next to her."

An awkward silence followed. Finally, Grady said, "So tell me a little more about this cop who's marrying my sister."

"Chief of police, remember?" She unwrapped a tea bag and asked, "Cups?"

"Next cabinet to where you're standing." He pointed. "Okay, so he's chief of police. Tell me about him. What's his background? What's his family like?"

"Spoken like a true big brother." She opened the cabinet and found a mug. "Okay. Well, let's see. He's former military and he—"

"What branch?"

"Army. Special Forces." The water had begun to boil and she turned it off.

Grady nodded without turning to look at her. He'd known more than a few Delta Force veterans. He wondered if he and Beck had any friends in common. "Keep going."

"He was a cop someplace else before St. Dennis. Actually, his dad had been chief of police there and he'd recommended Beck for the job when he semi-retired."

"They let him do that?" This time Grady did turn around. "They let this guy name his own son as his successor?"

"Hey, it's a small town. His father, Hal, was—is— very highly regarded, and Beck was a good cop and had great references. He was the best candidate they had, and before you say I'm prejudiced, I heard that from someone who doesn't particularly like Beck."

"Well, I guess I can see it. Small town, he probably lived there all his life—"

"Uh-uh." She shook her head. "Beck grew up around Chicago. When he was almost fourteen, his mother brought him to live with his father." She paused to pour hot water into her mug. "I should preface that by saying that Hal didn't know he had a son with Beck's mother. She never told him. They'd fallen madly in love when she was just eighteen, but he'd gotten drafted and shipped off to Vietnam before she knew she was pregnant. She was engaged to someone else at the time, and her parents made her marry the guy she was engaged to. His mother went through with the wedding but the marriage didn't work out."

"How much of this are you making up as you go along?"

"None. I swear. From what I've heard, Beck was a very wild and uncontrollable kid from the time he was ten or twelve. Right about that time, his mom re-married. That's when she took Beck to Hal and left him there."

"Wait a minute. You mean, she just . . ."

Mia nodded. "Rang the doorbell, handed over Beck's birth certificate, and told Hal he was going to have to take things from there because she couldn't handle his son."

"And she just left?"

"Yep."

Grady checked the water for the macaroni to see if it had reached the boiling point yet.

"Doesn't sound as if he comes from a very stable background, Mia."

"Sorry, pal, but this pot is not about to call that kettle black, if you get my drift. Not after Brendan."

"You do have a point there." Brendan had shattered any illusions anyone might have had about the Shieldses being a model family.

"Anyway, Hal took Beck in and really turned him around, though I did hear from some of the people in town that Beck was a bit of a hellion when he first arrived. But Hal hung tough." She sipped her tea. "He's an amazing man."

"Hal or Beck?"

"Both of them."

"And the mom?"

"I've never met her. Beck has no contact with her at all, though I think she's tried to contact him from time to time. Birthday cards, stuff like that. And I think his sister hears from her occasionally."

"He has a sister?"

"That's the other part of the story. He never knew about her. Didn't realize his mother was pregnant when she brought him to Hal, but he realizes now that she had to have been. A couple of years ago, Vanessa—that's the sister, Vanessa Keaton—showed up in St. Dennis looking for Beck. She said her mother told her it was time she met her brother."

"So Mama's a woman who likes to keep secrets."

"Apparently."

"Will we see her at the wedding?"

"Fat chance." Mia snorted. "Beck doesn't want anything to do with her. He never even refers to her as his mom, only by her first name, Maggie. According to Vanessa, Maggie is now on husband number whatever. She's living on a sheep ranch out west here someplace."

"The phone book is in that bottom drawer"—he pointed past her—"if you want to look her up, see if she's listed. Maybe you'd want to call. Introduce yourself."

"You are such a wiseass." Mia laughed. "I'd never do that behind his back. Besides, I don't know her last name. And I think she's in one of the Dakotas, not Montana."

"But you *are* curious." He dumped the macaroni into the pot of boiling water, then set the timer.

"Damn right." She grinned.

"You sure this guy doesn't have issues that you're overlooking because you love him?"

"Positive. Beck is the most stable person I've ever known." She smiled and added, "Like I said, more stable than some of the Shieldses have been for the past few years."

"And on that note, I'll go out to your car to get your things. I'm assuming you brought a suitcase or something?"

"There's a canvas bag on the backseat."

"I'll be right back. I want to check on Chance before I get too comfortable, so I'll grab your bag while I'm out there."

"Thanks, Grady."

Mia tossed him the keys, and Grady went out through the back door. It had grown dark while they chatted, so he switched on the outside lights before crossing the yard to the barn. Once he assured himself that Chance was good for the night, he locked the barn door and retrieved Mia's bag from the Jeep.

He paused halfway to the house and listened to the night sounds: an owl in the stand of pine trees at the far side of the property, the scurrying of something through the brush near his feet. He took a deep breath, savoring the clear air, and sensed a change coming that had nothing to do with the emergent spring. He wondered how many more nights like this there'd be, when he'd be here, with his memories, in this comfortable life he'd made.

"Maybe it's time," he said to the owl as it swept over his head. "Then again . . . maybe not . . ."

He hoisted the bag—what could she have packed

for an overnight that could weigh this much?—and went back inside.

"What the hell is in this thing? I've backpacked for a week and all my gear—including my tent and food—didn't weigh this much."

"It's my stuff. You know. Clothes and products and—"

"Products?"

"You know. Hair stuff and makeup and shower gel and—"

"Never mind." He waved her off. "I'll put it in the back room."

"Great." She laughed. "Thanks."

He went through the living room and down the hall to the last door on the right. Opening the door, he swung Mia's bag onto the bed without turning on the light. The room was small and not very fancy, but it, like every other room, had been painted and refurnished after Melissa died. He'd hoped to get the smell of death out of the house, but sometimes he thought he could still detect a faint lingering whiff.

"The macaroni's almost ready," Mia told him when he returned to the kitchen. "There are only a few more minutes on the timer."

He checked the pot and nodded.

"So how's the new job?" He searched a cabinet for a large colander, found one, and placed it in the sink.

"It's all right. The guy I work for is a real tool, but other than that, it's fine. Being a county detective isn't so different from what I was doing with the Bureau. Well, without the travel, which I don't miss at all. And without the great boss and the coworkers I loved like family. Other than that . . . it's all pretty much the same."

"And you're adjusting to small-town life okay?"

"I love living in a small town, and I love living on the Chesapeake. I've learned how to sail and how to catch crabs and how to back a boat into a slip. St. Dennis is charming, the people are friendly, and the seafood is amazing. I couldn't be happier."

"No small-town drama?"

Mia laughed. "There's always drama, but it's a pretty closely knit community. Everyone knows everyone else and everyone else's business and likes to discuss it. But in a good way, for the most part. Oh, there's a few gossipy types, but you just sort of watch what you say to them. For the most part, the people in town have been wonderful to me. They've made me feel very welcome."

She stepped back while he poured the boiling water from the pot into the colander. "I think even you would like it."

"Gee, even me?" He leaned away from the steam.

"Yup. Even you."

"I'll try to keep an open mind."

They continued to chat through dinner, but by dessert, the conversation had wound down and it was clear that Mia was falling asleep. Grady pointed her in the direction of her room and went back into the kitchen to finish cleaning up before turning in.

He'd had few visitors since Mia's last trip, the one she'd made with Andy, when they came to tell him about their father's fatal heart attack. They'd only stayed the one night, the three of them having flown to Virginia the following morning to plan the funeral.

That hadn't had the feel of a visit, though. Mia coming here on her own, to ask him to walk with her at her wedding—this felt like a visit, which meant they'd share, at the very least, the next couple of meals. He hadn't wanted to ask her how long she was staying—after all, she'd just arrived. He couldn't help thinking how strange it had been to hear another voice in the house, one that wasn't on the TV or a radio.

It wasn't that he didn't want Mia there. He was happy to see her and have her company all to himself for a few days, since it was so rare that he did. He just felt a little awkward. He'd never been good at small talk, but small talk wasn't what you were supposed to make with your family. And this was Mia, his little sister. It had never been difficult to talk to her.

He finished in the kitchen and checked that the back door was locked. He turned off the lights as he made his way to his room, thinking that there had been few enough happy occasions for the Shields family over the past few years. Mia's wedding would be a time to celebrate something positive and joyous. That she wanted him to play a special part in her big day, that she'd come all this way to ask him, warmed his heart. He'd never have turned her down, even if it did mean going back into his old world for a whole week. He'd manage. He'd do his part. He'd be social. But he suspected he'd be counting the hours until he'd board the plane and retreat again to this quiet place where even the ghosts had gone silent, and where the life he'd made was nothing like the one he'd left.

Chapter 3

I REALLY appreciate you coming with me to pick up my dress," Mia said as Vanessa slid into the front passenger's seat and secured the seat belt.

"I'm happy to do it," Vanessa assured her. "Not to mention that you've given me an excuse to sit for a half hour. I took deliveries of stock all day today and had to check everything in against my orders. I didn't have a minute to myself." To make her point, she eased the seat back as far as it would go, toed off her shoes, and stretched her legs out in front of her. "I couldn't close up fast enough tonight."

"I can't believe how quickly the last few weeks have passed and how much I still have to do. For one thing, I have to get into your shop before I pack for our honeymoon. I still need something to wear for sightseeing in Italy."

"Come in tomorrow. I just got in some darling sundresses that I was going to put in the window, but I'd be happy to hold off until you can look."

"I'll be in as soon as I get home from work," Mia told her. "I hope you have something in my size."

"I brought in one of everything in your size." Vanessa grinned. "Just in case."

"You truly are a goddess," Mia told her solemnly.

"I do have my moments." Vanessa rested back against the headrest and smiled.

"I'm so glad you're coming with me. It helps to have a friend to talk to. I seem to be getting more and more nervous, the closer we get to The Day."

"Are you having second thoughts?"

"About Beck?" Mia shook her head firmly. "He's the one thing I'm not second-guessing. Everything else is stressing me out. What if the florist can't get peonies and I have to carry carnations? What if I trip going up the aisle? What if they drop the cake? What if it snows? What if—"

Vanessa burst out laughing. "Sorry, Mia. But seriously? *Snow?*"

"Miss Grace said it snowed once in May when she was a girl."

"No offense to Miss Grace, but that was probably back in the Ice Age. I doubt there's been snow that late in the season here for half a century, at least."

"Okay, good. That's good." Mia nodded. "We'll cross snow off the list."

"Olivia at Petals and Posies is doing the flowers, right?"

Mia nodded.

"So I think you can safely cross off the flowers as well. Olivia wouldn't promise you peonies if she couldn't get them."

"Good point. Right."

"As for the cake being dropped, isn't the pastry chef at the Inn doing the cake?"

"Yes."

"And the reception is right there at the Inn?"

"Yes, but—"

"I think they'll know how to get the cake from their kitchen into their ballroom. They've probably done it before. Like maybe once or twice a week for the past million years."

"Another good point." Mia nodded. "You're very good at this."

"Now, on to the tripping-up-the-aisle thing." Vanessa rolled down the window to better view the shorebirds that gathered on the tiny tufts of land surrounding the Bay Bridge. The sun had begun to set and the light dancing off the bridge momentarily dazzled her. "You were successful in talking both brothers into giving you away, correct?"

"Correct."

"One on each side, right?"

"Right." Mia's face brightened. "Oh. Right. One on each side."

"Twice the security."

"Mind if I call when the next round of anxiety strikes?"

"That's what I'm here for. You just let me know if there's anything else I can do for you."

"Well, there *is* one thing." Mia glanced over at Vanessa. "There is something that I've been wanting to ask you."

"What's that?"

"It's about my brother Grady."

Vanessa motioned with one hand for Mia to continue, trying to project *Sure, Mia, anything you need,* rather than the *uh-oh* that was causing an ice-cream-type freeze to her brain.

"Grady is such a loner, and you're so outgoing and you know everyone in St. Dennis and he's going to be here for the entire week. I was wondering if maybe you wouldn't mind taking him under your wing, so to speak. You know, sit with him at the rehearsal dinner, make him get up and dance at the reception a time or two. Maybe show him around town, give him the tour."

"Sure." Vanessa hoped her smile looked sincere so that Mia wouldn't suspect that the last thing she wanted to do at her brother's wedding was to be saddled with a reclusive stranger. "I'd be happy to."

Mia breathed a long sigh. "Thank you, Ness. I can't tell you how relieved I am. I worry so much about him, and he'll be the only one in my family who'll be without a significant other at the wedding. Everyone else is married or engaged or in a totally committed relationship. I had visions of Grady holing up in his room at the Inn and only coming out when his presence was mandatory."

"Not to worry. We'll find things for him to do." *Things a guy like him might find exciting, like, oh, picking up litter on Charles Street. Counting the gumballs in the containers on the counter at the drugstore. Watching the pedestrians cross at the corner. Cool, fun stuff like that.*

"You know, he's really a terrific guy and he's had such a hard time of things these past few years. I just hate the thought of him not having a good time, or, you know, feeling left out of things because he's by himself and—"

"Relax." Vanessa patted Mia on the arm. "He'll be fine. Cross my heart. I'm sure we can find ways to keep him busy."

I may want to slit my throat from sheer boredom before the week's over, but I will see to it that Mountain Man has a full dance card.

The bridal salon where Mia found her dress was in a newly renovated two-story house right outside of Annapolis. There was parking at the door and a hostess who showed Vanessa to a lovely white damask sofa, then served her tea and small cakes while Mia tried on her dress for the last time before taking it home. Vanessa had never seen so many beautiful and expensive designer gowns in one place before, and she couldn't stop herself from going to the racks and thumbing through the dresses. Lace, satin, satin and lace, chiffon—there were gowns for all seasons and every time of day or night, from the most casual morning ceremony to the most lavish black-tie affair. The variety alone took Vanessa's breath away. She stopped to admire a strapless gown of pure white chiffon that had huge fabric flowers trailing down the back and another at the waist in the front.

"That would be absolutely drop-dead stunning on you." A saleswoman appeared at her elbow. "Would you like to try it on?"

"No! I mean, I'm not looking for . . . that is, I'm just waiting for my brother's fiancée. She's here to pick up her gown."

"Oh, so sorry." The saleswoman smiled. "That dress is a favorite of mine, and when I saw you looking at it, I couldn't help but think how perfect it would be on you."

"Well, perhaps in another life." Vanessa backed away from the rack and returned to her seat, where she sipped her tea and nibbled on her tea cakes and fought back the waves of regret that washed over her.

"Ness, what do you think?" Mia stepped out from the dressing area. "Do you think it's all right?"

"All right?" Vanessa stood and clapped her hands in glee. "All right? It's magnificent. Perfect. You look . . . perfect. Gorgeous. We should probably add a tank of oxygen to that list of yours. My brother is going to have trouble breathing when he sees you walking up the aisle."

"Oh God, I hope so." Mia fussed with the skirt. "Otherwise, what would be the point of all this?"

"True. Now turn." Vanessa motioned with her hand, and Mia pivoted slowly. "It's perfect, Mia. Everything about it, from that soft off-the-shoulder neckline to the full skirt. And that fabric is to die for . . . silk as thin as a sheet of tissue paper." She found herself tearing up. "You are going to be one stunning bride, girl."

"Thank you," Mia whispered, a bit teary-eyed herself.

"It *is* gorgeous on her, isn't it?" The saleswoman beamed and fussed with the row of covered buttons that ran down the back of the dress. "I swear, when I see a bride in a dress that looks as if it had been designed just for her, it makes my day. And this gown was certainly made with a figure like yours in mind, Mia."

"I knew it was the one the first time I saw it." Mia smiled and turned just a bit to see the back in the three-way mirror, where she met Vanessa's eyes. "I wanted a dress that would knock Beck's socks off."

"That's the very least it will do," Vanessa assured her.

Mia returned to the dressing room to change, the saleswoman disappearing with her behind the curtain to assist. When she emerged with the gown in hand, she turned to Vanessa and said, "Are you sure you don't want to take another look at that dress? You never know . . ."

"Trust me," Vanessa told the saleswoman. "I *know*. *Never* is the operative word there."

Mia's dress was carefully slipped onto a form, then tucked into its garment bag. The saleswoman accompanied Mia and Vanessa to the car, and gently secured it in the backseat. She hugged Mia and made her promise to send pictures of the big day.

Mia slid behind the wheel and eased her new Malibu into traffic.

"For the longest time, it seemed as if the wedding would never get here. Now it's eight days away and I can't believe it's going by so quickly. I don't know how I'll get everything finished in time." Mia shook her head. "I don't know what I was thinking when I decided to bake cookies for the favors instead of buying something."

"You were thinking it was your mother's favorite cookie recipe," Vanessa reminded her, "and that would be one way of having her there with you."

"She always made them for family occasions. She always let us help, all four of us. I just don't know how we'll get them done."

"We're going to bake on Thursday next week, and

we'll box the cookies and tie pretty ribbons around them on Friday. All will be done on time, so relax."

Mia grinned sheepishly. "You're probably so tired of hearing about this wedding, the flowers and the invitations and the seating chart and the favors and everything else. Since you've been through it all yourself, I guess it's old hat to you."

"Not really." Vanessa turned her head to look out the side window. "I never really had a wedding."

"What are you talking about? You were married before." Mia frowned.

"Twice. But I never really had a *wedding,* not like what you and Beck are having," Vanessa explained. "The first time was in a Las Vegas chapel, and I wore leggings and a sweater and my bouquet of silk flowers was borrowed from the wife of the Elvis impersonator who owned the place. I had just turned eighteen. The second time I wore a short blue dress I'd bought on sale at the department store where I was working and carried some yellow roses I'd bought for myself on the way to city hall, where a judge performed a two-minute ceremony."

Vanessa watched a shadow cross Mia's face, then added, "It's all right to say it."

"Say what?" Mia hedged.

"Say that you're sorry, or, 'oh, I didn't know,' or whatever it is that you're thinking."

"I was thinking that I was sorry that neither of them were right for you," Mia admitted. "That I'm sorry that you didn't have the hoopla."

"In retrospect, it would have been wasted hoopla, since neither husband number one nor husband number two was worth it."

"Ness, I'm sorry. I wasn't thinking that all this might bring up bad memories for you."

"Oh, sweetie, those memories are there, regardless," Vanessa assured her. "Some things just never go away, you know?"

"I'm sorry," Mia repeated.

"Why be?" Vanessa forced a brightness she didn't really feel. "You have every right to be excited and happy and chatty about your wedding. For heaven's sake, Mia, you're marrying one hell of a great guy."

"I am, aren't I?"

"The best. And it's going to be a glorious spring day, and it will be the most beautiful wedding ever. Everything will be perfect."

"It will, mostly thanks to you." Mia nodded. "I can't thank you enough for all your help."

"It's nothing. I'm a party planner at heart. Besides, Beck's the only brother I have. I want his day to be wonderful."

"Maybe someday we'll get to return the favor."

"Uh-uh. Don't even think those evil thoughts. Marriage is not for me. I learned that the hard way."

"Hey, you're young, and you never know . . ."

"Trust me." Vanessa shook her head. "Been there, done that. Got the scars to prove it."

The fingers of her right hand rose, and without thinking, she traced a raised line under her shirt, one that ran from just above her left breast to her collarbone. It was only one of the many scars Vanessa bore, one of the many reminders that "bliss" didn't always follow "wedded."

*   *   *

Hal Garrity draped his baited line over the index finger of his left hand and let the heavy string drop over the side of his boat into the shallow waters of the Chesapeake. He'd opted for the old rowboat this morning, since the shallows where he preferred to crab was no place for the *Shady Lady,* his cabin cruiser. This was his favorite time of day—just as the sun rose—and his favorite pastime: sitting in the small craft that had been seasoned by many years of crabbing and had weathered many a storm, much like Hal himself.

It was early in the season, so he didn't expect to bring in as many crabs as he might in the summer months, but that didn't matter. He'd take whatever he caught into the police station and fire up a pot of water and steam those blue claws for whoever was lucky enough to be on duty at the time. The size of the catch wasn't the point of spending a few hours out here or drifting along in the nearby river. The point was having a few hours away from everyone and everything, a few hours to think about things that were on his mind. Today, he had his family on his mind.

First there was Beck. It seemed like only yesterday he'd shown up on Hal's doorstep, surly and disrespectful and about as full of attitude as a boy could be. It had taken awhile, but he'd worked it all out of him, taught the kid the things he needed to know. By the time Beck graduated from high school, pretty near all of the rough spots had been ironed out. He'd grown into one fine man, and it had given Hal no small amount of satisfaction over the years to have watched his son grow into his own. In his heart, Hal knew that it was he who'd helped mold the unruly boy into the outstanding young man, and he secretly guarded the pride he felt in the job he'd done.

He and Beck had been their own little clan for a long, long time, and that had been just fine with both of them. They understood each other, knew each other's moods and silences the way parents and children do. Then one day, there was a tentative knock on his door, and when he'd opened it, there stood the loveliest young woman. She was tall and had long dark curly hair, and he'd suspected that under all that makeup, she was probably as beautiful as one of those magazine models. They were in the midst of one of those uncommon early snowfalls, and there were flakes melting in her hair and on her eyelashes.

"Are you Hal?" she'd asked in that scared-to-death voice.

"I am," he'd told her.

"I'm Vanessa," she'd said simply, and looked up at him with the palest blue eyes, and in that moment, he'd known exactly who she was. "My mother told me it was time I met you and Beck."

"How *is* Maggie?" he'd asked as he'd opened the door to invite her in, then closed it behind her.

And with that, Hal felt his family circle was complete. He had his son, and with Vanessa's arrival, he had a daughter. Oh, he knew he wasn't her biological father, and she was already in her twenties when she showed up at his door. But he'd taken the girl into his heart, and he'd been the kind of father she'd needed, and he'd never for a moment regretted having opened his door to her. In many ways, she'd suffered from a lack of good parenting—just as her half brother had—and God knows the girl had a lot of baggage, but inside, she was as sweet a girl as Hal had ever known. As sweet as Maggie had been, when he'd first met her, before he'd gone off to war and fate had had its way with the both of them.

Ah, well. He sighed and gently raised the string in response to the slight tugging he'd felt. That milk had been spilt ages ago, and he'd long since quit crying over it. He and Maggie had each traveled their own paths in the years that followed. Hal was a man with few regrets, but he'd never looked back on his time with her without wondering what might have been. He'd loved Maggie Beck with all his heart, and he'd never loved another woman since.

The string went taut and Hal held fast with one hand and grabbed the long-handled net with the other. He peered over the side of the boat slowly, and saw the large jimmy feasting on the chicken neck he was using as bait. He lowered the net into the water and scooped up the male blue claw in one motion, then dumped it into the pot that sat on the floor near his feet. He covered the pot with the lid, and dropped the nibbled-on chicken part back into the water.

And now, Hal reflected, his circle was about to expand again. Soon he'd be welcoming another daughter into the fold. Mia Shields was about as well matched to Beck as any woman could be, in Hal's estimation. She'd been an FBI agent for a number of years before quitting and moving to St. Dennis. It had been a case that had brought her to town, but it had been Beck who had brought her back when the case was over. She quit the Bureau, applied for a criminal investigator's job with the county when the first opening appeared, and as far as Hal knew, Mia never looked back. She and Beck were cut from the same cloth, in some ways, and were different enough in others to balance nicely, Hal thought. He was looking forward to the wedding, looking forward to letting that circle continue to grow. Who knows, there could be grandkids one day.

Wouldn't that be something, he mused, and couldn't help but smile at the thought. *An old confirmed bachelor like me, a grandfather. Wouldn't that just be something . . .*

Another tug on the line, another grab for the net, another crab for the pot. This one clung tenaciously to the net, and a few minutes passed before Hal was dropping his latest catch into the pot with the others and replacing the lid. He heard a clatter of claws inside the pot and hoped they wouldn't battle to the point where they dismembered each other.

"Settle down there, boys," he told them as he slipped his string into the water.

He hunched over slightly, leaning on the arm that rested on the side of the boat. The sun was up now, though not enough to bring any real heat yet. Still, he reached into his pocket with his free hand and took out his sunglasses and put them on. The dark glasses always made him smile.

"They're so Hollywood, Hal. You look mysterious and oh so very cool in those," Vanessa had told him when she'd given them to him as a just-because present.

Well, cool he was not, he knew that, but it tickled him that she'd thought of him on one of her buying trips.

They say that a leopard can't change its spots, but

that was one girl who sure did change hers. Smart as a whip she was, smart enough to take one look around St. Dennis and figure out that the women there in town did not apply their makeup with a trowel, and did not wear their clothes tight enough to look like second skin. She knew right away that she wanted to stay and she wanted to be accepted, but she knew she'd have to adapt to fit in, and she did, without anyone even telling her. She just knew her old ways were not going to cut it here, so she washed her face, chucked most of her clothes, and settled in to her new skin like she'd been born in it, like the clothes she used to wear and the makeup she used to hide behind had been waiting all those years to be shed.

Another yank on the string and another crab for the pot. He'd have to be careful, or there'd be nothing left of those fellows. They didn't especially like being crowded, though the ice should keep them somewhat sedated.

This brother of Mia's—Grady—Hal couldn't help but wonder about him. He wasn't sure he was getting an accurate read on the boy. He'd been in the FBI for nine years, then quit and moved out full-time to Montana to the house where his wife had been murdered. Murdered on orders from their own brother, because of something to do with some dirty business the brother had been into. Vanessa jokingly referred to Grady as Mountain Man, and last night at dinner she'd begged Hal to take him out on the boat while he was here.

"Please, Hal. Take him crabbing. Or take him out to fish," she'd pleaded. "I promised Mia I'd find things to keep him busy. Almost every night of the week before the wedding, there's something planned . . . dinners or whatever. But there's nothing during the days. Could you please take him out one day? I can't promise he'll be good company, but it's so important to Mia that he not be left to sit in his room at the Inn by himself."

"Now, Ness," Hal had replied. "Any man who spent nine years in the FBI can probably find something to occupy his time if he has a mind to. And if he's anything at all like his sister, he'll be pleasant enough to be around. I'm more than happy to offer to take him out on the boat, but if he isn't inclined, I'm not going to force him."

"That's good enough for me." Vanessa had nodded. "I don't know what he's like. My guess is that he's duller than dull—I mean, let's face it, he's been living alone in the mountains for a couple of years now, so he's bound to be a dud. And he's probably fat, you know, from lack of activity. But I don't want Mia to be worrying about a thing."

Hal had patted Vanessa's hand and assured her that he'd be around to help make the loner feel part of the group.

"Well, if anyone can make this guy feel at home, it would be you," she'd said.

"We'll give it our best. Mia's family now, so whatever it takes to make her happy is what we'll do."

And with any luck, the guy will have his sea legs before too long, and we can spend a little time out on the Bay, Hal thought. He and Grady were both former law enforcement, so they'd have that at least to talk about. Hal wasn't worried about entertaining Mia's brother.

There was a clatter in the pot, and he raised the lid to take a look. One of the males was getting feisty with the others, so Hal poured a little more ice into the pot, and decided to call it a day. He settled back on the seat and positioned the oars, and started to row back toward the dock. He'd drop the crabs off at the station, then go home and take a shower. He had an appointment to have his tux fitted that afternoon, and he didn't want to be late. On his son's wedding day, he wanted to look the part not only of a proud father, but of the best man.

And wasn't that something, he thought as he rowed through the gentle waves. He was going to be the best man at his boy's wedding. Yes, sir, that was sure something else.

Chapter 4

WHERE have you been?" Mia watched her brother climb the three short steps to the deck behind Hal Garrity's house, where a party honoring the upcoming nuptials was in full swing. She had one hand on the railing, the other wrapped around a flute of champagne, and a frown on her face.

"If I'd known such a warm welcome awaited me in St. Dennis, I'd have been here sooner." Grady smiled at his sister's indignation. He couldn't help himself. She looked almost fierce. "Is this the look you save for the bad guys? 'Cause I know that I would be shaking in my shoes if you stared me down like that. Specially if you were armed."

Mia laughed in spite of herself.

"I was getting worried when I called the Inn a few hours ago and they said you hadn't checked in yet," she told him. "I thought you would have been in town long before now."

"Did I miss something?"

"Well, no," she admitted.

He leaned over and kissed her on the cheek.

"Well, then. No harm, no foul, right?"

"Right." She grudgingly nodded. "You're pardoned."

"You said Sunday; it's Sunday. The invitation from Beck's dad said four in the afternoon. It's four-twenty," he pointed out. "Some people would consider that fashionably late."

She laughed again and handed him a glass of champagne, but he waved her off.

"Cowboys don't drink champagne," he told her, tongue in cheek. "I'm going for one of those manly beers over there in the cooler."

He moved through the crowd to the cooler. His hand plunged into the ice and came out with a cold bottle. He popped off the cap and took a long drink. After the long drive he'd made that day, the beer tasted terrific.

"Gray, you remember Beck." Mia was at his elbow with her fiancé.

"I do." Grady extended his hand to the man his sister would marry. "Congratulations, Beck. I wish you all the best."

"Thanks, Grady." Beck took the proffered hand and shook it. "We're really glad you could make it."

"Nothing could have kept me away."

"Awww, Grady. That's sweet." Mia hugged him. "Now, may I assume that your room at the Inn is okay?"

"It's terrific. It faces the bay and it has a balcony. Thanks for arranging it."

"Anything to keep you happy so that you'd want to come back for a visit sometime." She poked him in the ribs. "So where the hell were you and why haven't you answered your phone for the last three days?"

"Checking up to make sure I didn't chicken out?"

"Don't change the subject. Where were you?"

"Actually, I was hiking the Grand Canyon," he told her. "And my phone wasn't picking up signals."

"You went to Arizona?" She appeared horrified. "The week before my wedding? You could have fallen down one of those gorges and—"

"No, no. There's a Grand Canyon in Pennsylvania," he said.

"Pennsylvania?" Mia frowned.

"It's one of the fifty states. Right between New Jersey and Ohio. Surely you've heard of it?"

"Ha ha."

"Anyway, they have their own Grand Canyon, upstate, right near the New York border. Some hikers I know told me about it, so I read up on it. Since I was going to be so close on this trip, I thought I'd take advantage of the opportunity and come out a few days early and see for myself."

"How was it?" Beck asked.

"Beautiful. Not as rough as some of the hikes out west, but really nice. It was more challenging in some places than I'd expected—there are a couple of steep ascents—but all in all, it was great. I enjoyed it."

"It sounds as if you've been doing a lot of hiking."

"Hiking, backpacking, camping out. Why live near the wilderness if you're not going to explore it?"

"I guess everyone needs a hobby," Mia said, "especially since you have so much time to kill."

Grady fought the urge to smirk.

"Excuse me," Beck said. "I want to run inside and see if Hal needs a hand with anything."

"Let me know if there's anything he needs me to do," Mia told him.

Beck nodded and made his way through the crowd to the back door.

"I guess you couldn't have taken that hike after the wedding?" Mia turned back to Grady.

"I have a different hike planned for after."

From the corner of one eye, he could see a vision floating up the steps as if on a cloud. He took off his sunglasses and turned his head for a better look as the vision crossed the deck. She was taller than Mia and had dark hair worn long and free and curly. Her face was small and heart-shaped, her eyes huge and star-tlingly light blue. She wore a pale pink strapless dress of some sheer fabric that did nothing to hide her curves and all but foamed around her when she moved. He wondered what kind of material could do that—and he wondered who she was.

"Wow. It's true what they say." The pretty woman in the floaty dress walked directly to him and looked up at him through darkly fringed eyes.

"What's that?" he asked, his mouth unexpectedly dry.

"All you Shields guys *do* look alike."

Mia laughed. "Grady, meet Vanessa Keaton, Beck's sister, and a very dear friend of mine. Ness, this is my brother Grady."

"I figured that out." Vanessa smiled and offered her hand, which he reached out to take.

He was surprised by her strength. "Nice grip."

"Thanks."

"Ness owns a shop here in St. Dennis," Mia told him. "I'm a frequent and happy patron."

"What do you sell?" he asked.

"Girly things. Froufrou stuff. Clothes and bags and jewelry." She took a sip from her glass that held some fruity-looking drink, something that looked sweet and syrupy. Grady never understood why anyone would want to drink one of those things.

"Nothing a cowboy would be interested in," Vanessa added.

Grady gave his sister a withering look.

"I didn't tell her to say that." Mia protested her innocence. "Really."

"Sorry." Vanessa rolled her eyes. "I just figured, you know, Montana. Ranches. Cows. Cowboys. It was a natural association for me. I hope it didn't offend you."

"No offense taken."

"You know, like most people who have never been beyond the Mississippi, all I know about the west is what I've seen on TV."

"You should come on out sometime, see for yourself."

"Maybe I'll do that. Sometime." She turned her head and waved to someone in the yard. "Excuse me, would you? I see someone I need to speak with." She flashed a smile at Grady. "I'm sure I'll see you again before the week is over."

"Like every day between now and Saturday, according to the schedule Mia sent me."

Vanessa laughed, and floated away toward the yard on a cloud of pink. Grady tried not to watch her go, but he couldn't help himself.

"She's pretty, isn't she?" he heard Mia say after Vanessa disappeared into the crowd.

"What?" He turned back to her. "Oh. Yeah."

Mia grinned with what appeared to be satisfaction, and Grady frowned. "Get that look off your face, all right? Yes, she's a pretty woman. I'm not blind, you know."

"Good," Mia said. "I'm glad you like her. 'Cause you're going to be seeing a lot of her this week, and, well, you never know."

"I said I wasn't blind." He raised the beer bottle to his lips and drained it. "I didn't say I liked her *or* that I was interested."

Over the course of the afternoon and early evening, Grady met what he figured must have been the entire population of St. Dennis. He was having trouble keeping them all straight. Was the guy over there in the khakis and the navy V-neck sweater the owner of the Inn, or the owner of the art gallery? And the fiftysomething woman with the pale blond hair pulled back in a bun—did she own the antiques shop or the bookshop? The pretty, flirty blonde with the long legs . . . was she the ice-cream parlor or the restaurant that everyone said served the best crab cakes in town? He was pretty sure that the little old lady with the white hair and bright blue eyes behind her granny glasses was Miss Grace, who owned the local paper. She'd more or less interviewed him, but whether it had been for some article about the wedding, or merely for the sake of gossip, he hadn't been sure.

Grady couldn't remember the last time he'd seen this many people in one place. Maybe his dad's funeral, but even then, they'd been spread out over several rooms in Connelly's Funeral Home.

And were all these people invited to the wedding? He couldn't help but wonder. Most of the weddings he'd gone to had been mostly family affairs. This whole let's-invite-the-entire-town thing was a totally new and foreign concept.

Then again, he reminded himself, this was a small town, and it was Beck's town. His dad—Hal, Grady recalled—had lived here all his life, except for the time he spent in the service. He and Beck probably knew the names of every man, woman, and child in St. Dennis. Which meant that, by now, Mia probably did, too. Which would explain why most of the town was at this party to kick off what he'd come to think of as the "wedding week."

Tomorrow he had to pick up his tuxedo and try it on for any alterations it might need. Tuesday night was the bachelor party—he'd heard someone mention something about dredging for oysters but he was pretty sure that was a joke. Wednesday, Hal offered to take the guys from the wedding party out on his boat, which could be fun. And on Wednesday night, there was something for Mia and her attendants—he couldn't remember what that was all about, but it didn't matter because it didn't involve him. Thursday night was the rehearsal followed by a dinner. Friday night was some get-together for the wedding party that his brother Andrew had talked him into co-hosting. Saturday would be the wedding. And come Sunday—freedom!

He thought of the backpacking and hiking trails within a three-state radius that he'd researched on the Internet. There were several Civil War battleground hikes that had caught his eye, none of them particu-

larly strenuous, but interesting for their history, and
several others that led through the Appalachian
Mountains that looked as if they could be somewhat
challenging. He hadn't set his heart on any one in
particular—though the one through Virginia's Bull
Run Mountains had stuck in his mind—so he could
be flexible. As long as he was here, he might as well
make the most of the trip. He didn't have a scheduled
hike back in Montana until the end of next week.

He grabbed another beer and made his way around
the tables that had been set up in Hal's backyard to
the one where the Shields family had gathered. Andy
was already there with his wife, Dorsey, along with
several of his cousins and their significant others:
Aiden and his wife, Mara, and Connor and his fiancée, Daria.

"I was right, wasn't I?" a voice behind him whispered in his ear. "You can't help but notice it yourself."

He looked over his shoulder and found the pale
blue eyes of Vanessa Keaton looking into his.

"Excuse me?"

"That all of you look so much alike," she explained. "You look as if you're seeing it for the first
time."

"Oh, yeah." He was taken off guard, not only by
her unexpected presence but by the softness of her
breath on the back of his neck when she'd whispered
to him. "You're right. There is a really strong family
resemblance."

"Even Mia looks like the rest of you," she went on.
"Only prettier than you guys. No offense."

"She *is* prettier than I am. Thank God. And certainly, Mia's prettier than Andy here." He pointed to his brother, who looked up at the sound of his name. "Our cousin Connor, though—I don't know if anyone's prettier than he is."

The chairs emptied as the entire group rose with a collective whoop to descend upon Grady with hugs and slaps on the back. When the greetings had concluded and everyone gravitated back to their seats, Grady turned to introduce Vanessa, but she was gone.

From time to time throughout the evening, he caught a glimpse of her in the midst of this circle or that. It was clear that she knew everyone at the party, and was not only comfortable there, but an adept conversationalist as well, enough so that she chatted with each of the guests for what appeared to be more than a "hello, how are you?" Every once in a while, he caught the sound of her laughter, and he'd instinctively turned to it.

Once or twice, he'd caught her eye, but he never managed to speak with her again. When he left the party and returned to his room at the Inn for the night, he left alone. But he took with him the image of her face and the scent that had floated lightly around her, much as her dress had done, a scent that reminded him of some flower that his mother had liked so much that she always had them in the house when they were in season but he couldn't recall their name.

Then there was the disturbing thought that—his protestations to his sister aside—he just might be more interested in Vanessa Keaton than he'd like to be.

In his mind he went back over the scraps of conversation he'd shared with her, and realized he'd learned nothing about her except that she was Beck's sister, but he'd already known that—Beck's *half sister,* he recalled Mia saying—and that she owned a shop where she sold what she called "girlie things." Well, she was certainly girlie—in the way that Mia was, anyway. They were both pretty and soft and feminine. Of course, he recalled, Mia was also a deadly shot and had been top of her class in martial arts.

He opened the door and stepped out onto the balcony and caught the salty night air, and wondered what more he might learn about Vanessa Keaton before the week was over.

"Here you go, Miss Grace." Vanessa stopped in front of the old Federal-style mansion that had tall columns reaching to the third floor. It had been updated sometime in the 1800s by one of Miss Grace's late husband's great-somethings, adding porches to the second and third floors to match the one on the ground level. "Door-to-door service."

"I appreciate the ride all the way out here, dear." The older woman sat with her purse on her lap. "I wasn't ready to leave the party when my son was. Daniel had to get the kids to bed early. It may have been a party night for us, but it's a school night for them."

"I didn't mind a bit." Vanessa smiled. "I love to come out here. I love the drive down that long lane and seeing this beautiful house sitting there with the Bay behind it. I think it was wonderful that your family turned it into an inn so that everyone could enjoy it."

"Well, it was my husband's family, not mine. But

yes, the old place makes for a fine inn. We spent many happy years here, running it, Dan and I did." She nodded as if in satisfaction for those years. "Once he was gone, I didn't mind turning it over to our son. Daniel has turned out to be an excellent innkeeper. He's made some changes that I didn't understand at first, but I bit my tongue. Turns out all that stuff—the playground, the guided nature walks, all those classes for children, the art classes, the yoga—it all made my head spin when Daniel first started talking about it, but I have to admit, it's all been very profitable. Between all those activities and the children, he keeps very busy. Barely has a minute for a life of his own." Grace stared out the window toward the Bay. "I'm sure you heard about his wife's drowning . . ."

Vanessa nodded. "I did. It happened the year before I came to St. Dennis. It was such a sad thing."

"It was a terrible tragedy." Grace sighed as she unbuckled her seat belt. "I keep wishing that Daniel would meet someone. He's too young to be alone for the rest of his life."

"Well, maybe someday the right woman will walk through those big double doors and just knock him dead," Vanessa said.

"Now that's a happy thought for me to take with me tonight." Grace reached over and squeezed Vanessa's hand, then opened the car door. "You know, I've always prided myself on being quite the matchmaker—you wouldn't believe some of the couples I've gotten together—but when it comes to my own son, I just don't seem to have the right touch."

"He'll find the right person on his own, or she'll find him," Vanessa assured her.

"Of course, you're right, dear." Grace got out of the car, but before she closed her door, she said, "I've been meaning to tell you what a terrific addition Bling is to the shopping area. You've brought in some lovely things, Vanessa. Your windows are always such a pleasure to look at. We're hoping you're planning on staying for a good long time."

"Thank you, Miss Grace. I appreciate that."

"Will we see you for morning coffee tomorrow?"

"I'll be there."

"Good. And thank you again for the ride." Grace slammed the car door and walked to the Inn's front doors.

Vanessa drove slowly down the long lane between the Inn and the main road that led back into town. It was all she could do not to shout "woo-hoo!" as she peeled out of the drive, still smiling with pleasure at Grace Sinclair's compliment.

It hadn't taken Vanessa very long to figure out that there were two St. Dennises. There was the St. Dennis of the tourists and the summer people, and there was old St. Dennis. Miss Grace was about as old St. Dennis as it was possible to be. Not just her family, the Abernathys, but the family she married into, the Sinclairs, were land-grant families, here since the earliest days. Of course, Hal's family was, too, and Vanessa was certain that this fact had guaranteed that most people in town would be polite to her, if not accepting, since Hal had claimed her as one of his. But Miss Grace had always been just a little more warm, a little more kind, than most of the others had, at the beginning, anyway. These days, things were fine for Vanessa, better than fine, actually, with just about everyone in town. But Miss Grace still somehow managed to go above the level of ordinary kindness, to make Vanessa feel as if she really did belong there.

On the drive home, she repeated the compliments.

. . . what a terrific addition Bling is . . . brought in some lovely things . . . windows always such a pleasure . . . hoping you're planning on staying for a good long time.

Thank you, Miss Grace. Yes, I'm planning on staying. There's nowhere else I'd rather be.

This is my home now, she thought as she parked in her driveway. *Everyone and everything that matters to me . . . Hal, Beck, Mia, Steffie, my shop—my beautiful little shop—my wonderful little house . . . everything I love is here in St. Dennis.*

Oh, yes, Miss Grace, I'm not going anywhere.

Diary—

Attended a lovely party on Sunday afternoon for our own Chief Beck and his beautiful bride-to-be, hosted by the father of the groom, my dear friend Hal. Nice to have met so many of the bride's relatives, all in from out of town (and all booked at the Inn for the entire week—Daniel couldn't be more pleased that Beck recommended us). Mia's people are all in the FBI, except for one brother who lives in Montana and, if talk is to be believed, is a bit of a tragic figure. The story is that he's mourning the death of his wife at the hands of <u>his very own brother</u>! Tragic indeed! That is, of course, if it's true. . . . Small-town talk being such as it is, well, who knows what the whole story—<u>the real story</u>—might be?

But I must say, for one who is supposedly grieving, he certainly seemed to be smitten with a certain young lady at the party. Not that anyone would blame him if he couldn't take his eyes off her—the young lady in question is a beauty, and a personal favorite of mine, and one who has had more than her own share of heartbreak, so they say. Nothing would please me more than to see her meet a nice young man.

So—we shall see what we shall see!

—Grace

V ANESSA was leaning on the counter next to her cash register, writing her shopping list for Thursday's bake-a-thon, when it occurred to her that 252 guests times four cookies each equaled one hell of a lot of baking between now and Saturday. She picked up the phone and dialed Mia's cell.

"I think we should start baking before Thursday," she said when Mia picked up.

"Who is this and how did you get my number?" Mia asked calmly.

"I'm the person who's trying to figure out how much lemon glaze we're going to have to make to glaze all these damned cookies. And have you figured out how many cookies we're talking about here?"

Before Mia had a chance to respond, Vanessa told her.

"One thousand and eight, that's how many."

"Divided by twelve equals . . . eighty-four dozen," Mia told her. "So we take the recipe, which makes . . . let's see, I think it was—"

"Five dozen. I have the recipe right in front of me." Vanessa bit her bottom lip. "I don't trust that to be right, though. It's only five dozen if you make them exactly the same size as the person who wrote the recipe, and that never seems to work for me."

"Want to make ninety dozen, just in case?"

There was a long silence, after which both women began to laugh.

"Sure. Ninety dozen! What the hell!" Vanessa tried to make light of the task. "What's a few dozen more?"

"It won't take any time at all with both of us baking."

"Seriously, I think you're grossly underestimating the amount of time we're going to need. Today is Tuesday. I'm thinking maybe we start tomorrow and plan to keep on baking right up to the rehearsal dinner, after which we return to our respective kitchens."

"Maybe we need to do this in teams," Mia suggested.

"That might work if we could recruit a few more bakers. Can you think of anyone else who could be talked into pitching in?"

"I can probably get Dorsey to make some," Mia thought aloud. "And my cousin Aidan's wife, Mara. She loves to bake."

"What about your friend Annie? Isn't the matron of honor supposed to help the bride out with all the last-minute details?"

"Yeah, but she's in New Mexico on a case. We're holding our breath that she gets back in time to make it to the wedding. Otherwise, you'll be bumped from bridesmaid to maid of honor."

"We'll worry about that on Saturday. Today you

need to find out if Annie has a kitchenette in her hotel room. We need all the help we can get."

"We'll be okay. I'll just ask Dorsey and Mara. Between the four of us, we should be fine."

"Maybe. That breaks it down to"—she tried to mentally compute—"roughly twenty-two dozen cookies each, give or take a dozen or so. And this is going to take a lot of flour, sugar, and butter. I think I'll call over to the Market Basket while I'm thinking of it to see if I need to make a special order. I doubt they have this much butter on hand."

"Right about now is when you get to say, 'You should have gone with the truffles.' " Mia sighed. "I guess this wasn't such a great idea."

"Of course it's a great idea. You wanted to honor your mother's memory and we're going to do exactly that. I just thought I should point out that we should not wait until Thursday to start, and that we were severely understaffed."

"If we start baking on Wednesday, they'll be stale by Saturday."

"No, they won't. We'll freeze them and put the glaze on them all on Friday. They'll be fine."

"According to the schedule you made up, on Friday we're supposed to put them in boxes and tie on those pretty ribbons."

"So we nudge the schedule a little," Vanessa said to assure herself as much as she assured Mia. "We'll get them into their little boxes and we'll get the ribbons tied on and everything will be fine."

The bell over Bling's door rang and Vanessa looked up as a woman closed the door behind her.

"I'll check with Ken at the market and get back to

you if there's a problem. Meantime, think about maybe three cookies per guest. That would eliminate about twenty dozen cookies if my seat-of-the-pants math is right. Gotta run . . ."

She hung up the phone and replaced the receiver, then moved the phone to one side of the cash register. She smiled at the potential customer.

"Welcome to Bling. May I help you find something, or are you just poking?"

"Just poking," the woman replied.

"Poke away," Vanessa told her cheerfully. "Let me know if there's something you'd like to try on, or if there's something from one of the cases you'd like a better look at."

The woman smiled tentatively.

Vanessa watched the customer without appearing to, appraising her unconsciously. The woman appeared to be in her early thirties, her hair colored light brown but not done well. Vanessa suspected that the woman had done her color herself but wasn't very skilled at it. Her makeup was a little heavier than what she normally saw on the weekday tourists, who tended to be very conservative in their dress and appearance. This woman wore a long sleeved T-shirt with a mock turtleneck, long pants just a hair too tight, and faux-leather shoes that were far from new and probably rubbed her feet uncomfortably. She carried an out-of-season straw bag, and her unpolished fingernails were chewed to the quick. There was an air of hesitancy about her, as if she had just realized that she'd entered a shop where she couldn't afford to buy anything. Vanessa was no stranger to that sort of uncertainty because she'd felt it so many times before in her old life.

And, she reminded herself, *there'd been more than one time in my life when I'd worn shoes very much like hers. I'll bet hers are just as uncomfortable as mine were.*

Vanessa didn't have to look at her own hands to know that these days, her nails were buffed and polished and kept pretty with a once-a-week appointment with a manicurist, but once upon a time, the sheer stress of her life had caused her to bite her nails down to nothing, and she'd never had time for polish.

The woman walked around the shop, her eyes darting from one item to another, but her fingers never reached out to touch any of the lovely items on display. In the way she hung her head and the wariness in her eyes, Vanessa recognized something else of the woman she herself had been, once upon a time. She'd have bet her entire week's receipts that if she pulled up the sleeves of the woman's shirt, she'd find the imprint of angry fingers bruised into her upper arms.

"It's a gorgeous day, isn't it?" Vanessa said, hoping to put the woman at ease. "I think spring is finally with us for real."

"Yes. It's real nice out."

"Those shorts on the rack right next to you are on sale," Vanessa pointed out.

The woman paused to look through them. She stopped at a pair of madras plaid, glanced at the price tag, then pretended that she hadn't blanched when she read the number.

"Are you touristing today?" Vanessa asked.

"What?" The woman frowned. "Oh. Yeah. I'm just here for the day."

"Where are you from?"

"Oh. Um . . . Baltimore." The woman averted her eyes.

"What brought you to St. Dennis?" Vanessa persisted.

"I . . . I heard it was a pretty town, so I decided to take the day and check it out."

"You heard right. It's a beautiful town. One of the nicest on the Bay." Vanessa rested an elbow on the counter and her chin in her hand. "What have you seen so far?"

"Oh, not so much yet. I saw the place down there where all the boats are parked." She waved in the general direction of the Bay. "Down near the parking lot."

"Oh, the marina. It's always fun to walk along the dock there and look at the boats. Where else have you been?"

"I had coffee across the street."

"Good choice. I have coffee there every morning."

"You do?"

Vanessa nodded, wondering why that tidbit would seem interesting. "I'm afraid I'm terribly lazy. I fall into a routine and I just stick with it."

The woman, who'd turned her attention to a pile of lightweight summer sweaters, nodded vaguely.

"Is there any particular place you want to see while you're here?" Vanessa tried to keep her customer engaged.

"Oh . . ." She appeared to think it over, then returned her attention to the sweaters. "Not really. I was just passing by and saw your window displays and thought your shop looked really cool."

"Thank you." Vanessa looked around at the little world she'd made for herself. "I think it's pretty cool."

The woman walked around the shop for a few more minutes before lingering over a summer party dress of white eyelet.

"Would you like to try that on?" Vanessa asked.

"Oh. I . . ." the woman stammered. "I don't think . . ."

"Do I have your size?" Vanessa came out from around the counter and walked toward the woman, who watched her with some curiosity. "You look as if you're . . . what, a size ten?"

She flipped through the hangers with ease.

"You're in luck. One size ten left. Here you go." She handed the hanger to the woman and pointed off to the right. "The dressing room's right through that door. If you love it, maybe I could take a little off the price, since it's your first time in St. Dennis."

"That would be really nice," the woman replied, but made no move toward the dressing room.

"Did you want to look around a little more first?"

"Oh, no. No, I'll just take this in . . ." The customer backed toward the dressing room.

"Take your time."

Vanessa strolled over to a stack of khaki shorts and straightened out the pile, then refolded some cotton T-shirts.

"How are you doing?" she called to the dressing room.

"All right."

"Does the dress fit?"

"Yes. It fits just right." She hesitated before adding, "It sure is pretty."

A few moments passed before the woman emerged from the dressing room with the dress on the hanger.

"What did you think?" Vanessa asked.

"Oh, I'm not sure," the woman told her. "Maybe I'll come back with my husband and see what he thinks."

"That's perfectly fine," Vanessa assured her. "Would you like me to put a hold on it for you? Just in case?"

"Oh, I don't know . . ."

"It's not a problem. There's absolutely no obligation. But if you decided you wanted it, I'd hate to see you disappointed if you came back and found it had been sold. What's your name? I can hold it as long as the weekend. We start to get real busy on Fridays now that the weather is getting warmer. But I'd be happy to hold it until then for you." Vanessa took the hanger and hung the dress on a stand near the counter. "What's your first name?"

"It's Candy. Candice."

"Candice, it is." Vanessa wrote on a piece of paper, which she then attached to the hanger with a straight pin. "Hold till Friday for Candice," she read the note aloud.

"Thank you," the woman said softly.

"My pleasure." Vanessa reached for the little porcelain dish near the cash register that held a stack of business cards. "Take one, in case you need to call."

The woman picked up a card and appeared to study it.

"If you don't call or stop in by noon on Friday, it'll

go back onto the floor. And if you decide you'd like it, I'll take off twenty percent."

"That's real nice of you."

She appeared about to say something else when the door opened and Steffie came in, grinning and looking like she had a tale to tell.

"It'll be in the back room if you come back. If I'm not here, just tell whoever is that Vanessa put a dress in the back for you."

"So you're Vanessa," the woman said softly.

"Yes. But anyone can get it for you if I'm not here." Vanessa smiled as she walked toward the back room, the dress over her arm. "My brother's getting married this weekend, so I'll be in and out for the next few days."

"Oh. Will the wedding be in St. Dennis?"

"Will it ever." Steffie answered for Vanessa, who'd disappeared into the back of the store. "Ness's brother is the chief of police and he knows everyone in town."

"The police chief?" Candice repeated.

"Yeah, and the woman he's marrying is a county criminal investigator, and all her brothers and cousins are FBI agents. God forbid anyone should think about committing a crime in St. Dennis over the weekend."

"God forbid," the woman agreed as Vanessa came back out to the shop floor. "Well, thank you for letting me try on the dress."

"Of course. Come back anytime." Vanessa walked her to the door and held it open for Candice to pass through. She waved good-bye from the door and closed it behind her.

"What a slow day," Vanessa complained to Steffie. "That was it as far as customers go."

Steffie glanced at her watch. "It's early yet. It's a nice, warm sunny morning. By two this afternoon, the sidewalks will be packed."

"So what's put that shit-eating grin on your face this morning?"

"Guess who I had coffee with while you were trying to make your first sale of the day?"

"I couldn't even begin to guess."

"Mountain Man."

"Oh, Grady?" Vanessa tried to appear disinterested. "Where'd you run into him?"

"Across the street at Cuppachino. He was there with Beck and the other brother who's going to be in the wedding and his wife."

"Andy. Dorsey is his wife."

"Right. And I'm here to tell you, the man is not all that dull."

"Really? Couldn't prove it by me." Vanessa refolded a stack of T-shirts. "I met him at Hal's party the other night. I wasn't impressed."

"You lie."

"No, seriously. I wasn't at all . . ."

Steffie started to laugh.

"What's so funny?" Vanessa raised an indignant eyebrow.

"Did you know that when you try to tell a lie, your eyes shift to one side?"

"You've been watching too much TV," Vanessa grumbled.

"Seriously, Ness." Still grinning, Steffie rested her

elbows on the counter. "How could you not be impressed? He's good-looking, articulate, smart, interesting—"

"You got all that over one cup of coffee?"

"And a cheese Danish."

"A Danish?" Vanessa raised an eyebrow. "What happened to the water diet you were on a few days ago?"

"This was a special occasion."

"Well, since you so obviously think this guy's got it all, I say go for it."

"Thanks, but he's not my type."

"Stef, you just finished telling me that he's—"

"He's all those things I said. He's a really nice guy. But . . ." Steffie shrugged. "No spark. Know what I mean?"

Vanessa stared at Steffie. "I'm . . . speechless."

"I know." Steffie grinned. "I could hardly believe it myself. But you know how I always know the minute I meet a guy if there's ever going to be something there or not?"

Intrigued, Vanessa nodded.

"Well . . . nothing." Steffie held up both hands. "Nada. Zilch."

"Wow. Who'd have guessed it?" Vanessa's eyes began to twinkle. "The first really hot single guy to hit St. Dennis since I moved here, and Steffie isn't feeling the love. I guess stranger things have happened. Perhaps not in my lifetime, but still . . ."

"There is an explanation."

"Do tell."

Steffie leaned over the counter. "I heard that Beck invited Wade MacGregor to the wedding and that he's coming in on Friday. And that he isn't bringing a date."

"I saw the name on the guest list, but I don't know who he is."

"He's a guy who used to pal around with my brother. He and Beck used to sail together."

"Just a guy?"

"Just *the* guy. As in, the guy I wrote about in my diary. The guy I walked three blocks out of my way every day just to go by his house. The guy who broke my heart when he took Krista Blackwell to the prom junior year."

"How about senior year?"

"I don't remember who he took his senior year, but my senior year, I wanted to ask him but my mom wouldn't let me."

"Why not?"

"Because she thought he was too old for me."

"How much older?"

"Like, four years."

"That's a lot when you're in high school, Stef. He'd have been in college already."

"He was. I invited him to my graduation party, and he came and brought me flowers." Steffie's eyes took on a dreamy look. "I made him kiss me out back near the grape arbor."

"What happened next?"

"You mean after the kiss that set the standard for the entire rest of my life and has never been duplicated?" Stef made a face. "He was outta there so fast I barely even saw him leave. Left me brokenhearted. Never wrote, never called."

"So you would want to see him again . . . why?"

"I guess just to see what I missed."

"Uh-uh. Wrong answer."

"There's a right answer?" Steffie frowned.

"Yes. The correct response would have been, 'So that he can see what *he* missed.' "

"Well, that goes without saying." Steffie fluffed up her long blond hair.

"So where's he been all these years?"

"I don't know. No one ever really seems to talk about him. Everyone talks about his sister, of course. His sister is . . . wait for it now." Steffie paused dramatically. "Dallas MacGregor."

"Dallas MacGregor, the movie star?" Vanessa's eyes widened. "I did hear that she was a local."

"Not exactly. Her great-aunt is a local, lived here all her life. Still does, even though she's like a million years old by now. Dallas used to visit a lot when she was a kid. Believe it or not, she and my brother had a thing going once upon a time. When their dad died, her mother and brother moved in with the great-aunt for a while so that Wade could go to school here. Dallas was older than Wade and she was already in college by then. She did come back in the summers, at least, until Wade finished high school and their mom moved away. You always see stuff in the magazines and newspapers about Dallas, but I never hear much of anything about Wade. I imagine someone in town knows what he's been up to. Beck must hear from him."

"I'm sure Beck knows. Want me to pump him?"

"No, thanks. He'll know why you're asking and he'll tell Wade. I'd rather ambush him." Steffie grinned.

"Well, then, have you gotten a dress yet?" Vanessa walked to the front of the shop. "Because if you haven't . . ." She pulled a silk sheath in pastel watercolors from the rack. "This little number just happens to be your size."

"Ohhh. Gorgeous! The colors . . ." Steffie reached out with both hands. "Gimme . . ."

Vanessa laughed and handed over the dress. "You know where the dressing room is."

Minutes later, Steffie stepped out wearing the dress and pronounced, "I am an absolute goddess in this dress."

"Oh, my. You certainly are." Vanessa nodded. "It's perfect on you."

Stef looked at the tag and gulped. "Think I could get the same twenty percent off that you offered the woman who just left?"

"I can do better than that. Since it's so perfect for you—and I admit I did think of you when I ordered it in—I'll give it to you at cost."

"Gasp." Steffie held a hand to her heart.

"The offer comes with strings."

"Anything. You name it. Lifetime unlimited ice cream—delivered to your door. A flavor named after you . . ."

"Loan me one of your girls to cover the shop for Saturday afternoon until closing. Nan is working for me on Thursday and most of Saturday, but her grandson is being christened on Sunday in Virginia and she needs to leave on Saturday by four. I've asked everyone I can think of. I just need someone until seven. All she'll have to do is turn off the lights and lock the front door."

"What about your cash receipts?"

"They can wait until Sunday morning."

"Don't you think that might be tempting fate? Oh, I know, there hasn't been a robbery on Charles Street in years, but still." Steffie went into the dressing room to change.

"Maybe I'll stop in after the reception."

"I'll talk to Cathy about it. She's my best counter girl. I've had her close for me several times."

"That would be worthy of a deep discount," Vanessa said. "But that raises the question of what you'll do."

"I've had several of the others close for me from time to time." Steffie emerged from behind the curtain with the dress. "But even if I have to leave the reception for a bit to close up both our shops, I'd do it in a heartbeat." She opened her bag and withdrew her wallet. "And I'd say we have a deal . . ."

It was almost dark when Vanessa locked up and walked the three blocks to her house on Cherry Street. There had been a brief shower earlier in the afternoon, and the rain had washed some of the tree pollen from the sidewalks, leaving the air clean and fresh. She inhaled deeply as she strolled along, admiring the spring flowers her neighbors had planted. The entire front yard of the small brick Colonial on the corner of Cherry and Mavis was planted in yellow and red tulips that brightened the entire block. Three houses up, the owners had planted hundreds of mixed daffodils. And farther up, one house in from the next corner, sat Vanessa's pride and joy. She never minded the walk, because she never grew tired of catching that first glimpse of her house as it came into view.

Off-white clapboard with a high slate roof, gables on each side of the second floor, and two deep porches—one front, one back—the house was a hodgepodge architecturally, but she'd fallen in love with it the minute she saw it.

"It's a bit of a bastard child, architecturally," Hamilton Forbes, the Realtor, had told her while he unlocked the front door that Saturday afternoon back in September. "I'd be hard-pressed to put a name tag on it. It's not quite Colonial, not quite Victorian, though it does have features of each. The layout suggests a bungalow, but it was built before that style became popular. It's in desperate need of updating and hasn't been painted in God knows how many years, but it's sturdy and the mechanicals are decent. The estate is leaving the contents, so you'll have furniture. Some of it is pretty good, actually, and God only knows what's in that attic. Everything has been covered since Miss Ridgeway's death."

Vanessa had barely heard a word once she'd stepped inside. There were hardwood floors and an oddly placed mantel on one of the dining room walls. White sheets covered every piece of furniture in the place. There were several bay windows and a kitchen with a real nook that overlooked the backyard. She'd all but sprinted past the Realtor to get to the second floor, where there were three good-size bedrooms and one tiny one, and one and a half baths. A door led to an attic that had thick wooden rafters and lots of dark corners in which boxes holding who knew what were stacked. She'd run back downstairs to the kitchen, and unlocked the back door. She stepped out onto the porch, her eyes sweeping across the backyard hungrily. She knew next to nothing about plants, but her mind's eye filled in the empty beds with color and the dry fishpond with water, koi, and water lilies.

She wanted the house so much she could barely breathe.

". . . been on the market for quite some time . . ." Ham had droned on, but she hardly heard him. ". . . right before her one-hundredth birthday and she—"

"What?" Vanessa had been in the kitchen again, wondering how much a new stove and refrigerator would cost.

"I said, the woman who lived here died right before her birthday. She'd have been one hundred years old, if she'd made it another three weeks."

"Was she the oldest inhabitant of St. Dennis?"

"Not by a long shot. Penny Grassi's one-hundred-and-two-year-old great-grandmother lives in the Oakes Retirement Home, and old Mr. Ivens Sr. is almost one hundred and three. I'm sure there are others I don't know about." He grinned. "We grow 'em old down here on the Bay."

"You said the house has been on the market for a long time?"

"Close to a year now."

"Why's that, do you suppose?" Before he could respond, she walked back into the dining room and asked, "Do you suppose there's a fireplace behind that wall where the mantel is?"

"I'd certainly look into that." He followed her into the room. "It sure does look like it might have been a working fireplace. Let's take a look outside, see where the chimney is."

He went out the front door, and Vanessa followed him.

"Yes, see? There's your chimney." He pointed to the side of the house where the chimney rose past the roof. "You could look into opening that up. I'd call Stan Westcott and have him take a look."

Vanessa had nodded and gone back inside to take another walk from room to room, her head spinning.

"Why did you say the house had been on the market for so long?" Before she arrived, Hal had primed her to focus on anything negative as a bargaining chip. The only negative she could think of was maybe there was a problem with the deed, or the structure, something that wasn't readily visible, because to her eye, the place was perfect.

"I started to tell you about the previous owner. Alice Ridgeway was a little . . . eccentric. She never left her house except to water her plants, maybe toss some fish food into that pond, putter around in her backyard. Never came out the front, had one of the neighbor boys mow the lawn. Of course, the pond is dry now, but at one time, she had an impressive number of koi out there."

"But what does that have to do with the house not selling?"

Ham cleared his throat. "There are some who think Miss Ridgeway never did leave."

The silence hung in the air between them for a very long moment.

"Oh." Vanessa paused. "You mean, she might still be here?"

"In spirit only."

"I see." Vanessa wandered from room to room and tried to decide if she felt something otherworldly accompanying her. "Has anyone actually seen her?"

"A few of the neighbors claim to have, but who knows?" He shrugged. "Maybe we see what we want to see."

Vanessa thought that he might be sorry to have brought it up. Still, there was that full-disclosure thing.

"What was she like?" Vanessa asked. "When she was alive, that is."

"She was . . . well, as I said, a bit eccentric. Kept to herself, always did, as I recall. She read a great deal, I remember that about her. My sister worked for the library many years ago, and would bring books to her and pick them up when she was finished with them and take them back. Brought her a new stack twice a week."

"I'm not seeing where she was so eccentric. Lots of people don't like to leave their homes." Vanessa defended the home's departed—or not—owner.

"True enough. But to the best of my knowledge, Miss Ridgeway was the only true agoraphobic in St. Dennis."

"Well, then, that gave her some distinction, didn't it?" She gazed out the kitchen window. "I wonder what she had planted in those beds."

"Well, she did have a big herb garden, and they say she liked those bug-catching plants."

"What?" Vanessa turned to face him.

"Venus flytraps, that sort of thing." He hastened to add, "But I hear she liked mint, too. Had several varieties. And as I said, she had her herbs. Those who know say she had bunches hung over the doors and some of the windows. I noticed there's some still around, here and there."

"Her version of room freshener, I suppose."

"Miss Grace could probably tell you more about it. She grew up right around the block there." He pointed out the back door toward the rear of the property. "That's the old Abernathy place right through there. You can see the back of the carriage house right beyond those trees. I believe Miss Grace's mother may have known Miss Ridgeway."

They'd already been in the house for over an hour, and there was no mistaking the fact that Ham was more than ready to leave. With great reluctance, Vanessa followed him out the door and watched him place the key back into the lockbox. She'd wanted to grab it from him so that she could stay awhile longer, but she was supposed to meet Hal and Beck at Lola's for dinner and she was already late.

She'd been almost hyperventilating by the time she reached Lola's.

"So what did you think of the old Ridgeway place, Ness?" Hal had asked after Vanessa had taken a seat at the table.

"It's so . . . perfect. Just . . . perfect." The words came out in a rush. "There's a fireplace in the living room and maybe another one in the dining room but that one's boarded up so it's tough to know for sure if there's a fireplace there or not, but there's a chimney outside so it could be." She turned to Beck and grabbed him by the arm. "It has bay windows . . . I always wanted to live in a house with bay windows.

And this funky kitchen with old cabinets but I could paint them and maybe do something with the floor in there because it's—"

"Ness." Beck waved a hand in front of her face. "Take a breath."

She did.

"So I guess you liked it, then," Hal said.

"Oh, I loved it."

"I knew you would."

"Fat lot of good it does, but yes"—she sighed—"I love it. If I were in a position to buy a house, I'd be back in Ham Forbes's office signing the papers right now."

"Well, now, maybe we could give you a little help with that," Hal said gently.

"What are you talking about?"

"Ham probably mentioned that the house is held by an estate. It passed to a niece of Miss Ridgeway's who came down here once, for the funeral, and hasn't been back since. I heard she isn't hurting for money, but still, she has to keep up the taxes, keep the house heated so that the pipes don't freeze, and she pays one of the Morton boys to keep the lawn mowed." Hal rested both arms on the table in front of him. "Add to that the fact that the market's slow and we're headed toward winter, and I'm thinking we could make a low offer and see what happens."

Vanessa stared at him as if he were mad.

"Hal, we can't get the price down low enough for me to cough up a down payment. I have savings but not that much."

"I doubt the mortgage payments would be more

than what you're paying in rent for that apartment you're in now," Beck noted.

"That may be, but like I said, I don't have . . ."

Hal and Beck exchanged a conspiratorial look.

"What?" she asked.

"Beck and I have been real proud of the way you put that business of yours together," Hal told her. "You have a real fine work ethic, Ness, and a real head for business. You pay your bills on time, and from what I hear from the ladies in St. Dennis, you carry real nice stuff there in the shop. Classy, they tell me. You contribute to the community in a lot of ways, and you've made a place for yourself here in St. Dennis."

"Thank you." Her eyes welled. "It's the only place where I ever felt I belonged."

"Of course you belong here." Beck patted her on the back. "You've earned your place."

"Now, as you know, I've bought up properties here and there in town. Like the building your shop is in, and the ones on either side. I have a lot invested in St. Dennis, so I don't like to see vacant buildings. It's bad for the town's image, especially since we're trying to establish ourselves as a tourist destination. We've come a long way in the past five years, but we have a lot more to clean up before we can compete with some of the other Bay towns. That's why I bought some of those old warehouses over by the marsh. I'm thinking maybe something like an antique mall would be good in there, once I finish the renovations." Hal stopped and turned to Beck. "What do you think of that idea?"

"I think it's a good one," Beck replied, "but I also like the idea of a boatbuilding venture."

"That's another thing altogether, and a conversation for another day," Hal said. He turned back to Vanessa. "So I'm thinking that I'm going to buy Miss Ridgeway's property from the estate myself, then sell it back to you for whatever I pay for it." He took a sip of the one beer he limited himself to each evening. "That is, if you want it."

Vanessa's mouth moved, but nothing came out except a squeak.

"Nod if that was a yes." Beck elbowed her.

She nodded, her eyes as big as dinner plates.

"You'll make the mortgage payments to me," Hal continued. "I'm thinking a fifteen-year mortgage at four percent would be about right."

Still no intelligible sound from Vanessa.

"Cat got your tongue, Ness?" Beck teased, and she burst into tears.

Hal made his offer, and after some brief and half-hearted negotiations on the seller's part, the offer was accepted. They'd agreed upon a thirty-day settlement, much to the seller's delight. Vanessa moved in the day of settlement, and as soon as all the paperwork cleared, Hal resold the house to her just as he'd promised.

That had been last fall, and she hadn't missed a payment to Hal or an escrow payment for her taxes. Once a month, she took Hal to dinner, and she handed over her mortgage payment right before dessert and coffee. Sometimes Beck joined them, but more often than not, it was just Hal and Vanessa. In him, she'd found the father she'd never known. In her, he'd often said, he'd found the daughter he'd always wanted, the daughter he might have had if Maggie had stayed with him when she brought Beck those many years ago, instead of turning tail and running away again.

Even now, six months later, Vanessa's heart lifted when she drew close enough to see the pink and purple tulips she'd planted along the front walk and around the porch right after she moved in. From inside, a soft light glowed, the timer having turned on a lamp in the living room's bay window.

"My house," she whispered to herself as she unlocked the front door. "Mine."

Vanessa never once crossed the threshold of the house on Cherry Street without feeling immensely grateful that Maggie had sent her to meet Beck. It was the one truly good thing her mother had ever done for her. In coming to St. Dennis, Vanessa had found so much more than a half brother. She'd found herself.

Chapter 6

As far as Hal was concerned, any day that started out with him on the deck of the *Shady Lady* was a fine day indeed. His only wish was that this day had started earlier. When he'd invited Mia's brothers to spend a few hours on his boat, fishing with him on the Bay, he figured on leaving at his regular time, which was sunrise. There was something about watching the sky wake up and turn on the light that got to him, every time. Unfortunately, he'd made the mistake of asking, "What time's good for you?" And so he'd been stuck there, the boat still in its slip, till close to eight that morning waiting on the Shields boys, while the fish were running for someone other than him. When Grady showed up—ten minutes early but alone, because Andy had gotten a call on one of his cases and had to send his regrets—Hal was just as happy. If he'd had to wait another twenty minutes for someone else, he'd have fallen asleep.

"Things should be pretty quiet out here today," Hal told Grady as he cut across the river channel and out toward the Bay. "The herring run ended about a week ago, and the commercial crabbers won't be ready to head out for about another week, so we're sliding in between the two."

"Herring's fished out of these waters?" Grady sat in what Hal referred to as the copilot's chair, the one that stood opposite the captain's.

Hal nodded. "The blueback migrate into the Bay's freshwater rivers to spawn. Used to be a big business, but between the water being overfished and polluted, and the river habitats being destroyed, it's nothing like what it used to be. Conservationists are trying to help the fish make a comeback, though. We'll see how things go, another ten years down the road."

Hal cut the engine and waved to a passing boat. The woman behind the wheel cut hers as well, and steered in the direction of the *Shady Lady*.

"What's up, Hal?" she shouted across the water.

"Not much, Doreen." He waved back.

"You on your way back?"

He shook his head. "On my way out."

She laughed. "Good luck, my friend. I've been out since five-thirty and I've caught one rockfish and one puny flounder. Not even worth the gas I used getting out there today."

"Tell me where you were so I know to avoid it."

"Doesn't seem to matter," she told him. "I saw Pete Marshall and Joe Grant. They're both on their way back in, too. Said nothing's catching." She waved again and moved back to her wheel. "Have a good day, though, whatever you decide to do."

She gave the engine some gas and headed off in the opposite direction.

"Well, that's not sounding so good now, is it?" Hal

pulled his baseball cap down over his forehead a little more. "Want to give it a try anyway?"

"Sure. Why not? We're already out here," Grady said. "Of course, if you'd rather go back in, that would be fine, too."

"Nah. Nothing going on back there in town today. Let's just take our chances. I know a spot where we can tie up and see if the blues are hungry. If they're not, well, I've never been one to complain about having to spend an hour or two on my boat on a nice day like this one's turning out to be."

Fifteen minutes later, they'd dropped anchor, baited their lines, cast off, and were sitting on a couple of folding chairs Hal brought out of the cabin.

"Just put your rod right in there"—Hal pointed to a hole near the railing—"and sit back down and wait to see if there are any takers down there."

They sat for a few minutes, watching the lines, but nothing was happening.

"You do much fishing out there in Montana?" Hal asked.

"Just some lake and stream fishing."

"You have much luck with that?"

"Some." Grady nodded.

"You're talking trout, pickerel, bass . . . ?"

"Right, but mostly trout."

"I heard that can make for a good day."

"It can, yes, sir, if the fish are biting. Otherwise, it's pretty much like sitting right here. It's a pleasant enough way to pass some time on a nice day, like you said."

"So how do you feel about your little sister getting married?" Hal asked.

"I think she's made a good choice. Beck makes her happy. That's good enough for me."

"We're pretty pleased with his choice, too. Mia is good for Beck, in a lot of ways."

"I'm still trying to figure out why she needs a full week of events leading up to the wedding."

Hal laughed. "You know Mia. She's always looking for ways to get people together, especially people she loves. She did say that she thought it was important for her family to get to know Beck's. Of course, we don't have as much family as you do. It's just me, Beck, and Vanessa. Mia and Vanessa have gotten real close, you probably know, which is good for Ness. She never had a sister. At least, not one that any of us know about."

Hal slanted a glance at Grady. More than once that week, he'd seen Grady watching Vanessa when he didn't know anyone was noticing.

"Yup, she's like a daughter to me, Vanessa is. She's one hell of a girl. We're real proud of her, Beck and I are, despite her issues." Hal bit the inside of his cheek and told himself to shut up. Grady didn't press, and Hal was grateful for that. He'd already said more than he should have. The last thing he'd want to do would be to scare the boy away. There weren't any young men in St. Dennis that he thought were good enough for his girl. Mia's brother, now, Hal thought he might be a possibility, but Hal had opened the door for Grady to talk about her, and he hadn't, so maybe he wasn't all that interested after all. Damn.

"Beck mentioned the other night that you used to play semipro baseball." Grady glided smoothly right past the mention of Vanessa.

Hal nodded. "That was a long time ago. I got picked up right out of college. There were some who thought I could make it in the majors. But, like so many of us back then, I got drafted and sent to Vietnam. One minute on the pitcher's mound, the next minute jumping out of a low-flying plane into the jungle. Spent the next year trying not to get killed."

"What happened when you came back? Did you try to reconnect with your team?"

Hal shook his head. "I wrenched my shoulder a couple of times over there. My throwing arm was never right again. Besides, when I came back, I found the girl I left behind had married someone else. I came home to St. Dennis, got a job with the local police force. Made it all the way to chief." He paused for a moment. "I hear you were in law, too."

"FBI. Jokingly referred to as the family business."

"I heard about your dad and your uncle, your cousins, all going into the Bureau. That must have made for some interesting family dinners."

"There was never any lack of conversation, that's for sure."

"You have any thoughts about going back?"

Grady shook his head. "No. I knew what I was doing when I left. I'd had enough, seen enough. I figured I could find something else to do."

"Did you?"

Before Grady could respond, Hal's line took off, and both men lunged for the rod. A few minutes later, Hal had reeled in a nice-size bluefish. He slipped it off the hook and into the ice chest he'd brought with him.

An hour later, they still had only the one fish in the

cooler and no other nibbles. Hal didn't really care if the fish were biting or not, but by midmorning, he figured they'd spent time enough on the Bay for one day. He had other things to do, and he suspected Grady might as well.

The closer he got to 309 Cherry Street, the slower Grady walked. On a scale of one to ten, baking cookies with the girly girl would have been at point-oh-five. But Mia had all but begged him.

"Why me?" he'd asked after he had been summoned to the house she shared with Beck with a come-quick-I-need-you phone call on the morning after Grady's fishing outing with Hal.

"Because I have someone to help me and she doesn't," Mia explained. "We need about a thousand cookies for wedding favors by Saturday and we won't have time to bake them all if we don't double up."

"You're just now figuring out that you need a thousand cookies?"

Mia had nodded somewhat sheepishly.

"So what's the big deal? I passed a bakery on the way in. I'll bet they have cookies."

"I want *Mom's* cookies." She moved several bags of flour and sugar around on her kitchen counter. "Where did I put those measuring spoons?"

"Mom's cookies?"

"Mom's lemon cookies." Mia found the orange spoons under a bag of flour. "Remember them?"

"The little round ones with the lemon stuff on top?"

Mia nodded. "I wanted to have something special of Mom there on my wedding day. You know that if she was still alive, she'd be baking them for the wedding."

"That's really sweet, honey, but why don't you send *your* someone to Vanessa's place and I'll stay here and help you?" He thought that sounded reasonable.

"Because *my* someone is Mara, and she's baking at her house."

"So why can't Mara's cookies count for half of Vanessa's?"

Mia had stared at him as if he'd suddenly gone stupid, then replied, "Because they count for mine."

Her eyes began to fill with tears, and he'd given in. What insensitive oaf would make his sister cry over cookies just three days before her wedding?

"Just go back to Charles Street, then take a left onto Cherry." Mia seemed to recover quickly but he thought it best not to mention it at that point. "Vanessa's house is three blocks up. Number 309. You can't miss it. It's a white house with a blue door. It has some pink and purple flowers in the front yard."

"Yeah, well, no surprise there," he grumbled as he walked along.

It wasn't that he didn't like Vanessa. They'd run into each other several times over the past few days, and he'd found her to be funny and charming and smart. And yes, as Mia had noted, she was very pretty. He hadn't needed his sister to point that out. Some might even have described her as beautiful. But it wasn't as if he hadn't been around very pretty women before. It was just that there was something different about Vanessa. He couldn't put his finger on just what that something was, or how to react to it, but it set off an alarm inside his head. He'd been in the FBI long enough to know danger when he saw it, regardless of the form it took.

Halfway into her block he spotted the house on the opposite side of the street. To say there were "some" flowers out front had been an understatement. There were so many tulips—in every shade of pink and purple imaginable—that it looked as if someone had spilled bags of pastel jelly beans across the yard. It must have taken her days to plant them all.

But yeah, pink and purple. It figured.

He walked along the path that wound through the sea of blooms and took the porch steps two at a time, imagining what the house must look like inside. He'd bet that the furniture would be all white with flowery pillows and the walls would be shades of pink. He pictured Vanessa in the kitchen with her pink apron, wearing pearls and high heels as she measured out flour and cracked open eggs to bake Mia's cookies.

He rang the bell, not sure whether he was more amused or frightened by the image he'd conjured.

Vanessa unlocked the front door. "Mia just called to tell me you were on your way. Thanks for coming."

He stepped inside and found himself engulfed by the scents of lemon and vanilla. In a flash, he was transported back to his childhood, and could almost see himself sitting on his knees on a kitchen chair, his elbows propped on the kitchen table as he sniffed the air intently while his mother grated lemon rind.

"Careful," she'd teased him, "or there won't be any lemony smell left for the cookies."

"Just close the door tightly behind you so that it

doesn't blow open in this breeze we're having this morning." Vanessa's voice brought him back to the present with a thud.

Her voice trailed away as she disappeared toward the back of the house.

He followed and tried to will away the memory of the way life had been back then, before their mother died and childhood had changed for all of them.

The front hall was all polished wood, the walls the color of fresh cream. Grady gave a quick glance at the rooms on either side as he followed her. The living room was a deeper shade of cream, the furniture not at all what he expected. It was all vintage-y looking, in dark jewel tones. The dining room off to the right had deep red walls and an old Oriental carpet. No pink anywhere.

No pearls, either, he realized as he came into the kitchen several steps behind Vanessa. No cutesy apron, and no high heels. The apron covering her cut-off jeans and gray T-shirt was tan and had DISCOVER ST. DENNIS! in navy-blue block letters. Her feet were bare, and though her hair was pulled back into some elastic thing, enough escaped to frame her face with curls. She wore no makeup and, in spite of her smile, appeared just barely happier to see him than he was to be there.

The counters were crowded with baking supplies and cookie sheets. An open carton of eggs, half empty, sat on the kitchen table.

"What can I do to help?" he asked.

"Do you know how to roll out cookie dough?"

"I know how to mix it." He did his best to ignore

the cut lemons that lay side by side on a cutting
board. It was still his all-time favorite scent.

"I'm not ready to mix another batch yet," she told
him. "I'll roll and you cut."

"Cut?"

"With cookie cutters."

"Sure." He nodded. "I can do that. I used to be
good at that."

"Great. You're hired." She waved him over to the
table and pressed something into his hand. He looked
down at the smooth plastic object, then back up at
Vanessa.

"My mom always used a round cutter," he told her.

"Mia wants hearts."

"Oh." What, he wondered, had happened to kick-
ass former FBI agent, criminal investigator Mia Shields
in this town?

"You can work over here." Vanessa cleared a space
and tore a piece of waxed paper from a roll. She flattened it onto the counter, took a blob of dough from
the refrigerator where it had been chilling, and
dumped it onto the waxed paper. She sprinkled a
rolling pin with a little flour, then proceeded to roll it
out to the thickness she wanted.

"There you go," she told Grady. "You're up to
bat."

He hesitated for a moment, then realized there
would be no escape until the job was done.

*Oh, if only my old friends from the Bureau could
see me now . . .*

He grimaced at the thought. Where once he
tracked serial killers and child predators, he was now

reduced to cutting out little heart shapes in dough with Miss Fluff. How the mighty have fallen . . .

From the corner of his eye he stole a glance at her. He had to admit she wasn't looking quite so fluffy today. As a matter of fact, she was all business, in an intense sort of way that he found oddly appealing. He struck the thought from his mind as quickly as it had entered.

"Nice of you to offer to help Mia," he said to break the ice.

"Mia's my friend, and she's marrying my brother," Vanessa replied very matter-of-factly. "Why wouldn't I help?"

"She has other friends who didn't offer to hire someone to work for them so that they could help out."

"She'd do the same for me." Vanessa took one batch of cookies out of the oven and placed it on a cooling rack. Into the oven went another tray.

"What do you want me to do now?" A line of cutout dough hearts lined up across the table.

"That was fast." She glanced at his work, then nodded. "They look pretty good. You can put them on that tray on the counter there, as soon as I get a minute to clean it off."

"I'll do it," he told her.

He stepped around her and grabbed the tray and took it to the sink and turned on the water. He could feel her eyes on the back of his neck while he washed off the cookie sheet, then dried it.

"I think we need a sheet of parchment on that tray before you put the cookies on it." She was at the kitchen table measuring flour. "So they don't burn on the bottom."

"Okay." He pulled a sheet off the roll and fitted it to the tray. When he finished placing the cookies on the tray, he asked, "What now?"

"Now we have to wait for another tray to come out of the oven. I should have picked up a few extras but I ran out of time, so we have to shuttle them back and forth."

He left the tray on the counter and walked to the table.

"Hey, my grandmother used to have a table like this." He tapped his fingers on the blue-enamel-on-metal top. "Does yours have flowers in the corners?" He peered around her. "Yep. Just like Gramma's."

"Mia told me." She opened a stick of butter and dropped it into a bowl. "It was in the house when I moved in, as was most of the rest of the furniture."

"The previous owner just left it all here?"

"The previous owner was just shy of one hundred when she passed away. She had a grandniece who really wasn't interested in the house or the furnishings. She did come for the funeral, and while she was here, she took the things she thought had some value, but she just left everything else where it was."

"Aren't you lucky she didn't have a better eye." He took a seat in one of the chairs next to the table. "I noticed the stuff in the living room when I came in. That mohair sofa and the chairs with the nail heads look like they're from the forties, maybe the fifties."

Mia grinned. "I figure Miss Ridgeway must have had some kind of midlife crisis right around that time. You know, out with the old, in with the new?

Only she didn't toss the old, thank goodness. There's still a lot of lovely old Victorian pieces in the attic and in the garage loft. I'm figuring she probably put them into storage when she bought what you see in there now."

"I remember my grandparents having a sofa in their living room that was very similar to yours."

"Mia said it was even the same color." She opened the oven door and peered inside, then closed it again. "I asked Nita—she's one of the antique dealers in town—to look over some of the furniture and the artwork. She said she couldn't imagine what the grandniece had taken, judging by the quality of the items that were left behind. She either didn't take the time to really look through the house, or she didn't know what she was looking at." Vanessa covered the bowl holding the dough with plastic wrap and placed it in the refrigerator to chill as the recipe directed. "Nita took some pieces that I didn't particularly like on consignment in her shop."

"Did they sell?"

"Not yet, but she only took them a few weeks ago. She thinks they'll go quickly once the tourist season begins for real. We have A Day on the Bay coming up next month, and things will get pretty busy from then right through to the end of the year."

"What's A Day on the Bay?"

"That's when everyone brings out their boats and we have races. Sailboats, motorboats . . . you name it, we race it. People come from all over to compete as well as to check out the boats in the marina that are for sale. They even bring out the old skipjacks to show them off. They used to call it Harbor Fest but last year they changed the name."

The timer on the oven buzzed and she grabbed a mitt and removed yet another tray of cookies and set them aside to cool.

"Mia wants to glaze these for Saturday, but I don't know." Vanessa gnawed on her bottom lip. "I'm afraid they'll stick together."

"The glaze is that lemon stuff that goes on top?"

She nodded.

"My mom used to do that at night before she went to bed, so the icing would be solid in the morning," he told her. "What if you put that stuff on them today? Wouldn't it be hard enough by Saturday to not stick?"

"Maybe. I don't know. I guess we could try a few of the ones that have cooled and see how they are by this evening. I baked several batches last night but they're in the freezer."

He reached past her and picked up the recipe.

"Wouldn't this go faster if we doubled or tripled the recipe?"

"Yes, but we still have to chill each batch for about two hours, and we still only have one oven."

"So we'll stagger them." He looked around. "Why don't I wash up all the stuff that you'll need for the next batch while you roll out that one?"

"That would save some time." She nodded. "Thanks."

He ran water in the sink and gathered the used bowls and spoons and the beaters from the counters.

"I hear you went out on Hal's boat yesterday." She

stood across the room, at the table, and rolled out another batch of dough.

"Yeah. Nice of him to take me."

"Hal Garrity is the nicest man on the face of the
earth," she told him.

"He obviously thinks the world of you, too,"
Grady noted. "He said he thinks of you as a daughter."

"I wish to God he *was* my dad." Mia stopped
working and turned around. "I'm sure my life would
have been very different if he had been. Beck and I
had the same mother, but not the same father."

"Sorry."

"So am I. Not about Beck, but about . . . oh, whatever." She smiled wryly and turned back to the work
at hand. "So what did you think of the *Shady Lady*?"

"Who? Oh, you mean Hal's boat. It was great. I'd
never fished from a boat before. The only fishing I've
ever done has been in mountain streams—freshwater
fishing."

"That's with the skinny rod and reel and the funny
little things that are supposed to look like bait?"

"You mean flies. Also called lures. They're supposed to mimic, well, flies or other critters that the
fish in the stream would eat."

"I knew that part. I just couldn't remember what
they were called. It's been a long time since I thought
about fishing."

"So you've been?"

"No, but one of my mom's exes used to go all the
time. He had this metal box that he kept all his stuff
in."

"Tackle box." He finished washing and looked around for a towel.

"Right. He had one of those and he had all these little things in there with hooks on them. Some had feathers and some looked like little tiny fish." She gazed out the window, as if remembering. "And he had these little silvery things, like little weights, he sometimes tied onto the lures."

"Sinkers." He nodded. "Depending on what kind of fish you're after, you might want a lure that sits on the water, or one that goes beneath the surface. In the latter, you want something to take that lightweight lure under."

"Funny. I barely remember what that stepfather looked like, but I remember his fishing stuff. Oh, and he had these long boots. They came up to here." She tapped the top of her thighs.

"Waders. So you could walk into the stream." He couldn't help but smile at her. She looked so earnest, remembering.

"Do you have those?"

He nodded.

"And those rubber overalls?"

He nodded again.

"He used to bring home these fish and stand at the kitchen sink and cut them apart and pull the guts out." Vanessa made a face. "I couldn't watch."

"Well, if you're planning on cooking and eating your catch, you need to clean it."

"Do you do that?"

"When I catch for food, sure."

She wrinkled her nose, and he laughed.

"Well, you wouldn't cook it with the organs still

inside. I don't know for sure, but I imagine that could make you sick," he told her. "I guess I eat about a third of what I catch."

"What do you do with the rest of it?"

"I release the fish and let it go."

"What's the point of catching it if you're going to let it go?"

"You go for the sport."

"So you hurt the fish just so you can have a little 'sport'?"

"I usually flatten out the hook so it doesn't pull the fish's mouth when I take the hook out."

"Seriously?"

When he nodded, she asked, "What's the big deal with the whole sport thing, anyway?"

He hesitated before answering. He'd never really thought about why he did it, other than the fact that he liked it.

"Well, I guess because it makes for a peaceful day. You have to stand real still so you don't scare off the fish, and you don't talk or make any sound for the same reason. There's just the sun and the water flowing downstream and the fish, and you. It's just a good excuse to be outside, in nature, all by yourself."

"But aren't you always by yourself anyway?" she asked.

"When I'm home I am," he admitted. "Most of the time, anyway."

"Where else would you be?"

"Hiking, backpacking, camping in the mountains."

"Isn't that dangerous, to do that by yourself?

Aren't you supposed to always go with a buddy? At least, this article I read—"

"When I go for more than a day, it's almost always with a group that I'm taking on a prearranged trip," he explained.

"You mean, like a guide?"

"Exactly." He spotted a towel on the counter and he pointed to it. "Can I use that to dry this stuff?"

"Sure." She nodded. "So you take people on camping trips?"

"And hiking and backpacking through the mountains, sometimes the state parks." He picked up the towel and began to dry the measuring spoons. "Sometimes it's a day hike, sometimes it's for several days. Depends on what type of experience they want. Sometimes it's part of their package at one of the nearby resorts or lodges. When things get slow, I advertise in outdoor magazines, and on the Internet, but I've only had to do that twice."

"How did you get into that?"

"When I moved out to Montana, I spent a lot of time hiking on my own at first, to become better acquainted with the area around the house. I graduated to backpacking because I wanted to do longer hikes, then I wanted to try an overnight. As you mentioned, camping alone can be dicey, especially in areas where there are a lot of bears. But after a while, I got bored being off by myself all the time. I'd be walking along and I'd see something . . . maybe an eagle swooping down, or a stand of trees that had turned a brilliant color, maybe a bighorn sheep. You know, the sort of thing that makes you turn to someone else and say, 'Hey, look at that!' Not so much fun when there's no one else around. So I joined a hiking club and went out with them and a guide a couple of times. Since I was thinking about staying in Montana awhile, I looked into becoming a guide myself. I took some courses at a wilderness training center, then I took a few more. I stopped in at the lodges and a couple of resorts in my part of the state, talked to the managers, gave out my cards."

"How often do you take people out?"

"A couple of times a month in good weather." He grinned wryly. "Not so often in the winter, unless it's a really experienced group, I know the terrain really well, and there are no storms forecasted for that week but that's really rare."

She sat on one of the chairs and rubbed the small of her back with her hand. "Wait. Do people pay you to take them into the mountains?"

He nodded. "Sure."

"Does Mia know about this?" Vanessa looked puzzled. "Because to hear her tell it, you never leave your house and you go for weeks without talking to anyone, and you don't work."

He laughed out loud. "Mia has never asked me if I have a job. She assumes that I don't, so I haven't brought it up. If she ever asked, I'd be happy to tell her. But she doesn't ask. She has this image of me as a tragic loner, so I just let her hold on to that pitiful picture."

"That is just flat-out evil." Vanessa's eyes narrowed but there was a glint of humor there. "Your sister's worried about you and the solitary life she thinks you're living. She believes that you hole up in that house and only occasionally venture out into the hills with no companion other than a horse."

"My sister is going to have to learn not to assume." He paused. "You're not going to tell her, right?"

"She's my friend. Come Saturday, she'll be family."

"Well, then, let's just consider this a family secret for the time being."

The oven timer went off, and Vanessa appeared to be thinking while she took one tray out and put the latest one in.

"Doesn't it bother you to know that your entire family thinks you're a pathetic recluse?" she asked.

"My entire family doesn't. Only Mia."

"You mean everyone else knows?"

He nodded.

"Even more evil than I thought." She laughed. "But all right. Your secret is safe with me. Of course, it will cost you."

"What's the price of your silence?"

"Why, I don't know." She tilted her head, as if thinking. "Certainly I couldn't be expected to squander an opportunity like this on something trivial. I'll have to give it some serious thought." She nodded solemnly. "Oh, yes. This needs to be good. I'm going to have to get back to you."

"Take your time," he told her. "I'll be around for a few more days."

"Are you hungry?" she asked.

"I'm always hungry." He started to glance around at the stacks of cookies.

"Uh-uh," she warned him. "Don't even think about it."

"What did you have in mind?"

She went to the refrigerator and opened it. "I have soup. And corn bread."

"What kind of soup?"

"Chicken rice and cream of broccoli."

"Either is fine."

"Really?" She looked over the top of the door at him. "I'd have expected you to shy away from the broccoli."

"I don't shy away from much."

"Great." She took a container out of the fridge. "We'll have the chicken."

She moved the cookie trays from the stove top and found a pan into which she spooned the soup. While it heated she cleaned off a spot at the table and set two places. Grady sniffed the air and looked into the pan, where chunks of chicken were warming in a fragrant yellow broth thick with rice.

"This smells homemade," he observed.

"You get points for that," she told him.

He shrugged. "Do I lose points if I admitted I sometimes make soup for myself at home?"

"Actually, that would earn extra extra points. I think it's great when a guy can make stuff. It says a lot about him."

"Like what?"

"Like, he can take care of himself. Guys who can't do for themselves . . ." She made the thumbs-down sign. "And it says that he's not hung up on some macho image of himself." She smiled. "Too mucho macho . . ." Another thumbs-down. "Besides, a guy who can make his own soup will never have to depend on a woman—or worse, wait for a woman to do it for him, and that is very liberating, as far as I'm concerned. I really like a guy who does things for himself."

"I feel the need to confess I only know how to make two kinds of soup."

"Which two?"

"Potato, and beef with vegetables."

"Good ones. Nothing to be ashamed about there." The soup began to boil and she turned down the heat. "Seriously. I'm impressed."

"Thanks, but you should know that liberating someone else never entered my mind. Winters are harsh where I live. You can be snowed in for a long time. There was a clear choice between learning how to cook and starving to death."

"Whatever the reason, I like it." She brought the pan over to the table and spooned soup into the bowls. "I've known too many men who expected women to do everything for them. From my step-fathers right down to my . . ."

She paused. "Well, let's just leave it at that." She placed the pan back on the stove, then returned to the table with a plate of corn-bread squares and sat across from Grady. "Did you teach yourself to cook after you went to Montana?"

"No, actually, our mom died when we were all fairly young. Our dad never seemed to get the hang of getting home in time to make dinner for us kids." He hastened to add, "I'm not criticizing him. He was in the Bureau and passed up several promotion opportunities so that he could be home most nights, but he rarely made it by dinnertime and he wasn't much for putting meals together once he got there."

"So who cooked for you kids?"

"Sometimes one of our aunts came over, but most of the time, our older brother cooked dinner. Mia was too young when Mom first passed away. Mia never did like to cook."

"I think she still avoids it as much as possible. Beck is pretty good, though, and Hal is even better." She stirred the soup to cool it. "I learned to cook early because I grew up in a home where I learned that if I wanted to eat, most nights I'd have to take care of myself."

"Did your mother work?"

"Sometimes. Mostly when she was between marriages." Her smile was touched with a bit of irony. "Mom was never one to do for herself what she could get someone else to do for her, so she was fine with me taking over."

"I see." He saw that, to her credit, Vanessa wasn't interested in following Mom's example.

"She also liked to go out after work, and sometimes she forgot that she had a child at home."

She grew quiet and seemed to be concentrating on the rice in her soup. They ate lunch mostly in silence after that, and returned to baking as soon as they'd finished eating. By late afternoon, they'd completed their share of the wedding cookies. Vanessa mixed up a batch of glaze and frosted a few cookies, which she left out on the counter to dry.

"I'll try to stack them when I get back tonight to see if they stick together," she told Grady as she checked the time. "Meanwhile, we're due for the rehearsal in a little more than an hour."

He glanced at his watch. "I better get back to the

Inn. Andy was going to stop by for me at six forty-five."

She grabbed several cookies from the counter, wrapped them in a napkin, and handed them to him with a smile. "For your service."

"Thanks. I was wondering how I was going to manage snitching a few."

"You'll have to let me know how they measure up to your mom's." She walked along with him to the front door. "Thank you so much for giving me a hand today. If you hadn't come over, I'd be up all night trying to finish my quota."

"I was glad to help," he said, and realized he meant it.

She unlocked the door and walked outside with him, pausing to deadhead a tulip here and there.

"Well, I guess I'll see you later." He paused at the end of the walk. "Thanks for lunch."

"You're welcome." She straightened up, a handful of dead petals in one hand, and dazzled him with a smile. "Thanks again for your help."

He nodded and began his walk back toward town, thinking that everything he'd assumed about her had been pretty much wrong. He chastised himself for being as bad as Mia, making assumptions based on incomplete information. He had to admit that, at second glance, he'd found nothing fluffy about Vanessa. She'd come across as independent and strong, if somewhat guarded, but a woman who stood on her own two feet. He couldn't help but wonder what else he might find if he got the chance to take an even closer look. He almost wished he was going to be around a little longer.

Funny the way some things come back to you, he

thought. Some memories come when you hear a certain song, some with the sight of something that reminds you of another place, and sometimes, like today, with the hint of something that takes you to another time. Until today, he hadn't even realized how closely he associated lemons in general—and those lemon cookies in particular—with his mother and his childhood. Maybe it was because he'd lost her when he was young, but one of his most vivid memories was of them all in the kitchen when it was time to bake, with the three boys and Mia around the table, each with a job to do. Brendan was the oldest, so he always got to break the eggs. Andy got to measure the flour and sugar, Grady got to cut out the cookies, and Mia got to pick them up off the table and place them on the cookie sheet. There had been an innocence to those times, a closeness to each other and to their mother that had held them together for years after they lost her.

Mia remembers, too, he realized. That's why it was so important for her to bask in those memories as her wedding day drew near, why she wanted to share that special treat with her guests, why she wanted to dwell on those days and surround herself with the best of her childhood. Before she left on her honeymoon, he was going to have to thank her for pulling him back with her, so that he could bask in them, too.

Chapter 7

THE outdoor wedding rehearsal—held on Thursday night rather than Friday because of a scheduling conflict with the officiant—had proceeded without a hitch, from the procession up the aisle to the string quartet's playing of Clarke's "Trumpet Voluntary," to the recessional Vivaldi's "Spring." Was there anything more perfect than violins playing at dusk on the shores of the Chesapeake, a lone sailboat silhouetted against the setting sun? Vanessa couldn't think of anything that even came close.

She stood at the makeshift altar and watched a smiling Mia walk up the aisle between Grady and Andy. *There will certainly be no dearth of eye candy at this wedding,* she thought. She caught Grady's eye as he drew closer with his sister on his arm. There was something in the way he hovered over Mia that Vanessa found endearing.

Reverend Quinn explained how the ceremony would proceed on Saturday, then put them all through their paces one more time.

"I think that after the ceremony, on the way back down the aisle, Dorsey should walk with Andy, and

Vanessa should walk with Grady." Mia stood on the grass at the front of the imaginary aisle they'd all just walked a second time. "See, when they walk me up the aisle, they move to stand on the side."

"The father of the bride usually returns to his seat in the front aisle," the minister told her.

"I know, but they're not my father. I want them to stay up here with me."

The minister shrugged. He obviously knew better than to argue with a bride about where her brothers would stand during the ceremony, whether they were standing in for their father or not.

"So after Beck and I walk back down, the matron of honor—that would be Annie—meets up with the best man—that would be Hal—here"—Mia pointed to a spot in line with the center of the aisle—"and they start to walk together. Then, Andy, you meet up with Dorsey, and after they start walking, Ness, you meet up with Grady. Okay?"

Everyone nodded.

"Anyone have questions?"

No one did.

"Great. Let's head on out to dinner," Beck told the group. "Everyone has a ride? Good. See you all in the bar in about ten minutes."

Vanessa chatted and laughed with the other members of the bridal party as they made their way to the parking lot, then led the line of cars back into town for the rehearsal dinner at Captain Walt's, a local landmark that had started life as a waterman's shack and had been added onto over the years.

One by one, the cars pulled into Walt's lot, and one by one, the members of the party filed into the bar for a predinner drink on the house since their room was still being set up. Vanessa ordered a glass of white wine, and sipped it while the others crowded around the few available stools. It was the first time she'd taken part in such an event and she felt more an observer than a participant. She knew that by the time most people were her age, they'd taken part in any number of weddings, funerals, christenings—all those rites of passage that were based around family and tradition and ritual. She had none of that in her past. She couldn't decide if she felt more included than excluded, or vica versa.

The one thing she had decided was that Grady Shields was no tongue-tied recluse who needed to be led around by the hand.

She'd been on edge from the minute Mia had called her that morning and told her that Grady was on his way over to pitch in with the cookies. Vanessa hadn't wanted him there—hadn't invited a man into her house since she moved in, other than Hal, Beck, and the occasional workmen—but before she knew it, he was standing on her front steps and she'd had to let him in. Far from being the shy dolt his sister had described, she'd found him funny and easy to be with and sexy. Definitely sexy.

Watching Grady now, with his fingers curled around the neck of a bottle of beer, she felt a tension growing inside her and twisting into a knot. She liked the way he looked—well, who wouldn't?—and she liked the way he laughed. Add that to the fact that he hadn't been the least bit hesitant to admit to his cooking skills, and that he'd spent almost the entire day cutting out little heart shapes in cookie dough just because it would make his sister happy on her wedding day, even though he'd probably wished to be somewhere else, and you had one damned attractive package. Certainly Vanessa was attracted.

He was such a contrast to the men in her past. God knew that neither of her ex-husbands had so much as opened a can on their own. Make their own soup? Wash their own dishes? Ha! In her dreams!

As if he'd read her mind, he glanced over at her and smiled.

"Do you need a drink?" he asked.

She held up her wineglass in response. He grabbed a basket of peanuts from the bar and made his way toward her, stepping between Andy and Connor, who were arguing over who would kick whose butt at darts later that night. As Grady drew closer to Vanessa, he held the basket out to her.

"No, thank you." She shook her head. "If I'm going to eat anything before dinner, it's going to be the artichoke-and-crab dip."

"It's good?"

"The best ever."

"In that case . . ." He handed the basket to Andy to return to the bar.

"You won't be sorry you saved the room," she promised.

"Dinner, everyone." The hostess waved them to the private room Hal had reserved.

Grady stepped to the bar to put down his empty bottle, and Vanessa lingered a moment, waiting for him while trying to appear not to be. Suddenly she had the strangest sensation of someone's eyes boring into her. She glanced around the room but saw no one who appeared to be looking in her direction. Still, the feeling was almost overwhelming, strong enough to accompany her into the room where their dinner would be served.

Vanessa stood in the doorway, her discomfort momentarily edged aside while she studied the table. As she'd requested, the centerpiece was low and long and packed with all of Mia's favorite flowers: white hydrangeas tinged with green; lush, fragrant dark pink peonies; fat pale pink rosebuds, all set off by the drama of purple anemones. At each place setting was a gift bag in either lime or navy—the primary wedding colors—tied with a floppy pink satin bow. Into each Vanessa had tucked a DISCOVER ST. DENNIS! mug, a jar of honey from a local farm, a box of truffles from Sweetie Pie's, the confection shop that opened last fall, a walking map of St. Dennis, and a certificate good for breakfast on Sunday morning at Let's Do Brunch, the newest eatery in town. At the last minute, she tucked in one of the snow globes from the gift shop on the first floor of the Inn at Sinclair's Point. Beneath the glass dome was a perfect likeness of the Inn, right down to the Adirondack chairs that overlooked the Bay. Shaking it, watching the white whirls engulf the stately old building, reminded her that she'd first arrived in St. Dennis on just such a snowy day.

"The flowers are lovely and so is the table," Mia whispered in her ear. "I see your touch in everything."

"I may have suggested a little something here and there." Vanessa straightened a bow on one of the bags. "But Olivia did the flowers."

"After you told her what the centerpiece should look like."

"I merely mentioned what you like." Vanessa smiled modestly. "Olivia did the rest."

Once everyone found their place at the table, there were toasts and speeches, the most memorable being from Hal.

At Beck's insistence, Hal was seated at the head of the table. When he rose silently, a glass in his hand, one by one, everyone's eyes turned to him. Several times he appeared to be about to speak, but several moments passed before he finally did.

"A long time ago, I fell in love with a lady who, I believed back then, loved me, too. War and time came between us. When I returned from Vietnam, I'd discovered she'd married another man. I came back here to St. Dennis to lick my wounds and get on with my life."

The room had fallen so quiet, Vanessa could hear Grady breathing over her right shoulder.

"A long time passed. I thought I'd meet someone else and fall in love again, but I never did. I'd always wanted a family to raise here in my hometown—a son, maybe even a daughter—but that didn't seem likely, either. Until one day, my doorbell rang." Hal cleared his throat, his emotions beginning to catch up with him. "I opened the door, and there on my porch stood the woman I had fallen in love with years before—and a sullen-looking boy of about thirteen who looked like he was ready to bolt. The lady handed the boy over to me and said something like, 'Here, see what you can do with him. He's an awful handful.'

Well, by the time I recovered from the shock, the woman had gone, but the boy was still there."

"Hal, you don't have to—" Beck's voice cracked.

"Oh, but I do, son." Hal took a minute to compose himself before continuing. "The woman was right: the boy was an awful handful. Tested me at every turn, in ways I could never have imagined. But one thing was true: he was my boy. My son. Eventually, somehow, we made our peace, and that awful handful of a kid . . . well, he turned out to be the son I'd always prayed for, a son any man would be proud of. And I am proud of you, Beck."

Hal turned directly to Beck.

"I always thought you were a smart boy. But falling in love with Mia . . . well, that just proves the point, doesn't it? If it had been up to me to pick a bride for you, I couldn't have done better. I'm hoping that you'll both be as happy as you deserve to be. And maybe one day, you'll ring my doorbell and bring me a little one to add to our family."

He looked as if he had something else to say, but instead, he tilted his glass to toast the couple. When no more words came, Beck stood and embraced him. The two men clung to each other for a very long moment. A teary-eyed Vanessa stood and completed the toast.

"I think what Hal was trying to say was, may you have a long and happy life together."

"Here, here!"

"Amen!"

Glasses clinked as they touched across the table and cameras flashed as pictures were taken to record the moment.

Andy spoke next, about how the three brothers used to play tricks on their little sister, until they discovered she was a better shot than any of them, which lightened the mood at the table. Mia's matron of honor, Anne Marie McCall, the profiler from Mia's old FBI unit, spoke of how Mia had grown up in the FBI and how much she was missed, but how happy all her former co-agents were that she'd found exactly what she'd needed in St. Dennis.

Vanessa had wanted to make a toast of her own, but after listening to Hal, she found she was incapable. Every thought she had stuck in her throat. How to put into words, in a room full of near strangers, what his acceptance of her had meant to a young woman who had felt so lost, so unsure of herself, so totally alone? How the welcome she'd been given by Beck and Hal both had given her direction and the sense of place, the sense of herself, that she'd needed?

Well, maybe tomorrow at the wedding I won't feel so weepy, she told herself. *Or maybe not. Either way, it'll be all right. Beck and Mia know how much I love them, how I want so much for them to be happy. And that's the important thing, right?*

She cleared her throat and blotted under her eyes with her fingers. When she felt Grady's eyes on her, she turned to him and said, "Sorry. I usually don't cry in public."

"Me, either," he said, and they both laughed.

He leaned closer and whispered, "You may not have noticed, but there's hardly a dry eye in the place. Like Andy said in his toast, Mia was the only girl in the family, and she's had a rough couple of years lately. To see her this happy . . . well, let's just say we're all happy for her, and we'll leave it at that."

"Were you all overbearing big brothers when she was growing up?"

"We were merciless," Grady admitted. "We all kept an eye on her. Made her life a living hell when she started getting interested in boys. Any guy who looked at her twice got worked over. You know how it is."

"Actually, I don't. But I wish I had. I might have made some better choices." She regretted the words as soon as she'd spoken them. To change the subject, she told him, "Hal said he was thinking about taking the boat out again tomorrow. It's supposed to be a beautiful day. You might want to go. I'm sure he'd be happy for the company."

"Are you going?" He repositioned his leg under the table, and for a moment, it rested against her bare thigh, so that the soft fabric of his khakis brushed her leg. The old Vanessa—the one who'd been so needy for attention—would have taken that casual bumping of knees as an invitation. The new Vanessa—the one who'd learned a lot about herself since she moved to St. Dennis—kept her shoes on her feet and her feet to herself.

"I wish I could, but I need to work," Vanessa explained. "I've been out of my shop so much already this week, and I'll be out all day Saturday. I have someone really good filling in for me, but you know that no one takes care of your own business as well as you do."

"True enough." He moved slightly to the right while the waiter refilled his wineglass.

Vanessa put her hand over the top of hers to indicate she didn't care for a refill. She smiled at the waiter and he moved on to the other side of the table.

The staff served an excellent meal, and soon the chatter inside the room was almost deafening. It was fun, though, Vanessa thought, to be part of a group like that, even if it was for just a little while. It was almost like being part of a big family. She studied the easy way the Shields cousins teased each other, the playful way they traded insults, the stories they told about each other, the shared history that bonded them and kept them close. She listened wistfully, wishing she'd had that growing up. Much of the time, Maggie wasn't around when she got home from school or in from play. Most days, there was no one to tell that she'd fallen in the school yard and hurt her leg, that she'd been laughed at when she didn't know how to properly pronounce a word, that she'd gotten the highest grade on her history test, or that the teacher had hung her artwork on the bulletin board outside their classroom. Her childhood was not one she cared to look back on very often. She'd been lonely and neglected, and many times, she'd been afraid. She squeezed her eyes closed for a moment to squeeze away the images that haunted her.

"Are you all right?" Grady leaned over to ask.

"I'm fine." Vanessa flashed a smile.

"You look like you're a thousand miles away," he said.

"Close enough," she murmured.

The pretty cake she'd ordered from Sweet Somethings was served with coffee, and before long, it was clear that the evening was winding to a close.

"Are you coming back into the bar with us?" Grady asked. "Andy's challenged me to a game of darts."

"It's tempting, but actually, I was just thinking that I should be getting home. I have an early day tomorrow." She pushed her chair back and stood.

His hand was on her wrist as if to hold her there.

"You sure?"

She nodded. "I have a lot of catching up to do since I was out all day today."

"Well, thanks for letting me join in the fun today. And thanks for saving me for the crab dip. You were right. It was the best."

"You're welcome. Thank you for your help today. If you hadn't come by, I'd still be in the kitchen, rolling out endless little hearts." She was tempted to grab onto the hand that encircled her wrist and just hold on for a moment, but she resisted. "By the way, how did the samples measure up?"

"There's not a crumb left. That should tell you something."

"Good. Then I suppose they'll do."

"So, I'll see you tomorrow night." He let go of her wrist, then pushed back his seat and caught Andy's eye. "What time is dinner tomorrow night?"

"Seven," Andy replied as he held the chair for his wife. "Hey, Grady, do you have a minute? There's something I want to run past you . . ."

"Sure." He turned back to Vanessa. "Let me know if you need any help icing those cookies."

"I know where to find you."

She kissed Hal and Beck and Mia, waved good night to everyone else. She went back through the bar and the main dining room, and was almost to the door when she felt it again: that feeling of being watched. It was so strong that for a moment she thought of going back and asking someone to follow her home.

Silly, she told herself. *Shake it off.*

She left by way of the side door that opened directly into the parking lot. She walked across the macadam and opened her car with the remote when she was almost upon it. She'd read somewhere that if you used the remote to unlock your car while you were still a distance away, anyone following you would know which vehicle was yours, and that it was open, and that could put you in danger. The parking lot was still full. Who knew who or what could be lurking there?

She shook her head as if to shake out the uneasy feeling and drove home with one eye on the rearview mirror. There were no cars behind her as she made her way from Walt's at the far end of the pier to Kelly's Point Road past the municipal building where the police department had its offices, and past the long parking lot that, at the height of the tourist season, would be filled even at this hour. No car followed her onto Charles Street, and she drove up Cherry alone.

She pulled into her driveway, and noted for the first time how dark it was between her garage and her house, how the trees along her neighbor's side of the drive made it seem even darker. She really should have a light installed outside, she thought; one that would illuminate not only the garage, but the entire yard and drive. Maybe one of those motion-sensor things that lit up when someone came within so many feet of the house or the garage.

She was glad she'd had the presence of mind to leave some lights on in the house, and once she was inside, the door closed securely behind her, the feeling that unseen eyes were following her lifted. She even felt a little silly for letting her imagination get the best of her. Still, first thing tomorrow she'd call Stan Wescott, and have him get right on those outside lights. Tonight, she'd lock her doors, check her windows, and try not to spook herself any more than she already had.

Grady's participation in the impromptu darts tournament had been short-lived. Beck had knocked him out in the second round, and he'd spent the rest of the evening spectating and cheering on his brother, who lost to Hal in the finals. The losers paid up in beers at the bar, and soon they were all sitting around a table trading dart stories. Then they talked cars, followed by fish tales of questionable veracity. Finally, the topic of conversation turned to law enforcement, and everyone had a story or two to share.

"The worst crime scene I ever saw . . ."

"The dumbest guy I ever arrested . . ."

"There was this time I was sent to Maine to work on a serial-killer case . . ."

"I was in Arizona on a child abduction . . ."

Grady tuned it all out. He'd been a damned good agent in his day, but he left the Bureau because he found he could no longer separate the good memories from the bad. He'd found peace in his mountains, but even that was proving to have run its course. He'd told Mia that he'd made a life for himself there, and it was a good one. But if nothing else, being back with his family this week, seeing his old friends again, reminded him that the life he'd left behind hadn't been so bad, after all. The thing was, he liked what he was doing, really enjoyed being a wilderness guide. He loved hiking, camping, and he'd found it easy enough to support himself doing just that. Of course, his expenses were minimal in Montana. He owned the house outright, and his car had long been paid for. His biggest expenses were food and enough wood to keep the woodstoves going in the winter when the oil truck couldn't get through.

It both amused and annoyed him that his sister seemed to think that he spent his days sitting in a corner, sucking his thumb and watching game shows. Amused, because it was so far from the truth, and annoyed because, well, because it was so far from the truth that he couldn't believe that she honestly believed it. He'd have to set her straight one of these days.

The entire wedding-week extravaganza amused him, as well. There'd been many weddings in their large family over the past few years, but none of them had taken a week to build up to. His own wedding to Melissa had been spur of the moment. They'd eloped, an act he'd later regretted when he realized how it had hurt his family to have been shut out. He'd never make that mistake again. Not that he was looking to get married again anytime soon, but still, these few days with his family reminded him why sharing the moments of your life with people you love who love you back was important. Sometimes you just needed a little tap on the shoulder.

He was enjoying spending some time with his brother and his wife, and was looking forward to the cousins all returning to St. Dennis over the weekend, a place he was enjoying as well. The town had a pace of its own, certainly different from Montana, and definitely different from any other place he'd lived in the past. He'd never lived near water before, but he was finding that he liked seeing the sun on the Bay every morning from the window of his room at the Inn. Yesterday, after his trip with Hal, he'd walked back down to the dock and watched the other fishing boats come in, and he'd lingered to listen to the banter of their occupants. There was an easy rhythm to life here in St. Dennis, one he found appealing.

He leaned back in his chair, one arm over the back of Mia's, and watched her face as she looked up at Beck. There was such love in her eyes, and in the eyes of her future husband. He and Melissa must have looked at each other that way at one time, but he couldn't remember. There were more and more days when it was harder to recall what her voice sounded like, or what her skin felt like against his. It wasn't that he was trying to forget her, it was just that life moved forward, not backward.

Someone put money in the old jukebox at the far side of the room, and music began to play. Tables were pushed aside, and several couples—two middle-aged and a pair in their twenties—moved onto the makeshift dance floor and swayed to a song he didn't recognize. Moments later, an older couple joined them. They appeared to be in their eighties, the woman spry, the man not so much. He moved slowly, his feet shuffling side to side, but he held the woman in his arms and held her gaze lovingly in his. They continued to sway together, the woman looking up at her partner as if he were the only man in the world.

Well, Grady thought, *I suppose for her, he is.*

The man leaned down and placed a kiss on his wife's cheek, and Grady looked away. The moment had held such bright intimacy and love, it was almost blinding, like looking into the sun.

That's what he wanted for Mia, he thought: The kind of love that lasted through all the years and all the changes and all the stages of life.

And for himself? He didn't think the cards held a great love for him. He'd been more aware of his aloneness tonight than he'd been in a long time. He didn't feel especially lonely, most times, but just, well, *alone.* He watched the other dancers on the floor for a few more minutes, his mind drifting along with the music. Another song began to play, this one soft and sensual, and it took his mind to other places. Like back to the dinner table, where his leg had been pressed up to Vanessa's, and she hadn't moved it away. He'd been trying to avoid thinking about her, but three truths came to mind, now that she was in his head. One was that he hadn't felt so alone yesterday, at her house, when they'd shared cookie duty. The second was that he'd been very much attracted to her from the minute he first saw her. Pretending that he hadn't been hadn't made it so.

And the third was, if Vanessa had stayed, he'd have asked her to dance.

Chapter 8

WHEN Vanessa strolled into Cuppachino a little before eight on Friday morning, she found a few of the Charles Street merchants already at the table they favored near the front of the room. She waved to them on her way to the counter to order her usual—half decaf, half regular, whole milk, half an artificial sweetener—and joined them after Carlo, the owner, served her in her personal mug. It was brown and had BLING! in pink in the same feminine script as on the sign that hung over the shop's door and on the shopping bags in which her customers carted home their purchases. Carlo's wife was a potter, and every merchant in St. Dennis who frequented their shop had their own mug decorated with the name of their business. He kept the mugs lined up on a shelf behind the coffee bar, in order of their geographic location on Charles Street.

"Morning, Vanessa." Barbara Noonan, the owner of Book 'Em, the book and magazine shop several storefronts down from Bling, moved over to make room for Vanessa. "Grab a chair from that next table and sit for a few."

"Yes, have a seat," Nita Perry, whose Past Times sold antiques, chimed in. "Bring us up-to-date on the wedding."

"It's rolling right along," Vanessa told them. She slid a chair across the floor from one table to the other. "So far, so good."

"I was just saying how nice it was that Beck found such a lovely girl." Grace Sinclair held her mug between her hands as if to warm them. Grace actually had two mugs on Carlo's shelf, one for the Inn at Sinclair's Point, which technically belonged to her son, Daniel, now that she'd signed it over to him, and one for the *St. Dennis Gazette,* the newspaper she inherited from her father. Today, in honor of the upcoming wedding, Grace was using the Sinclair's Point mug.

"God knows he took his time looking." Barbara grinned. "There's going to be a lot of broken hearts in St. Dennis come Saturday."

"There aren't too many young, eligible men left," Nita added. "I don't know where these young girls are going to go to get a date."

"I heard Wade MacGregor will be back for the wedding," Grace said.

"That's one, and he doesn't count since he won't be staying. Besides, that one always was a handful."

"I always rather liked Wade." Grace smiled.

"You didn't live next door to him." Barbara frowned with disapproval. "Him and that batty old aunt of his . . ."

"Great-aunt." Grace corrected her. "Berry is his great aunt."

"Beryl Townsend was nutty as a fruitcake when she was a girl, and she's even nuttier now that she's an old woman," Barbara huffed. "My mother told me some stories about her that would singe your eyebrows."

"Watch who you're calling an old woman." Grace's eyes narrowed. "Berry isn't so very much older than I am."

"Yeah, well, you grew up." Barbara raised her mug to her lips. "She never has."

"Berry's just a wee bit of a free spirit. Always has been. She was a stage actress in her youth, you know," Grace told them.

"I guess that's where Dallas got the acting bug," Nita chimed in.

"Dallas was always a lovely girl," Grace recalled. "And Wade was a good boy. He was just a little unsettled. After all, his only sibling grew up to be a huge Hollywood star. I think after she became famous, people more or less forgot there was another MacGregor. That couldn't have been easy for the boy."

"I still say he was a pain in the butt, regardless of the reason." Barbara turned to Vanessa. "Now, where do you go to look for a nice young man these days?"

"Who, me?" Vanessa shook her head. "I'm not looking."

"Pretty young girl like you ought to have lots of dates," Barbara persisted. "You don't want to end up an old spinster like me or Nita."

"Speak for yourself," Nita said. "Besides, I was married. Once."

"Well, I think Vanessa has plenty of time to look for someone. When she decides she wants one." Grace patted Vanessa's arm. "Seemed to me that handsome brother of Mia's had his eye on you at the wedding rehearsal."

Vanessa felt a tinge of pink creep upward from her collar to her hairline.

"Oh, were you at the Inn last night?" she said to divert attention from her blush.

"I was on the veranda," Grace explained. "I think everything is going to be beautiful once Olivia decorates the trellis leading into the rose garden and the chairs are all lined up on the lawn. I heard that the weather is going to be spectacular tomorrow."

"We're keeping our fingers crossed."

The door opened and a small crowd of tourists came into the coffee shop.

Barbara glanced at the newcomers, then at her watch. "It's only eight-fifteen. Unusual for this time of year."

"Well, as I said, the weather's been glorious all week and it's going to last right through the weekend," Grace said. "All that sunshine always brings the visitors out."

"I'll bet if Beck had known that there'd be so much traffic coming into town today, he'd have gotten married last weekend. You know how he likes to keep an eye on things," Nita noted.

"Well, he deserves to have a lovely wedding day." Grace set her mug down. "I can't remember when that boy took off more than a few days at a time. He deserves to have a week off."

"Two weeks, actually," Vanessa said. "He's taking two full weeks."

"Good for him." Grace smiled. "Like I said, he deserves it."

The door opened again and another group came in. The coffee shop was beginning to get crowded, the noise level rising.

"It looks as if you all have a busy day ahead of you," Grace noted.

"From your lips to God's ears, Gracie." Nita toasted the older woman with her coffee. "The antiques business has been slow so far this year. Slower than I can remember."

"Books are holding their own," Barbara told them. "A little mystery, a little romance, a little crime fiction. Add a cup of good coffee, and for a lot of people, you have the perfect day."

Vanessa had just raised her mug to her lips when she got that feeling of unseen eyes boring into her again. She turned in her chair and glanced around. The room was packed now, and she saw no one overtly staring in her direction.

"I should get going." Vanessa stood and drank the rest of her coffee. "I need to get over to the shop and see what's what before I open."

"Ness, what do you have in dangly earrings?" Barbara asked.

"I have lots. What are you looking for?"

"Something fun to wear to your brother's wedding," Barbara explained. "Just because you're not interested in Mia's good-looking brother doesn't mean no one else is."

"He's young enough to be your son," Grace reminded her. "That makes you a dirty old woman."

"The term these days is *cougar*." Barbara pretended to be in a huff.

"Ugh. What a gross term. I don't want to hear

about it." Vanessa covered her ears and grimaced as she made her way to the counter. She smiled at Carlo and handed him her mug. Once outside, she had to move to avoid a group of five or six women who were headed in.

"Be careful," someone whispered in her ear, "or you'll get knocked to the ground. I heard that the coffee stampede around here can get ugly."

She looked over her shoulder and into Grady's eyes.

"Hey, I know how it feels to need that first cup of the day." She laughed.

"You're on your way out?" he asked.

Vanessa nodded. "I have to get my shop opened."

"I knew I shouldn't have gone back for that extra forty winks. We could have had coffee together."

"That would have been nice." She moved out of the way of a couple who were intently studying the visitors' guide. "So who won the dart game last night?"

"The game turned into a tournament. In the end, Hal was the last man standing. He beat Andy in the last round. That man can throw a dart."

"I should have warned you. He and Beck play all the time. They're both pretty good."

"I noticed. Beck was the one who knocked me out in the second round."

"So where are you off to so early?" she asked.

"Hal is taking me out on his boat to do a little crabbing. He said no one should visit the Bay without having eaten crabs he's caught himself."

She nodded. "That's Hal's idea of going out to pick

up lunch. He knows all the best spots. You should have a good day."

"You know, I never did get that tour of St. Dennis that you promised," he reminded her.

"If you can wait until Sunday, I'd be happy to show you around."

"It's going to have to be early. I'm leaving on Sunday."

"Oh. Well, you'll be staying for brunch, right? Maybe we can fit something in then, before or after. Whatever works best." She looked across the street to her shop, where several women were gathered in front of the window.

"I have to go. My customers are arriving before me."

"I'll see you tonight, then."

"Right. Dinner at Lola's," she recalled. "Seven o'clock."

"Seven. Right."

She turned and crossed the street. She looked back while she unlocked her door, but he'd already disappeared into the coffee shop.

"Good morning, ladies." She greeted the group who stood by patiently. "Welcome to Bling . . ."

It had been a hectic day. Vanessa called Nan to ask her to come in early, but she wasn't available until two, and could only stay until six, which wasn't ideal, but it was better than no Nan at all. Vanessa hoped for a break so she could reorganize things a bit, but the customers seemed to come in waves for hours. As Grace had noted earlier that morning, the warm weather brought the tourists. Well, St. Dennis was a great place to spend a few hours on a sunny day, Vanessa mused during one of her few brief lulls. You could shop, have a great lunch, take a walk along the dock, or, she smiled, you could shop.

She stepped into the back room she used for an office and saw the white eyelet dress still hanging there. She was tempted to return it to the floor, but hesitated, remembering how the woman's eyes had shined when she looked at the dress.

It can wait another day or so, Vanessa reasoned. *Just in case she does come back over the weekend. I'd hate for her to be disappointed. She looked like a woman who'd had her fair share of disappointments.*

The bell jingled over the door and she went back out to the floor. Three very stylish-looking women clustered around the jewelry counter.

"Welcome to Bling." Vanessa smiled. "Was there something you wanted to see in the case?"

"The wide silver cuff there . . . the one with the red stone." One of the women pointed a well-manicured finger at the top shelf of the glass case. "That *is* silver, isn't it?"

Vanessa slid behind the counter and unlocked the case. "The wide cuff with the big hunk of carnelian? Yes, that's solid silver, and the stone is real. Would you like to try it? There's a pendant that matches, by the way . . ."

Before ten minutes had passed, the bracelet and the pendant had been sold, along with a pair of long, dangly citrine earrings that Vanessa had thought to put aside for Barbara to try. She probably should have taken them out of the case when she first arrived that morning, but she'd barely had a minute to breathe. Who could have predicted such crowds on a Friday afternoon weeks before the season began?

Her last customers left at seven-ten. She'd hoped to have them out of the store sooner, but they'd lingered over the belts she'd unpacked earlier in the week, and she sold three of the pricey accessories to a woman who purchased one for herself and one for each of her daughters. Vanessa straightened up stacks of shorts and sweaters as quickly as she could, tucked all the hangers back onto their racks, checked the dressing rooms and the displays where handbags and scarves had been moved around. One last look to ensure that everything was neat for Nan to open in the morning, then she locked the cash in the safe and the front door behind her.

Vanessa dashed across the street to Lola's, where Grady greeted her with a warm smile that sent a tingle down to her toes.

"I was just about to walk over to your shop to see if you'd forgotten," he said.

"I was so busy today, I could hardly keep track of who was coming in and who was going out." She looked for the waiter. "I could really use a glass of wine."

Grady grabbed a bottle from the table. "Is white okay, or would you rather have red?"

"White is fine, thank you." She eased into a chair and sighed as she slipped her feet out of her shoes.

"Would you like a glass, or should I ask for a straw so you can drink it straight from the bottle?"

"A glass would be fine." She laughed.

"So you were saying you had a busy day." Grady took the chair next to her.

"Amazing. I'm usually not this busy until the end of May. Caught me totally unprepared." She spotted Mia in the group at the other side of the table, and blew her a kiss.

"Don't you have help?"

"I have an employee, Nan, who comes in part-time, several days each week starting in June, though she's helping out this week. I may have to add a full-time person, though, if this keeps up. Not that I'm complaining—I love that my shop is doing so well—but it's hard keeping up." She took a sip of wine and leaned back in her chair. "Steffie is loaning me some-one to close for me tomorrow night, though, so that I don't have to make the choice between closing up in the afternoon or leaving the reception at seven."

"Steffie owns the ice-cream shop?"

Vanessa nodded. "She's a good friend."

"I stopped in there with Hal today, after we got back from crabbing. I had two scoops of Mocha Berry Vanessa, by the way."

"What?"

"She said it was a brand-new flavor. Mocha Berry Vanessa."

Vanessa thought about her deal with her friend, and the way Steffie's eyes lit up when she first saw herself in *the dress*.

"She really did it! She named an ice-cream flavor after me." Vanessa laughed. "What's in it? And more importantly, was it any good?"

"Mocha ice cream and raspberries. Highly recom-mended with a sprinkling of chocolate chunks and pecans."

"I'm definitely going to have to sample that before

she retires the flavor." She took another drink, then sat the glass on the table. It felt so good to be off her feet, sipping a glass of excellent wine. She had to admit, the company went a long way to improving her mood. "So you crabbed today. Where did Hal take you?"

"Everywhere. Name someplace. That man knows more places where crabs hide. We were in the river—"

"The New River? The one that runs along St. Dennis, then into the Bay?"

He nodded. "And we went out to some island, then along a cove. To a nature preserve to see the migrating birds."

"Ah, you got the full tour."

"Only by water. After we docked, we went back to the police station and steamed the crabs we caught." He took a sip of beer. "Don't forget, you're walking me around town on Sunday."

"I won't forget." She paused, then asked as casually as she could, "What time are you planning on leaving St. Dennis?"

"I'd like to be on the road by around three."

"Are you catching a flight back to Montana?"

He shook his head. "No, I'm driving to Virginia, staying over, and doing a hike on Monday morning."

"Oh."

"Bull Run Mountains. I heard it was a good climb. I've been looking forward to it."

"Oh," she said again, because she couldn't think of anything else to say.

The waiters came in to serve dinner, and everyone sat at the table. More toasts were made again this night, and more tears shed. By the end of the evening,

Vanessa's head was pounding, mostly, she thought, from all the champagne she drank at the end of every toast. When she got up to leave, she wobbled.

"Whoa, there." Grady stood and took her elbow.

"Sorry. Just a little unsteady. Sorry. I'm not used to this much champagne."

"I'll walk you out to your car." He was still holding on to her arm.

"Actually, I walked to work this morning, so I'll be walking home." She leaned on the back of the chair to steady herself.

"Are you sure you're all right?"

"Hey, you try standing in these four-inch heels for . . ." She checked the wall clock. It was nine-thirty. ". . . thirteen and a half hours."

He looked at her feet. "I don't think they'd fit."

She peered down at his. "Well, the straps are adjustable."

"Yeah, but I don't know how that plum color would look with my white athletic socks."

"Oh, dear God, don't put pictures like that in my head," she groaned, and Grady laughed.

"Come on," he said, "I'll drive you home."

"I need to say good night to everyone first."

"Let's do that."

They made the rounds—hugs and kisses and see-you-in-the-mornings—then made their way out to Grady's rental car.

"You just go to the stop sign and take a left at the first street," she told him as he opened the passenger-side door for her.

"I remember." He slammed the door and walked around to the driver's side and got in. "Your house is almost to the end of the third block. Lots of pink and purple tulips in the front yard."

"Right." She smiled to herself, pleased that he'd remembered, that he'd opened the car door for her, that he'd offered her a ride home. "Thanks for the ride, Grady."

"I couldn't have you walking three blocks after"— he checked the clock on the dashboard—"fourteen hours in those shoes."

She was still smiling when he pulled into her driveway.

"So what do you think of our little town?" she asked.

"I like what I've seen of it, land and sea. I noticed a lot of old buildings—like, late 1700s, early 1800s— around the square. But I'm not going to ask about them now. I'm saving all that for my tour on Sunday."

"I wouldn't think of spoiling it for you." She unbuckled her seat belt. "But I will tell you, that's the oldest part of town. Hal lives up in that area, right off the square. His great-grandfather built the house he lives in."

"He's one really interesting guy. While we were out on the boat the other day, he was telling me about how when he was younger, he played with a minor-league baseball team. He might have had a shot at the majors if he hadn't been sent to Nam."

Vanessa nodded. "All true. He has a scrapbook with all these press clippings in it. Pictures of him when he was a young man. He was quite the good-looking fellow in those days."

"I guess that's around the time when your mother met him."

She stared at him for a long moment. Before she could respond, he said, "Sorry. Wrong thing to have said, apparently, judging from your reaction. I apologize."

"It's not that. I just wouldn't have expected him to bring her up. And yes, that's when my mother met Hal, when he was a dashing, soon-to-be-professional ballplayer."

"He talked about her when we were out on the boat today."

"He did?" Vanessa was wide-eyed. "He never talks about her to me or to Beck. What did he say?"

"Just pretty much what he said last night, that he'd always thought he'd have a family, but it didn't work out for him the way he thought it would. That having Beck in his life, even if he hadn't had him as a little boy, and having you, even as late as you came to him, made it all right, in the end."

"He said that?"

Grady nodded. "He's really proud of both of you."

She stared out the window. "I don't know what I'd be doing, or where I'd be, if not for Hal. It's really hard to explain what he means to me."

"The father you never had. I get it."

She shook her head. "That isn't the half of it. I mean, yeah, it's true that he filled that role, since I never had a father, but it isn't the whole of it. Before I came here, no one had ever had any expectations of me, including me. I never figured to amount to very much."

"Why would you feel that way?"

"I was the girl in high school who wore too much makeup and who dated guys who were way too old for me. The girl with the flighty mother who moved around a lot. I never asked much of myself because I didn't know I could—or should. No one ever had. Hal was the first person in my life to believe in me, to make me understand that I could be more than what I was, but that I had to demand more from myself." She shrugged. "I was late catching on."

"Hey, that's a lesson that some people never learn."

"You know, if he and Beck had just been friendly and cordial to me when I first came here, I'd have gone back to where I came from, or gone somewhere else and had the same kind of life I had before, because I didn't know any better. But they took me in, right away, made me family, never asked a damn thing of me, gave me a place, but even more than that, they made room for me in their lives. And because of them, now I do know better. And I will never go back and I will never settle for less."

She cleared her throat, surprised that she'd said so much, revealed so much. "Too much information, right?"

"Not by a long shot." He shook his head. "Not enough."

"Well, maybe enough for tonight. Right now I have several dozen unglazed cookies waiting for me and I have an early day tomorrow. I appreciate the ride home."

"It was my pleasure. But I could help out with those cookies, you know."

"Thanks, but I can handle it."

"If you're sure . . ."

"I am." She unbuckled her seat belt and opened the car door and stepped out onto the drive. She turned to say, "See you tomorrow," when she realized he'd gotten out of the car, too.

"I'll walk you to your door," he told her.

She smiled to herself. *Does the cowboy think he's about to get lucky?*

He took her arm, but when the space between her fence and the car narrowed, his hand slid down her arm to her hand, and they walked single file to the sidewalk. He began to say something, when Vanessa stopped cold in her tracks.

"Oh my God. What the hell . . . ?" She stood openmouthed at the foot of the path leading to her front door.

He followed her gaze to the ground, where here and there, tulips lay scattered, bent and broken.

She could barely believe her eyes. "It looks like a tornado went through here."

"How do you suppose this happened?"

"I don't know. Cujo, maybe."

"Cujo?"

"The Kleins' dog. They live behind me and over a couple of properties. They have this dog that gets out every chance he gets. He always runs through my yard on the way to the park."

Grady squatted and picked up a broken stem. "How much does this dog weigh?"

"Probably forty or fifty pounds. Why?"

"Because whatever flattened this flower had some heft behind it. I'm guessing more than forty or fifty pounds' worth." He picked one up and held it for her to see. "Any kids in the neighborhood who might be prone to a little vandalism now and then?"

"The Carr boys from around the corner get into trouble once in a while." Vanessa began to pick up the flowers that lay on the ground, gathering the ones with stems intact into a bouquet.

"What kind of trouble?"

"Eggs behind the car tires and toilet paper in the trees on mischief night. That sort of thing. Nothing serious. But I wouldn't want to accuse them. I've never had a problem with any of them myself." She held the flowers in one hand. "If you knew how long it took me to plant these bulbs . . . damn. I was so proud of my little garden."

"Why don't we just clean this up right now," he suggested.

"There isn't enough light out here," she said. "I think it's going to have to wait until the morning."

"You sure?"

She nodded. "I picked up the ones I could see in the porch light, but if I start raking up the broken ones and the leaves, I may end up making an even bigger mess. I planted different varieties so they'd bloom at different times. I figure I have another few weeks of blooms to go yet. If I try to clean up in the dark, I'm likely to break some of the ones still in bud."

"I'm sorry you had to come home to this. I can see it's upset you."

"Well, like I said, more will bloom over the next few weeks, and of course, they will bloom again next year." She smiled wistfully. "Maybe by then the Kleins will have decided to fence their yard."

She held the bunch of tulips in her arm while she searched her bag for her keys.

"Well, anyway, thanks for driving me home. I'll see you tomorrow at the wedding." She brightened at the thought of the wedding. "Wait till you see your sister. She's going to be the most glorious bride ever."

She located her keys and went up the porch steps to the door. As she did, the flowers slipped in her arms and the keys clattered to the ground.

"Let me do that." Grady came up behind her and placed one hand on the small of her back while he picked up her keys with the other. He fitted the key into the lock and started to push the door open, then stopped. He stood behind her, one step lower, so that when she turned around to thank him, there was barely breathing room between them.

Later, she tried to decide who had moved first. She thought it might have been him, but she wasn't sure, because at that moment, the urge to kiss him had been overwhelming. All she knew for certain was that one minute she was looking down, watching those sure fingers unlock her front door, and the next minute, her mouth was locked with his. She hadn't been expecting it, but by the time she realized that she was kissing him back, the kiss was over and those lips that had been pressed to hers were whispering, "I'll see you tomorrow."

"Right." She'd managed to nod. "See you tomorrow."

He'd started down the sidewalk, walking backward the way he'd done on Thursday. "Go on in, now," he'd said. "You know I can't leave until I know you're safely inside your house."

"What do you think could happen between now and the time you get into your car?"

"Old habits die hard," he'd told her, and she'd gone in and locked the door behind her.

From the dining room window, Vanessa watched him get into his car and back out of the drive, then onto Cherry. She watched until the tail lights disappeared halfway into the next block. She listened to a few voice-mail messages—Nan reminding her that she would be leaving the shop early on Saturday, so she hoped Vanessa had found someone to lock up—and Steffie thanking her again for the deep discount on the dress she'd be wearing to the wedding because "I realized just how hot I look in that dress and I saw Wade MacGregor this afternoon when he hit town, and if I ever needed to look spectacular, tomorrow would be it. To celebrate, I named a flavor after you . . . which Mountain Man sampled when he stopped by, you should know. Just sayin' . . ." There were two hang-ups then, and she checked the caller ID, but both calls were from private numbers.

She kicked off her shoes near the bottom of the steps and left them there, then went into the kitchen. She checked the glaze on the cookies and found it had hardened to an acceptable degree.

She ran upstairs and changed her clothes, then came back down and slipped on her apron. She looked amid the clutter on her kitchen counters for the lemon-glaze recipe. She found it, but before she started to gather the ingredients, she flipped through a box of CDs. She wanted something she could sing along with, something with a little bit of beat. She decided on Keith Urban, slipped the disc into the little

Bose system she kept in the kitchen on one of the wide windowsills, turned up the volumn, and began to sing.

Tomorrow, before she went to the Inn, she would box the cookies and tie them up with the pink grosgrain ribbon Mia had picked out, then load them up and drive them to the Inn, where they'd be placed on the table with the guests' name cards.

It was almost two by the time she'd glazed every last one of the cookies and turned out the light on her bedside table. She lay back against her pillow, closed her eyes, and raised her fingers to her lips to touch the place where Grady's lips had been. Judging by that one kiss, she'd have to rate him pretty high on the kissing scale. It had been, she'd decided, a pretty damned fine kiss. She tried to remember the last time she'd really, really wanted to be kissed, and realized that she couldn't. She fell asleep wondering whether she'd get the chance to kiss him again.

Diary—

Daniel has been beside himself getting the Inn ready for Saturday's wedding and reception. I've been telling him for the past year that he needs to hire an event coordinator, but he says he just hasn't gotten around to it. I say he isn't willing to hand over control of anything connected to the Inn to anyone else. For example, I said that he could ask his sister to come home and do her wedding-planning thing right here at the Inn, but no. "Lucy will come back when she's ready, and apparently <u>she isn't ready yet</u>." Says he. Hmmph, says I.

Anyway—earlier this evening I just happened to be on the balcony off my suite enjoying my after-dinner coffee when the bridal party arrived to rehearse! Mia looked so tiny walking up the aisle between her two brothers—Hal said their father died last year, so it's nice that she has them to accompany her. I just happened to be in the flower shop today when the flowers for the wedding arrived—such glorious colors! Oh, the shades of pink! The peonies! The roses! The hydrangeas! I can't wait to see what magic Olivia performs with those blooms!

I daresay this will be a wedding everyone will be talking about for a long time to come!

—Grace

Now, just you calm down there, honey." Hal stood in Vanessa's foyer watching her run around to gather everything she needed before they left for the Inn. "We've got plenty of time. I promise the wedding won't start without us."

"I need to get there a little early." She ran past him on her way upstairs for the third time since he arrived. "I have all these favors to take with me so they can be put out on the table with the place cards, and I have to run back upstairs for my dress and I can't find my shoes."

"Take a deep breath, slow down, and put one foot in front of the other." Hal looked amused, and in spite of herself, the sight of the older man in his tux, a silly smile on his face and the box of prettily wrapped cookie boxes in his arms, made Vanessa smile, too. "I swear, even Beck didn't seem to be as excited as you this morning."

"Beck doesn't have an appointment to get his hair and makeup done in fifteen minutes," she called down the steps as she ran up them.

"Well, it would be a first if he did."

"What?" she asked as she flew down the steps, the dress over one arm, shoes in her hand, and a tote over her shoulder.

"I said, Beck didn't mention having made an appointment to have his hair and makeup done this morning."

"Oh, you . . . ." She swatted at him with her free hand. "I think I have everything." Mentally she went through her checklist.

"Does this mean we can leave? This box is getting heavy."

"Oh, you could have set that down, but yes, I'm ready. Let me just find my keys. You go on out, I'll be right with you."

Hal went out through the front while Vanessa searched her bag for her keys with her free hand. She found them in the pocket of her jeans where she'd stashed them while looking for her shoes. When she joined Hal outside, he was in the middle of the yard, looking over the debris that had been her carefully planted tulip bulbs.

"What the heck happened here?" he asked.

"I'm not sure, but I think Cujo might have gotten out last night and gone on a tear." She locked the door and dropped the keys into her bag. "It was like this when I got back from Lola's. I picked the ones that had a stem and a flower still attached to it and brought them inside and put them in a vase, so at least they've gone to good use. First thing this morning I gathered up the loose leaves and petals that were scattered around and trashed them. It actually looks better than it did."

"Jason is going to have to do something about that

dog." Hal frowned. "I know he isn't vicious, but he's fast, and he could hurt someone, or at the least, give someone one hell of a scare if he bowled them over. You should say something to them."

"I really don't want to do that." She shook her head as she walked to Hal's car. "For one thing, they're good neighbors except for their dog occasionally taking a shortcut through my yard. For another, I don't know for sure that the dog caused the damage. It could have been some kids up to mischief."

Hal opened the trunk of his car and set the box of favors inside. "That's vandalism, not simple mischief."

"I don't know if little kids would see it that way." Vanessa carefully placed her dress across the backseat and got into the front passenger side. "Anyway, some of the bulbs hadn't bloomed yet, so there will still be a little bit of a show over the next few weeks."

Hal slammed the trunk and got into the driver's seat. As he backed onto Cherry Street, Vanessa said, "Thanks for picking me up this morning."

"Well, I thought it would be nice if we got to ride over to the Inn together. It's a family sort of day."

"It is." She returned the smile, and wanted to say something like, *Thank you for letting me be part of your family, Hal.* But the words wouldn't come, so she simply said, "Anyway, I appreciate the ride."

"I would have driven you home last night, but I hear Grady beat me to it."

"We were leaving at the same time, so he gave me a ride." She tried to shrug it off and make light of it. "I didn't have time to hang around much after dinner because I still had so much to do here to get ready for the wedding. For some reason, Grady thought I shouldn't walk home alone in the dark. I think he spent too many years in the FBI. As if anything ever happens in St. Dennis."

"Well, we do have a pretty safe town here, and your neighborhood is generally a good one. That business a few years ago, though . . . all those girls being murdered." He shook his head. Vanessa knew it was still painful for him and Beck to look back on the killer who'd taken several young lives, including that of the first woman police officer on their force. "But Grady probably knows better than most of us that there's no such thing as a place that is one hundred percent safe, one hundred percent of the time. God knows he's been closer to the devil than any of the rest of us have, and I've been in law enforcement for more than thirty years."

"Maybe so, but one of the things that I really like about living here is that I can walk to and from work every day. It's not just the exercise, and it's not just that I'm saving gasoline. I like the peacefulness, the quiet mornings before everything comes alive, and the hum of things winding down at the end of the day, know what I mean? This town is so slow to wake up and early to bed most days."

Hal chuckled. "Well, for another few weeks, anyway. Then we get full into the season and things won't be slow around here again till September. But I do know what you mean. The rhythm around here is more downbeat than up-tempo."

"That's exactly what I meant."

She turned her head to look out the window as Hal made a left onto Charles Street and headed out toward Sinclair's Point. They passed marshes where the cattails were growing tall and green again and the migrating birds had already stopped to forage for food and rest. A red-winged blackbird sat atop a reed that swayed in the morning breeze, and a hawk rose on a thermal to see what it could see. Vanessa had never been much of a nature girl, but that had changed when she moved to St. Dennis and Hal taught her to notice things she'd overlooked before.

"If you're going to live on the Bay, you need to know the Bay, and all its inhabitants," he'd told her, and took it upon himself to teach her what he thought she should know.

Vanessa took no small amount of secret pride in the fact that she could now recognize several birds by their calls alone, and could tell a wood duck from a mallard, a mallard from a blue-winged teal from a northern shoveler. She knew more about crabs— the Chesapeake being the home of the famed blue claws—than she ever suspected there was to know. She learned to tell a sook—an adult female crab— from a jimmy—an adult male—and the best way to catch them as well as the best ways to cook them. All tiny triumphs, but to her, triumphs all the same.

The car slowed as they approached the entrance to the Inn at Sinclair's Point, marked by a handsome sign adorned with a painted life-size great blue heron, to which someone had tied a very large bunch of pink, navy, and lime-green balloons.

"I guess this is the place," Hal said as he made the turn.

"I'm so excited." Vanessa could barely contain her-self. "This will be the first wedding I've ever been in."

Hal shot her a look of surprise but said nothing.

"No, neither of mine were anything like this." She sighed and wished she didn't feel the need to explain. "Anyway, I'm excited for Mia and for Beck."

"I am, too." Hal parked near the entrance to the Inn. "Let's get you and your gear inside, then I'll park over in the lot."

He got out of the car and walked around to the trunk. One of the staff who'd been hired for the special event appeared to give Hal a hand with the box of favors.

"Give those directly to Claudia," Vanessa called after the young man who was hurrying up the walk with the box. "She's probably waiting for them."

"Will do," he assured her.

Vanessa gathered up her dress, her shoes, her bag, and stood on her toes to plant a kiss on Hal's cheek.

"Thank you again. It makes it extra special for me to be here with you." She swallowed what she knew would be only the first of many lumps that would come and go in her throat over the course of the day. "I don't thank you often enough for all you do for me, not the least of which is to always find ways to remind me that—"

"You don't have to say it, Ness." Hal patted her on the back. "Now go on in and help your almost sister-in-law get ready for her big day."

Vanessa nodded. "Right. The photographer will be here any minute. Maybe I'll get lucky and she'll start taking pictures of the guys first."

She hustled into the Inn and stopped at the desk to get directions to the suite the bridal party was using for hair, makeup, and dressing. She ran up the wide

central stairway and down the hall to the last suite on
the right. Mia, Annie, and Dorsey were all in various
stages of prep. The hairdresser provided by the Inn
had started with Mia, whose long hair had been carefully worked into a French braid, and was just finish-
ing up with Annie and getting ready to move on to
Dorsey. Mia's makeup was almost complete, and the
chatter and laughter seemed to be calming everyone's nerves. Before Vanessa arrived, a cart had been
wheeled in with plates of fresh fruit and croissants
and coffee, and Vanessa helped herself while waiting
her turn. She stepped through the French doors onto
the balcony and looked down on the lawn where the
actual wedding would take place and the reception
tent had been set up. An altar had been erected for the
ceremony, and it was now completely covered with
garlands of magnolia leaves and white hydrangea,
baby's breath, and pink roses. Shepherd's hooks lined
the aisle, and silver cones hung from the hooks.

"The cones are going to look gorgeous after Olivia
finishes with them," Vanessa called back into the
room to Mia.

"I noticed the cones earlier," Annie said. "What's
going in them?"

"Bunches of peonies and hydrangea." Mia's eyes
sparkled. "And Olivia is going to scatter rose petals
up the aisle and there will be large urns of flowers at
the ends of the front two rows of chairs. It's going to
be gorgeous."

"It will be," Vanessa agreed, and leaned on the railing to watch the staff set up the guests' chairs in a fan
shape in front of the altar.

She continued to watch all the scurrying below and

wondered what it would be like to have a day like this. It was painful to admit even to herself, but secretly, she couldn't help but envy the fairy-tale wedding, with Mia a bride so beautiful she could have stepped right out of the pages of a magazine, and Beck a real life Prince Charming. In her heart, Vanessa most envied that Mia had found someone wonderful who truly loved her, someone who would love her for better or for worse, in sickness and in health, and all the rest of the promises that people made on their wedding day. For Vanessa, none of those promises had been kept. For Mia, Vanessa was certain that Beck would keep every one.

She deserves it all, Vanessa reflected, *and I truly am so very happy for her. She deserves to have it all: the dress and the fabulous day and the wonderful guy and the happily-ever-after—and yes, even the one-thousand-plus glazed lemon cookies. Mia has done the right thing all her life, has made all the right decisions, and had the good fortune and the good sense to fall in love with a very special guy who loves her deeply.*

Vanessa couldn't help but wonder what it would feel like to have such a day, such a life. The envy she felt wasn't the soul-killing, turn-green-and-spit-fire kind, but more a wistful, I-wonder-what-it-would-have-been-like-if-I'd-been-more-like-her envy. And maybe it was also partly because Mia was the person Vanessa wished she'd grown up to be.

"Ness?" Mia was calling to her. "Ness?"

"Oh. Sorry." Vanessa planted a huge smile on her face before turning around. "I was just watching the goings-on and must have zoned out."

"Well, zone back in. It's your turn."

Vanessa came back into the room, her smile intact, and placed a kiss on Mia's cheek as she walked past on her way to the chair where the hairdresser waited.

"What was that for?" Mia asked.

"Just because I'm happy for you," Vanessa said, and meant it.

"Aw, thanks, Ness. I'd kiss you back, but I just had this mouth painted on." Mia pointed to her very rosy lips.

"I spent ten minutes on that mouth," the makeup artist reminded her. "Do not mess with the mouth."

The chatter started back up again with the arrival of the photographer. Vanessa sat while her hair was being blown out, watching and listening, happy to be there, grateful that she was part of this wonderful day when all was right in the world.

She held on to that feeling while her makeup was being applied and she slid into the light-as-a-feather green silk dress; while she floated down the stairs with the other members of the bridal party; while she listened to the strings begin to play. She felt as if she had a part in a magical play—until she started down the aisle and made the mistake of glancing to her right. There, in the last row of seats, in the chair closest to the aisle, stood a woman who looked so much like her mother they could have been twins. Vanessa did a double take.

The woman winked and waved.

Dear God, it *was* her mother.

Feeling a bit like a deer caught in the headlights, Vanessa somehow managed to make it down the aisle without missing a step.

How had Maggie found out about the wedding? Surely Beck hadn't invited her. Beck never spoke to her. Hell, he rarely spoke *of* her.

What in the name of all that's holy was she doing there?

And oh, God, what was Beck going to do when he saw her?

Vanessa took her place at the head of the aisle and maintained a fixed smile, even when she met Beck's eyes. She detected no hellfire burning there, so he apparently hadn't gotten the good news yet. She focused on Anne Marie, and then on Mia, who appeared at the foot of the aisle between her handsome brothers.

Mia was a picture-perfect bride, with every detail just so, from the flowers in her hair to the amazing gown. Vanessa stole a glance at Beck, who looked positively gob-smacked, and definitely close to needing oxygen. Then her gaze locked with Grady's for a moment, and she felt the color rise in her cheeks, as if he could read her mind to know that she'd awakened that morning thinking about him.

The minister stood at the flower-covered altar and stepped forward to begin the ceremony. Vanessa barely heard a word, her attention divided between thinking about Grady and the big uh-oh back there in the last row.

The minister pronounced Beck and Mia husband and wife, they kissed, and Annie handed Mia her bouquet, which Annie had held while the rings were exchanged. The bride and groom turned to their guests and the strings began to play the recessional. The newly married couple was halfway down the aisle when Beck momentarily froze. Vanessa closed her eyes as Annie and Hal fell in behind Beck and Mia as they'd rehearsed, followed by Andy and Dorsey.

"Vanessa." Grady was at her elbow.

"Oh." Her eyes flew open and she took his arm just as a smiling Maggie took one step toward the aisle to greet Beck and Mia. Vanessa held her breath as Beck walked past Maggie, apparently without giving any sign of recognition, judging by Maggie's reaction.

"Oh, dear God," Vanessa muttered. "Why did she have to do that?"

"What?" Grady leaned closer.

Vanessa just shook her head and craned her neck to see if Hal had noticed Maggie, but she guessed he had not. Not yet, at least. Hal never would have ignored her the way Beck had.

But how would the tenderhearted Hal react when he realized that Maggie was there? Remembering the toast he'd given on Thursday night, one might suspect that Hal had always carried a torch for the woman who had given birth to his son and whom he'd once hoped to marry.

Well, Beck once said he wanted fireworks at his wedding, Vanessa recalled. *I don't think this is what he had in mind, but if you toss a thought out into the cosmos, you better be prepared for whatever form it takes when it comes back at you.*

The guests followed the wedding party onto the veranda, where the cocktail party was to take place.

"How about a glass of champagne?" Grady asked.

"Oh, yes. Please," she replied.

He signaled the waiter as Maggie stepped onto the porch.

"On second thought"—Vanessa grabbed Grady's arm—"ask him to bring the whole bottle . . ."

From the corner of her eye, Vanessa tried to keep track of her mother in the crowd. For most of the cocktail party, Maggie kept to herself, standing alone at the doorway to the lobby, or on the lawn, sipping her champagne and looking uncomfortable.

Well, what did she expect? Vanessa thought. *Did she really think that Beck would welcome her with open arms?*

Apparently, she had. Otherwise, why would she have come, uninvited and unexpected?

Vanessa sighed deeply.

"Excuse me," she said to Grady. "There's someone here I need to talk to."

She walked to the doorway and stopped in front of her mother.

"Hello, Maggie," she said.

"Well, at least you remember me, which is more than your brother seems to do."

"Oh, come on. What did you expect him to do? Seriously."

"I guess I didn't think about it, other than, oh, my son is getting married. This might be the opportunity I've been waiting for all these years." She wiped a tear from her face. "I can't believe he looked right through me like that, as if I didn't exist."

"Maggie, don't play that card. Don't pretend to be the injured party. You abandoned him, it wasn't the other way around."

"What could you possibly know about that?"

Maggie's eyes narrowed. "What could you possibly know—"

"I know what Beck's told me, that you brought him to Hal and dumped him and went back to your life. Are you going to tell me it happened any other way?"

"It wasn't quite that simple."

"Whatever you say, Maggie." Vanessa felt a monster headache coming on. "How did you know about the wedding?"

"Well, obviously not from either of my children."

"Did Hal tell you?" As soon as she said it, Vanessa knew he had not. Knowing how Beck felt about his mother, Hal never would have done such a thing behind his back.

"Of course not."

"Then who . . . ?"

"I called your shop the other day, and when I told the girl who answered that I was your mother, she said you were home baking cookies for Beck's wedding. Well, of course I wanted to be here. I took the first flight I could get—I had to take several connecting flights; it was not a pleasant trip, let me tell you. But I got into town early this morning, took a room here at the Inn, and here we are."

"Where's . . ." Vanessa tried to recall the name of her mother's current husband. "You know. Mr. Turner."

"He passed away six weeks ago. That's why I've been calling you and leaving messages that haven't been returned."

"I'm sorry to hear about your loss, Maggie."

Vanessa conveniently passed over the part about the unreturned phone calls. She would have called to offer condolences if her mother had left a message that had gone beyond "Call me."

"Well, you know, he was so much older than I, and he'd been ill for a long time now." She shook her head imperceptibly. "I do wish you could have met him, Vanessa. He was the best of all the ones I married."

"Well, knowing you, Maggie, I'm sure you'll land on your feet."

"That was a mean-spirited thing to say to a woman who's just been widowed."

Before Vanessa could reply, Mia swept across the brick floor and grabbed Vanessa's hand.

"We're doing pictures." When she realized Vanessa had been in conversation, she apologized. "I'm so sorry. I didn't mean to interrupt . . ."

"That's all right, dear," Maggie told her. "We were finished."

Mia hesitated. "Do I know you?"

"Ah, no." Vanessa squeezed Mia's hand. "This is . . . ah, this is my mother, Maggie Turner."

"Oh." Mia looked momentarily startled, but recovered nicely. "Well. It's nice to meet you."

"It's lovely to meet you." If Maggie had anything else to say, she kept it to herself. Mia saved the awkward moment. "I hope you'll stay for the reception, Mrs. Turner."

"I don't believe my son would like that, but I appreciate the thought."

"I know there will be room. We had a few unexpected no-shows, so please stay."

"Mia." Annie poked her head through the door. "The photographer is getting antsy."

"Right. We're coming." Mia smiled at Maggie. "Stay."

"Thank you," Maggie said noncommittally.

Vanessa all but dragged Mia into the lobby.

"Are you crazy? Beck is going to have a fit. He doesn't want Maggie here. I think he made that very clear."

"She's come a long way, right? From somewhere out west? She should stay. If Beck doesn't want to speak with her, that is his choice. Not the one I'd make, if it were up to me, or if she was my mother, but he has that right. And I have the right to ask her to stay." Mia slowed her steps. "She looked so sad, Vanessa. When I saw her standing there with you, my first thought was, 'Who is that sad woman?' It isn't going to hurt anyone if she's here for a while. Besides, I bet Hal will be happy to see her."

"Now see, that's the one thing that's bothering me the most about her being here. I don't want Hal to get all sentimental over her. I don't think he's ever gotten over her. She married someone else way back then— and she's married several other someones since—and she's just lost another husband, which means she's going to be looking for a new one sometime real soon. Maggie is never without a man in her life. Besides, she isn't good for Hal."

"Well, I think that would be for them to work out."

The conversation dropped because the photographer had the shot lined up and was only waiting for Mia and Vanessa to take their places, Mia in the center with her new husband, Vanessa on the end with Grady.

"So did you get rid of him?" Grady whispered as she posed.

"Get rid of who?" she whispered back.

"Whoever it was you had to see."

"It's a long story." She sighed. "But it wasn't a *him*. It was my mother . . ."

"Oh."

"Mia had the same reaction when I told her. Just . . . 'oh.' I guess no one knows what else to say."

"What did you say when you realized she was here? Or did you know she was coming?"

"I think my first reaction might have been, 'Oh shit, that can't be her.' But I can't be sure because I was walking up the aisle when I saw her and I think my mind went temporarily numb. And no, I didn't know she even knew about the wedding."

"Are you upset that she's here?"

"I'm upset that she upset Beck by coming uninvited. I'm upset because she knows better. And I'm upset because I'm afraid she'll . . ." She could barely get the words out.

"You're afraid she'll what?"

"She's newly single and I'm afraid she'll hit on Hal."

"Well." Grady cleared his throat. "I didn't see that coming. But, if I could point out, you're upset for everyone except yourself."

"I can handle Maggie being here."

"You sure about that?"

"Of course."

"Then maybe you should let everyone else handle her presence here on their own terms, too."

She fell silent, and was grateful when the photographer switched their placements so that all the men were on one side and all the women on the other. After the last frame was shot, it was time for dinner to be served, and the wedding party went as a group to the tent that had been set up on the south lawn, facing the Bay. There were toasts before and during dinner, and dancing on the wooden dance floor in the center of the tent. Vanessa tried to push from her mind the whole unsettling mess of her mother being there and her brother refusing to acknowledge it.

Grady is right, she told herself as she swayed in his arms to a seventies ballad. *We'll all have to deal with this on our own.*

At that moment, all she really wanted to deal with was Grady. She pushed everything else from her mind, and moved closer when he drew her in, reluctant to move away when the band stopped playing. She liked the feel of his body next to hers, the way they moved together, the way he held her, the way she almost came up to the tip of his chin—well, at least in these shoes she did.

She knew the exact moment she decided to seduce him.

The band had just finished playing two slow dances back-to-back: a fairly decent cover of Journey's "Open Arms" led right into the brassy female lead singer's somewhat cheesy version of the Bangles' "Eternal Flame." Grady never let Vanessa out of his arms, just held her, his eyes looking into hers as they moved from one dance into the next. In that moment, her entire body seemed to come to life, and she wanted the music to keep playing on and on. When the last note faded away, it took all of her willpower not to wrap her arms around his neck and draw him into the longest kiss he'd ever had.

Oh, my. Wouldn't Cuppachino be buzzing in the morning.

The best part was she knew that he was thinking— feeling—exactly the same way, that her thoughts had somehow become his, and her wants mirrored his own. Had it been anyone's wedding other than her brother's, she would have suggested that they leave right then and there.

But it *was* her brother's wedding—his sister's, too, she reminded herself—and there'd be no sneaking out early. It was all right, though, she told herself. She could wait. They'd have all night.

And there was still Maggie . . .

"Are you going to introduce me to your friend?" Maggie caught Vanessa's arm as she and Grady made their way back to their seats at the head table.

"Maggie, this is Grady Shields," Vanessa said levelly. "Grady, meet my mother, Maggie Turner."

"Nice to meet you, Mrs. Turner." Grady greeted Maggie politely, as Vanessa knew he would do.

"Well, you're certainly a tall one, aren't you?" Maggie appraised him. "But very good-looking. Vanessa, don't you think he's—"

"Ah, Grady, now would be a good time to maybe scout up a glass of wine for me, if you wouldn't mind." Vanessa forced a smile, something she felt she'd gotten plenty of practice doing that day.

"I don't mind at all." He turned to Maggie. "Mrs. Turner? Could I bring something for you?"

"Why, a glass of champagne would be lovely, thank you." Maggie flashed him her best smile, one Vanessa was certain was not fake. Maggie loved nothing more than flirting with a good-looking man.

"Should I bring the bottle?" he deadpanned, and Vanessa nodded slowly.

"Well, he certainly is something." Maggie appraised Grady as he walked away. "Did you say he's the bride's brother?"

"No, I didn't say, but he is." Vanessa sighed and sat in the nearest chair. "I see you decided to stay."

"And I'm glad I did. It's a lovely reception." Maggie scanned the room, her eyes fixing on Mia. "Is she as nice as she seems?"

"She's wonderful. Beck couldn't have found anyone nicer."

"I'm glad." Maggie's face softened. "He deserves . . . well, I guess we all deserve to be happy, don't we?" She forced a brightness into her voice that Vanessa suspected she didn't really feel.

"I suppose."

Maggie patted Vanessa on the arm. "I'm sure you'll find someone just as nice, honey."

"I'm not looking for another husband, Maggie. I'm not going that route again. Twice was enough."

"Oh, you say that now. But I bet you'll change your mind when—"

"I doubt anything could change my mind."

"Life can get very lonely when you're by yourself."

Vanessa rolled her eyes. "When were you ever by

yourself? I can't remember a time when you weren't with someone."

If Vanessa had intended to wound, she'd hit the mark.

"You don't know everything, missy," Maggie snapped.

"I know that there was never a time in my life, growing up, when there wasn't one man leaving and another coming in to take his place."

"Is that really what you remember, when you look back on your childhood?" Maggie appeared surprised.

Vanessa nodded.

"Oh, honey . . ." Maggie moved toward her daughter, but Vanessa stepped back, both hands up as if to ward off her mother.

"It's a little late, Maggie," Vanessa told her. "Besides, that's a conversation for another day."

"All right." Maggie nodded. "We'll talk about something a little less . . . charged." She appeared to think for a moment, then said, "So, I guess you were surprised to hear from Shannon."

"Who?"

"Shannon. Your best friend from high school."

"Maggie, I didn't have any friends in high school."

"Of course you did, honey. Don't be silly. Why else would she have called to get your address so that she could get in touch about the reunion?"

"What reunion?" Vanessa frowned. "Who wanted my address?"

"Haven't you been paying any attention? Shannon called about your high school reunion."

"Shannon who?"

"I don't know." Maggie's exasperation was evident. "She was your friend."

"I don't know anyone named Shannon, and I cannot imagine that anyone I went to high school with would give a rat's ass whether I showed up at a reunion or not."

"So, I guess that means you haven't heard from her."

"I haven't heard from her or anyone else." Vanessa rubbed her temples. The headache had all the makings of a monster. *Please,* she begged the tiny man she imagined was responsible for all the pounding inside her head. *Please go away. Not tonight . . .*

"That's strange, because she called over a week ago, and seemed so eager to get in touch. She was so interested in hearing about where you lived and what you were doing these days. I'm really surprised that you haven't heard from her."

"Well, if I ever do, I suppose the mystery will be solved."

The band started up again, and Vanessa watched Steffie lead a tall, ruggedly handsome man onto the dance floor, and she wondered if this was the enigmatic Wade MacGregor.

Steffie does look fabulous in that dress, Vanessa thought. *I'm going to have to tell her . . .*

". . . but I'm not sure that I want to do that," Maggie was saying.

"Not sure you want to do what?" Vanessa tuned back in.

"I'm not sure I want to stay in St. Dennis for a few more days."

"Why would you?"

"Hal said he had some things he wanted to talk over with me." Maggie's eyes took on a soft shine. "You know, he's still the most wonderful man I have ever—"

"Uh-uh." Vanessa took her mother by the hand. "Please, don't get involved with him, don't get his hopes up. Don't get him tangled up with you again after all these years. Leave him alone, Maggie."

Maggie looked as if she'd been slapped. She backed away from Vanessa, and walked through the dancers toward the opposite side of the tent.

"Was it something you said?" Grady handed Vanessa a glass, and poured from the bottle he'd managed to talk one of the waiters out of.

"I'm afraid so." Vanessa bit the inside of her bottom lip and wondered if she should have just kept her mouth shut and let Hal take care of himself.

"Want to talk about it?"

"Maybe later." She took a sip of champagne and stood, slipping her arm through his. "Right now, it looks as if Mia and Beck are about to cut the cake. Let's go watch."

And after that, she thought as they joined the bride and groom at the cake station, they'll leave.

And then, so will we . . .

Chapter 10

EVERYTHING about the evening was perfect.
The moon was high and cast golden shadows on the Bay. There was music outside the tent as well as within: the gentle lapping of the water upon the sandy shore, the soft call of an owl, the hush of the breeze playing through the reeds at the far end of the lawn.

If I were ever to believe in romance, which I most certainly do not, Vanessa mused as she and Grady strolled through the Inn's lobby into the night air, *I almost could believe tonight.*

Hand in hand, Vanessa and Grady walked with their hips lightly touching as they descended the front steps.

"The car's at the far side of the lot. I'll run and get it," Grady told her. "I'll be right back."

She opened her mouth to say she didn't mind the walk, when she saw Steffie flying up the circular drive as if in a royal snit. Seeing Vanessa, she stormed toward the steps.

"You are not going to believe this." Steffie was wild-eyed.

"That ass Wade MacGregor, with whom I thought I was having the perfect evening, walks me outside, and of course I'm thinking, 'Yay, big night ahead.' But it turns out he's walking me to my car and he tells me he has a plane to catch, but it was sure nice seeing me and catching up and maybe we'll run into each other the next time he's in town."

"Oh, Stef . . ." Vanessa began, hoping to spare Grady the full Steffie blowout.

"No, no. I'm not finished. That was just the first part." Steffie was on a roll. There'd be no stopping her now. "So I say, well, don't let me keep you from your flight, and I stomp off to get into my car, and there are four cars parked behind me. Not one, but *four* boneheaded fools who think it's okay to block someone in have parked behind me. I can't even make a grand exit and blow cinders all over his car as I do wheelies and screech by him in a cloud of exhaust. Then Tina calls to tell me she can't lock up because she just realized I forgot to leave her the key."

Steffie blew out a long, angry breath.

"Why don't you go in and see if someone can give you a hand finding out who owns the cars that are blocking you?" Vanessa suggested. "Write down the license-plate numbers and ask the band to announce it."

Steffie waved a piece of paper. "I did that. It's going to take forever, though. Want to bet that at least two of these blockheads are in the bar, drunk, and at least one of them is in the restroom? I told Tina I'd be there fifteen minutes ago."

"I can't help you with the guy, but I can drive you to your place so you can lock up," Grady offered.

"By the time we bring you back, the cars may have been moved."

"Really? You wouldn't mind?"

"Not at all. We were just on our way out. You two wait here," Grady told them.

"Wow. He is really hot," Steffie told Vanessa when Grady disappeared into the lot. "And nice. Hot *and* nice. I'm having serious envy here. I'm really sorry you saw him first."

"I'm not." Vanessa grinned.

"What happened to 'I'm not interested in finding anyone, I don't want another guy in my life' . . . I can't recall your exact words, by virtue of the amount of champagne I drank tonight, but I definitely remember you saying you were not interested."

"That was then," Vanessa said. "Besides, it's just for tonight. He's leaving tomorrow. I probably won't even see him again unless Beck and Mia have a baby and he comes to the christening."

"What is it with these guys who blast out of here like St. Dennis is the Village of the Damned?"

"He's made plans to do something." Vanessa shrugged. "And that's fine. He doesn't have to stick around. I was serious when I said I don't want anyone in my life. I just want someone for tonight." She watched the car approaching, the headlights flashing across the grass.

"God, Ness, you are the very soul of romance."

"Well, not just any someone. Him. I want him. Which doesn't necessarily mean I want to keep him."

"Can I have him when you're done with him?" Steffie stage-whispered when the car stopped in front of the Inn and Grady got out to open the car doors for the two women.

"Awww," Steffie sighed as she got into the backseat. "I love it when a guy does that."

Grady got back behind the wheel and started out of the lot.

"Well, at least you'll get to try Mocha Berry Vanessa," Steffie said, and poked Vanessa's arm to get her attention. "I did tell you that I named a newly created special flavor in your honor?"

"Grady told me." Vanessa turned in the front passenger seat and looked around the headrest to Steffie. "And I am honored."

"You should be. It's pretty terrific, if I do say so myself. Right, Grady?"

Grady nodded. "It's very good, Steffie."

"Yeah, it's been pretty popular," Steffie went on. "I think I'll keep it on the board for a while."

They merged onto the main road and headed toward the center of town.

"Hey, Ness, did I tell you I saw Candice coming out of Sips this afternoon?"

"Candice who was in my shop this week and put that white eyelet number aside?"

"Uh-huh. I'm certain it was her."

"Oh, good. Maybe she stopped in and picked up that dress after all. I left it in the back room over the weekend, just in case she didn't get a chance to come in yesterday." Vanessa smiled in the dark. "I hope she did. It looked really nice on her, and she looked like someone who needed something pretty and new."

"That could have something to do with the company she keeps. The guy she was with today . . ."

Steffie shuddered. "Let's just say he didn't look like a very nice guy." She paused. "Then again, he probably didn't dump her after a few hours of playing cozy at a friend's wedding, either. God, men are so annoying." She paused again. "Present company excluded, of course."

Grady looked at Steffie through the rearview mirror. "I guess it depends on who you talk to. I admit to having been called annoying a time or two. Actually, I've been called much worse than that."

"Not by me," Steffie told him. "I think you're a prince."

Grady laughed and made the left onto Kelly's Point Road, which, except for the occasional streetlamp, was dark until they approached the municipal building, which was well illuminated. The reserved parking spots for the police cruisers were all filled.

"So do you think there's anyone actually on duty tonight?" Steffie asked as they drove past. "I could swear I saw the entire police force at the wedding."

"You did. Beck wanted everyone to come, but obviously they couldn't all attend at the same time. So the night shift came early, for the ceremony and the cocktail hour, though of course they weren't drinking anything stronger than club soda. The day shift came for dinner and dancing after the night shift clocked in."

"Nice. Oh, Grady, turn left here into the parking lot and drive all the way down to the end," Steffie instructed. "Go all the way to the back corner."

"Why all the way down there?" Vanessa asked. "That's the darkest corner of the lot."

"Yeah, but it's right behind my shop, see? We can

go right down that path to my back door." Steffie opened the car door as Grady came to a stop. "And there's some light down there. See? Over the door?"

"I hope you don't park down here when you're working alone at night." Vanessa frowned her disapproval.

"It's not that far." Steffie set off for the shop. "Looks like there are still some customers. Come on, you two. Yours is on the house."

"You up for some Mocha Berry Vanessa?" Grady asked.

"Sure." Vanessa got out of the car and waited for him. "I swear she must have cat eyes. I don't know how she can see where she's going."

He held out his hand for her and they stumbled along together in the dark over the uneven ground. Little pieces of crushed shell from the parking lot lodged in her instep and she stopped and took off her shoes.

"You know, everyone thinks that crushed shells in the parking lots is so atmospheric, so in keeping with the whole beachy-bay thing," Vanessa grumbled. "I think it's one big pain in the butt."

They reached the back door and Vanessa put her shoes back on before they went inside. Steffie had tossed an apron over her beautiful dress and was serving the few late customers who'd wandered in.

"Tina, go latch the front door after these customers leave and tell anyone else who might wander up that we're closed. Oh, and put the 'Closed' sign on," Steffie told her employee. She rang up the customers and scooped up two dishes of ice cream, which she handed to Grady and Vanessa.

"Here you go, with my thanks for the ride. I really appreciate it, Grady," Steffie told him.

"You had to get a ride from the Inn?" Tina latched the door behind the last two customers. "What happened to your car?"

"I got blocked in."

"So do you need a ride back?" Tina asked. "I go right by there on my way home. I don't mind taking you."

"That would be great. Thanks." Steffie turned to Grady and Vanessa. "I guess you guys are free to go to . . . wherever it was you were headed when I so rudely interrupted."

Vanessa nodded. "Great. But you're going to close up right now, right?"

"We are. I'm just going to do a quick count and I'll take the receipts with me, drop them off at the bank in the morning." Stef smiled. "You're free to go. Dismissed. With my eternal thanks."

"You're welcome," Grady said as he made his way to the door.

"Great ice cream, Stef," Vanessa told her.

"Oh, you like it?" Steffie grinned.

"I do. We're doing brunch tomorrow around eleven at Let's Do Brunch. Meet us there, if you're up," Vanessa suggested.

"I'll be awake. And I might just take you up on that if my Sunday-morning help arrives on time." Steffie opened the cash register and began to count. "Tina, lock the back door behind them, please."

"See you." Grady waved and held the door for Vanessa. Once outside, they heard the lock snap with a click. "Want to walk down to the dock? The Bay looks pretty with the moon on the water."

"Sure."

They walked around the building to the boardwalk that led to the water.

"It's really quiet down here," he observed.

"Most of the boats have already been brought in and tied up," she replied. "There's not much activity this time of night. Once in a while, some kids— teenagers—gather over there to just hang out at the little park"—she pointed to some vague spot well beyond One Scoop or Two—"but that's about it. And around the bend there is Captain Walt's, but they probably don't have much of a crowd tonight. Walt and Rexana were still on the dance floor with most of the rest of St. Dennis when we left the wedding."

He finished his ice cream and tossed the cardboard dish into a trash receptacle on the pier.

"Here, take mine, too." Vanessa handed over hers to be disposed of. "I've had enough to eat and drink to last the next twenty-four hours."

Headlights flashed across the dock momentarily, then were gone.

"There goes Tina and Steffie." Vanessa watched the taillights disappear at the end of the road. "Good thing Stef doesn't have too far to drive from the Inn to her place. She probably shouldn't be driving at all."

"I think she'll be okay," Grady said. "Getting pissed off seemed to have cleared her head."

He took her hand and they walked back to the car, through the ever-darkening parking lot. He unlocked her door and reached for the handle, but she turned to him before he could open it. She backed against the door, her arms around his neck, and drew him to her. Her lips parted as his mouth met hers, and she sighed softly. She'd been thinking of this moment all day. She leaned back slowly against the side of the car and brought him with her so that his body was against hers. He moved in closer, and she urged him closer still. His tongue parted her lips and teased hers, then traced the inside of her mouth slowly. Vanessa thought for a moment that her entire body had caught flame, the heat rushed through her so rapidly, blocking out everything but his mouth and body. She moved against him just the slightest bit and she heard the breath catch in his throat. His hands ran down her back to her waist to the back of her thighs and back again, the heat increasing at the touch of his fingers. His hands moved to her breasts, and she felt a shot to her core.

"Ah, you're not wearing . . ." he whispered, his mouth on her neck, her throat, his fingers skimming her body.

"Nope." She brought his mouth back to hers and kissed him deeply, her tongue tempting him, inciting him to take more. She felt his body respond and he pressed even closer, his hands kneading the soft mounds beneath the silken fabric. When she realized she'd implode if she didn't feel his hands on her skin, she reached behind her to the buttons that fastened the halter top of her dress, and one by one, undid them. Slowly she peeled down the top, his mouth following every inch of skin as she exposed more and more. His lips sucked gently on her skin until they reached her breast, and she arched her back to offer more. Need and desire overtook her mind and her body, and she wanted nothing more than to have him right then and there. Every cell in her body hummed: she could have sworn she heard bells.

There. There they were again. Bells. Vanessa pulled back from him and tilted her head to listen.

Not bells. Sirens.

Grady tensed and turned toward the municipal building, where the police department appeared to be emptying, the cars flying out of the lot, lights flashing and sirens blaring, and up Kelly's Point Road.

"I wonder if there's been an accident," Vanessa said.

She stared at the flashing lights, which had stopped at the top of the street where Kelly's Point met Charles Street. It took a moment for her to realize that the patrol cars were not moving on. "Something's going on up there."

She watched for a moment.

"My shop is up there." She continued to stare, an uneasy feeling flooding through her. The abrupt change from totally-turned-on-what-are-we-waiting-for to going stone cold made her knees shake. "I wonder—"

"Let's go check it out. Here, let's just fix this . . ." He pulled up the top of her dress and she redid the buttons, her eyes still on the lights. He took her hand. "We'll walk up. If we drive, they probably won't let us stop. Come on, Ness. We'll see what's what."

She held on to his hand as they made their way past the police station and through the dark passage, moving more quickly with each step until they were running by the time they reached Charles Street. Vanessa's heart all but stopped when she realized that Bling was the center of all the activity.

"Oh my God. My shop!" She rushed across the street and through the front door. "What's going on?" she cried to the officers who were gathering near the rear of the building. "What's happened?"

"You had a break-in." Sue Dixon, one of the officers, walked back to meet her.

"A break-in?" Vanessa wasn't sure she'd heard correctly. "Someone *broke in* to my shop?"

"Apparently." Sue nodded. "Unless you or your help left the back door wide open and smashed the counters and tossed your merchandise all over the place."

Vanessa followed Sue's pointing finger to the jewelry case beneath the glass counter. "Oh, man . . ."

She went to the case and started to put her hand inside when Grady grabbed her by the wrist. "You probably shouldn't touch anything until they've run prints."

"Agent Shields, I'd appreciate you staying near the door," Sue told him. "Nothing personal, but—"

"I understand about contamination." He smiled. "But it's not 'agent.' "

"Oh. Sorry." She turned back to Vanessa. "Gus just went out to get the kit out of his car. We'll want to print you, Ness, to eliminate your prints."

Vanessa frowned. "There have been dozens of people in and out of this shop for the past week. You'll never be able to isolate the burglar's fingerprints."

"You're probably right." Carl Silver, another officer, came to the front of the shop from the office, holding a trash can in his gloved hand. "There are some used paper towels in here, and there's a bottle of glass cleaner in the vanity in the powder room. Looks like the guy wiped everything down before he left."

"We always clean the counters at the end of the day," Vanessa told them. "I had someone new in for me tonight, but I did ask her to just give the glass a quick swipe before she left. I hate to come in to open in the morning and be met with smudgy counters. It's one of my pet peeves."

"Then maybe we'll get lucky," Sue ventured.

"Anyone smart enough to get past that lock would not be stupid enough to come in here without gloves," Carl said. "Whoever it was did a masterful job."

"I've seen a lot of smart people do stupid things since I started on this job," Sue told him.

Vanessa glanced around her shop and almost cried to see the stacks of pretty sweaters tossed onto the floor in a heap, as if someone had simply swiped at the pile as he went past. Dresses that had been hanging on racks when she left the store the night before were now strewn across the carpet, and she could almost imagine a hand grabbing that last hanger to push the lot of them to the ground. Feeling sick to her stomach, she started toward the back of the shop.

"Do I have to stay near the door, too?" she asked.

Sue shook her head. "Your hair and fingerprints are already all over this place. Slip these on your feet, though."

Vanessa took off her shoes and pulled on the plastic booties Sue handed her and walked into the office. Papers were strewn across her small desk and several garments that had been left on a stand, waiting for customers to pick them up, were on the floor. Thankfully, they were in their garment bags. It was all she could do to keep herself from righting the stand and picking up the dresses that lay there.

She was on her way out of the room when she thought of the white eyelet dress. She looked back at the mass on the floor, but the dress was not among the casualties.

Good for you, Candice. The woman must have been on her way into the shop when Steffie saw her leaving Sips, the takeout-only beverage bar two doors away that specialized in fresh juice drinks.

She returned to the front of the shop, where Gus Franklin was busy lifting fingerprints from the counter tops.

"I called Hal's cell a couple of times, but he didn't pick up," Gus told her.

"The band's pretty loud. He probably didn't hear the phone. He'll probably check his phone before long and he'll give you a call."

"Probably." He nodded. "I'll get your prints as soon as I finish here."

"Fine. Whenever you're ready." Vanessa sighed and went to Grady, who was still seated patiently near the front door. "I'm sorry," she said softly.

"Sorry for what?"

"Well, you know . . ." She gestured in the direction of Kelly's Point Road and the general direction of the parking lot where fifteen minutes earlier they'd been hot and heavy and well on their way to what should have been an unforgettable night.

He reached out and took her hand and slowly ran his thumb across her knuckles. "You have nothing to apologize for. Your shop has been broken into, vandalized, and it looks like you've been robbed of some valuable merchandise. You do not owe me an apology, Ness. I'm just sorry this happened to you. I know how upset you must be."

She was on the verge of tears when Sue's phone rang. The officer unhooked the phone from her belt and looked at the caller ID.

"Oh," she said. "It's the chief."

"Do not tell him about this." Vanessa spun around. "Sue, don't tell him. He'll feel obligated to come back here and he'll miss his honeymoon."

"But if he asks me what's going on . . ."

"Tell him it's just another quiet Saturday night. Please. His honeymoon will be over before it starts." Seeing that Sue was still hesitant, Vanessa added, "I will take full responsibility for this."

"I can't lie to him," Sue told her. "He's my boss. If he asks, I have to tell him."

"Only if he asks."

"Dixon." Sue answered the call. "Oh, hi, Chief. Yeah, I had a great time. Sorry I couldn't have stayed longer. I hear the band kicked ass. I hope someone reminded Hal where he is to bring the leftover cake." She met Vanessa's eyes and shrugged her shoulders. "Oh, sure, I'll take care of that. Not a problem. Are you still at the airport? Is your flight on time? Good . . . yes, will do. Have a great time, Chief. And congratulations to you and to Mia . . ."

Sue ended the call. "He didn't ask," she told Vanessa. "He just wanted someone to run past his house and make sure his back door was locked."

"Thank you for not volunteering . . ." She waved her hand around the shop.

"Yeah, well, I hope I can count on you to give me a good reference when he finds out we were here when he called." Sue shook her head and walked outside.

Gus motioned Vanessa over to the counter he'd just finished dusting. "I thought the glass would be stripped of prints but I found quite a few smudges and a few good prints, one a partial palm print. I'll run them through the records when I get back to the station. Meanwhile, I'll get your prints now."

One by one, he dipped her fingers in ink, then pressed each onto a card.

"Will this wash off?" she asked.

"Sure," Gus told her. "Eventually."

Not sure if he was kidding or not, she went into the powder room and proceeded to scrub at the ink. When she was satisfied she'd gotten off all she was going to get that night, she came back out to the shop floor. Carl was near the cash register, pulling on a pair of thin rubber gloves.

"Vanessa, I need to ask you to prepare a list of what you think is missing," he told her as he squatted down.

"I have no idea how much the sales were from today. I'll have to call Cathy Williams and ask her." She looked over the counter and saw he was picking up a pile of receipts. "Those would help. May I see them?"

He tossed her a pair of gloves and she slipped them on.

"I'm going to want her to stop by tomorrow so I can take her prints as well. She might be able to help you figure out what was sold as opposed to what was taken." Gus glanced up from his work on the contents of the jewelry case.

"Cathy was only here for a few hours. Nan Silvestri was here most of the day, and several days this week. She's away until tomorrow night, though."

"We'll catch up with her." Gus picked carefully through the broken glass. "You think you could tell what jewelry might be missing?"

"Not without knowing what was sold today. It's mostly costume, not fine jewelry. The best pieces I have are silver with some semiprecious stones. Nothing real expensive, certainly nothing rare. No gold. No platinum. No precious gems." She looked over each receipt, touching them only on the edges to lift them or turn them over. Even wearing the gloves, she felt as if she were doing something she shouldn't be doing. "Do you need to know everything that's missing tonight?"

"No." Gus shook his head. "But the sooner you can get it together, the better."

Vanessa stripped off the gloves.

"Vanessa, have you noticed any strange activity lately? Customers who acted peculiar? Anyone hanging around the store?"

She shook her head. "No, no one strange. Gus, if you don't need me anymore, then I think I'd like to leave now."

"Go on home. We'll call you if anything comes up," Gus told her without looking up from his work.

Grady was still leaning against the doorjamb. She walked over and said, "We can go."

"Do you want me to run down and get the car and come back for you?"

"No." She took his hand. "I want to stay with you."

He nodded and they walked out of the shop and across the street. The town was pin-drop quiet, the only sounds the *tap-tap* of her heels on the pavement. There was a fine silver mist rolling in off the Bay that made her skin feel damp. She wanted to go home and take a very hot shower and she wanted to take him with her. She was tired and worn out and dispirited and she felt sick. Bling was everything to her, and someone had trashed it. She'd have to close for God only knew how long and she probably was out hundreds of dollars' worth of her carefully selected merchandise. The day that had begun so perfectly had turned out to be perfectly awful.

They went through the dark area off Charles Street and passed under the streetlights that marked the end of the municipal building's lot. Across the road was the lot where Grady had left the car. Before her, the walk through the unlit lot appeared endless. Their shadows, cast by the lights from the municipal building, grew longer and longer as they walked farther and farther into the lot. Finally, they were at the car and Vanessa let out a breath she hadn't been aware she'd been holding. She'd never been afraid of the dark, but tonight, on the heels of the break-in at Bling, she felt spooked.

At first, Vanessa thought the loud crunching she heard was the sound of the oyster shells in the lot crushing beneath their feet. But something sharp stabbed through the sole of her shoe and she cried out.

"What?" Grady caught her arm as she stumbled.

"Something went right through the bottom of my shoe." She stopped and stood on one foot. She removed the shoe, and when she touched the side of her foot, she felt something wet and thick. "I think my foot is bleeding. I must have stepped on a piece of broken glass."

Grady started toward the car for a flashlight, but after he'd taken two steps closer, he began to curse softly.

"What?" she asked. "What is it?"

"Do you have a tissue in your bag?" he asked.

"I think so. You never go to a wedding without tissues." She opened her bag and felt around inside until her fingers closed around one. "Here you go."

He reached out in the darkness and took it, then walked to the car, using the tissue to cover the handle as he opened the car door and reached inside to turn on the headlights.

Vanessa stared at the ground, then at the car door. "Grady, is that . . ."

"Yeah. Glass. Someone's broken all the windows out of the car."

"What . . . ?" She stepped closer.

"Don't. I don't want you to step on anything else." He held a hand out to stop her. "Let's go back to the police station and get someone over here."

"I can't believe this." She felt stunned. "This whole night has turned into one big nightmare. My shop, your car . . ."

"My *rental* car."

"This is such a quiet town, this is just crazy, that someone would break into Bling and someone else would vandalize your car."

They were nearing the edge of the lot, and in the dim light, she could see him shaking his head.

"I'm not so sure it was someone *else*," he told her.

"You think the same person did this? The shop and the car?"

He nodded.

"Damn. That is the most bizarre coincidence, isn't it?"

"Stop and think, Ness. First your shop, then the car you were riding in? Uh-uh." His jaw was squared, and for the first time since she'd met him, he was angry. "No coincidence there, babe. I think someone's trying to send you a message."

He opened the front door of the municipal building and held it for her to enter.

"What's that supposed to mean? What kind of message?"

"I'm not certain, but I'm guessing it isn't a love note."

"You're scaring me."

"You should be scared," he told her. "You have every reason to be scared."

"Maybe you're wrong. Maybe it isn't what you think. Maybe it's kids, just out causing mischief."

"What happened in your shop is more than mischief. The smashing up of the car? Coming immediately after the break-in? I don't think this is the work of mischievous kids. Whoever did this is angry, and that anger is being directed at you for some reason. You must have really pissed off someone." He took her by the hand. "Which way is the police department?"

She pointed to the hall on the right. As she did so, Sue walked out of one of the offices. Seeing them, she said, "Did you forget something?"

"No. We're here for round two," Grady told her.

"Round two?" Sue raised her eyebrows.

"Someone took a sledgehammer or something equally heavy and knocked out all the windows of my car while we were at the shop."

"Son of a bitch . . ." Sue's eyes grew wide. "What are the chances of that?"

"Yeah." He nodded wryly. "Go figure . . ."

Chapter 11

"Hal's still not answering his phone," Gus told Vanessa, "so I'm going to take a ride over to his place, let him know what's going on."

"Don't do that, please. Right now, he's probably sitting in the Inn's bar, catching up with old friends who came to the wedding," Vanessa pleaded. She had a sinking suspicion of just which old friend Hal might be catching up with, and if that was the case, she really didn't want to know. "Anyway, there's nothing he could do tonight except worry."

"Or he could be home, sleeping soundly," Grady offered. "In any case, Vanessa is right. You've got two people out there going over the car, two people over at Vanessa's shop. You probably don't need Hal, too. At least for now."

"All right," Gus said. "We'll let it go until the morning. But you just pray that this guy"—he pointed across the parking lot toward Grady's bashed-up rental car—"is done for a while."

"If he has any sense at all, he's got to be thinking that he's pushed his luck enough for one night. He did get away with the break-in without anyone seeing him, but . . ." Vanessa said.

"Not so sure about that. We'll be canvassing the neighbors in the morning," Gus reminded her. "Right now, we don't know who saw what."

"True enough," Grady agreed. "But he walked away from that and from the car without getting caught. This guy is no amateur. He picks and chooses his time and his target, but he's also opportunistic. He hit the shop when half the town was at the wedding, and he hit the car when everyone was focused on the burglary. Now, I'm pretty certain that the break-in was planned in advance, but vandalizing the car . . . that couldn't have been planned. He'd have had no way of knowing that you'd be with me, in that car, and that the car would be parked in the lot down here, but he took advantage of the opportunity. If we believe that he's targeting Vanessa for some reason— and I believe that he is—he must have seen her get out of my car, possibly when he was finished at the shop."

"Why would he have even been back near the lot? If he'd just burglarized Bling," Vanessa wondered, "wouldn't he want to be far away?"

"I think he wanted to watch—which is another reason I think this is personal. Look, there's that long dark section of the road out there. He could have been hiding just about anywhere. He'd have watched the police cars head for Charles Street, and he'd have known that was the focus of everyone's attention. So while the breaking glass would have made noise, there wasn't anyone around to hear it. Steffie was gone by then, and she was the last one who'd have been in that area of the parking lot, other than Ness and me. Once we were drawn to the shop, he had the lot to himself." Grady paused to think.

"Or," Vanessa suggested, "he hit the shop because it looked like exactly what it is: an upscale women's boutique that does a good business."

Before Grady could counter, she continued.

"As far as the car is concerned, who's to say it wasn't a couple of kids taking a shortcut from the park through the parking lot?"

"What park?"

"On the other side of the trees that run along Steffie's, there's a small park. The generally accepted shortcut to Charles Street is through the parking lot."

"It's possible," Grady conceded, "but that's not what my gut's telling me."

"Is your gut psychic?" she asked.

"Instinct, then." He tried to explain. "I spent nine years in law enforcement. After a while, you develop certain instincts, and you learn to trust them. Yes, it's possible that Bling was targeted because it looks like a shop that brings in shoppers with money, and is likely to have a few dollars in the cash register at the end of the day. But don't many shop owners now make their deposits at night? Do you usually leave money in the drawer when you leave?"

"No," she admitted. "I usually lock it in a safe that I have hidden or I take it to the bank. There was money in the shop last night, though, since I wasn't going to be there to lock up or to make a deposit."

"How many people knew that?" Gus asked.

"Just the person who locked up last night, and me. I might have mentioned it to Steffie, but that isn't something she'd discuss with anyone else."

"I'm going to have a few officers walk the area from Charles Street through the parking lot and down to the playground, just in case he dropped something or left something behind," Gus told them. "The more I think about it, the more I'm thinking you're right about the path he took down toward the parking lot. I think he hit the shop, hid somewhere close by while he waited for the call to come in here so he could watch us answer it. He had to know that in a town like this one, a crowd would be gathering to see what the commotion was, then he'd stroll on up and blend in." Gus was thinking it all through. "I agree with your friend here, Ness. He wouldn't have expected to see you get out of that car, but after he did, he couldn't resist the opportunity to give you just a little more to think about. Besides, with you walking around down on the dock, then in the parking lot, you might have ruined his chance to sneak up to Charles Street, catch the action. That could have pissed him off. First thing in the morning, when it's light, I'll have that area gone over with a fine-tooth comb. No telling what they might find."

Gus walked them past the reception desk toward the door. "Well, with any luck, you folks won't be needing us again tonight."

"I understand that the raccoons are making a racket, ma'am. We'll have a patrol car over there as soon as we can." Bill Mason, the night dispatcher, waved to Vanessa as she passed. He put a hand over the phone and told Gus, "The raccoons are in Mrs. Brophy's tree again."

Gus rolled his eyes. "Tell her I'll be coming by in about ten minutes."

He opened the front door and held it for Vanessa and Grady and exited with them.

"I'll drop you off at home," Gus told Vanessa, then turned to Grady. "You staying at the Inn?"

Grady nodded and took Vanessa's arm as they walked to Gus's patrol car.

"I'll drive you out after I take Vanessa home."

"Grady, why don't you take my car back to the Inn? That way, you'll have some transportation in the morning to get back into town," Vanessa said.

"Are you sure you won't need it?" Grady asked as they got into Gus's cruiser.

"I walk into town all the time," she reminded him.

"Then thank you. I'll take you up on the offer."

Gus stopped in front of her house. "Maybe I should come in and take a look around. You know, just in case there's someone in there who shouldn't be."

"I'll take care of it, Gus." Grady opened the rear passenger door and slid out, then leaned in to give Vanessa a hand and helped her out. "I'll check it all out before I leave."

"Hal would skin me alive if anything happened to her." Gus put the car in park. "Not to mention what Beck would do when he got back."

"Good point." Vanessa checked her small evening bag for her keys.

"You used to wear the badge, though, right?" Gus asked as they walked up the front walk.

"Former FBI."

Gus nodded. "I thought I heard something like that."

Grady held out his hand and Vanessa handed him the keys. He unlocked the front door, and Gus held him back, his hand on his holstered handgun.

"Give me a minute to clear it," he told them.

Grady and Vanessa waited in silence in the dark until Gus came back and turned on one of the living-room lamps.

"Everything looks fine," he told them. "No sign of anything amiss."

"Thanks, Gus," Vanessa told him.

"Anything weird happens, you hear any noises, you call the station and I'll be right out." He went out onto the front porch. "And we'll be driving by throughout the night. Make sure you lock that door as soon as Grady leaves."

"Will do," she told him.

The key was still in the outside lock. Grady removed it and used it to lock the door from the inside. Vanessa smiled and held out her hand. "I'm guessing we won't need this until the morning."

"There's no way in hell I'm leaving you here by yourself." He walked into the living room, his jacket over one shoulder, his tie undone. "I can sleep down here."

"Oh, I don't think so." She met his eyes from the doorway. She wanted to put the events of the evening behind her. She'd had all she could handle of being afraid and being upset. Tomorrow, her shop would still be a mess and Grady's rental car would still be smashed and there'd still be someone out there who was really angry with her for reasons she couldn't know. But tonight . . .

"I don't think Gus checked under the bed or any of the closets. What if someone's hiding up there?"

"Good point." He draped the jacket over the back of a chair. "I don't want you lying awake all night worrying that someone will pop out from that closet. I'd better come up with you and check."

She turned off the lamp and started toward the stairs.

"Do you have a basement?" he asked.

"What?" She frowned.

"A basement. You know, an excavated area under the first floor."

"Yes, I have a basement."

"Is the door inside or outside?"

"It's right through there." She stood on the bottom step, her hands on her hips, and watched him disappear into the kitchen.

He was back in less than a minute. "You could use a better lock on that door. It's just a slide bolt. You should have dead bolts that require keys on it and the back door."

"I have a dead bolt on the back door."

"It has a latch that's located right under the glass panes."

She started up the steps slowly, glancing over her shoulder. He was following her, his eyes on her face.

"So?" she asked.

"So someone could break the glass, reach in, turn the latch, and just like that, they're in."

"Oh, thanks for that mood breaker." She stopped midway up the stairwell and glared at him.

He came up behind her, chuckling softly. "If the mood is broken, we'll just have to find a way to get it back again."

"Think you're up to it?" She tugged on both ends of his tie.

"I guess we'll find out."

She laughed and led him by the tie to her room facing the back of the house. Three arched windows framed a bay, and moonlight streamed in through the sheer curtains. She backed toward the bed, then stopped at the side and raised her hands to undo her dress.

"Are you sure you aren't too rattled from the break-in and everything . . . ?"

"I don't want to think about it anymore tonight. You're here to protect me, right?" She dropped the dress and it puddled on the floor at her feet. "Besides, do I look rattled to you?"

"You look beautiful. In or out of that dress."

He reached out for her and she walked into his arms. His hands slid up and down her back, and she unbuttoned his shirt, pulling the tails out from the waist. She pulled up the T-shirt and ran her hands over his bare chest, then fell back on the bed, taking him with her. His mouth met hers halfway to the pillow, and she parted her lips to his tongue that thrust inside and teased the corners of her mouth. His hand reached for her left breast, but she moved it, offering the right one instead. She felt crazed with wanting him, could not seem to get close enough. She felt as if she were on fire, inside and out, everywhere he touched seeming to burn. His mouth moved to her throat, and she all but purred as his lips made an agonizingly slow descent to her shoulder, then lower, and she arched her back, but when his mouth sought her breast, she moved slightly to offer the right one and he took it between eager lips. She moaned far back in her throat and reached down to tug on his waistband.

"As good as you look in this tux," she gasped, "I think it's time to retire it for the night."

Later, she would wonder how he'd managed to undress without his mouth ever leaving her skin, she was so totally lost in sensations she barely recalled ever having had before. She wrapped her legs around his and drew him inside almost frantically while his mouth drove her to the edge of madness. Wordlessly, the rhythm natural, he began to move inside her, slowly at first. She took him in deeper, as the pace increased, until she could no longer tell her cries from his. He slowed for a moment and raised his head to look into her eyes, then drove them both to completion on waves of sensation that she thought would never end.

He nuzzled the left side of her face without speaking, and before she realized it, he'd run his hand from her neck to her breast. His hand stopped moving, then slowly, with one finger, he traced the jagged line that ran from the nipple to just under her collarbone.

"What happened here?" he asked.

"I, ah, walked into a knife." She moved his hand away and pulled the blanket around her, but he pushed it down again.

"Who was holding it when you walked into it?" His voice was calm but she detected something disquieting below the surface.

She pushed him away and sat up.

"Ness?" He sat up with her. "Who did this to you?"

Her insides twisted and her stomach knotted and she couldn't get any words out. She hadn't wanted him to see, hadn't wanted anyone to ever see the disfiguring scar that had kept her from wearing clothes that didn't cover it, had kept her from getting naked those few times she'd almost let a guy get close. Why had she dropped her guard with Grady? Now that he saw, now that he knew, he'd be outta there.

Yeah, well, he was leaving anyway, she reminded herself.

"Vanessa, look at me." He turned her face to his. "Tell me who did this to you. What's this scar . . . ?"

She wet her lips and took a breath.

"Just something I could have avoided if I'd been smarter and faster. It's not a very interesting story."

"Let's say I'm interested." When she didn't respond, he reached over her to turn on the light on the bedside table.

"Don't. Please don't."

He sank down next to her.

"All right. But from what I can feel, I'm guessing it's not a surgical scar. It's too ragged. Any doctor who cuts like this should be behind bars."

"He *is* behind bars but he wasn't a doctor." Vanessa sighed. It was clear Grady wasn't going to give up.

"Who was he?"

"My second husband."

"Why would he do something like this to you?"

"Why?" She laughed, her voice harsh. "Because he was angry with me, and because he could."

Grady ran his finger along the scar very gently. "You loved him?"

"I thought I did."

"That boils down to the same thing, doesn't it?"

"I suppose."

"You loved him, and he did this to you?"

"He was very angry because I told him I was leaving. He didn't want me to. He picked up a knife, said that he'd make it so that no one would ever love me again, no one would want to make love to me again. He'd cut off both of them." In a defensive motion, she raised her arms to cover her breasts.

He was so silent for so long she wasn't sure he was still awake. Then he gathered her to his chest and stroked her back softly, but he still didn't speak.

"Such a cliché, right?" She covered her face with her hands. "Woman wants to leave an abusive husband, he disfigures her."

"How did you stop him from cutting the other one?"

"I kicked him straight up the middle, and he dropped the knife, and I ran outside, to a neighbor's, and they called an ambulance and the police. As you can imagine, there was quite a bit of blood—"

"Did you press charges?"

"I did. Yes, I did." She twisted the end of the sheet into a point, first one way, then the other. How to tell him what that time had been like? Why even try? "And there was a trial. That was the worst part of it."

"It couldn't have been worse than the abuse."

"Oh, yeah. His whole friggin' family was there in the courtroom all day, every day. They whispered at me when I came in, and they whispered at me when I came out. They threatened me with everything you could imagine. The day he was sentenced, at Maggie's insistence, I went back to Illinois with her. That night, they set my house on fire. Burned it to the ground. I lost everything I owned."

"I'm guessing the police figured it out quickly enough."

"Oh, sure. One of his brothers and one of his cousins were arrested and brought to trial, but there was no physical evidence and the jury didn't convict them."

"Where is he now? Your ex-husband?"

"He's still in prison. He got seven years and he had to agree to anger management while he's in prison."

"How long ago was that?"

"Three years and a couple of months."

"Any chance he's out?"

She shook her head. "No. Someone would have contacted me. The district attorney promised me that if I'd testify, they'd make sure that I was notified before he was released."

"And where did all this happen?"

"Back in Wisconsin." She sighed. "Anyway, that's why there's that scar. And that's why I didn't want to turn on the light. I didn't want you to see how ugly my body is."

"You're kidding, right?"

She shook her head.

"Vanessa, there is nothing ugly about your body. If anything, yours is the most beautiful body I've ever seen up close and personal."

"You're just saying that because you think you'll get lucky again."

He cupped her face in his hands.

"I got lucky the day I walked into Hal Garrity's backyard and stood on his deck and watched this beautiful woman float across it. She took my breath away," he told her. "She takes my breath away every time I look at her."

She felt as if something inside her cracked, then broke.

"Stop it." She swatted at him, tears welling in her eyes.

The tears became a torrent. She had no words, only emotions, too many at one time for her to separate shame from the relief that he had not recoiled in disgust, or from the mind-numbing pain she felt every time she thought about the night that Gene had pushed her back against the kitchen table and sliced through her shirt into her flesh. It had been hard for her to admit even to herself that she'd left one bad marriage only to fall headfirst into another. She was embarrassed to remember what she had been like back then. It had been a long time since she'd talked about it, longer still since she'd cried for the woman she had once been.

"You must think I'm the stupidest woman in the world, to let someone do this to me," she sobbed.

"I doubt very much that you *let* him do that, Ness. I don't think abuse was what you were looking for when you married him."

"But I took it, and I kept taking it." She hiccuped. "I let it get worse. I should have walked that first time but . . ."

"But he promised he wouldn't do it again, and you believed him because you loved him, right? You made excuses for him because you loved him."

"I am such a cliché, aren't I? Pathetic," she wailed.

"What's pathetic is a man who is so small that he has to hurt someone else in order to feel like a man."

He gathered her up, blanket and all, and let her cry until there were no tears left to fall. When finally she stopped, he asked, "What's his name?"

"Gene Medford."

"Is that Eugene?"

"Yes. Why?"

"Just curious. He's in prison in Wisconsin now?"

She nodded, then rested against him, sniffing and wishing she'd left that box of tissues on her nightstand instead of taking them into the bathroom on Saturday morning.

"Damn good thing that makeup woman used the waterproof mascara." She swiped at her eyes with the back of her hands. "Otherwise, I can't even begin to imagine what I'd look like. Bad enough the nose is red now but I could have raccoon eyes to go with it."

Grady leaned back against the pillow and tucked the blanket around them both.

"Grady?" she whispered.

"Hmm?"

"It's been one hell of a night, hasn't it?"

"Yeah. It's been one hell of a night."

She lay against his chest, watching the shadows from the branches of the tree outside her window move across the floor until she closed her eyes, and, feeling safe for the first time in a very long time, fell asleep.

Grady lay awake in the dark, unable to get the image of a bleeding, terrified, wounded Vanessa out of his mind.

So many times as an agent, he'd seen the victims of vicious attacks not unlike the one Vanessa had survived. Husbands attacking wives, wives attacking husbands, their children, parents, siblings, best friends, strangers . . . there seemed to be no end to the number of ways in which to hurt someone.

He'd certainly seen injuries a hundred times worse than Vanessa's. More than once, he'd seen women for whom the threat to cut off one or both breasts had been carried out. But this ate at him. How heartless could a man be that he'd do something so heinous to a woman who loved him? No one deserved to be treated like that.

Vanessa was as sweet, caring, funny, smart, capable, and yes, as beautiful and as sexy, as any woman he'd ever met. She wore her heart on her sleeve when it came to those she cared about and he really liked that about her. In fact, there were a lot of things he liked about her.

And she was strong. She hadn't fallen apart when she realized her shop—which obviously meant everything to her—had been broken into, nor did she freak out when he told her that he thought both the burglary at the shop and the vandalism to his car were somehow a message intended for her. She hadn't backed away from what was obviously a strong physical attraction between them, but met it head-on without pretense. She'd been brave enough to walk away from a bad situation, and courageous to have faced her abuser and his entire family in open court, and despite their threats, she hadn't blinked. And somehow she hadn't lost her sense of humor. What she had lost, however, was her self-confidence. How could she see herself as anything less than beautiful? Anything less than wonderful? What did that tell him about her? How had she come to believe that her scar defined her?

As if she knew he was thinking about her, she stirred slightly, then sighed in her sleep, one hand on his chest like a badge.

That she'd suffered made his heart ache—that she'd suffered at the hands of someone she'd loved made him sick to his stomach.

The longer he thought about it, the sicker—and more angry—he became.

First thing tomorrow, he was going to contact someone at the Bureau and have him check the release status of Eugene Medford.

He awoke to the sound of water driving against glass. He sat up and realized that Vanessa was not beside him, and the sound was coming from the shower in the bathroom across the hall. He got up and dressed in the tuxedo he'd worn to the wedding. Vanessa came out of the shower, her hair in a towel, a robe wrapped around her.

"Hey, you're awake." She came into the room with a smile on her face. "And I know I said it before, but you do look good in that tux."

"Thanks. Admire it while you can."

"Oh?" She looked momentarily disappointed. "Are you leaving?"

"Yeah. The tux goes back to the shop tomorrow. And right now, I'm on my way back to the Inn. I want to grab a shower and change. There's a black-and-white parked out front, by the way, so you won't be alone. I already checked the rest of the house. There's been no unwanted visitors overnight." He glanced at his watch. "It's already nine-thirty, and the brunch is . . . what, eleven?"

She nodded.

"So I'll take your car, and come back to pick you up around ten of eleven?"

"All right." She found her keys on her dresser and tossed them to him, and he caught them with one hand. "But I'd like to be there on time since I am hosting the brunch. Are you punctual, or are you more of the, I'll-get-there-when-I-get-there type?"

"I worked for the FBI, remember? I'll be here at ten-fifty."

He took her face in his hands and kissed her mouth.

"I will be here on time," he promised.

He started out of the room, when the phone began to ring. On his way down the steps he heard Vanessa say, "Good morning, Hal. Yes, I'm fine. Well, we didn't want to disturb you . . . yes, I really am fine . . ."

By the time he'd showered, dressed, and returned for Vanessa, and arrived at Let's Do Brunch, it seemed that everyone had already heard about the break-in and the vandalism to Grady's rented car. The discussion of last night's crimes even threatened to overshadow the rehash of the wedding.

"Did you call your rental company yet?" Andy asked Grady.

"I called this morning before I left the Inn," Grady replied. "They need a copy of the police report, and they want to come for the car as soon as the police release it. In the meantime, they'll give me another car.

I just have to go pick it up at someplace right outside of St. Dennis. Vanessa said she'd drive me out."

Hal came into the room two steps behind Maggie. Grady glanced around for Vanessa, to see if she'd noticed, but she was conferring with the hostess and had her back to the group.

"I can fax the police report to your car company if you give me the info." Hal had apparently overheard Grady. "Speed things up a bit for you."

"I'd appreciate that." Grady nodded. "Thanks."

"Don't mention it." Hal lowered his voice. "I hear you kept an eye on my girl last night."

Grady nodded, wondering what else Hal might have heard.

"Thank you." Hal folded his arms across his chest. "Anyone hurts Vanessa, he'll bring down the wrath of God. I guess you know what I mean."

Grady nodded again. He was pretty sure he knew exactly what Hal meant.

"Yeah, when we get this guy who broke into her shop, tossed her place, there will be hell to pay. Like I said, no one hurts our girl." Hal slapped Grady on the back and went for the coffee.

Vanessa's mother had helped herself to coffee from the large carafe that stood on the buffet table, and had strolled over to the doorway to look out upon the passing cars. Grady grabbed a cup for himself and joined her.

"So did you enjoy the wedding, Mrs. Turner?" he asked.

She turned and looked up at him as if surprised that he'd sought her out, but she smiled and said, "It was just beautiful. I'm so glad I came, even if my son wasn't happy about it. I must say, though, that your sister made me feel welcome."

"She's a welcoming kind of person."

"I hope Beck appreciates her."

"I'm sure he does." Grady toyed with an idea for a moment, then asked, "Mrs. Turner, whatever happened to Vanessa's first husband?"

"Craig?" She shrugged her shoulders. "Last I heard, he was remarried and the father of three little ones and living in New Mexico. Why?"

"Just wondering." He took a sip from the cup. "And the one she sent to prison . . ."

Maggie wrinkled her nose to show her displeasure. "Gene. The bastard."

"Do you know for a fact that he's still in prison?"

She nodded. "He was, last I heard, maybe six, seven months ago."

"Has anyone in his family ever contacted you to find out where she is?"

Maggie shook her head. "Nope. Not a one. Fact is, no one has ever even asked about her." She paused. "Well, except for that girl a week or two ago."

"What girl?"

"A girl Ness went to high school with was sending out notices about their upcoming reunion and wanted Ness's address."

"Now, which reunion would this be?" he asked.

"Well, let's see now." Maggie thought it over. "She graduated in 1998 . . . that would make it her twelfth reunion."

"That's odd, don't you think?" Grady said. "Usually reunions are the tenth, or the fifteenth. Did anyone notify her about the tenth reunion?"

Maggie shook her head. "No. Nothing before this."

Vanessa walked over, a mimosa in her hand. She eyed Maggie suspiciously.

"I was just telling Grady about Shannon calling about your upcoming reunion," Maggie explained.

"I still have no idea who she is," Vanessa said.

"You didn't have a friend named Shannon?" Grady asked.

"I had no friends at all back then," Vanessa told him.

Maggie frowned. "That is simply not true, Vanessa. Don't make this nice young man think you were a social outcast."

Vanessa turned to Grady. "I was."

"I guess you wouldn't have a copy of your high school yearbook handy?" he asked.

"I never got one. There wasn't anything I wanted to remember. Why? You want to see how weird I was back then?"

"Maybe if you looked at Shannon's picture, you'd remember her."

"There was no Shannon in my class," Vanessa insisted.

He was staring, prompting her to ask, "What?"

"I'm going to have someone track down this ex of yours. I want to confirm that he is in fact still in prison."

"I told you, the D.A. promised to let me know if he was going to get out." She sighed, exasperated.

"Did you provide the police back in Wisconsin with a forwarding address?"

"Well, no. But I'm sure they'd contact Maggie."

"How many times has Maggie moved since the trial?"

"Twice," she told him.

"Maggie"—Grady turned to Vanessa's mother, who'd fallen silent—"have you given the D.A. your new address?"

"Ahhh . . . well, actually, now that you ask, I didn't." Maggie appeared slightly embarrassed to admit it.

"So the D.A.'s office would find you, how?" he asked.

"I don't know." Maggie shrugged her shoulders. "I guess the same way Shannon did."

"And how was that?" he persisted.

Maggie tilted her head, as if considering the question. Finally, she said, "I don't know. I guess she could have asked around the neighborhood where I was living during the trial. I still have friends there."

"You moved to Indiana after that," Vanessa reminded her, "and from there, you went to North Dakota."

"Yes, but Shelley always knows where I am. We've kept in close touch." Maggie turned to Grady. "I suppose someone could have come around asking about me. My upstairs neighbor from those days knows where I live."

"Would you mind giving her a call and asking if someone's done that lately?" Grady couldn't believe how easy it would have been for anyone looking for Vanessa to have found her.

"I gave that girl your address and your phone number." Maggie was shaken.

Vanessa frowned. "You think that Shannon was someone of Gene's?"

"How many high schools have twelfth reunions?" he asked.

"You think maybe he's out and no one told us?" Vanessa's face drained of color.

"Someone has you targeted for something that is not good. If your ex was released early on parole, he could be that someone. He'd certainly be the prime suspect."

"You think he could be here, in St. Dennis?" Vanessa blanched. "You think he could have broken into my shop?"

"It's possible. Look, maybe you should go stay with Steffie until this thing is figured out."

Vanessa shook her head. "I'm not going to make her a target."

"Then Hal."

"No. If anything happened to him because of me, I'd kill myself."

"Hal can probably take care of himself."

"No." She shook her head again.

"Do you have a gun?" He suspected she did not, but wanted to be sure.

"A gun?" She stared at him as if he'd lost his mind. "*A gun?* No, I don't have a gun. What would I do with a gun? Guns can hurt people."

Grady's phone began to ring. He glanced at the caller ID, excused himself, and walked outside to take the call.

"Grady, it's Will Fletcher," the voice on the other end said. "John called this morning and asked me to run something down ASAP. He said it was for you."

"Yeah, thanks for getting right on it."

"How've you been, man? We all miss you," Will told him.

"I occasionally miss a few of you, too. How's that fiancée of yours?" Grady asked.

"Miranda is fine," Will said. "I keep asking her to make an honest man out of me but she keeps postponing the date."

"Hey, if you were engaged to marry you, how much of a hurry would you be in?"

"You have a point." Will paused. "What are the chances we'll be seeing you back in the office sometime soon?"

"Unlikely." Grady hated having these discussions, and he hoped Will wouldn't press. To his relief, he didn't.

"Well, anytime you're in the neighborhood and just want to hang out, give us a call, hear?"

"I will, thanks."

"So, back to Eugene Medford."

Grady heard some papers rustling on Will's end of the line.

"I ran a check, traced him to a prison in Wisconsin, where he was sent to serve a seven-year term for assault."

"I know that part," Grady told him. "I need to know if he's still in there now."

"Well, he was, up until three weeks ago."

"He was paroled?" Grady asked.

"No," Will told him. "He was in a fight with another inmate and his neck was broken."

Grady hesitated before asking, "Are you telling me . . ."

"Yeah," Will told him. "The guy is dead."

Diary—

When I said the wedding would be one people would be talking about for a long time, I never dreamed . . . Well, where to begin? I'm fanning myself with the program from the ceremony and hoping that my poor old heart holds out! The day ran the gamut from the sublime to the scandalous to the . . . well, I hardly have words for what happened here!

First—the wedding. It was, in a word, perfect. The bride was as beautiful as a fairy tale princess, the groom her story-book prince. The Inn looked fabulous—if I do say so myself—the flowers glorious, the food divine. The weather was warm and balmy. What more could one have asked for on their wedding day?

Next—the scandal. The mother of the groom showed up uninvited! Yes, _that woman_ who to the best of my knowledge hasn't laid eyes on that boy of hers since she dumped him— yes, I said dumped—on the front doorstep of his unsuspecting father. She had the gall to show up at the wedding, and unless my hearing is going, _she_ was put out because Beck wouldn't speak to _her_! Can you imagine? What in the name of decency was that woman thinking? There will be more on this, I feel certain!

Finally—the unthinkable. Vanessa's sweet little boutique, Bling, was broken into and robbed! Right there on

Charles Street, while her brother's wedding reception was taking place, someone broke into the shop and—from what I heard at the day-after-the-wedding brunch—the burglars trashed the shop before they left! Yes, that's what I said— as if it wasn't enough to rob the poor girl, they tossed her lovely merchandise on the floor and broke the glass in some of her cases!

Now, I ask you: What kind of person would do something like that? Obviously, it's someone from out of town. No one in St. Dennis would stoop so low! And then . . . just moments later, the car that nice young Grady Shields rented and which he left parked in the lower town lot while he took Vanessa to inspect the damages at Bling . . . didn't someone come along and smash out every window? I hear through the grape vine that Hal believes both acts were committed by the same criminally-minded individual.

Breaking into shops! Smashing car windows! What kind of riff-raff are we allowing into our fair town? What has this world come to?!

I must work on an editorial for this week's paper. . . .

—Grace

Chapter 12

HAL did his best to talk Vanessa out of taking a walk through town that afternoon.

"Honey, I agree with Grady that something's afoot, that someone here has got it in for you. I don't think you ought to be putting yourself out there."

"There are tons of walkers out today," she pointed out. "We'll be on the main street, and you can have an armed guard follow me if it makes you feel better, but I need to focus on something besides the fact that I'm afraid and confused right now. All this conjecture is making me nuts." She softened. "Grady will be with me. He won't let anything happen to me."

"Then just do the short tour." Hal knew when to compromise. "Just up to the square and back. Leave the side streets for another day."

There isn't going to be another day, she wanted to remind him. Grady would be gone in a few hours, and chances were good he wouldn't be back anytime soon.

Playing tour guide actually did relax her, in spite of the fact that patrol cars seemed to be constantly driving by, circling the block like black-and-white sharks.

"The town was under siege during the War of 1812, but no buildings were destroyed. The townspeople had a plan, you see," she told Grady as they walked along. "The British approached the harbor at night, but as soon as they started firing, all the candles in town were snuffed out so that the entire town was dark. Some houses closest to the water took direct shots—a couple even still have cannonballs lodged in their walls—but none came down."

"If I remember my American history, that was the war when the British attacked the city of Baltimore and Francis Scott Key saw the flag flying above Fort McHenry the next morning and was inspired to write 'The Star-Spangled Banner.' "

"Well, here's a little did-you-know. The commanding officer wanted a really huge flag to fly over the fort, so he commissioned a woman from Baltimore to make one. And it *was* huge, like thirty feet high and forty-two feet long. That was the flag that Key saw the next morning."

"I did pay attention in my American history class. Major George Armistead was the commander. He wanted to make sure that the British could see the flag from their ships." Grady added, "I suppose it was the 1814 equivalent of getting in someone's face."

"Do you know the name of the flag maker?" she countered.

"No. Do you?"

"You betcha. Mary Pickersgill. There's a book in the Historical Society library that talks about how she was asked to make that flag and she only had a very limited time to do it. The flag is in the Smithsonian now."

Grady had made a move to take her hand but she walked with both hands linked behind her back so they were out of reach. When her arms grew tired, she switched her shoulder bag to her left side and looped her hand through the strap to occupy it. It wasn't that she didn't want that casual contact with him—she did. In fact, she'd been aching to touch him all day. But he'd be leaving town in a matter of hours, and a public display would only invite questions. She was under constant scrutiny by the police department, and all day long, people she knew had been driving past and waving. She couldn't bear the looks of pity she knew she'd get when she walked into Cuppachino in the morning. Or the questions that would inevitably come, the speculation that would be made. St. Dennis was still, after all, a small town, and there was little that could stop the gossip once it got rolling. There'd be enough attention on her in the coming days, with her shop having been the victim of the first burglary since the town started trying to attract tourists. To have that same light shining on her love life right now would be overkill.

"This area up here, we call the square," she continued. "The houses on each corner were among the first built when the town was officially laid out in 1685. Before that, there were land grants, maybe around 1650 or so, that pretty much defined the village area. The brick was all locally made, and the wooden sections that you see were all from trees cut down to clear the area." She smiled. "Sometimes I like to walk along here and try to picture the way it was back then, with only those few houses, and dirt paths between them. No roads, no cars . . . just horses and a wagon here and there." She pointed beyond the square. "You see those woods off to the right? There are trees there that have been standing for more than three hundred years. It's believed that's the last of the forest that the early settlers found when they first came here."

"You're really into this, aren't you? Hard to believe you're not a native." He seemed so casual, so nonchalant, yet Vanessa could not fail to notice that his eyes were constantly moving, from the passing cars to other pedestrians.

"I've learned a lot from Hal. His family has been here since the early 1700s. Imagine that? Being able to trace your family back that far?"

"I guess it's easy if no one ever left town. There'd be records in the churches of births, marriages, deaths," he pointed out. "And depending on how well the town kept records of the deeds changing hands, you could trace that, too."

"I suppose. But for someone . . ." She stopped herself from saying *someone like me*. ". . . someone whose family records are scattered or missing or inaccurate, or just plain unknown, it's a revelation to find out that some people even know who their first ancestors were who came to this country, and even what ship they came on." She shook her head and added, "I've never even met my real father. I took Keaton from a step-father, but my real dad . . . I know his name but I don't know anything about him."

"Maggie never told you?"

"There's a lot Maggie hasn't told me," Vanessa said drily.

"Have you asked her?" He stopped at the corner when she did. "About the things you don't know?"

She shook her head from side to side. "I always figured if she felt like talking about him, she would." She made a face. "Maybe that's not really true. Maybe I was afraid to ask because—oh, I don't know. Because she'd blow me off, or maybe not tell the truth, you know, maybe just tell me what she thinks I want to hear."

"What do you want to hear?"

"Just the truth." She was taller in the four-inch heels she wore, but still not eye to eye with him. "I would like to know about my father. I always told her it didn't matter, that I didn't want to know, but it does matter. I do want to know."

"If you weren't honest with her, why would she be honest with you?"

Vanessa frowned. "Whose side are you on?"

"Yours." He took her arm when she wouldn't give him her hand. "If you want the truth, ask for it. Don't assume people can read your mind. That's game playing. I didn't figure that for your style."

She crossed the street and started walking back toward town, and he kept in step with her.

"Ness?"

"I heard you."

"I can see that I upset you," Grady said. "I'm very sorry. But you brought up—"

"I know I did." She exhaled a long breath. "I'm not upset with you. I'm upset with myself."

"Why?"

"Why?" She snorted. "Why should I feel annoyed

with myself for telling a man I slept with last night all my deepest secrets?"

"If you can't share something of yourself with the man you sleep with, maybe you shouldn't be sleeping with him."

"We don't 'sleep with' each other. We slept. Past tense," she corrected him. "We just slept together last night."

"So you're telling me I was just a one-night stand?" He stopped in the middle of the sidewalk. "I feel so . . . cheap. So . . . used."

"You're not funny." She kept walking.

"What do you expect me to say?" He caught up with her in one stride. "Ness, I don't do one-night stands."

"Of course you do." She brushed him off. "All guys do."

"That's not fair."

"You stayed with me last night. You're leaving today," she pointed out. "One night."

"So if I leave town today, that means I can't come back?"

"You mean, like once a year? Or whenever you felt like it?"

Grady whistled, long and low. "You really have a low opinion of men, don't you?"

When she didn't answer, he said, "Every guy isn't out to love you and leave you, Ness, or to hurt you if he stays."

They walked along in silence for a while.

"You are the oddest man I have ever known." She shook her head, then fell silent again for the rest of the walk back to the center of town.

"Want to stop for coffee?" he asked as they approached Cuppachino.

She shook her head.

"How 'bout we stop in the art gallery across the street and just take a look around?"

"It won't open for another few weeks. Rocky, the guy who owns it, usually doesn't come back to St. Dennis until June first. He has a home in Arizona, and he stays there except for the summer. Anyway, don't you have to get going?"

"Are you trying to get rid of me? Tired of me already?"

"You said you had to leave St. Dennis by three. It's almost that now, and you still have to go back to the Inn to get your stuff and check out."

"I'll get to it."

They crossed the street, and Vanessa stopped in front of Bling. She hadn't noticed last night, but one of the side windows must have been cracked, because it was boarded up on the outside. Through the front window she could see the mess. There was yellow crime-scene tape wrapped around the entire building, and she noticed several passersby stop to speculate. She wrapped her arms around herself and willed herself not to cry.

"Maybe they'll let you go in soon and clean up," Grady said. "Maybe Hal can speed that up for you."

"He said tomorrow I could go in. I asked him this morning. After the shock of seeing him walk in with Maggie wore off."

"That bothers you, doesn't it? That Hal and Maggie seem to have so much to talk about?"

"How is it that you just always seem to know exactly which scab to pick at?" He'd just played on her last nerve.

She walked ahead of him and turned up Cherry Street without looking at him. He walked alongside her, his hands in the pockets of his Dockers, his dark glasses hiding his eyes.

When they got to her house, he said, "I just seem to set you off, no matter what I say. I'm sorry. I don't mean to pry or get into your business, but when you throw stuff out there, you shouldn't be surprised if I pick up on it. That's part of the whole conversation thing. You say something, I listen and say something back to you that pertains to whatever it is that you said. Then you say something else, and voilà. A conversation."

"I'm not used to talking about . . . certain things . . . with anyone. I don't know why my mouth has been so free this morning. I don't talk about my father, and I rarely talk about my mother, and as for this . . ." She placed a hand on her scar and shook her head. "So I don't know what's gotten into me. You seem to bring out the blabbermouth in me."

"Sometimes it's healthier to talk about things, than to not." He smiled. "You can blabber on to me anytime you want."

And I probably would, if you were sticking around, she thought.

"Now, here, all this time, I'd been led to believe that you were the strong, silent one. The loner. The recluse." She snorted. "I swear I never met a man who asked as many questions or who talked about as much stuff as you do."

"How else do you get to know someone?" Grady

shrugged. "Besides, I like to talk to you. You're not like most of the women I've known."

"Yeah, well, back atcha there, pal."

He laughed, and she found herself laughing, too. She tugged on his hand.

"Come on in and get some cookies to take with you for your hike. I must have miscounted my batches, because I had some left over."

"There were cookies here last night and you didn't bother to mention it?"

"You were busy checking for intruders," she reminded him as she unlocked the door.

His hand was on the small of her back while they walked toward the kitchen.

"Coffee or milk?" she asked.

"With cookies? Not even close."

She opened the refrigerator and took out a carton of milk.

"Glasses are in the—" She stopped short, her attention drawn to a box wrapped in white paper and tied with red ribbon that sat in the middle of the kitchen table. "Did you put that there?"

His eyes followed her gaze to the table. "No. Maybe Hal dropped it off. Does he have a key?"

She nodded. "He does. Maybe it's from Beck and Mia. You know, like a thank-you for being their unofficial wedding planner."

She put her purse on the counter and unwrapped the present. When she opened the box and looked inside, she stood for a moment, staring at the contents.

"What is it?" Grady asked.

She reached into the box and held up crudely torn strips of white eyelet.

"It used to be a dress," she told him. She dropped it back into the box. She looked up at Grady. "I think I know who broke into my shop. There was a woman in Bling the other day who came in and tried on this dress. She wasn't sure if she wanted it or not, so I put it in the back to hold it in case she came back."

"Get Hal on the phone," Grady told her. "Tell him what you just told me."

She did, and Hal arrived within minutes of her call.

She wasn't as happy to see Maggie as she was to see Hal.

"Are you riding shotgun in the cruiser these days?" she asked her mother, who trailed into the house with Hal.

"Don't be a smart-ass," Maggie replied. "I have the right to worry about my daughter."

"Don't start with me." Vanessa had led them into the kitchen.

Hal went straight to the box. "Ness, I'm assuming you opened this. Grady, did you touch it?"

"No. I doubt you'll find any prints on there except Vanessa's," Grady told him.

"This was here when you came back from your walk?" Hal asked.

Vanessa nodded. "We came in through the front door—"

"Which I'm assuming was locked?"

"Yes."

"Any idea how someone could have gotten in?" Hal asked her.

"Back door," Grady said. "The lock was picked. Expertly done, I might add."

Grady walked through the small back entry and

pointed to the door. "An amateur would have taken out the lower glass pane and turned the latch. The door was unlocked as you see it when we came in, but it wasn't obvious until we started looking after Ness found the box."

"So tell me again about this woman you mentioned on the phone. When she was in the shop, what she looked like, any conversations you might have had with her." Hal took out a pad and pen.

Vanessa ran through the woman's visit to the store.

"She said her name was Candice," she told him as she finished up, "but that's probably not her real name. Oh, and Steffie saw her coming out of Sips yesterday when she—Stef—was on her way to the Inn for the wedding."

"How did Steffie know who she was?" Hal asked.

"Stef was there the other day in the shop when 'Candice' came in."

"I'm going to want to stop down and have a chat with Steffie, then, see if she can add anything to what you told me." Hal folded the notepad and tucked it into the inside pocket of his jacket.

"She might. I went into the back of the shop for a moment while Stef was there, so they might have had some conversation," Vanessa recalled. Then, thinking about how considerate she'd been to her would-be customer, she began to steam. "You know, I felt sorry for her. She just looked so . . . I don't know, unhappy or downtrodden."

"Like she was having a bad day?" Maggie asked.

"More like she was having a bad life. I offered to hold the dress for her—and I did, it was still on the hold rack in my office yesterday. And I even offered to give her a nice discount on the price because I felt sorry for her."

"Why?" Grady stuck his hands in his pants pockets and leaned against the wall.

"Because the dress was a little on the pricey side, and I thought it might make it easier to make the sale." Vanessa stared at Grady for a moment, then added, "Oh, all right, it was because she wasn't dressed well and she looked like someone who didn't have a lot of nice things and she said the dress had looked nice on her when she tried it on. She sort of lit up a little when she brought it back out of the dressing room. I wanted her to have it, okay?"

"Let's assume for a minute that she was the person who broke into your shop last night," Grady offered. "If she liked the dress all that much, why wouldn't she have just taken it with her? Why destroy something she really wanted?"

"That's the odd part, that she'd take the dress only to rip it to shreds. Why would someone break in, take the dress, destroy it, and then wrap it up and give it back to me? She'd have to know that I'd make the association to her right away."

"No woman in her right mind would do that," Maggie thought aloud. "That'd be like painting a big sign on her back: 'I Did It.' "

"Well, she may have been involved, but I don't think she was behind it," Grady said. "I don't think she was the person who broke into the shop and beat up on the car."

"Those instincts of yours again, eh?" Vanessa asked, and Grady nodded.

Hal pulled on rubber gloves and replaced the lid on the box.

"Ness, do you have a paper bag?" he asked.

She nodded and got one from the pantry.

"Here you go." She handed it to him.

He tucked the ribbon into the bag.

"Guess that's it for now." He picked up the box and the bag. "I'm going to take this down to the station and see if I can lift some prints. I'll send someone down this afternoon to see what we can lift from that back door and the table."

"I'll bet you don't find any." Vanessa followed him from the room. "I'll bet she wore gloves when she wrapped that box."

"Was she wearing gloves when she tried on the dress?" Grady asked.

"Of course not . . . Oh." Vanessa followed his thought. "Can you get prints off of fabric?"

"Depends." Hal walked out onto the porch. "We'll see what we can find."

"I'll bet there are prints on that price tag," Maggie said when she reached the front door. "I never saw a woman yet who picked up something in a fancy store and didn't sneak a peek at the price."

"She did. She looked at the tag." In spite of herself, Vanessa was impressed that Maggie had thought of it. "And she looked at some other things. A pair of shorts . . . madras plaid. They're probably still in the shop. There's only one pair like them. Red, blue, yellow, green, and white plaid, Hal."

"I'll stop and look for them. Sue down at the station is real good with lifting prints. If we're lucky, we'll find prints on the tag and dress that match prints from the box. And then if we're really lucky, we'll find them on record somewhere," Hal said over his shoulder as he walked toward his car. "I'm going to send Sue over, see what she can get from the door and the table. We'll get back to you, Ness."

He stopped midway down the path and turned around. "In the meantime, I'd feel a lot better if you'd stay over at my place."

"Why can't you just park a police car in front of my house all night?" She frowned. "I hate that someone could drive me out of my house and I don't even know why."

"Well, it's going to be easier to figure out the *why* once we figure out the *who*." Hal continued walking to his car. "Regardless, you shouldn't be staying here alone."

"Vanessa, maybe I could—" Maggie began but Vanessa cut her off.

"Thanks anyway, but no."

Vanessa waved good-bye and watched Hal and Maggie get into the car and drive away.

Vanessa went down the steps and picked up a few dead tulips she'd missed the day before. She could feel Grady's eyes on her.

"What?" she asked.

"Hal's right. The least you can do is have someone stay here with you," he reasoned. "I guess it's out of the question that you take Maggie up on her offer."

She glared at him. "What do you think?"

"I think that narrows the field," he muttered.

"What?"

He shook his head. "Nothing."

"I am so mad at this woman." Vanessa began to

rail. "This 'Candice.' Who the hell is she and why is she doing these things? What could I have done to her that she'd want to destroy my business and scare me?"

"Let's finish this discussion inside." He held the door for her, and she followed him into the living room, sat when he did.

"Maybe it's someone you've had words with."

"I don't 'have words.' I hate confrontations. When it comes to arguing, I'm always the one to back down. I'm such a wuss. I've apologized for things I didn't do just to avoid having someone yell at me." She pulled her feet up under her. "How else to explain not one, but two abusive marriages? I just wish I knew who this woman is and why she's so angry at me. And after I was so nice to her."

She tried to think of someone she'd offended in the past, and other than a woman who'd bought a leather bag and returned it because the strap broke after she'd used it three times, Vanessa could not think of anyone who'd be holding a grudge against her.

"You know, maybe your first instinct was the right one. Maybe Eugene did get out early for good behavior or something—hard to imagine his behavior being that good, but I suppose people can change. Maybe the D.A. forgot to let me know. Couldn't find my address. That's possible, right?"

Grady put a hand on her shoulder. "I have some bad news about him, Ness. I had someone make some calls this morning."

"Oh God, I'm right, aren't I?" Her face went ashen. "He's here in St. Dennis, isn't he? He's been inside my house." She started to hyperventilate.

"No, no. He wasn't here, Ness. He couldn't have been. He's dead."

"What?" Both hands flew to her heart. "Dead? Did you say Eugene's *dead*?"

Grady nodded. "I'm sorry, I—"

"He's dead." She blinked a few times. "Dear God, I feel like one of the Munchkins."

"Munchkins?"

"Yeah, you know, the little people from *The Wizard of Oz*? 'Ding dong, the witch is dead?' "

"Let's go into the kitchen. I'll get you a glass of water."

"I'm fine." But she let him lead her into the back of the house. "It's wrong to be happy that someone died, right? I mean, maybe he changed while he was in prison, maybe he found religion and he's turned himself around. It would be bad to be happy that someone who's rehabilitated himself is dead."

"He was in a fight with another inmate and his neck was broken." Grady turned on the cold-water faucet. "I doubt he was rehabilitated."

"Oh, good." She fanned herself. "Because I'd hate to be this happy if he died a good man, and—"

He filled a glass of water and held it to her lips.

"Drink," he told her. "You're on the verge of babble."

She took several long sips, then grabbed the glass from his hands.

"I'm okay. Thank you." She took some deep breaths. "He's really dead? You're sure?"

"Unless someone in the prison system thinks it's skippy to lie to the FBI, I'd say, yeah, he's really dead." He watched her for a moment. "Are you okay?"

"Okay? Gene is really dead." She shook her head. "I never saw that coming but yes, I'm okay with that. When did you find out?"

"I asked my old boss if he'd have someone check, just to make sure this guy was still behind bars. I honestly thought we'd get confirmation that he'd been released on parole. I had him pegged for the break-in. But I got a call while we were at the brunch this morning. Gene Medford is definitely dead. I didn't want to tell you at the restaurant, and then later, we were walking, and I was just happy being with you, and you seemed so relaxed. For a while, anyway. The truth is, I didn't want to bring him along with us. I didn't want to spoil that time together." He looked a little sheepish. "Well, I ended up doing that anyway, I guess. But I thought it would be better to wait until we got back here to tell you."

"You didn't spoil anything. Sometimes you make me think about things that I don't necessarily want to think about, but that's on me, not on you."

She put her arms around his waist and rested her head on his chest.

"I'm not sorry that he's dead, Grady. He made my life a living hell." She thought of all the times in the past she'd wished that something—anything—would happen to remove Gene from her life. "I used to dream that his car would get stuck on the train tracks and he couldn't get out in time. Or that he'd be eating lunch at work and he'd choke to death. Stuff like that. And in the dreams, someone would come to my house to tell me, and I wouldn't cry. I'd just say, 'Oh, thank you for letting me know. Bye.' And I'd close the door, and then I'd wake up. I never really thought he'd die, ever. Like someone that mean couldn't die like ordinary people."

He wrapped his arms around her.

"But you were married to him. You loved him once. You could cry for him if you wanted," he told her. "Don't feel like you can't cry because I'm here."

"Are you serious?" She pushed out of his arms and raised her shirt up, then turned around so he could see her back. "One of the ways Gene liked to wake me up when he'd come in drunk was to put his cigarette out on my back." She looked over her shoulder and met his eyes. "Do you really think I'd waste a tear crying over him?"

"Jesus, Ness." Grady was visibly stunned. He touched the scars gingerly, as if afraid that they had not healed. "Jesus."

Vanessa pulled her shirt back down.

"I wasn't showing you so you'd feel sorry for me. I just wanted you to understand."

He nodded, but as if still stunned, he didn't reply. He just held her.

Finally, he said, "Maybe this woman, Candice, maybe she was involved with your ex. Maybe she blames you because he's dead."

"Maybe. She had that look about her."

"What look is that?"

"The look of a woman who's afraid of being hurt," she told him. "A woman who's used to being hurt. Just because he was in prison doesn't mean he couldn't have hurt her. He could have just beaten her down with words, the way he used to beat me down."

"Give Hal a call and run that past him." Grady

stood and took his phone from his pocket. "Meanwhile, I'll see if the FBI can get a list of all of Gene's visitors."

She called the station, and he called John Mancini and had a long talk with him. Grady walked out into the backyard to improve reception, and when he returned to the kitchen, Sue was already setting up to start taking prints.

"It's all yours," Vanessa was saying. "Doors, counters, kitchen table, whatever."

"Thanks. I'll try not to get in your way." Sue looked over her shoulder and smiled at Grady. "I'll be out of here as soon as possible."

"You won't be in our way." Vanessa turned to Grady. "I'm going to drive Grady to pick up his rental car."

"Oh, and Hal said to tell you he called a locksmith. He's having your locks changed. He said he'd leave the new keys at the station if you weren't here when the guy finished up."

"Great. Thanks." Vanessa turned to Grady. "You ready?"

He nodded and waved to Sue. Vanessa grabbed her handbag from the counter, where she'd earlier tossed it.

Grady had left Vanessa's car in the driveway and he now returned the keys to her. They got in and she backed out, maneuvering carefully around the patrol car that Sue had parked a little too close to the end of the driveway. She drove to the rental car's location on the highway.

"Look at all the pretty cars." Vanessa pulled into the lot and stopped behind a gorgeous black luxury sedan. "You don't suppose they'll let you take this one?"

Grady laughed. "It's a beauty, but it won't do me any good where I'm going."

"Oh, right. Nature man. Wilderness hiker." She nodded. "I guess you wouldn't want to leave something that pretty out all by its lonesome while you explore the wild."

He laughed again and opened the car door. "This might take a few minutes. Come on in."

"I can wait here."

"I'd rather have you come inside with me."

"All right." She got out of the car and locked it, then followed him inside. While Grady tended to his paperwork, she walked around the reception area. There was a radio playing somewhere in the back of the building. She could hear U2 singing about a beautiful day, and she almost laughed out loud.

Oh, it's been a beauty of a day, all right.

She stood at the window and looked over the cars in the lot, and tried to pretend that it didn't matter that he was picking up the car that would take him away from St. Dennis, and from her. She tried to block Candice's sad face from her mind. She tried to forget that Maggie was in town and spending way too much time with Hal. The only good news she'd had that day had been about Gene. That was one demon she could put to rest forever. It was almost surreal to think she would never have to be afraid of him ever again.

"Got it." Grady was at her elbow, keys in hand. "Thanks, Ness. Let's go."

When they got outside he said, "How about I follow you back into town? I need to pick up some things at the Inn."

"Sure." She was still smiling when she got into her car, and when she drove from the lot, waving to him as she pulled her sedan in front of the four-wheel-drive SUV he'd just picked up. But her smile faded as she merged into the line of traffic and forced herself to take several deep breaths.

You knew he was leaving today, he told you that right up front. You knew and you let yourself get involved with him anyway, her little inner voice lectured. *And don't make this more than what it was: a fun weekend. A fling. You used to do flings.*

"I don't do flings anymore," she said aloud.

Well, you had one this weekend. Let it go. Move on.

Traffic on the highway had built up and the stop and go was annoying her, so she turned off the main road and followed the backstreets. He was still behind her, so she meandered down toward the river side of town, not wanting to end the drive. Once the drive ended, once they were back on Cherry Street, they'd be saying good-bye, and she could barely stand how awkward it was going to be. He'd be saying something like, "Well, I'll call you," or maybe, "Hey, the next time I'm in St. Dennis . . ." but only because he'd feel obligated to. Most one-night stands didn't run well into the next day the way this one had.

As for his claim that he "didn't do one-night stands". . .

"Bull," she said aloud. "Guys live for the one-night stand. It's in their DNA."

And it isn't like I won't have anything to think about after he leaves, she reminded herself. There was her trashed shop, for one thing. Her home, which apparently was no longer her castle, since someone had found a way in, uninvited and intending her harm, for another.

Oh, and let's not forget Maggie.

Was it Vanessa's imagination, or did Maggie really have her sights set on Hal again?

Dear Lord, please say it isn't so . . .

She was not going to think about Maggie. Or Grady, for that matter. Uh-uh. Not going there.

She drove back to her home then, still not thinking about Grady.

He slowed down when she turned into her driveway, then beeped his horn and waved when she got out of her car. Then, incredibly, he kept on going, and drove past.

Vanessa stood on the sidewalk next to Sue's cruiser, her mouth open. Had he just blown her off?

She knew he had plans, but still. Damn. That was just unbelievably . . . unbelievable. Not even to say a real good-bye? That "Thanks, Ness" back there at the car rental place . . . *that was it?*

Numb, Vanessa went into the house. Sue was still dusting for fingerprints, but she'd finished the back door and had moved into the kitchen.

"Hal called a while ago," Sue told her. "He said that he thinks you should reconsider and sleep at his place tonight."

"I'll think about it." Knowing full well she wouldn't, Vanessa went upstairs and into her room.

The bed was a tangle, the sheets and blanket every which way. She stared at it long and hard before pulling everything off and stuffing it all—the blanket along with the sheets and pillowcases—into a laundry basket that stood near the closet door. She took fresh linens from the closet and remade the bed, taking the blanket from the spare-room bed and exchanging the pillows from one bed to the other.

She stood back to assess the newly pulled-together bed. The blanket wasn't as pretty as the one in the basket, and the pillows were not the ones she preferred, but the important thing was that there was no scent of him there, no valley in the pillow where his head had lain.

"There."

She took off the skirt she was wearing and hung it in the closet, and changed into her favorite jeans. She'd just slipped her feet back into her shoes when she heard the front door slam.

"Ness?"

And damn it, didn't her heart flip just a little at the sound of his voice?

"I'm up here," she called.

"Got my stuff from the Inn . . . hey, you look pretty." He grinned as he came in the room. "Got a hot date?"

He crossed the room and kissed her.

He came back, was all she could think of. *He came back . . .*

He looked down at her feet. "Do you have any other shoes?"

She was still trying to catch up to the fact that he hadn't left her after all.

"You are kidding, right? Of course I have other shoes. Shoes are my life." She walked to her closet, opened the door, and pointed to a row of shelves lined with boxes. "Shoes."

"I meant, any other kind. Shoes you could walk in."

"I walk in these." She turned her foot to show off the pretty brown leather pumps with their four-inch heels. "I walk to work every day in shoes like this."

"How 'bout shoes you can comfortably walk a distance in."

"Oh. Well, sure. I have some really cute flats." She pulled a box from the shelf. "Aren't these the cutest? I just got these."

"Let's rephrase." Grady's mouth twitched at both ends. "What would you wear if you went walking in the woods?"

"Nikes?" She frowned.

"You'd wear hiking boots. Where's your computer?"

"It's in the kitchen."

"Come on. We'll look up the closest athletic equipment store."

"We don't have to look it up. Mickey Forbes has a place right outside of town."

"Great." He tugged on her hand. "Let's go."

"Well, God knows I'm not one to pass up on a shopping opportunity, but I thought you were leaving to go on your hike."

"I am. You're coming with me."

"What?"

"You don't really think I'd leave you here, with all that's going on?"

"You want to take me with you?"

"Sure. You won't mind roughing it a little for a couple of days, would you?"

"How rough is rough?" She frowned again.

"Not as rough as it could be if whoever is stalking you catches up."

"As much as I'm sure I'd love roughing it with you—there's no one I'd rather share a tent with—but I can't leave St. Dennis. I have to go into Bling tomorrow and figure out what I'm missing so I can meet with the insurance company. We're coming into our busy season. I have to get Bling open as quickly as I can, or I won't make enough this summer to carry me through the winter." She sat on the side of the bed and he sat next to her. "I appreciate the thought, I appreciate you offering to take me with you, but I can't go."

Grady nodded. "I understand. I probably should have thought of that myself. In that case"—he leaned over and kissed her—"I suppose I better go get my stuff."

"What stuff?"

"My clothes."

"I thought you said you just picked them up from the Inn."

"I did. They're in the car. If you can't come with me, I'm just going to have to stay with you. So until this is over, I'm afraid you're stuck with me. Think you can handle sharing your space? Unless you'd rather stay at the Inn—"

"What about your trip? The hike you had planned?"

"The mountain will be there when all this is over." He started toward the steps. "I want to make sure you are, too . . ."

Chapter 13

D IDN'T I tell you she hated me?" Maggie slumped in the front seat of Hal's car.

"Well, now, *hate* might be too strong a word." Hal drove away from the curb, mindful of the group of teens who for unknown reasons did not seem capable of walking on a sidewalk in this town. "I think she's got issues, Maggie, but I don't know that she hates you."

"She'd rather take her chances with some crazy guy in a ski mask than have me stay with her."

"Let's be fair, now." He paused, trying to choose his words carefully. "I'd guess that she's a little put out on Beck's behalf. You know he wasn't expecting to see you at the wedding, Maggie."

"You think I was wrong to come."

"I think if he—"

"You think if he'd wanted me at his wedding he'd have invited me."

"That isn't what I was going to say, but yes, I think that's probably true."

He rolled to a stop sign, looked both ways to see

what was what on Rayburn Road before continuing on his way.

"So what were you going to say?"

"I was going to say, if he'd had some time to prepare himself, if he'd had some contact with you over the past few years, he'd have taken it a little better."

Tears welled in Maggie's eyes. "I've never done a damned thing right where that boy was concerned. I didn't know how to handle him when he was a child, or when he was a teenager, or now that he's an adult. I've never known how to talk to him, Hal. I think it would have been easier for all of us if you'd been there . . ." She swallowed hard. "That was not what I intended to say, so forget that part."

"Maggie, once something's been said, it's said." He drove around the block to Charles Street. "You can't take words back and pretend they weren't spoken." His voice softened. "Just like you can't take the last twenty years back, and expect your children to pretend those years never happened."

Maggie stared out the window.

"What should I do, Hal?"

"You have a lot of explaining to do to both of them," he told her. "If you want them to let you into their lives, you have to let them into yours. From what you've told me, you've made a lot of mistakes in your life." He hastened to add, "We all have. But you have to own up to them if you're going to move past them."

"What if I tell them, and they still don't like me?"

"Well, then, I suppose that's a chance you have to take. The way it stands right now, they both have problems with you but they don't understand why you acted the way you did. There is a chance that they could hear the truth and still have a problem with you. That's the chance you take. But they're your kids, and if you want them back in your life, you're going to have to step up and talk to them, and tell them everything you've told me over the past twenty-four hours. Maybe they'll understand and forgive, maybe they won't. I'm seeing that as fifty-fifty. But if you don't have those conversations with them, your chances of reconciling with your kids are zero."

"What if they dislike me even more?"

"Like I said, that's the chance you take."

"Where should I start? What would you do, if you were me?" she asked.

"I guess I'd start by taking Ness out to dinner and just talking to her. Get to know her a little, find out what's happened in her life since she's come here."

"Well, I know what's happened in her life. I know that you took her under your wing and helped her to get her business started. I know that you financed that little house of hers. I know that she thinks of you as the father she didn't have."

Hal couldn't tell if she sounded happy or annoyed.

"You know that much, seems to me that's a starting point."

He drove down Kelly's Point and parked in the spot that was reserved for the chief of police. He never got tired of remembering that the chief was his son. He opened his car door and started to get out.

She reached for the door handle and asked, "Do you hate me, Hal?"

He shook his head. "No. I never hated you, Maggie."

"Not even when you came back from Nam and found out I was married to someone else?"

"Maybe for a while, back then," he admitted. "But I started thinking about how hard things must have been for you. Pregnant, not knowing if I'd come back alive, your parents pressuring you to marry this other man. After a time, I realized you did what you thought you had to do. I understood."

He slammed his car door and walked around to the passenger side.

"The fact that I understood doesn't mean that I liked it." He fell in step with her and they walked down the road toward the Bay.

"I was scared."

"Of course you were. Who wouldn't have been?"

"My father kept telling me that the baby and I would end up like these homeless people we had in the town where we lived." Her step slowed. "My parents owned a restaurant, and every night, there'd be people cleaning out the Dumpster out back. My parents would leave the leftovers in these Styrofoam containers and they'd leave plastic knives and forks out there so that people wouldn't have to eat with their hands." She shook her head. "It sounds so crazy now. But my father used to make me watch out the window when they came. 'See that?' He'd hold my face to the glass. 'That's going to be you if you don't marry Vic.'"

She clasped her hands together in front of her as they walked, and Hal suspected that the hands were probably as shaky as the voice.

"I don't blame you, Maggie. We already talked about this," Hal reminded her.

He'd heard it the night before, and he didn't want to hear it all again. He understood how one thing had led to another in the past, how everything had gone downhill and why she felt powerless to stop it. He just didn't want to hear it again now. He wanted to put it all behind him. He wasn't sure where that would take them, but one thing he knew for certain: looking back was no way to move forward.

Which was all well and good as far as he was concerned, he supposed, but apparently she hadn't gotten it all out of her system yet, in which case he'd be hearing about it again and again. But if that was what Maggie needed to work it all out, that was the way it was going to have to be. The thing was, he wasn't sure that even Maggie fully understood the choices she'd made over the years. Maybe she'd have to talk it through a little more before she did. And that was okay, because the longer she talked, the more time he'd have to look at her. It was a pleasure he thought he'd never experience again, and he wasn't about to pass up the opportunity.

He took her by the arm and led her down the path to One Scoop or Two.

"Oh," she said, surprised. "Are you taking me for ice cream?"

"Yes, I am," he replied. "And while we're here, I'm going to have a little talk with Steffie about this Candice person who was in Ness's shop the other day. She may have noticed something that Vanessa might have missed."

"And after that, are you going to take me back to the Inn?"

"Nope. After that, I'm going to take you for a cruise around the Bay on the *Shady Lady*."

"The *Shady Lady*?"

"My boat." He opened Steffie's screen door and waited for Maggie to catch up.

"Did you name your boat after me?"

Hal smiled, and stepped back to allow her to pass.

"You won't believe who that was on the phone." Vanessa came into the spare bedroom, where Grady was hanging his tux in the closet. He'd meant to give it to Andy to return when he took his own back, but he hadn't been able to locate his brother before he left the Inn.

"Let me guess. It was Candice, apologizing for having trashed your store and wondering if you could get her another one of those dresses." He looked over at the doorway, where she stood leaning against the jamb. "Maybe one that's in one piece."

"I wish. Maybe her number would show up on my caller ID so that we could track her down and sit her phony little ass in one of my brother's cells." She plopped down on the chair in the corner. "Maggie was on the phone. She's with Hal, and they wanted to know if I wanted to meet them for dinner."

"What did you tell them?"

"I told them I had plans." She crossed her legs.

"Do you?"

"I do now." She grinned. "Unless of course, you have plans with your family . . ."

"I don't. I did try to catch up with Andy and Connor at the Inn, but they're either playing tennis or sightseeing, and they weren't in their rooms."

He tossed his suitcase on the bed and opened it.

"Mind if I use one of those drawers?" he asked.

"Help yourself. They're all empty."

He wondered if it felt as odd to her to see him put his clothes in her dresser as it felt for him to be doing it. He could have kept his room at the Inn, but that would have defeated the purpose of him staying in St. Dennis. He hadn't planned on hanging around, but he could not in good conscience leave her while he still suspected that someone meant her harm. There had been one or two times in his life as an agent when he'd felt, in hindsight, that some action on his part might have prevented something from happening to someone who'd ended up a victim. For the past several years, he'd had to live with wondering if he could have saved Melissa. If he'd been able to see Brendan for what he really was, would she still be alive?

No way was he going to leave St. Dennis with similar regrets. Uh-uh. If something happened to Vanessa, too, he wouldn't be able to live with himself.

He thought about the guided hike he had scheduled for the end of the coming week. Well, if other arrangements for her safety could not be made, he'd just have to take her with him back to Montana, maybe leave her at the lodge while he took out his tour. Right then, the only thing he knew for certain was that he *wasn't* going to leave her alone and vulnerable in St. Dennis.

"Grady?" She was sitting in the chair, her knees primly together, her arms resting on her thighs. "I'm glad you came back."

He put the last of his things in the drawer and closed it.

"Thank you," she added.

He turned around and studied her face. "Why wouldn't I have come back?"

She shrugged. "I guess I just thought that you weren't going to."

"Didn't I tell you that I'd be stopping at the Inn?"

"Maybe you said something about the Inn . . ."

He went to the chair and leaned down to kiss her. "Do you really think I'd have done that? That I'd have waved good-bye and never come back?"

"I suppose I don't have great expectations when it comes to men."

"Then I guess we're going to have to raise your expectations." He kissed her again. "What do you want to do between now and dinner?"

She smiled and pulled him close. "Unfortunately, Sue is still here."

"Well then, we'll just have to find something else to do until Sue is finished." He thought about it for a moment, then pulled her up. "Let's walk down to Steffie's for ice cream. You know you're dying to talk to her about what happened last night at the shop."

"Actually, yes, I admit I am. How did you know that?"

"I have a sister."

They stopped in the kitchen to tell Sue they'd be gone for a while. The locksmith still hadn't arrived, but she said he'd called and was on his way.

"I'll still be working on this counter, so I can let him in," Sue told them. "There are a lot of prints here."

"Some are probably mine," Grady said, recalling that he'd spent most of Thursday in Vanessa's kitchen. "But I can get a copy of mine sent from the Bureau to your department so you can rule those out."

"Thanks." Sue never raised her eyes from her work. "That would be helpful."

The air was cooler than it had been when they'd walked through town earlier in the day, but it was still pleasant. When they got to the corner at Charles Street, Vanessa raised her right hand to her face and said, "Let's keep walking. I don't want to see it. I'll deal with the shop tomorrow."

There was still a lot of foot traffic in town, and he could have told her that more than one pedestrian had stopped to look at her store, where the police tape still wrapped around the front. Grady took her hand as they crossed the street and headed down Kelly's Point, and tried not to think about the fact that she'd believed he'd left her with nothing more than a beep and a wave. She wasn't kidding when she said she had low expectations of men.

Well, the only thing he could do was try to raise them, and he was determined to do just that. If he could have gotten his hands around Gene Medford's neck, he'd have choked him for what he'd done to this woman. Grady was almost sorry that one of Gene's fellow inmates had gotten to him first.

"Grady?" Vanessa tugged on his hand.

"Oh, sorry. I guess I just wandered for a minute."

"I said, it looks like half the town had the same idea we did."

"It's really crowded." He could see through the

side windows. "I think we're going to have to wait until a few people come out before we can go in."

"We could walk down to the dock, and . . . oh, there's Miss Grace." Vanessa smiled and waved.

"Oh, Vanessa, dear." The older woman sat alone at one of the small outside tables. "I heard about your shop. I am so sorry. I can hardly believe it."

"I can hardly believe it myself, Miss Grace."

"Do the police have any suspects?"

"Not yet. I know they're working on it, but so far . . ." Vanessa shrugged. "Nothing."

"Was much stolen?"

"I won't know until tomorrow. The police were still combing through the shop this morning, looking for evidence, so I didn't go inside today."

"Well, it must have been someone from out of town," Grace pronounced. "I cannot imagine anyone from St. Dennis doing such a thing."

"I feel the same way," Vanessa said. "I don't want to think that anyone I know would do this to me. But we do think it may have been someone who took advantage of the fact that everyone's attention was on the Inn yesterday."

"I wouldn't think that anyone other than the locals would have known about the wedding." Grace frowned. "Was there much damage to the shop?"

"One of the glass cases was broken, and one of the windows on the side was damaged. I think I probably lost some inventory, and I'm clearly going to need a new lock and a new alarm system, since both failed last night."

"Terrible, dear. Just terrible." Grace waved a thin hand as if to fan herself as she turned to Grady. "And what's this I'm hearing about your car being smashed to smithereens?"

"Not quite smithereens," he replied, "but yes, someone broke the windows out of my rental car while Vanessa and I were in Bling following the burglary."

"Such crazy business. What next, do you suppose?" Grace patted him on the arm. "But it was certainly good of you to accompany Vanessa to the scene of the crime. I'm sure Beck will appreciate you giving her a hand last night."

The corners of Vanessa's mouth twitched.

Grady pretended not to notice. "Yes, ma'am. I was glad to do it."

"Well, I hope they catch whoever was responsible." Grace paused. "Do you think it was the same person? It seems awfully suspicious to me, one happening right after the other. Especially since we rarely have such goings-on in St. Dennis."

"I think we all agree with you there." Grady nodded.

"But let's talk about that lovely wedding yesterday. Grady, your sister was a beautiful bride. I made sure we got several photos for this week's paper. Along with a fascinating interview I had earlier today with Dr. McGowan." Grace was almost beaming.

"Dr. McGowan?" Vanessa frowned. "You mean Daria? The woman who's engaged to Connor? She's a doctor?"

"Daria has a doctorate in archaeology," Grady told her.

"She's quite well known in the field," Grace added. "One of the girls working at the Inn on weekends is a freshman in college, and she's majoring in archaeology. Dr. McGowan offered to send her some photos she took at a dig in Turkey. The girl is simply over the moon."

"That was very nice of her." Vanessa's attention turned as several patrons emerged with their ice cream. "Oh, Grady, look. People are leaving. Let's dash in before anyone else does."

"Well, you'd better hurry. There's a small army coming up there on the left." Grace pointed. "He who hesitates . . ."

"Has to wait in line." Vanessa waved to Grace as she and Grady entered the shop.

The little bell over the door jingled but Steffie didn't look up.

"Boy, she looks beat, doesn't she?" Vanessa whispered from the corner of her mouth.

Grady nodded as they stepped in line. He looked around the shop, and met Hal's questioning eyes from across the room.

I guess he's wondering why I'm standing here holding Vanessa's hand. Well, I suppose if I were him, I'd be curious, too. But curious *is probably not the word I'd use to describe Vanessa's reaction when she sees that Hal is sitting there with an arm over the back of Maggie's chair.*

He stood so that his body was between Maggie and Vanessa, then realized how silly it was for him to try to protect her from seeing her parents together. He understood why Vanessa would object, would want to protect Hal just as Grady wanted to protect Vanessa, but it was silly. Hal and Maggie were going to do whatever it was they were doing, regardless of what Vanessa or Beck or anyone else thought, and that was the way it should be. If Vanessa had a problem with it, she was just going to have to deal.

They were still three people back in the queue but the line was moving. Steffie had apparently called in recruits.

"You know, I get more steamed every time I think about that woman, Candice," Vanessa told him, her hands in the pockets of her jeans, a deep frown on her pretty face. "I was going to give her a twenty percent discount on that dress. And then she destroyed it. Doesn't that just stink?"

"It does." He fought to control a smile. She was so seriously put out over that one factor. But the longer Grady thought about it, the more it began to bother him, too, albeit for totally different reasons.

"What can I get for . . ." Steffie raised her head, then smiled. "Oh, hey, guys. Ness, I was going to call you as soon as I had a break. I heard about what happened. Look, anything I can do . . . I mean anything, you got it."

"Thanks, Stef. I appreciate that."

"We need to talk about this. I need to hear everything."

"You will. I'll be at the shop tomorrow morning to start cleaning up."

"I'll be there to help if you need me. I'll see if Tina can open for me. She was looking for extra hours." Steffie's eyes followed several new customers into the store. "Do you believe this? You'd think I invented ice cream, the way people are streaming into this store. Honestly, Ness, it's been like this since I opened at noon." She grinned and added, "And I should mention that Mocha Berry Vanessa has been a big seller."

"We'll have two of those," Grady told her.

Steffie scooped the ice cream into bowls and stuck a plastic spoon in the top of each before handing them over.

"What time are you planning on going to Bling tomorrow?" she asked.

"I'd like to keep my regular hours, so I guess I'll be in town for coffee by eight," Vanessa told her.

"I'll see you then." She waved Grady away when he took his wallet from his back pocket. "I can help the next person in line. . . ."

"Wow, she's really doing quite the business," Grady noted as they stepped out into the sunlight.

"It's a nice warm day, and people like to get out and walk in the sunshine after a long cold winter. Besides, Steffie's good at what she does, and she was at the right place at the right time. Unlike me, however, she always knew exactly what she wanted to do."

"She always wanted an ice-cream shop?"

"She always wanted to make her own ice cream. Make up her own flavors, sell from her own little place. At one time, this little building was a crabber's shack. She told me that her dad and her uncle and her grandfather were all watermen. This was where they picked the crabs, her grandmother and her mother and her aunt. Crabbing fell off a few years ago, the grandfather died, the uncle moved away, her dad retired from commercial crabbing, took out some loans, and went back to college."

"What does he do now?"

"He's an environmentalist. He's working on writ-

ing the new conservation regulations for the Chesapeake Watershed."

"There's a switch of hats."

"Not so much. Stef said he saw firsthand what pol-
lution was doing to the Bay, and wanted to work to
correct it." Vanessa licked ice cream from the spoon.
"Anyway, she wanted a place to do her thing, so her
dad let her have their old shack. She worked on it for
six months, fixing it up. She said it had leaks, it had
bats, the windows needed to be replaced, and the
floor needed repair."

"She did all that work herself?"

Vanessa nodded. "Mostly by herself, though her
brother did help her out when he could. He's the vet
here, owns a small animal and waterfowl clinic down
on the river."

"Small animal and waterfowl," Grady mused.
"Now there's an interesting combination."

"Stef said that when he went away to school, he
wanted to come back to St. Dennis to practice someday, so I guess he knew what they needed most
around here."

They'd reached the wooden walkway, as far as one
could go before stepping into the Bay. The water had
rainbow swirls from fuel that leaked from the motor
of one of the boats tied up just a stone's throw farther
down toward the pier. They stood and watched the
boats ease in or out of their slips, the motors muffling
as they maneuvered slowly around the pier. Once out
in the channel they could open up their motors and
the boats could soar and scream like wild things, but
here, on their best behavior, they whispered.

"Well, now, I thought that was the two of you back there in Steffie's place."

Vanessa turned in time to see Hal take Maggie's arm.

"Look here, Maggie. Vanessa and Grady are out enjoying the day, too."

"I was," Vanessa muttered.

"We're just on our way to take the boat out for a spin. Maggie says she's never been out on the water. Imagine that, Ness." He looked her directly in the eye. "Imagine living your whole life, and never getting to feel the spray in your face, the wind in your hair . . ."

Vanessa's smile was fixed and frozen.

"I was just telling Maggie about taking you out this week, Grady," Hal went on as if everything was just peachy, as if Vanessa wasn't staring daggers at Maggie, and Maggie wasn't trying to ignore her daughter, choosing instead to focus on Grady.

"I enjoyed both trips," Grady told them. Addressing Maggie, he said, "I'm sure you'll have a great time. Hal really knows his way around the Bay."

"After sixty-some years around here, I'd better know my way around. Say," he said as if it just occurred to him. "I thought you were leaving this afternoon."

"I had a change of plans," Grady replied.

"I see. Well, then, why don't you join us for a spin around the Bay? It's been a while since you and I were out together, Ness."

"Some other time, Hal, but thank you," Vanessa replied.

"All right, then. See you later." He took Maggie's

arm and started to turn toward the dock. "You know what would make me very happy? If you two would meet us for dinner later at Walt's."

Grady watched the conflict cross Vanessa's face. She loved Hal and wouldn't hurt him for the world, but she still clearly had issues with Maggie.

Finally, she said, "Grady, did your brother ever get back to you about having dinner tonight?"

"No," he replied. "I haven't heard from him."

"Oh, Andy you're talking about?" Hal adjusted the dark glasses on his face. "I ran into him earlier at the Inn. He said he'd be heading over to Cannonball Island. He and his wife and a couple of your cousins left around three. I wouldn't be surprised if they were to have dinner while they're there."

"In that case, I guess I'm free." Grady turned to Vanessa. "Are you free?"

Still watching Hal's face, Vanessa nodded. "What time is good for you, Hal?"

"I suspect we won't be out as long as an hour." Hal looked across the Bay and seemed to study the sky. "No point in it, since the sun is going to be setting soon enough."

"Let's say an hour then." Vanessa nodded.

"Good. I'll be looking forward to it. Now, to get that boat out of her slip without nudging into that fool Carter Harwell. Will you look at the way he's parking that Whaler of his?" Hal set off down the walk, his eyes on his precious boat, one hand on Maggie's arm, the other raised to his face as he yelled across the pier, "Hey, Harwell! Watch where you're going. . . ."

Grady looked down at Vanessa, who was looking up at him.

"Way to stand firm," he said.

"I can't say no to him. If he wants me to do this, I'll do it. If he wants me to make nice to my mother, I'll make nice."

"I think he's hoping you're doing this for the right reasons, not because you want to please him."

"Pleasing Hal *is* the right reason." She shook her head. "It's the only reason why I'd sit down with her right now."

"Well, then, I guess that's going to have to do. For now." He took her hand and walked to the end of the pier.

Even from a distance, they could hear Hal berating his old sailing buddy, who still hadn't gotten his boat into the slip.

Listening to Hal, Vanessa started to laugh. "He's such a paper tiger. He'll rail away on Carter, and Carter will rail away on Hal, and in an hour, they'll be buying each other a beer at Walt's. Hal just loves to bluster sometimes."

They stood and listened to the harangue-fest for a few more minutes before Hal leapt from the dock to the deck of the Whaler and helped navigate the craft into position. Within minutes, the boat was tied up and both men were stepping up onto the dock. They chatted a few minutes—Hal introducing Maggie to Carter—before apparently forgetting all about the *Shady Lady* as the three headed directly to Walt's.

"She's up to no good." Vanessa's eyes narrowed. "Her last husband died recently so she's on the loose. She's come to St. Dennis and she's realized that Hal is pretty well off and she's setting her sights on him again."

"You don't know that."

"Oh, yes I do. I know that look."

"Look, I'm sure after all these years, they have things to say to each other. They were in love once, they had a child together . . ."

"Which she never even bothered to tell him about until she couldn't handle him. Let's not forget about Beck and the way she told Hal that he had a son."

When Grady didn't comment, Vanessa stopped walking. "What?" she asked.

"I think you need to leave that part to them to work out."

"How would you feel if Melissa—that was her name, right?" she asked, and when he nodded, she continued. He had a feeling he knew where this was going. "How would you feel if she disappeared from your life and came back years later with a child she said was yours?"

"She did disappear from my life," he said softly, "and if she showed up today with a child of mine, I'd be very happy to have that child. I would have loved to have had a child. But since she's dead, that's not a possibility."

"Oh, God, I am such an idiot. I am so sorry." Vanessa's face flushed as scarlet as the sun dropping into the Bay. "I can't believe I said that."

"It's all right, Ness. . . ."

"What a boneheaded thing to say." She was wide-eyed. "Boneheaded and thoughtless and insensitive and—"

"Enough." He put a hand over her mouth. "I understand the analogy you were trying to make. It's all right. We can talk about Melissa, Ness. Just as we can talk about Gene."

"That's very different." Her face grew very serious. "Gene and I got divorced because I knew that sooner or later, he was going to kill me. That's why we're not together. You and Melissa—you'd probably still be together if she hadn't died, right?"

It was a question he hadn't anticipated, and once asked, one he found himself hesitating a little too long to answer.

"I don't know," he said finally.

"You don't have to say that just because you're here with me. I can take honesty."

"That's an honest answer." He sat on the edge of a stone bench that looked out over the water. "There were some things that . . . that didn't set right with me."

"Oh, hey, everyone has things about their significant other that drives them crazy." She waved a hand as if to dismiss what she perceived must be inconsequential.

"This isn't like, she always left her shoes in the middle of the floor, or that sort of thing. This was bigger. Much bigger."

"You mean like maybe she was having an affair?"

"No, it was more like she lied to me about the half million dollars she'd hidden in the bookcase."

Chapter 14

THE silence was overwhelming. For a moment, Vanessa could not speak. When she finally did, her words came almost as a squeak.

"A half a mil . . . half a mil . . ." She cleared her throat and tried again. "A half a million dollars in the bookcase?"

"Inside a bunch of those fake books, you know, the hollow ones? I found them when I started packing things to do some remodeling. The whole house needed repainting . . . you can probably imagine what the place looked like and smelled like. Before I could do any real work, I had to clean it out, so I started easy, packing up the small stuff."

"What did you do next? After you realized what was in the fake books?"

"I sat on the floor and counted it. And I did exaggerate a little," he confessed. "It was more like four hundred and seventy thousand."

"Close enough to half a mil in my book," she said. "Melissa never told you she had all this money?"

"After she moved, she told me that someone had paid her to quit the Bureau, but that she didn't know who it was, and while she said it was a lot of money, she never told me how much. I later found out that she hadn't quite told the truth."

Vanessa digested this for a moment. "Why would someone pay her to leave her job?"

"I suppose sooner or later, I need to tell you about Brendan." His arm rested along the back of the bench, his fingers absently toying with the ends of her hair, which lay loose around her shoulders and partway down her back. He appeared to be deep in thought.

"You don't have to feel that you have to tell me. If it bothers you to talk about it, you don't have to."

"Remember earlier, I said if you can't share something about yourself with the person you sleep with, that maybe you shouldn't be sleeping with them?"

Vanessa nodded.

"Well, I guess it's my turn to walk the walk." He turned to her slightly. "I guess the easiest place to start is the night my cousin Dylan—Connor's brother—was killed. The short version is there was a sting operation in the works, a couple of drug dealers. Connor was supposed to be undercover to meet these guys and make the deal. At the last minute, Connor got pulled off the op and Dylan was sent in his place." Grady paused and took a deep breath. It was obvious that it still bothered him deeply.

"The official version was that Dylan was killed by one of the drug dealers being set up that night. But the truth was the shots were fired before the targets were even out of their cars. Melissa was part of the backup team; she was there. She saw someone slipping out of the building where the shots had come from carrying a high-powered rifle. Later, she realized this person was not on the roster for the operation. She didn't realize at the time that he wasn't supposed to be there because she'd yet to see the final list of agents who were assigned that night."

"Who had she seen coming out of the building?"

"My brother Brendan."

"No one else saw him?"

"Apparently not. Anyway, a week or so after that, out of the blue, Melissa told me she was quitting the Bureau—that she was burned out—and she was going to move to Montana. She and I had been dating for quite a while, and we started talking about me putting in for a transfer out west. She said she'd wait for me there, that she couldn't wait to get away. I've known other agents who just got fried from the stress, so it didn't strike me as particularly odd. But that wasn't the real reason why she was quitting."

"What was the reason?"

"The threat against her and her family, and the money she was offered to walk away and forget what she saw that night, came from Brendan."

"She told you this?"

"No. She never discussed this with me. If she had, Brendan would be in prison right now, instead of in hell, where he belongs. I was able to put it all together after Brendan died."

"Why did your brother want Connor dead?"

"Brendan was involved in some very nasty business in Central America, and he thought that Connor was onto him. So he planned to use this op as a means to get Connor out of the way."

"Except at the last minute, Dylan went in Connor's place."

Grady nodded. "Brendan was afraid that Melissa had caught on to the fact that he'd fired the killing shot. His way of dealing with her was to make her disappear. Unfortunately, Brendan's partner—Luther Blue, another agent—wasn't convinced that Melissa would keep her mouth shut, so he killed her."

"But there was still Connor . . ."

"By then, Luther had figured out that Brendan had lost all interest in killing close to home, so he was a liability. Luther set up Brendan, then killed him."

"And then he would have killed Connor, too?"

"There would have been no need for that. Connor had seen Brendan, not Luther. He had no reason to connect Luther to Brendan's dealings in Santa Estela."

"Where's this Luther guy now?"

"He's in a maximum-security federal prison serving several life sentences. He offered to name names— give up all his international contacts, from the very top of the trafficking organization to the bottom, in exchange for life in prison and the guarantee that he would not be turned over to any foreign government for prosecution."

"Trafficking? You mean, as in, people . . . ?"

"Kidnapping and selling kids from Central America on the international black market."

"That's just . . ." She shook her head. There were no words.

"Yeah. Tell me about it."

"But if Melissa didn't tell you all this, who did?"

"It came out in Luther's confession."

"And it bothers you that you had to hear the truth from him."

"The consequences of her lies bother me. If she'd told me the truth, she'd still be alive. Brendan would have been brought to justice along with everyone else in that organization. The operation would have been shut down sooner."

"I understand all that. But didn't it hurt you on a personal level that she hadn't been truthful with you?"

"Well, yes," he admitted. "That, and the fact that after I realized that she'd known that Brendan was the one who'd bought her silence, I couldn't help but wonder if she thought that marrying his brother might not have been a form of cheap insurance in case he got the idea later on to shut her up permanently."

"Oh, Grady, you don't really think . . ."

"It's crossed my mind. The whole let's-run-off-and-get-married thing was her idea, and while at the time it seemed spontaneous, now I have to ask myself if maybe she hadn't seen it more as a survival tack than anything else. But . . ." He slapped his hands on his thighs, then stood. "I guess I'll never know for certain."

"Your story makes mine sound like a soap opera."

"We're not comparing. I hope you don't think I was trivializing what happened to you."

"I didn't for a second think you were. I thought you were sharing things that mattered with the person you sleep with."

"That's exactly what it was."

"Then maybe you should finish it."

"I did finish it. I told you everything that happened."

"But you didn't talk about what *didn't* happen." She tugged on his hand to pull him back down to the bench. "You didn't get to confront Brendan and ask him why he did what he did. You didn't get to ask Melissa all the questions you think you have answers to but want to hear her say that you're right. You are so angry that they both died before they could fess up."

He sighed and leaned against the back of the bench, his hands in her lap since she held both of them.

"You may not want to hear this, but it's something that I have to say. And remember that you opened the door for it with what you just told me."

"Go on."

"Sometimes people do things that hurt us so deeply, we're certain that we're never going to be right inside again. We want justice for the wrong that's been done to us, but we can't always make that happen. So then we have a choice. We can hold on to those questions that can never be answered and those feelings that hurt us so much, and we can make them a part of our lives forever. Of course, if we do that, we'll always hurt, and we'll always be looking for answers that we'll never get."

"Or . . . ?"

"Or we can put them aside, and make them not matter anymore."

"Excuse me, but are you the same woman who wanted to do a happy dance when I told her that her ex-husband was dead?"

"That would be me. But here's the thing. I started to put him behind me the day I put him in prison. Yes, I still have scars, inside and out, but they remind me to never let anyone else take charge of my life ever again. And yes, I have issues, but I don't let them define me. I've made a life for myself, and I'm very happy here. I could make having been abused the most important thing in my life, but I've chosen to put it aside and focus on what I've done to take control of my life."

"What's your point?"

"My point is, that you might want to think about what it's costing you to hold on to the anger you feel toward your brother and your wife. You can't change what happened in either of those relationships. You will never know what motivated either of them. Do you know that you can't seem to mention your brother without your jaw going tight?" Before he could respond, she added, "And why do you stay in that house, Grady? Your wife was murdered there. Why would you want to stay?"

The bells from the church two blocks away began to chime.

"It's seven," he told her after all the bells had rung. "We're supposed to meet Hal and Maggie now." He stood and took her hand.

"All right," she told him. "I'm sorry if I went too far."

He held up a hand as if to stop her from saying anything further. "No need to apologize."

They walked hand in hand to Walt's at the end of the pier. When they were almost to the door, Grady said, "So I'm guessing this whole leave-the-anger-behind thing doesn't apply to Maggie?"

"Well, of course not. That only applies to *old* stuff that you have no chance of resolving." She swung the restaurant door open. "Maggie's going to be a thorn in my butt for a long, long time . . ."

"There they are." Maggie elbowed Hal. "They're just coming in the door now."

"I see them." Hal patted her arm. "I want you to calm down, now. Take a deep breath."

Maggie inhaled deeply several times.

"One more for good measure," Hal whispered as Vanessa and Grady approached the table.

"Are you all right, Maggie?" Vanessa asked as she hung her bag over the back of the chair next to Hal's.

"I just . . ." Maggie paused. "I just had the hiccups."

"Oh, I hate it when I get those." Vanessa turned to Hal. "So what happened to your cruise around the Bay?"

"Aborted." Hal smiled. "Old Carter was having trouble docking that whaler of his, so I had to give him a hand. Then we started talking, one thing led to another, and the next thing I knew, we were seated out there at the bar having a cold one."

"How is Carter?" Vanessa took a sip of water from the glass the attentive waiter poured for her.

"He's doing better. Misses the wife, of course, but he's keeping it together."

"Glad to hear it. I always liked him."

The waiter handed Grady and Vanessa menus.

"Did you two already order?" Vanessa asked.

"We were waiting for you," Hal replied. "The specials are on the board there by the door. They have one of your favorites, Ness."

Vanessa turned and looked over her shoulder.

"Yum. We know what I'm having." She closed her menu.

"I'll join you there," Hal said, and closed his as well. "No one does a better grilled tuna than the man Walt has working in his kitchen."

"That sounds great. I'll have that as well." Maggie added her menu to the pile.

"Grady?" Hal asked.

"I'm going with the swordfish."

Hal signaled for the waiter and gave the orders.

"So how did you two spend the rest of the afternoon?" Hal asked.

"We just walked around a bit, then sat and watched the sun float down onto the Bay," Vanessa told him. "That's how we knew you never made it out of your slip."

"Well, now, you know how old men are once they get talking about their boats." Hal turned to Maggie. "I guess we bored you to death."

"Not at all," Maggie assured him. She took a deep breath and asked Grady, "Are you planning on staying in St. Dennis for a while?"

"I'm not sure," he replied. "I'm playing it by ear."

Hal took that to mean Grady would hang around until they figured out who was targeting Vanessa and why. He liked that about the young man, that he'd been concerned enough about Ness not to be so quick to leave when no one was really sure how serious the threat was. A man would be a fool not to know when two young people were circling around each other the way these two were over the past four days. Hal had been hoping the circling hadn't been all on Vanessa's part. Knowing that Grady was willing to change his plans to keep an eye on her . . . well, Hal couldn't help but approve of that.

"Hal tells me you live in Montana," Maggie said.

Grady nodded. "Not too far from Great Falls, if you know where that is."

"I do." She nodded. "I was in that airport once, when my flight to Fargo got redirected due to bad weather."

"How do you like North Dakota?" Grady asked.

"I like some things—I like all the space, and the scenery is beautiful. But it's so cold, and the summer's so short. But of course, you could say the same thing. We probably have similar seasons."

"Yeah. Winter and July."

Maggie laughed. "Yes, that's it exactly."

"What part of the state do you live in, Mrs. Turner?"

"Oh, call me Maggie. Everyone does. Even my children." Maggie slanted a look at Vanessa. "I live a little southwest of Fargo."

"Did Vanessa tell me you raised sheep?"

"Oh, no, no." Maggie laughed again. "No, that was my late husband's deal. He raised Cotswold sheep. They produce a very nice, long wool fleece. They tell me that people who spin their own wool like it, but since I don't spin and I don't knit, I wouldn't know."

"Who's minding the ranch while you're here, Maggie?" Vanessa asked.

"Oh, my late husband's sons have been working the ranch for the past several years, since he—Carl Senior, that is—got sick. Wayne and the Carls have—"

"The Carls?" Vanessa raised an eyebrow.

"Carl Junior, and his son, Carl the third." Maggie turned to Grady. "Yes, I know, the Turners were in a bit of a rut when it came to naming their children. Anyway, Carl's boys have been taking care of the ranch and they say they're staying on. This year they started raising turkeys as well, so I guess they're determined to keep it going."

"Is that awkward for you?" Vanessa asked. Hal glanced at her over the top of his glasses, and she rephrased the question. "What I meant was, since your husband died—"

"I understand exactly what you meant, and yes, of course, it's awkward. Neither one of them would throw me a line if I fell in the middle of that Bay out there." Maggie pointed out the window. "I understand why, of course—their father was an older man of some means when we married, he'd been widowed for about twenty years, and he'd neglected to tell the boys that he wanted to remarry. So I had three strikes against me going in.

"But it wasn't what either of the boys thought. I didn't want the property, and they are welcome to the house and the money their dad left behind." She smiled somewhat wryly. "I'm just as happy to be someplace where it's warm at this time of the year."

"So, are you planning on going back there?" Vanessa asked.

Hal was pretty sure he could tell by the look on

Vanessa's face that she was afraid of what Maggie's answer was going to be.

"I will." Maggie nodded. "But mostly just to pick up my things. These past few years, I spent most of my time taking care of Carl. Now that he's gone, there's no place for me there."

"So where *will* you go?" Vanessa's eyes narrowed as they focused on her mother.

"I have no idea, and right now, I have no plans." Maggie flashed her best smile. "Why, dear, were you thinking of asking me to stay with you for a while?"

"I was just curious," Vanessa replied, ignoring Maggie's obvious plea for an invitation.

"So, Grady"—Maggie turned her attention back to him—"what do you do in Montana? Do you ranch?"

"No. I only have a few acres, not enough to raise much of anything," he told her.

"What do you do for a job? I understand you're no longer with the FBI."

He nodded. "I left the Bureau a few years ago. Since then, I've qualified as a wilderness guide. I take groups or individuals camping, hiking, backpacking; that sort of thing."

"Can you make a living that way?" Maggie asked.

"Maggie," Vanessa admonished. "Why would you ask him that?"

"Well, sweetie, you've been spending a lot of time with this young man this weekend."

"He's . . . sort of . . . a bodyguard." To Hal, Vanessa sounded defensive.

"Well, then, let's just say it's maternal prerogative."

Vanessa set her glass on the table. "Where was your motherly concern when your just-turned-eighteen daughter wanted to marry a man who was twelve years older than she was?"

"Vanessa, I told you at the time that I did not think that marrying Craig was a good idea." Maggie's glass hit the table as well.

"You didn't try to stop me."

"I could never stop you from doing a damned thing you wanted to do. You said you wanted to marry him and—"

"No, no. I said *he* wanted to marry *me*. You were supposed to stop me. You were supposed to say he was too old and you weren't going to let me do it." Vanessa's eyes flashed anger, and for a moment, Hal thought she was going to get up and walk out. "What did I know? I was only eighteen years old."

The ensuing silence was so dense, Hal thought he could cut through it. He cleared his throat, trying to think of something to say that might salvage the moment. Fortunately, the waiter appeared with their dinners.

"Well, now, the tuna looks great, doesn't it, ladies?" Hal said. He got a nod from Vanessa and a distracted glance from Maggie, which was, he supposed, about the best he was going to get.

The silence returned and lingered right through the rest of the meal. When it came time to order dessert, Vanessa excused herself.

"I'm going to have to call it a night," she said. "I have to be in the shop first thing in the morning to start my inventory, and it's been a very long weekend." She leaned over and kissed Hal on the cheek. "Thank you for dinner."

"You're welcome." He leaned close and whispered,

"Thanks for humoring me. I appreciate the effort. Oh, I almost forgot." He stuck his hand in his shirt pocket and removed a set of keys. "The keys for your new locks. The locksmith left them at the station." He handed them to her. "They both fit all the locks on the house."

"Thanks, Hal." Vanessa rummaged in her bag for her key ring.

While she was removing the old and sliding on the new, Grady asked Hal, "Do you happen to know if anyone's working on getting a match for those prints?"

"Garland worked on it this afternoon, but so far, nothing. Of course, there were so many prints in the shop, it's going to take some time," Hal explained.

"I thought it was premature, but I thought I'd ask anyway." Grady stood and shook Hal's hand. "Thanks for dinner, Hal. I'm sure I'll see you again. Maggie, it's been a pleasure."

"You don't mean that, but I appreciate the thought, Grady," she replied. "It was nice meeting you. Take care of my little girl. Don't let anything bad happen to her."

"Oh, Maggie, for God's sake," Vanessa muttered.

"I will try my best to keep her safe," Grady promised.

"Good night, you two." Vanessa took Grady's hand and headed for the door.

"What do you suppose his intentions are?" Maggie murmured after Grady and Vanessa were gone.

"Well, now, I think he'll do whatever it takes to keep her from harm's way, just like he said."

"You could do that just as well."

"Maybe, maybe not. He's a lot younger and stronger, and he's had the benefit of a lot of training that I didn't have."

"Yes, but you've got a gun, right?" Maggie asked. "Do you think he has a gun?"

"Probably not," Hal said after thinking it over. "I doubt he set out for his sister's wedding thinking he needed to come armed."

"Maybe he should have a gun."

"Maybe he should." Hal thought it over. Maybe he should . . .

Maggie turned to Hal. "I know what you were trying to do tonight, and I thank you from the bottom of my heart. I know you want for Vanessa and me to get along, and I appreciate that so much." She paused. "It didn't go too badly, do you think?"

"Not too," he agreed, and signaled for the check. He'd hoped for better, but he knew it could have been much worse.

Well, he thought as he finished the rest of his beer, it was a start. They were talking—maybe not so much friendly talk, but at least they were talking. Judging by what Maggie had told him last night, it had been a long time coming.

He felt protective of both of them, the woman he'd once loved and the girl he'd taken into his heart and come to love as his own. Over the next few days—for however long Maggie was staying in St. Dennis—he'd do his best to help them make their peace. But in the end, he knew, it was up to them. And then there was Beck. Hal shook his head. If he thought it was rough trying to get Maggie and her daughter on the same page, the thought of getting Beck to come around to even discussing Maggie made Hal's head hurt. Well, he reminded himself, he had almost two full weeks before he'd have to deal with that. One problem at a time, his father always told him. One problem, one solution. He smiled as he signed the credit slip for their dinners, remembering all his father's clichés that could apply. Rome wasn't built in a day. You can lead a horse to water but you can't make him drink. And Hal's personal favorite: miracles take time.

Well, maybe a miracle was what it was going to take to make this all work out right for all of them. Where to find one . . . now, that was another matter altogether.

Chapter 15

YOU'RE awfully quiet," Vanessa observed as she and Grady walked the last block to her house.

"I'm just trying to stay observant," Grady replied.

"You mean in case someone's following us? It's still light out. It's tough to stalk someone in this neighborhood when all the kids are still outside playing and so many people are sitting on their porches or out for an evening stroll."

"Someone came into this neighborhood in broad daylight and broke into your house," he reminded her.

"True enough. But they weren't following me down the street before they broke in."

She waved to a neighbor across the street.

"I heard about your shop, Vanessa," the woman called to her. "I'm shocked."

"So was I, Andrea," Vanessa called back.

They reached Vanessa's house and she took the keys from her bag as she started up the walk.

"Wait." Grady took her by the arm. "I want to check around the outside first."

"Why?" She frowned.

"In the unlikely event that someone's been back while we were gone, I want to know before we go in."

"Oh."

Grady walked up the driveway and to the backyard, and Vanessa followed. He checked the plants under the windows and found none of them trampled down. Next he looked over the area around the back porch and the door that led to the stairs down to the basement, then he walked around to the other side of the house. Vanessa paused to pull a few weeds from one of the flower beds as she passed.

"Doesn't look as if anything's changed since this morning when I looked, so I guess we're okay so far," Grady told her when he returned to the backyard.

"Good." She shook the dirt off the weeds. "Oh, these smell nice. I wonder if this is one of Alice Ridgeway's herbs." She looked up and smiled. "The previous owner grew a lot of herbs and some flesh-eating plants as well. Isn't that an interesting combination?"

She raised the thin stalk to her nose and sniffed. "It's definitely something." She passed it to Grady, who took a sniff of his own.

"I can't place it, but it's nice."

"Well, I guess I have my work cut out for me back here," she noted. "I should get all these beds cleaned up, but I'm afraid of pulling out the wrong things. I don't know the herbs from the weeds from the flowers."

"From the man-eaters?"

"Flesh eaters," she corrected him. "Mostly Venus flytraps, the Realtor said."

Grady walked around the entire yard, pausing to

take a closer look at this or that. At the back corner, he stopped.

"Fishpond?" he turned and asked.

Vanessa nodded. "I heard she used to have koi. As soon as I find some time, I'm going to clean that out and refill it, buy some koi and some water lilies. Maybe I'll get one of those little stone waterfalls." She loved the thought of having a little water garden and the sound of the water trickling over her very own falls, no matter how small they might be. She'd never appreciated how soothing the sound of water in any of its many forms could be until she lived near the Bay.

An empty black flowerpot sat on the bottom step leading up to the porch, and she tossed the unidentified plant matter into it as she climbed the steps, her keys in her hand.

"The new key works just fine," she told him as she pushed open the door and went inside.

"Give me a minute to check things out." Grady walked through the kitchen and into the front of the house.

She heard his footsteps on the uncarpeted stairs and the floorboards squeak overhead as he went from room to room.

When he came downstairs, he called to her from the front hall, "Everything seems secure. No visitors. No pretty wrapped packages."

"Good." She went into the kitchen and tossed her bag onto the table. For the first time in days, she felt uncomfortable in his presence, so she found little things to do. She washed a few dishes that were in the sink, and she dried them. She heard him behind her when he came into the room and sat at the table over-looking the driveway.

"What's that bundle of dried stuff that's hanging over the back door?" he asked.

"Oh, that weedy stuff?" She shrugged. "I don't know, exactly. It was there when I moved in. I suspect it was some herby thing that Miss Ridgeway nailed up, probably some good-luck thing. I keep meaning to ask Miss Grace about it and I keep forgetting when I see her. I heard some things about her—that is, Miss Ridgeway—and I want to see what Miss Grace knows. She grew up right around the corner."

He leaned back in the chair and stretched his long legs. "What kind of things did you hear?"

"Oh, that she put spells on people."

"Good spells or bad spells?"

"I guess it depended on whether you were a friend or a foe." Vanessa dried her hands and turned around. "I'm thinking that might be why she had so many herbs planted out back, so she could use them in her spells."

"My, don't we have an active imagination." He smiled for the first time since they left the restaurant.

"A lot of people believe that certain herbs have certain powers."

"Are you one of them?"

"Maybe." She sat across from him at the table, try-ing to keep her distance. Something had changed be-tween them over the course of the evening, and she wasn't sure what it was. "I found some books that be-longed to Miss Ridgeway in the living-room book-case and I started to read them a few weeks ago, then we got busy with the shop and with the wedding and I had to put them aside for a while."

"Maybe your Miss Ridgeway was a witch."

"I don't believe in witches."

"Where are the books now?"

"Back on the shelf in the living room. Why? Did you want to see them?"

"Yeah. Let's take a look."

She turned off the kitchen lights and followed Grady into the living room. He sat on the floor in front of the sofa while she opened the glass doors in front of the bookcase and removed several volumes.

"These look pretty old." He picked one up and turned to the title page. "This one was copyrighted in 1921." He opened a second book. "And this one is even older: 1894."

He paged through them slowly. "This is about the uses for different herbs. Medicinal uses, mostly." He closed the book and handed it to her. "No spells."

"Is that what you were hoping to find? A book of spells?"

"It could be interesting."

She sat on the sofa, her legs curled up under her, and he stayed on the floor. Finally, she sighed and asked point-blank, "Are you angry with me?"

"With you?" He seemed puzzled by the question. "No. Why should I be angry with you?"

Vanessa shrugged. "Since we left the restaurant, you've been . . . I don't know. Quiet, I guess."

For a moment, she thought he was going to let that pass and not reply at all, which led her to believe he was in fact annoyed about something. She sighed. It must have been her big mouth back there on the bench, telling him what he should do about the baggage he was dragging around. He probably couldn't care less about her opinion of his wife or on his life.

"Was your first husband really thirty when you married him?" he asked.

Surprised by his question, she nodded. "That was one of the dumbest things I ever did."

"Did you love him?"

"I think mostly, I was just flattered that someone older, someone smoother than the boys I knew in high school, wanted to be with me. When he asked me to marry him, though, it was kind of exciting. I thought I'd look like a stupid little schoolgirl if I said no." She looked up at him and added, "I really was hoping my mom would put her foot down. I was surprised when she didn't."

"Were you really such a handful back then?"

Vanessa nodded. "I suppose. But understand, Maggie and I have always had a somewhat fractious relationship. When I got to high school, it only got worse. Her men friends started looking at me the way they looked at her, and I guess she didn't like that very much. I had wanted my mother to intervene and forbid me to get married, but when she didn't, I figured she was just happy to be rid of me. Like, I'd be someone else's responsibility and she wouldn't have to bother anymore."

"I didn't get that impression from her today."

"She's looking at herself in her own rearview mirror and she's seeing what she wants to see." Vanessa couldn't mask her irritation. "Maggie is finding herself alone for the first time in a long while and she doesn't know what to do with herself. She's hoping to snare Hal again so she'll have a home and someone to take care of her."

"So you don't think she's really trying to patch things up with you?"

"I think *she* thinks she's really trying. I don't know what I feel." She thought for a minute, then said, "That's what you're angry about, then. That I didn't tell you about Craig."

"I'm not angry with you, and whether or not you want to tell me something about your life, that's your choice." His face softened. "But I have to admit that it pisses me off that these things happened and there was no one there to stand up for you."

"You mean you're not mad *at* me," she said thoughtfully, "you're mad *for* me?" The thought that someone might be angry on her behalf had never occurred to Vanessa.

"Something like that, yes. And I think Hal was, too. As much as he cares about Maggie—and I think that's a given—I could tell he wasn't happy that she hadn't stepped in there for you."

"I don't like to think back on that time," she told him frankly. "It just makes me angry with her and angry with myself. Maybe she's right and I would have blown off anything she might have said to try to dissuade me, but she didn't even try, and that makes me see red every time I think about it. But I was stupid for going through with a wedding with someone I knew I wasn't in love with—that's all on me. I shouldn't have had to depend on her to tell me no. I just wish that she had."

"How many times had Maggie been married by then?"

"Oh, three times, maybe. But she'd had a bunch of live-ins, too."

"Maybe you didn't take the whole thing— marriage—as seriously as you should have because you'd never seen it portrayed as a serious pursuit. Maybe in your house it seemed more like a more casual arrangement."

She smiled. "You have the funniest way of putting things." Before he could ask what she meant, she added, "When you got married, did you think of it as a 'serious pursuit'?"

"Sure. Marriage is a big deal in my family. It really bothered me a lot that Missy didn't want my family at the wedding, that she didn't even want them to know we'd gotten married. She said it was because the fewer people who knew, the less likely the person who had threatened her would find out where she was. In retrospect, I think it was because she knew it was a sham. The only person she needed to think we were married was Brendan, and she made sure he knew."

"You really think she played you?"

"It's hard not to, when you take an honest look at the facts."

"Did you love her? When you married her, did you think it would last forever?"

"Yes, and yes."

"Me, too. Oh, maybe not so much the first time. It didn't take me long to figure out what Craig really liked was having a young wife he could show off to his drinking buddies. I didn't know much, but I knew that wasn't going to last."

"Were you disappointed?"

She shook her head. "I just wanted out. Craig had become verbally abusive, and it was awhile before he let me leave. By the time I was able to go, it was with great relief because the bad stuff was escalating. So when this good-looking guy with a pretty car and a nice apartment and a good job came along and wanted to sweep me off my feet, I let him." She looked up at Grady and fixed a stare. "I'm going to tell you something I never admitted to anyone. But you can't ever tell anyone else."

"Okay."

"When I was a little girl, I believed in fairy tales. I believed in happy endings. I believed in romance before I ever heard the word. I believed it was all real, would be real, and if I could find the right prince, we'd live happily ever after." She grimaced. "Fat lot I knew."

"And now?"

"And now, what?"

"Do you still believe that? That if you met the right prince, you could live happily ever after?"

She looked at him as if he had three heads. "Are you crazy?" She snorted. "Do you still believe if you met the right 'princess' that you'd live happily ever after?"

"Actually, I do."

"How can you say that when you just finished telling me that you think that possibly your wife only married you to protect herself from your brother?"

"Wrong princess." He shrugged.

"Like I said, you are one really strange man." She leaned back against the sofa, and he chuckled.

It had grown dark, and the streetlights outside had

turned on. They sat in the dark for a while not talking, but he reached up and took one of her feet in his hands and rubbed the arch with his thumbs for a moment.

"I'll give you until tomorrow morning to stop that," she murmured.

"And if I don't?"

"Then you'll have to start on the other foot." She slipped down onto the floor next to him, then moved onto his lap. Straddling him, she took his face in her hands and kissed him, her tongue flicking the tip of his. They teased each other for a long moment, then he clasped the back of her head and filled her mouth with his probing tongue. She placed her hands on his shoulders and eased him back onto the floor and covered his body with hers. She grabbed a throw pillow from the sofa to slip under his head. She lowered her mouth to kiss him again and he repositioned her hips so that she could feel him hard against her. His hands slid under her shirt and tugged her bra down to release her breasts and she leaned up slightly to fill his hands with her softness. A soft moan escaped her parted lips, and she pulled her skirt up around her waist and sought his zipper, pulled it down to release him to her busy hands. When she lowered herself onto him, he groaned and pushed himself up into her to fill her. When his mouth found her breasts, she rose and fell above him, taking him along with her, on an ever-faster ride to oblivion.

"Oh my God," she said when she could catch her breath. "I should have pulled those shades. I hope no one's looking through the windows."

"You mean, like the guy there on the front porch with the baseball cap?"

She started to turn to look, then realized he was teasing her. "Oh, you." She swatted at him before snuggling down against his chest to listen to his heart beat.

"Ness?"

"Hmmmm?"

"We have to get up. My neck is breaking."

"I gave you a pillow," she murmured sleepily.

"It slid across the floor. I think it's in the front hall now."

"All right." She sighed and reluctantly removed herself, sitting back against the sofa to reposition her clothes.

"Are you getting dressed?" he asked.

"Uh-huh."

"Why?"

"Because I can't walk through the front hall and up the steps half naked, that's why. And neither can you. If someone was walking by . . ."

"And happened to be staring through your windows, they might see something you don't want them to see." He laughed, but pulled his clothes on.

"Right." She stood and reached a hand down to him. "Besides, we can take them off again when we get upstairs."

"So, I guess this makes it a two," he said when they reached the top of the steps.

"Two what?"

"A two-night stand."

"You think you're funny, don't you?"

"Well, sometimes, yes, I do." He chuckled as they found their way across the darkened room.

"Guys say the dumbest things," she muttered, and he laughed good-naturedly.

Later, she sat against the headboard, her knees pulled up to her chest and her arms wrapped around her legs, listening to him breathe and wondering what her life might have been like if either of her ex-husbands had been a man like Grady Shields.

Chapter 16

"ARE you sure you're all right here by yourself?" Grady stood in Bling's doorway and assessed the damage, which somehow, in daylight, looked even worse than it had on Saturday night.

"Of course. Why wouldn't I be?" Vanessa moved through her shop with apparent determination. "Even if the person who did this was inclined to return, I doubt he'd do it on a bright sunny morning when half of the population of St. Dennis is looking for an excuse to be outside and strolling along Charles Street. And I will have the door locked." She disappeared into the back room and emerged a minute later with an apron, which she slipped over her head and then tied around her waist. "I think I'll start back here in the office, what do you think?"

"I think you should do what feels most natural to you. But are you sure you don't want company?"

"I'm sure. I really want to get this over with. I want my inventory checked and I want the floors cleaned and I want my shop back. Besides, you have something to do. Aren't you calling someone at the FBI about those fingerprints?"

"I need to check with Hal first to see if the prints they took on Saturday were submitted to IAFIS yet."

"Tell me again what that means?" She disappeared through a curtain on the right, but came right back out again. "Well, at least the dressing rooms were spared. I thought some things might have been tossed around in there but there's nothing."

"IAFIS means 'Integrated Automated Fingerprint Identification System.' It's a database. Law enforcement agencies can submit fingerprints, which are cataloged. Then, when they have prints they're hoping to match up, they'll send them in and request a search. If the prints are on file, they'll get a confirmation with the name and criminal history of the person to whom the prints belong."

"So, if the person who broke in here the other night committed a crime before, and his prints are already on file there in that system, when Hal sends in the prints they took here, the FBI can tell him who that person is?"

"As long as the prints are already on file so there's something to match to, yes."

"But if they hadn't committed a crime before, their prints wouldn't be there?"

"Not necessarily. If the agency that arrested him the first time didn't submit the prints, they wouldn't be in the system. And there are prints in the system that were submitted for other reasons—employment background checks, firearms sales, that sort of thing. So it isn't a definite, but maybe we'll get lucky if this guy's been arrested before and his prints were submitted and we'll find out who he is."

"Well, we can only hope." She looked distracted, so he waved a hand in front of her face.

"I'm going to walk down to the police station and talk to Hal. You have my cell number if you need me." He kissed her on the side of her mouth and smiled at her belated attempt to kiss him back. "I'll let you make good on that one later," he told her as he walked to the door. "Come on over here and lock this."

She took the key from her pocket and walked him to the door. "Tell Hal I said good morning."

"Will do."

Grady left the cool of the shop and walked out onto a sunny weekday morning. There was little traffic at this hour—the school buses had collected and discharged their riders and the locals who had to be at their jobs before nine were already there. But there was still a good crowd in Cuppachino as he crossed the street, and he decided to stop in and pick up a cup of coffee to go.

He bought his takeout and was on his way to the counter where the sweeteners and creamers were located, when he heard someone calling his name. He turned to see Grace Sinclair waving to him.

"Good morning." He waved back.

"So are you enjoying our pretty little town on this fine morning?" Grace asked.

"I am, thanks." Grady stopped at the table where she sat with an open notebook in front of her.

"Just working on my column for this week," she explained. "Between the wedding and the break-in and the upcoming historic house tour, it's more news than we generally have to talk about around here."

She hastened to add, "Not that I equate one with the other, of course. The police blotter doesn't appear on the same page as the social news, and the calendar of events is always on the back page by its lonesome."

"You have so many events here that you need an entire page to list them?"

"We don't simply list them. We have articles that correspond. For example, for the house tour, I interviewed the president of the Historical Society and several of the homeowners whose houses will be featured this year. All with photographs, of course, and advertisements from the merchants who might be offering special sales that weekend." Grace smiled. "It does keep us all busy. We like to say we have something for everyone at some time during the year. Makes me wonder what we used to do around here before we became such an attraction. Now, what are you interested in, Grady?"

"Me?" He thought it over. "Well, I like to hike . . ."

"Then you'll likely want to look into our marsh-and-wetlands walking tour. That's always the weekend following the Fourth of July." She started to rustle through a pile of notes on the table. "I have the dates here somewhere . . ."

"I doubt I'll still be around in July, but I appreciate the information." Grady doubted that even if he were in St. Dennis, a walk through some wetlands was hardly what he was accustomed to. Still, it was nice of her to ask.

"Oh." She appeared surprised. "I was thinking perhaps . . . well, no matter. If you do happen to be here that weekend, you're more than welcome to join us."

"I appreciate that, Miss Grace."

"I suppose you'd better go fix that coffee before it gets cold," she told him.

"Good idea. Nice to see you." He took a few steps away from the table.

"Oh, Grady," she called him back. "I noticed you coming out of Bling. How is Vanessa doing?"

"She's just starting to clean up, get her merchandise organized, see what was taken." He added, "She's doing all right. She was—still is—upset, but she's just trying to get it all under control so that she can re-open as soon as possible."

"What a shame." Grace shook her head. "She's worked so hard to make that shop the little gem it is. I've been saying since she opened, that girl is one of the hardest-working people I've ever known. It makes me so darned mad when I think of someone going in there and breaking up her shop and stealing from her." She looked up at Grady. "Are there any suspects yet?"

"Not that I know of. I was just on my way down to the police station to talk to Hal."

"Oh, you just missed him by about twenty minutes. He was in here earlier with . . . I'm not sure of the woman's name. Beck and Vanessa's mother."

"Maggie Turner."

"Ah, Maggie Turner." Grace nodded. "I noticed she was at the wedding the other day. Have she and Beck reconciled, then?"

"I wouldn't know anything about that." Grady shook his head. No way was he going to feed into small-town gossip.

"I was just wondering. It seems like such a shame,

being estranged from your children. I have three children, Grady. Only one lives close enough for me to
see on a regular basis." A cloud crossed her face. "It
isn't easy to be a parent sometimes."

"I'm sure it's a tough job."

Grace laughed lightly. "Would you listen to me?
Go. Fix your coffee and get on your way. It's a beautiful morning. Enjoy it. And walk on down to the Bay.
It's a wonder with the sunlight sparkling on the
water."

"I'll do that," he said. "Thanks for the tip."

"You're welcome." She smiled and picked up her
pen and turned her attention back to her notes.

He poured a sugar packet and some cream into the
cup and replaced the lid, then waved to Carlo and
Grace on his way out. It was slightly disconcerting to
him that people here seemed so comfortable discussing the business—both private and public—of
their friends and neighbors. Grady had never been exposed to small-town life, so Grace's inquiry about
Maggie had taken him aback somewhat. He hadn't
sensed any malicious intent on the older woman's
part, though; her questions appeared based more on
concern than on gathering information to be ran-
domly repeated and passed along, but still, it wasn't
his place to give out information about the family his
sister had just married into.

From the top of Kelly's Point Road, he could see
the Bay beyond. Grace had been right. It was sparkly
and beautiful in the morning sunlight. In the distance,
sailboats skimmed along in the breeze, and a catama-
ran was just edging out from its slip. It was all very
peaceful and gentle on the eyes. He'd never lived on

the water—had never considered it—but he could see its appeal.

He soaked up sun and small-town atmosphere as he walked to the municipal building and resisted an urge to whistle. It was that kind of morning.

He stopped at the reception area and gave his name and asked to see Hal. The day dispatcher, Garland, introduced himself and reminded Grady that they'd met at the wedding on Saturday before buzzing Hal's office.

Of course we met at the wedding, Grady mused. *Was there an adult living in St. Dennis who I did not meet at the wedding?*

"Grady, come on back." Hal waved to him from the end of the hall. "I see you stopped for coffee. A wise move on your part. I'm ashamed to say our coffee is as bad as most other police stations I've been in." He shook his head. "We really need to do something about that. It's such a cliché . . ."

Grady laughed and followed Hal into a conference room, and Hal closed the door behind them.

"I'm acting chief this week but I hate to use someone else's office, so I set myself up in here," Hal explained. "Gives me more room to spread out the morning paper and put my feet up, if nothing else." He rolled his chair out from under the table, and sat. "That was a joke, by the way."

Grady smiled to acknowledge the comment. "I just thought I'd stop in and see if there's been a response on those prints that Sue lifted over the weekend."

"I was just getting ready to call you." Hal had a stack of papers in front of him, which he gathered in one hand. "I had Gus print out everything that came in. We have a couple of matches. There's no doubt in my mind that these are the two we're looking for."

He slid a couple of sheets across the table. "Jackie Weston here is probably the woman who called herself Candice. She was picked up on bad-check charges in Wisconsin about six months ago but didn't serve any time, not sure why, but I've requested her picture, so we're going to need Vanessa to take a look, see if that's the woman who was in her shop. The other one, this Edmund Dent, he's the one who has me worried. Check out his criminal history."

Grady's eyes scanned the second sheet. "He's got a history, all right." He read down the list, then glanced up at Hal. "Assault, assault with intent to kill, sexual battery . . . and this guy is out on the street?" He shook his head.

"This arrest for arson in Wisconsin . . ." Grady tapped his finger on the section he read from. "Vanessa told me that one of her ex's brothers and a cousin burned down her house after Medford was sentenced."

Hal nodded. "The date's just about right. I'm still waiting for his picture. If this is the cousin, Vanessa will be able to identify him."

"Why don't you just call her? She'll know the name, right?"

"I'd rather not do that over the phone."

"If you get the pictures, I'll take them up. She's at the shop."

"By herself?" Hal looked up, his eyebrows raised.

Grady nodded. "With the doors locked and Grace Sinclair sitting at the front table at Cuppachino."

"No one's likely to get past Gracie, but still . . ."

Hal got up and poked his head out the door. "Gus? How're we doing with that picture we're waiting on?"

"It's just starting to come through now. You'll have it in a minute," the officer called back.

"You have anything you can arm yourself with?" Hal asked, and Grady shook his head no. "You licensed to carry in Maryland?"

"Not anymore."

Hal rubbed his chin and thought it over. "You a decent shot?"

"I've qualified as a sharpshooter. The only person in my family who's better is Connor." Grady smiled. "Maybe."

Hal left the room and came back a few minutes later with a Glock in one hand and a clip in the other. "How 'bout we swear you in as a part-time, temporary officer of St. Dennis?"

Grady raised an eyebrow.

"I know you're . . . well, spending a lot of time with my girl, son. I'd like to know you're watching her back with something more than your eyes and ears. Unless I'm way off base, this Dent is going to want to push on her a little more before he's through. I'd like you to be able to push back."

Grady nodded. "All right."

"Come on into Beck's office and we'll fill out the forms and make it nice and legal . . ."

When the paperwork had been completed, Hal handed over the Glock and got Grady a holster to clip onto his belt.

"I hope I don't need this," Grady remarked.

"I hope you don't, either. But I'd rather you had it and didn't need it than need it and not have it."

Gus came in with the photocopy of Edmund Dent. Both Hal and Grady studied it.

"I feel I might have seen him somewhere," Grady said. "Maybe passed him on the street one day last week."

"It's sure possible. I imagine he took his time, watching her. Figuring out her routine, where she went, where she lived . . ."

"Hal, you don't spend all that time studying someone just to break into their shop and steal a dress that you're going to destroy and leave in their house."

"I know. And that's what's worrying me . . ."

"I think you're right to be worried," Grady told him. "I've seen this type of pattern before. The first attack is on property, but it escalates. He's already shown her that he can get to her, at her shop or at her house. I think when Vanessa completes her inventory, she's going to find that nothing was taken except that dress and the cash receipts."

Hal nodded. "That's how I'm seeing it, too. And the woman—you think she was involved?"

"Not really. I think he only brought her along to go into the shop and see what's what. But I'm betting she wasn't in on the break-in. She wouldn't have ripped up that dress. But an arrogant man who wanted to take a poke at Vanessa, though, yeah, he'd do that. Especially if he wanted to take a poke at the woman—Jackie—too."

Hal sighed heavily. "If he tries to take another poke at her, take him down, Grady. Don't let him get close enough to touch her."

"I'll do my best."

Hal slapped Grady on the shoulder. "Thank you.

I'm real glad you decided to stay awhile in St. Dennis. Real glad."

"Thanks."

Grady left the station wondering what he'd gotten himself into. When he agreed to come to his sister's wedding, he had no idea he'd end up playing small-town cop. Then again, he hadn't counted on Vanessa, either. He still wasn't sure what was going on between them, but he didn't want to examine it too closely yet. It was enough to know that whatever it was, it made him happier then he'd been in a long time.

If things had gone differently, he'd be hiking on the Bull Run Mountains right about now. But the mountains would be there when this was all over, and he was pretty sure it would be over soon enough. Men like Dent didn't bother with finesse or restraint. He'd strike fast and he'd strike soon—and Grady would be there when he did.

It had taken her awhile to decide where to begin, until finally she told herself, *Oh, hell, just pick a spot.* She opted for the office, thinking she might as well start at the back of the shop since the glass man would be coming later that day to take the measurements to replace the cracked window and the glass counter. After she finished with the office, she picked up all the merchandise that had been tossed on the floor. She refolded everything, looking over each garment to assess its condition. Except for having been tossed onto the floor—which had been relatively clean, because it had been vacuumed on Saturday— nothing seemed to be damaged. Still, they had been tossed around and spent the past two days on the floor, so maybe she couldn't sell any of them as perfect and new. *Maybe I should have an after-the-break-in sale. "All merchandise tossed around by the burglar—thirty percent off!"*

She made a mental note to ask Stef if she thought thirty percent was enough of a discount.

The mannequins were still in the front window dressed up for the wedding. Vanessa stood, hands on her hips, looking them over.

"Oh, hell, the wedding is over anyway," she said aloud. "Time to move it all out. I wonder if it's too early to move all those cute golf and tennis things to center stage."

She needed music and wanted something upbeat, so she brought her CD player from the office and plugged it in on the counter. Odd he didn't take this, she thought, since it was right there on the desk in plain sight. She put in a few CDs and turned it on loud enough to drown out her own singing. The music lightened her mood, and before too long, she had the windows stripped and ready for the glass people to do their thing.

She turned her attention to the jewelry case, and was surprised to see that very little, if anything, appeared to be disturbed, other than the glass counter and shelves. She checked the sales slips for Wednesday through Saturday, and when she finished, she could account for every piece of jewelry she'd had in that case. As far as she could tell, the only things missing were pieces that had been sold. She was wondering why someone would take the time to break the glass but not steal anything from the case, when she heard a tap on the door.

Vanessa unlocked the door. "Hi, Miss Grace. Come to view the carnage?"

"No, I came to bring you some coffee. I figured you would be needing a break right around now." Grace handed her a cardboard cup with the Cuppachino logo on it.

"That's so thoughtful of you. Thank you."

"Thank Carlo. When I told him who it was for, he wouldn't take a dime for it." Grace looked around the interior of the shop. "Well, this doesn't look too bad . . ."

"I've been picking up in here for the past two hours, but for the most part, it really *isn't* too bad. The glass will be replaced and the contents are insured. I called my insurance agent, and surprise, surprise, she'd already heard about the break-in."

"You use the Radell Agency?"

Vanessa nodded.

"So do we at the paper and the Inn. That Alice Radell is the best insurance agent I ever worked with."

"She's been very helpful. But speaking of Alices . . . I've been meaning to ask you about Alice Ridgeway."

"What about her, dear?"

"I heard that you knew her fairly well."

"Oh, yes. I grew up in that neighborhood, you know."

Vanessa nodded. "I heard that, too. I was wondering if we could get together sometime to talk about her."

Grace frowned. "She isn't . . . *bothering* you, is she?"

"Ah . . . no."

"Because she's really harmless, you know."

Vanessa stared at her. "You mean, when she was alive?"

"Oh . . ." Grace laughed. "Of course. I meant, she *was* harmless."

"I see," Vanessa said, although she wasn't sure she did.

"What did you want to talk about, then?"

"I'd just like to know a little about her, that's all. All I know is that she kept to herself a lot, and that she grew a lot of herbs."

"Well, she wasn't completely antisocial. She did have friends," Grace made a point of telling her, "but she didn't care to go out. Everyone visited her at her home."

"Did you visit with her?"

"Oh, of course. We were friends, even though I was a lot younger. I've often wondered if anything still grew in her garden."

"A lot of herbs, but I'm not sure what they all are. There's a bunch of what appears to be herbs hanging over the back door."

"Really? What do they smell like?"

"I don't think they smell like anything, Miss Grace. They're very dry."

"Oh, of course they would be." Grace smiled. "I'm sure it's just something she put there for good luck."

"Good luck," Vanessa repeated flatly. Yes, her luck had certainly been swell lately.

Grace glanced at her watch. "I'm going to have to dash. I need to get these articles to the printer or we'll have no paper this week."

"Thanks for the coffee." Vanessa walked her visitor to the door. "And maybe sometime we could chat about Miss Ridgeway . . ."

"Yes, I'd like that." Grace was halfway out the door when she turned and asked, "You haven't happened to find any of her books. Her journals or . . . anything like that?"

Vanessa shook her head. "No. I've looked through the books on the shelves in the living room, and there are several books about herbs, but I haven't found any journals or . . . anything like that."

Grace started to close the door behind her. "Have you been in the attic yet?"

"Yes, several times. Although I haven't had time to look through the boxes that are up there. I've been so busy with the shop and then in the off-season, painting the downstairs and the bedrooms and trying to get the kitchen in order. You'll have to stop over sometime and see what I've done in the house."

"I'd like that very much." Grace turned and smiled again. "Yes, I would like that."

"Anytime. And thanks again for the coffee . . ."

Grace waved before she hustled down the sidewalk in the direction of her newspaper's office. Vanessa was shaking her head as she closed the door behind the tiny woman. *Well, she took my mind off feeling bad about this place. And it was nice of her to bring me coffee . . .*

Vanessa's cell began to ring, and she searched her pockets until she found it.

"Hello?"

"I wasn't kidding when I said I'd take him when you didn't want him anymore."

Vanessa laughed.

"You think I'm jesting but I am so serious. I just passed him on Kelly's Point Drive. He's seriously fine, so whenever you're finished with him, just toss him my way." Steffie paused. "I hope this doesn't interfere with our friendship."

"It won't, because he'll be leaving for Montana any day now," Vanessa said.

Steffie sighed. "So I suppose I will need to schedule some consolation time. We'll be busy at Scoop but I can work it in."

"What are you talking about? I won't need consolation."

"Please. It's Steffie you're talking to here. You know you're going to miss him, Ness."

"Well, sure. The sex has been great."

"Is that all you can say?"

"It has been." Vanessa bit a cuticle and frowned.

"Get off it. You're not that shallow."

"What shallow? It's the truth. And sex matters."

"What about the rest of it?"

"Yeah, well, the rest of it matters, too," Vanessa admitted. "But it's all moot. So it doesn't matter—it can't matter—beyond the next few days or however long he's going to be here."

"A girl can still dream, Ness," Stef protested.

"I don't dare dream, Stef. Any dream involving Grady is bound to have an unhappy ending. I've had enough of those." She caught herself before she could say more. "And speak of the devil; he's just crossing the street and walking in my direction."

"Well, I'll let you go, then, so you can chat with that guy who doesn't really matter all that much . . ."

"I didn't say that, damn it," she whispered as

Grady pushed open the door and came in. She slipped the phone into her pocket, knowing as well as Stef did that she'd been lying through her teeth.

"I thought you were keeping this door locked." He frowned.

"It was locked. I just opened it to let Miss Grace in. She just left."

"I had a little talk with her over at Cuppachino when I left here this morning."

"Well, I hope your conversation with her made more sense than mine did. I asked her about Alice Ridgeway, the woman who used to live in my house. She asked me if Alice was *bothering* me. As if she expected the woman to still be there. And then she asked me if I'd found any of Alice's journals. Like she was interested in those." Vanessa's hands were on her hips. "I suspect that Miss Grace might have known Alice Ridgeway a lot better than I'd previously thought."

She paused. "What's that in your hand?"

"Photocopies of the people we suspect broke into Bling and your house." He pulled the sheets of paper out of the envelope Hal had given him and laid the photo of Jackie Weston on the counter. "Look familiar?"

"That's Candice," she said as she leaned forward. "Her hair wasn't blond like this—it was brown—but that's definitely her."

"And this?" He placed the picture of Edmund Dent next to Weston's.

"Oh my God, that's Gene's cousin." Her eyes grew wide. "Edmund Dent. That slimy, sleazy little son of a bitch burned my house down. Not that there was anything in there worth saving—I didn't have very much—but the fact that he thought I was inside—"

"What?"

"Oh, yeah. He thought I was inside the house. That's why he and Gene's brother torched the place."

"How do you know this?"

"Because the doors and windows were all nailed shut. The arson expert testified that there was no reason to do that unless they were trying to trap someone inside."

"And yet they were still acquitted?"

"The jury couldn't decide which of the cousins and which of the brothers were involved, even though the circumstantial evidence pointed to Edmund and Gene's brother, Calvin. I never doubted that it was them. They were both really angry with me for calling the cops on Gene."

"Well, apparently, Edmund is still pretty pissed at you."

"I imagine they all blame me for Gene dying in prison." She leaned on the counter, one hand holding her stomach. "I guess he's not going to stop until I'm dead, too."

Grady put his arms around her from behind.

"That is not going to happen," he told her. "I will see him dead before he lays a hand on you."

"You can't watch over me twenty-four hours a day, Grady." She turned and put her hands on his chest, her fingers toying absently with the collar of his shirt. "Besides, sooner or later, you have a life to go back to. Don't you have some hikes or something lined up?"

He nodded.

She started to say something else, when she froze momentarily, then looked down.

"Is that a gun in your pocket, or are you just glad to see me?" She grinned and pulled up his shirttail. "I always wanted to be able to say that but never thought I'd get the chance."

"Hal put me on the force as a temporary part-time officer."

"He can do that?"

"He's acting chief in Beck's absence."

"He hired you just to watch over me?" She frowned. "That's not a very good use of taxpayers' money."

"We didn't discuss remuneration, and I don't expect any. He just wanted to be able to give me a handgun. Just in case."

"I do not like guns, but if Edmund Dent is in St. Dennis, I'm not going to argue." She picked up Jackie Weston's picture. "I feel real bad for her. I could be very wrong, but I didn't get the sense that she was a bad person. I'm sorry she got involved with that family. They're not nice people. That bad-news gene—and yes, the pun is intended—seems to run in the family. And I believe he's been abusing her. All the signs were there."

"I reviewed his criminal history. Their neighbors called the police several times to report screams and loud banging coming from their apartment, but she always insisted it was the television."

"I knew it. She just has that defeated look about her." Vanessa sighed. "If her fingerprints were in the database, she must have been arrested before, right?"

He nodded. "About six months ago, for passing bad checks."

She looked back at the woman's photo. "I can't decide whether or not to be mad at myself for having been so nice to her."

"If it makes you feel better, I don't think she had anything to do with the break-in."

"I hope not. There ought to be a law against men like that."

"Well, there is, but unfortunately, too many women ignore it."

"Some habits are very hard to break, Grady. Once you start believing that you deserve what you're getting, it's real hard to convince yourself otherwise. It took me a long time to realize that I could make it stop."

"I'm surprised you ever took that kind of treatment from anyone. You are so strong, so self-assured."

"It was hard-won, believe me." She smiled. "Just something else I have to thank Hal for."

"What do you mean?"

"If you'd seen me when I first arrived in St. Dennis . . ." She laughed ruefully. "Not just the way I looked, which was way inappropriate for anyone other than a teenager—I was just a mess all the way around. Looking back, it's a miracle Hal even opened his door when he saw me standing on his front porch."

She stopped and took a drink from the coffee Grace had brought her.

"I was scared to death that someone in Gene's family would come looking for me—prophetic, huh? I couldn't sleep, couldn't eat. Here I was, bunking in with strangers who had no real reason to take me in except the goodness of their hearts, and I sure wasn't used to people like that. I had no money, I couldn't pay Hal room and board. I told him I'd get a job, but it was winter and there wasn't much tourist action. Besides, there wasn't much I was qualified to do. Long story short, Hal asked me what I would do if I could do anything, anything at all. I told him the only thing I ever dreamed of was owning a little dress shop, since the only job I ever had was in retail. He told me that if I did two things for him, he'd help me to have that little shop. One, I had to take classes at the community college—business classes, math, that sort of thing—and two, I had to go talk to a therapist. He promised me he'd never ask me what we talked about—and he never has, though I often volunteered. Anyway, I went to school and I did really well— surprised the hell out of me, how well I did—and I went to therapy every week for almost two years, which Hal paid for. It helped me to put a lot of things in perspective. Dr. Campbell—she was my therapist— helped me to understand that sometimes, you just have to let certain things go."

She smiled up at him. "So yes, I am strong now. It took me a while, but I don't let my past dictate what my future is going to be. That's one of Dr. Campbell's mantras, by the way."

"Smart woman, your Dr. Campbell."

She nodded. "Very."

"You really have a lot to be proud of, you know that, right?"

"I got lucky, I had Hal and Beck and Dr. Campbell on my side."

"I think you're overlooking the fact that you must have had a lot inside you that you didn't realize was there. Friends and family and even professional therapists can't give you what you don't already have. They can only help you to find what you've got and tap into it."

"That's what Dr. Campbell always said. Were you in therapy, too?"

He shook his head. "Psych major."

"I should have known."

He laughed and looked around the shop. "Speaking of moving on, let's finish this up so that you can reopen as soon as the glass is replaced."

"The glass guy should be here soon."

"Do you have a large trash container? I can get this broken glass up for you while you try to figure out what's missing."

"I already made a list for the insurance agent," she told him. "He took the money and the dress that Candice—excuse me, Jackie—tried on. She must have been with him, for him to have known which one to take."

"She could have just described it," he replied. "I doubt he would have taken her with him on the break-in. There'd be less chance that he'd be seen coming and going if he was by himself."

"Maybe. I hope you're right, for her sake. If he's arrested, he'll go to prison, so maybe she can get away from him." She paused on her way to get the trash container for the glass. "I'd like to think that could happen for her. I'd like to believe she'd get another chance to make things right for herself. She didn't seem like someone who should be involved with someone like that." She thought over what she'd just said, then laughed ruefully. "Then again, neither was I . . ."

Diary—

Well, didn't I say that Grady Shields was a nice young man? Apparently Vanessa thinks so, too. I noticed he hangs around Bling quite a bit, in a most protective manner, I might add. Which is only right, since our chief of police is away on a honeymoon with Grady's sister—not that that obligates him, of course, but it is lovely that Grady is keeping an eye on Vanessa. But one cannot help but notice there's nothing brotherly in the way that young man looks at her!

As for Vanessa, she's come across some of Alice's old herb books! Oh, yes, I'm dying to get my hands on them, since so much information has been lost to me since dear Alice passed, and let's face it, my memory isn't what it used to be. Blessings on Vanessa, she invited me to come to the house and look at those books—I will take her up on that as soon as I can without appearing overly anxious. I did inquire if she'd found any of Alice's journals, but so far, she says she hasn't seen them. I cannot even begin to imagine what she might think should she open any one of those and read about the activities that once took place in the very house she now calls home . . . and more shocking still, the names of those who participated!

Oh, dear—how would one explain . . .

—Grace

Chapter 17

T<small>HE</small> woman stood in the doorway of the municipal building as if she wasn't sure she wanted to
go in. Hal noticed her when he crossed the hall from
Beck's office to the conference room, then when he
came back out again and walked to the reception
desk. He'd just opened his mouth to complain to Garland about having started three times to pick up his
messages but had been distracted three times, when
he realized why the woman looked familiar.

He walked toward her, half expecting her to turn
and run back out through the double doors, but the
closer he got to her, the more he realized that wasn't
likely to happen. She stood firm and watched him ap-
proach.

"I need to speak with the chief of police," she said
in a voice that was barely audible, as if she wasn't
sure she really wanted to be heard.

"I'm the chief," he told her. "This week, anyway."

"Something really bad is going to happen," she
said, her face as white as the T-shirt she wore. "You
need to stop it. He's going to hurt her."

A chill went through him, but he never blinked.

"When?"

"Right now."

"Where? At the shop?"

She shook her head. "I don't know. All he said was that it was time, and we'd be leaving as soon as he took care of her."

He took her arm and led her to the conference room.

"You've got to warn her," the woman whispered. "He's going to kill her."

He did not have to ask who either *he* or *her* was. He turned the woman over to Gus and set off running up Kelly's Point Road. It would be faster than getting the car and waiting for traffic to permit him to cross at Charles Street. As he ran, he dialed Vanessa's cell.

When she answered, he said, "Is Grady with you?"

"Yes, he's right here," she told him. "Did you want—"

"Tell him to stand at the door and watch for me. I'll be there in a minute."

"Is something wrong?"

"Just tell him . . ." Hal hadn't realized just how out of shape he was until he started to run up the hill to the main street. He had a mental picture of himself passing out in the middle of the street, but he made it to the shop without collapsing and was happy to see Grady in the doorway.

"Lock the door," Hal panted. "We have a problem."

"What? What's wrong?" Vanessa cried. "Dear God, Hal, did you run all the way from the police station?"

He nodded, and she went into the back room and grabbed a bottle of water from the refrigerator.

"What the hell is going on?" Grady was asking when she came back to the front of the shop. She twisted the cap off the bottle and handed it to Hal.

"The woman—Jackie—just came into the station. Told me that something very bad was going to happen, like now. To Ness." Hal paused to take a drink. "That Dent is planning on 'taking care of her' and then he and the woman were going to leave town."

"She told you this?" Vanessa felt the blood drain from her face.

"Yeah." Hal fought to get his breathing under control. "She doesn't know what he has in mind, only that it's going to be soon. As in now. This morning."

"Well, he isn't likely to be able to get past the two of you," she noted warily.

"Is the back door locked?" Hal asked.

"It was earlier," she replied.

"I'll check it." Grady walked to the back of the shop and tried the door. "It's locked and dead-bolted," he told them when he returned.

"So what do we do now?" Vanessa tried to keep the rising panic under control.

Hal rested his upper body on the counter. "I guess now we just have to wait to see what his next move is going to be."

"Swell," Vanessa muttered.

Maggie couldn't remember the last time she felt this good. It seemed that ever since Carl had passed away, things had just gotten better and better for her. Oh, not that she was happy that he died. Far from it.

His death had saddened her greatly. Carl had been a really good man and he'd adored Maggie. While he was lacking in certain of his husbandly duties, he'd made up for it in other ways. He'd been her friend, and he'd provided very well for her. It was the first relationship Maggie had ever had with a man who'd demanded nothing more of her than her companionship. So she'd kept him company every day, and when his eyesight began to fail, she'd read the newspapers to him as well as the crime novels he loved so much. In return, Carl had given Maggie a lovely if somewhat isolated home and the first financial security she'd ever had. But lately, she was beginning to secretly think of Carl as her geriatric guardian angel.

She smiled to herself as she walked up Vanessa's driveway with the bag from the plant nursery in her arms. Hal had said that Vanessa wanted water lilies and koi—well, then, water lilies and koi she would have. Maggie could hardly wait to see Vanessa's face when she realized that her mother had single-handedly cleaned out the old pond and brought it back to life again. There'd been so few times in Vanessa's life that Maggie had done something unexpected and just for fun. Well, this was the new Maggie. She was aware that her daughter was annoyed that she'd come to Beck's wedding uninvited and that Vanessa had, well, *issues* with her. But she was going to do everything she could think of to win her daughter's affection. She'd move heaven and earth, she told herself, why, she'd even—

Maggie rounded the corner of the house and went into the yard, and walked smack into a man who stood near the door leading down into the basement.

He was dark-haired, short and stocky, and had long sideburns, an unkempt mustache, and eyes like a ferret.

"Oh my God!" Maggie gasped when she recognized his face. The realization took her breath away. "You. It's been *you* . . ."

She started to turn back to the driveway, her only thought being to run like hell, but he moved more quickly. In one stride, he had one arm around her waist and the other hand over her mouth. The bag slipped from her grasp and fell to the ground.

"Don't make a sound," he hissed in her ear. "Not one little peep. And stop struggling, damn it, or I will put a hole the size of Ohio through the back of your head right now."

She froze.

"That's better." He began to move backward, dragging her along with him. "I'm going to turn you around, and you're going to go down the steps ahead of me."

He pointed to the basement, which loomed dark and deep before her eyes.

"No, no, please . . ." The thought of what might lie below in the dark terrified her, and the old movie mantra—*don't go down into the basement*—rang in her ears. She pushed against him, and he laughed.

"You have a short memory, Mrs. . . . I can't remember what your last name is, but it doesn't much matter. I know who you are. I know that you helped that bitch after she put my man Eugene in that damned prison so he could die there. I know you took her out of town before any of us knew she was gone. So it's going to give me a real thrill to do you, lady. An unexpected pleasure, but it's going to be a pleasure all the same. Now, walk down those steps, or I do it right here." He pulled the gun from his waistband and held it to her forehead.

Maggie descended the steps, Edmund Dent at her back, his gun pressed hard between her shoulder blades. The air below was close and redolent of dried herbs. It was dark and twice she fell slightly forward, and twice more she tripped over something before the toe of her shoe struck the bottom step.

"Lift your foot and find the stair," he told her.

She counted as she climbed, thirteen steps to the top. He reached around her and pushed open the door. Maggie blinked several times at the bright sunlight that flooded the kitchen. He led her across the room to the table and pushed her into the nearest chair. A length of rope lay coiled on the countertop, and she guessed that it had not been placed there by Vanessa. That, and the fact that the basement door was already open, told her that he'd been in the house earlier today. What else had he brought with him? she wondered. What did he have planned for her daughter?

"What's her cellphone number?" Dent demanded.

"What?" Maggie frowned.

He leaned forward, so close to her that she could smell his breath. She had to force herself not to gag.

"I want her cellphone number."

"I don't know it."

"You're her mother." He remained literally in her face. "How could you not know her number?"

Maggie shrugged and tried to move back away from him. "We're not particularly close."

"You were close enough a couple of years ago when Eugene's trial was going on that you were in the courtroom every damned day. You were close enough when he was sentenced that you drove her straight out of town."

"Yeah, well, that was then." Maggie looked him in the eye. "This is now."

The slap across her face was totally unexpected.

"I'm going to ask you again. What's her cellphone number?"

"I can't give you what I don't have. She never gave it to me. Up until Saturday, I hadn't seen her in three years."

She braced herself for another slap, but instead he put his hand in his back pocket and took out his wallet. He opened it and searched through some bills— bills most likely stolen from Vanessa's cash register, Maggie thought. He removed a card and reached for the house phone on the wall.

"Got something just as good." He smirked. He began to dial, turning the card around to show Maggie. It was one of Vanessa's business cards, taken, she suspected, from the shop when he robbed it. "I know she went to that shop of hers today. I watched her from the coffee shop across the street. When she answers, I'm putting you on the phone, and you're going to tell her to meet you here, you understand?"

"I won't do that," Maggie told him.

"Oh, I think you will." He pointed the gun directly between her eyes. "As a matter of fact, I'm sure of it . . ."

Chapter 18

S o what do we do, just stand around here staring at each other until Edmund shows up?" Vanessa asked.

"That's about it," Hal replied.

"Well, I'm just going to keep on doing what I was doing before . . ." She returned to the pile of sweaters she'd earlier started to fold, anything to keep her mind occupied. Knowing that someone was planning on killing you *that day* was terrifying. If she gave in to the panic, she'd be useless. She envisioned herself as a weeping heap in the corner of the room. Terrified and cowed wasn't a good look for her.

The phone on the counter began to ring. Vanessa reached for it and Hal stopped her.

"Check the caller ID first."

She leaned forward and read the number.

"It's my house." She frowned and looked up at Grady. "Who'd be in my . . . oh."

"Well, I guess we know where," Grady said to Hal, then nodded to her. "Pick it up, Ness. If it's Dent, sound surprised that it's him. Don't let him know we're onto him."

"Hello?"

"Vanessa. It's Maggie."

Maggie's voice vibrated with fear.

"Maggie, what are you doing at my house?" She shot a confused glance at Hal.

"I'm supposed to be luring you here, because—"

Vanessa heard the sound of a struggle, then a slap before Maggie cried out.

"Maggie? Maggie? What's happening?" Vanessa cried into the phone.

"Maggie isn't playing by the rules, so she took a penalty," a mocking male voice told her.

"Who is this?" *Don't let him know we're onto him . . .*

"This is your worst nightmare, baby," Edmund crooned, and Vanessa grimaced at Grady. She pointed to the phone and nodded. *It's him.*

"I've had a lot of nightmares lately," she said. "Who is this?"

"You're going to have to come on over here and find out for yourself. But you come by yourself, you hear? Do not call the old man or the guy who's been banging you." He snickered. "I saw his clothes in the closet upstairs. It must be nice and cozy around here at night."

"What do you want?" she asked curtly.

"I want you, here, in this house, in nine minutes. I know it takes eleven minutes to walk from your shop to this house because I timed it. I'm giving you nine. For every minute you're late, your mother will have another hole in one of her body parts. A foot, a hand, maybe shoot off a couple of fingers. If you don't come at all, I aim for the heart. I see anyone but you coming this way or anywhere near this house, I kill her. Come now. I'll be watching for you."

"Listen—"

"You're down to eight minutes, Vanessa, and so is your mother." He hung up.

"I have to go," she said. "He's going to kill Maggie if I'm not there in eight minutes."

She ran for the door.

"Hold up there." Grady grabbed her arm as she ran past. "I can't let you just walk in there."

"I have to. *He's going to shoot my mother.*"

"If you go into that house, Ness, he's going to shoot you, too," Hal told her.

"You're the survival expert, right?" She turned to Grady. "You figure out how to save us both." She shook herself free. "I have to go. He said he'd be watching for me."

"Ness, where's your cell?" Grady asked.

"It's in my bag." She pointed to the counter.

He grabbed her bag and dumped the contents onto the floor. He picked up her phone and dialed a number. His cell rang inside his pants pocket. He answered his phone as he handed Vanessa's phone to her.

"Leave the call open in your pocket so we can hear what's going on. He's going to have to be in the front of the house, so try to keep him there to give us time to get in through the back."

"How do you know he'll be in the front of the house?" she asked.

"You just said he told you he'd be watching for you. He'll only be able to see the street from the front door or from the living room." Grady turned to Hal.

"There's a stretch of woods that runs behind her house. You know where we can cut through to get to her yard?"

Hal nodded.

"All right, let's go." Before Grady opened the door, he kissed Vanessa soundly on the mouth. "Keep the phone open, and keep him talking for as long as you can. He's got to be feeling pretty clever right about now, so let him brag. Keep him talking, Ness. Act like you're impressed that he found you, whatever strokes you think his ego needs. Keep him focused on you. Keep your interactions with Maggie to a minimum."

Vanessa nodded and started out the door. "What if he's already shot Maggie? What if he just shoots me when I walk through the door?"

Before he or Hal could answer, she shuddered and said, "I have to go." She fled out the door, with both men at her heels.

"We can cut through the Eakinses' backyard," Hal said.

Hal and Grady were right behind her, but when she took off to the left toward Cherry Street, they turned right for the street that ran behind it.

Vanessa ran. She was scared to death and her heart was racing so fast she thought she was going to have a heart attack before she ever made it home.

Then he'll think I'm not coming and he'll shoot Maggie, she told herself.

She talked to herself the entire time.

Why am I doing this? I can't not. I can't let him kill her because he can't get to me.

What if he kills me? Grady won't let him kill me.

Grady and Hal. They'll save us.

How? How are they going to save us?

By the time she reached her house, she was scared out of her wits.

Don't let him know I'm afraid. Let him brag, Grady said. *Keep him talking. Let him brag. Act impressed. Keep him talking . . .*

Unless, of course, he shoots me the minute I walk through the door, she thought as she walked up her front steps on wobbly legs. *Maybe I should have waited until we came up with a Plan B . . .*

She pushed open the front door and stepped into her foyer. Edmund Dent stood at the bottom of the stairwell, Maggie in front of him, a gun to her head.

"Edmund?" Vanessa asked as if she hadn't known who had summoned her. "Edmund Dent?"

"Yup." He pushed Maggie away from him, into the living room and onto the sofa.

Vanessa kept her focus on Edmund.

"Bet you never expected to see me again," he taunted.

She shook her head. "How did you find me?"

He smirked. "It was easy. Your old lady left behind some very talkative neighbors everyplace she went. And she's pretty talkative herself. 'Hello, I'm looking for Vanessa Keaton . . . we're having a high school reunion and it wouldn't be the same without her.' " He mimicked a woman's voice.

"You . . . you made that call?" Vanessa asked, then turned to Maggie. "Maggie, couldn't you tell that that 'Shannon' person was really a man?" Before Maggie could answer, Vanessa had turned back to Edmund. "You had her fooled. She really thought you were a girl named Shannon, even though I told her I didn't know anyone named Shannon."

"Yeah, pretty clever, I thought."

Vanessa nodded. "I have to give you that one."

"Thanks." He sat on the bottom step and waved the gun. "I want you to sit over there with your mother. I want to tell you a story."

Vanessa moved slowly and backed onto the sofa. She made no move toward Maggie, nor did she make eye contact with her.

"So tell me a story," Vanessa said.

"When I was a kid, I was very small. And I stuttered. Everyone made fun of me, knocked me around. Nobody ever stuck up for me, except for one person. Know who that person was?"

Oh, shit, she thought. *I think I can see where this is going . . .*

Aloud she said, "Who, Edmund?"

"The man you sent to prison. The man who died there, beaten to death like a dog. My cousin Eugene." He stared at her through flat black eyes. "You should have taken it, Vanessa. Whatever you did to make him put you in your place, you should have taken it. You had no right to call the cops on a family matter. You should have taken it, then worked it out with him later. It's your fault he's dead, Vanessa. The Bible says an eye for an eye, right?"

He got off the step and started toward her, the hand that held the gun swaying, his free hand clenching and unclenching. She was pretty sure the first blow would be with a fist. He wasn't going to shoot her before he hurt her. Grady had been right about that. She braced herself for the punch that was coming.

"No! Don't touch her!" Maggie jumped from the sofa and lunged toward him. Just as he raised the gun there was the sound of something hitting the floor in the dining room.

Edmund smacked Maggie with his free hand and swung toward the sound just as a black plastic flowerpot rolled across the floor.

"What the f . . ." he muttered.

From the kitchen doorway, Grady leaped forward and landed on Edmund's back and slammed him, face-first, onto the floor. The gun Edmund had been holding slid on the hardwood almost to the front door.

"What the hell took you so long? And where's Hal?" Vanessa rushed to help Maggie up.

"I'm all right, honey." Maggie stood shakily. "I'm all right."

"Pick up that gun, Ness," Grady told her. "Put it on the table near the window."

She picked it up between her thumb and forefinger, as if it had a life of its own, and placed it on the table.

"Grab the cuffs from my back pocket, would you?" Grady asked as he twisted Edmund's hands behind his back.

She assisted Maggie onto the sofa, then pulled the cuffs from his pocket and handed them to Grady.

"Hal's out back, probably still trying to catch his breath," Grady told her as he cuffed her would-be assassin. "He ran the entire way, but he's just not in shape. He was breathing so hard I was afraid you'd hear him before I could create a distraction, so I told him to wait outside. He's called for backup but told them to hang back."

"Hal's outside?" Maggie started to rise, and Vanessa hurried to help her up. "Is he all right?"

"I think he's better off than you are right now." Vanessa tilted Maggie's face to get a better look at her injury.

"What if he's having a heart attack? Maybe we should call an ambulance . . ." Maggie ran to the back door.

"Tell him to let his backup know it's time to move in," Grady called after her.

"Get off me. I'm gonna sue you for excessive force . . ." Edmund yelled.

"Nothing I haven't heard before," Grady told him, then read him his rights. He turned to Vanessa. "You okay?"

"I'm fine. Maggie got the worst of it. He was just winding up, though. You didn't arrive any too soon, you know."

"I know. I was paying attention." Grady grabbed Edmund and pulled him to his feet. He held him by the back of the neck with one hand; with the other, he pulled his cell out of his shirt pocket. Vanessa smiled, and did the same.

"Hello," she said into her phone.

"Hello," he replied, then snapped his phone closed and said, "You'd have made a good cop, Ness. You followed instructions to the letter, you never lost your cool, you kept focused just like I told you."

"I was scared to death," she admitted as the first patrol car came screaming to a stop out front. "I had no cool. I thought I was going to pass out or throw up."

"You did just fine, babe," he said softly. "Just fine . . ."

She opened the front door for Gus and Sue and pointed to the man on the floor. "He's all yours, Officers . . ."

Vanessa and Maggie sat across from each other at Hal's conference table waiting to give their statements regarding the day's events while Grady paced in the hallway talking on his cell.

"Vanessa, I don't know how to thank you for saving my life this morning," Maggie said. "You didn't have to come."

"Do you believe he would have killed you?" Vanessa asked.

Maggie nodded. "There's no question in my mind. Several times, I thought he was going to pull that trigger . . ." She shivered at the memory. "Anyway, I just wanted you to know that I will never forget that you put yourself in danger to save me."

"Maggie, you're my mother." Vanessa sighed. "Whatever else has happened, whatever issues we have, the fact remains that you're my mother, and I could not let him kill you in my place."

Tears rolled down Maggie's cheeks. "Look, I know I screwed up as a mother. There are so many things I did back then that I'd never do now. I never meant to hurt you or Beck, Vanessa. I did love you—I still love you both—but I screwed up big-time. Every good relationship I ever had, I screwed up."

"Yes, you did." Vanessa faced her and met her eyes

without blinking. "You screwed up your life, and you screwed up both of ours. But here's the thing: in screwing up, you gave us both what turned out to be the best thing that could have happened to either of us. You sent us to Hal. He saved us—both of us—so for that I have to thank you. It makes up for everything you didn't do."

Maggie covered her face with her hands. "I'm sorry, Vanessa. I know I was a poor excuse for a mother."

"A piss-poor excuse, when you get right down to it. But maybe instead of beating your breast and crying about everything you did that hurt us . . ."

Maggie's head shot up.

"Yes. Hurt, Maggie." Vanessa took a deep breath. There were things she'd waited a lifetime to say. Now might be her only chance. "From the time I was seven years old until I was about fifteen, I was afraid all the time. Did you know that?"

"Afraid of what, honey?"

"Afraid that the men who came home with you at night would come back during the day when I was there alone. I hated the school day to end, because all the way walking home, I'd be getting more and more scared." Even now, years later, Vanessa could feel that cold finger of fear on the back of her neck. "What if someone was there when I got home? What would I do? What would I do if you were out at night and one of them came looking for you? What would they do to me?"

"Oh, baby, I'd never have let anyone hurt you. I'd have died before I'd let anyone touch you," Maggie wept.

"Good to know now, but it would have been even better to hear when I was a child."

"Dear God, I'm sorry. Look, I know I was a mess back then. I did so much wrong when I was too young to know better. I made a million bad choices and few good ones. I lost the best man I ever knew—the only man I really loved—because I was too weak and too scared to stand up to my father. You can't imagine what it was like for me back then, Vanessa." Maggie patted her eyes with a tissue she'd taken from her purse. "I was bullied and forced into marrying someone I didn't love. My entire life went wrong from that one wrong turn."

"This isn't all about you, Maggie. A simple I-screwed-up-my-life-and-I-screwed-up-yours-too-and-I'm-sincerely-sorry is probably all that's necessary at this point. The rest of it—the explanations, the attempts to excuse yourself that you've been making all these years—they don't matter so much anymore to anyone except you. I can't help you to clear your conscience but I can give you some of the best advice you'll ever get." Vanessa scanned the table and found a pen and a sheet of paper. She wrote something and handed it to Maggie. "This is the therapist who helped me. Maybe she can give you a referral to someone in North Dakota that you could make an appointment with."

Maggie frowned.

"You have issues that you've been dragging around for years, Maggie. You haven't been able to resolve them on your own, so maybe someone else can help you. It might be worth a try." Vanessa shrugged. "Of course, it's up to you."

Maggie studied the paper for a moment.

"You're right, of course." Maggie folded the paper and tucked it into her bag. "Thank you."

"Ladies, if you're ready to give your statements"— Hal appeared in the doorway—"Sue is ready to take them. Maggie, come on into the office across the hall, and we'll get started with you first."

"All right." Maggie stood and walked to the door. She turned back to her daughter and said, "Thank you, Ness. For everything."

Vanessa swiveled in the chair, trying to put it all into perspective. She did love her mother. She'd realized that earlier in the day when she'd willingly gone to the house where Maggie was being held hostage. There'd been no question in her mind whether to go or not go. She simply went, understanding that no one does that sort of thing—no one chooses to put themself in harm's way—unless they value the person whose life was at stake. For all their differences, they were still mother and daughter. Vanessa hoped that she and Maggie could put aside their unhappy past and find out what that meant as adults. Maybe Maggie would make that phone call . . .

A noise from the doorway drew her attention, and she looked up to see Grady standing there.

"Hey," she said.

"Hey yourself," he replied.

"Come on in," she beckoned him. "Keep me company until it's my turn to give my version."

He came into the room but did not sit.

"I guess you'll have to give your statement, too?" she asked.

"I already wrote it up." He smiled but to her he appeared troubled. "And handed in the gun Hal gave me."

"I was so glad you didn't have to fire it."

"Me, too."

"Can you sit?" She pulled out the chair next to her.

He shook his head. "Actually, I just wanted to let you know that I'm going to be heading back to Montana. I spoke with the head of the group I'd contracted to take out on Friday and they're really psyched for this camping trip. I hate to disappoint them—I've taken them before and it's a great group—plus they've already paid for the trip." He seemed to have trouble meeting her eyes. "With Dent in custody, I figured . . ."

"Oh. Of course." She nodded. "You don't need to stay. Especially since you have that trip lined up, you should go. How fortunate that it worked out the way it did so that you could get back there in time."

"Well, I figured if I got back tomorrow, I'd have enough time to get all the provisions that we need, and I can check the weather and figure out the best route, that sort of thing. We get snow in April and May sometimes, especially at the higher elevations, and I don't want to take them into unknown conditions."

She held up a hand to stop him. "I understand totally. You have a job to do. I appreciate that. And I appreciate that you extended your stay on my behalf. It was good of you to do that for someone you hardly know."

"Don't do that, Ness," he said softly. "Don't make it sound like we're strangers. From that day on Hal's deck, we haven't been strangers. Don't make it less than what it was."

"I'm not quite sure what it was." She stood and tried to force back the lump in her throat. She knew she'd be saying good-bye to him, but she hadn't expected it now, and here. "Maybe 'two-night stand' says it best."

"That doesn't say it at all, and you know it." He reached for her but she crossed her arms over her chest as if to put distance between them. He put his arms around her anyway and kissed the side of her face when she tried to turn away from him. "I'll call you when I get back from this trip."

She nodded. "Be careful," was the only thing she could think of to say. *Good-bye* stuck in her throat and she couldn't make herself say the word. "The house is open, so go on by and pick up your things."

He nodded, and then he was gone.

Just like that, he was gone.

Diary—

The events of these past few days have my head positively spinning! Remember I said that Hal believed the same person who robbed Bling was responsible for the vandalism to Grady's rental car? Well, he was right on the money, which just goes to prove once again that Hal Garrity was among the finest police chiefs this town has ever had. But when the identity of the perpetrator was revealed—well, let me just say that I wasn't the only shocked soul in town!

Now, the story that I heard—and I have this on very good authority—is that Vanessa's ex-husband was a violent and abusive man (can you imagine?!). I'd heard that she'd had not one, but two bad marriages, but I never heard the details. And let me assure you that I was not one of those who assumed that she was a wanton young thing. No, I just knew there was more to that story than met the eye.

Vanessa had this fiend arrested, but after he was convicted, relatives of his threatened her and burned down her house! If not for her mother spiriting her away in the night and sending her here to Hal, who knows what would have happened to her? It makes me ill to think of it! Now, it seems that the husband died recently in prison and one of those same vengeful relatives came after Vanessa, breaking into her shop, then into her home, where he ran into

Vanessa's mother, Maggie—who'd hung around St. Dennis after the wedding and has been seen with Hal a great deal, which has every tongue in town wagging, as you can imagine—and took the poor woman hostage!

Whew! Take a breath, Gracie!

Then, this evil man held the woman at gunpoint and forced her to call Vanessa and tell her she had to come home or he was going to shoot her mother! Well, didn't that courageous girl run home to save her mother's life?! God only knows what would have happened if Grady hadn't dashed to the house, created a distraction, then disarmed the villain! Talk about a knight in shining armor!

I have it on excellent authority that Vanessa is just not herself these days since Grady returned to Montana. This simply will not do. . . .

Yes, yes, I know. I swore off the spells after that fiasco with Rocky and that sweet young woman from Rock Hall last year (well, who knew that he was gay?). But there are times when one must take matters into one's own hands, and I do believe this is one of those times. Now, how to get my hands on some of those herbs Alice kept in those glass jars in her basement. . . .

—Grace

Chapter 19

"Ness, you shouldn't be alone at a time like this," Steffie told her. "If you don't want dinner and you don't want to drink, at least let me bring you some ice cream."

Vanessa paused. "Ice cream would be good."

"I'm on my way."

Less than fifteen minutes later, Steffie arrived at Vanessa's door with a bag filled with numerous paper containers, some napkins, and a couple of plastic spoons.

"I couldn't decide what flavor, so I brought a bunch," Steffie explained when Vanessa opened the door.

"Good." Vanessa grabbed the bag and took it into the living room, where she plopped into a chair. "Let's see . . . we'll start with this one."

"Don't you want to see what flavors?"

Vanessa shrugged. "Flavor, schmavor. It doesn't really matter."

She handed Steffie the bag.

"You've had one hell of a day, girl." Stef picked a

random container out of the bag and opened it. "Maybe we should put the others in the freezer."

"They won't last long enough to melt," Vanessa told her. "And yes, this was one hell of a day. To reiterate: my second husband's crazy cousin Edmund breaks into my house, takes my mother hostage, and threatens to kill her unless I come here so that he can kill me . . ."

"Why'd you do it, Ness?"

"Why'd I do what?"

"Why'd you come back here knowing that crazy bastard had a gun?"

"I couldn't live with myself if I'd just sat back and let him kill her." Vanessa finished her first dish and went back into the bag for another. She opened the lid and looked at the contents. "This looks good. What is—"

"No, put that one back. Better yet, give it to me." Steffie reached for it.

"Why? What's wrong with it?" Vanessa dipped her spoon in. "It's yummy."

Steffie sighed. "I made it yesterday and named it after Grady because he'd been such a sport about driving me to Scoop when it was very clear he had private plans for you."

"You named an ice cream after him?" Vanessa's spoon wavered halfway between the dish and her mouth. "What did you call it?"

"Mountain Man Fudge."

"Mountain . . ." Vanessa started to giggle, then couldn't stop, and before long, she was in tears, sobbing.

"Oh, sweetie, I'm sorry. I should have made up

some other name when you asked. I shouldn't have brought him up at all."

"It's okay," Vanessa wept. "It's just that I didn't expect him to leave so abruptly. I'll be fine. I'm just going to have this one cry, then it'll be done."

"I should have followed my first instincts and brought a couple of bottles of wine," Steffie muttered.

"No, no, I'll be fine. I just need to cry it out." She picked up the bag and swung it to Steffie. "This may take a while, though . . ."

"Take as much time as you need." Steffie helped herself and returned the bag to the coffee table. "But just so I know . . . is he, Grady, a bastard for leaving that fast, or what?"

"I knew he was going. I knew he had this trail thing he does. Camping trip he was taking some people on. That's how he makes his living." Vanessa got up and went into the kitchen and came back with a box of tissues. "So it's not like he misled me or deceived me or anything like that." She blew her nose and appeared to think for a minute. "I think what hurts is that it feels so . . . unfinished. You know? Like there should have been more, but there isn't going to be."

"You liked him that much, huh?"

"I never knew anyone like him," Vanessa said. "I guess if I were looking for someone for the long run . . . and we both know I'm not . . ."

"Right."

"But if I were, I'd be looking for someone like him."

"Ness?"

"What?" Vanessa sniffed and grabbed another tissue.

"He'll be back."

"Oh, sure, someday. Like when Mia and Beck have kids." She rolled her eyes. "Oh my God, could you see it if we were both godparents for the—"

"Stop it. He'll be back. It won't take that long."

"What makes you think that?" Vanessa stopped sniffing.

"Because of the way, I don't know, the way he looked at you when you were dancing the other night at the wedding. Like there was no one else in the room, no one else on the dance floor."

"He was counting on getting lucky, Stef."

"Maybe so, but I think it was more than that. I'm not always right when it comes to guys, but trust me on this one." Steffie polished off the last bite of Mountain Man Fudge. "He'll be back."

Steffie's words came back to Vanessa the next day when she was at the shop and taking delivery of an order of walking shorts, and later that same day when the glass cutter came to measure for replacing the window and the glass counter and shelf. And later still when she walked home that night to her quiet house and took a few frozen lemon cookies from the freezer. He'd called around midnight, apologized for the late hour, and said something about the different time zones, but the connection hadn't been good, and eventually the line went dead.

Didn't that just sum it all up?

She tried to read, and she tried to watch TV. She put her favorite movie into the DVD player and tried to find the humor, but even *Ghostbusters* couldn't keep her focused. Her mind wandered, replaying the moments of the past ten days that she'd spent with Grady. It had all seemed surreal. She'd dated now and then over the past few years, but she hadn't gotten involved with anyone since she moved to St. Dennis. Alternately, she berated herself for having fallen into a relationship with him so easily, and regretting that it had ended before she was ready to let him go.

The rest of the week brought more of the same. She met with her insurance agent, met with Hal and Sue and went over the very short list of items stolen by Edmund Dent. The only difference was that she was now sleeping in the spare bedroom. She'd tried sleeping in her own bed, but even after washing the bed linens, she swore she could still smell traces of his aftershave on the pillows, and that had made for one too many sleepless nights. She needed to be able to function if she were to get her shop organized to reopen as soon as the window was repaired. They were into June already and the foot traffic on Charles Street was picking up with every passing day. Her agent showed her how to calculate the amount of business loss she'd sustained—how much she was losing every day the shop was unable to open—so while she could expect some compensation for the interruption of her business, it wasn't the same as having her shop open and dealing with the public. She loved Bling, her customers loved Bling, and she couldn't wait till she could reopen. She missed the interaction, the fun of helping a customer find that exactly right something that made their face light up. Then, she figured, life would return to normal. All she really wanted was for things to feel normal again.

It was hard not to think that fate had been incredibly and deliberately unkind to her. The simple fact was that she'd met the best guy last. Everything about him had been right, except the timing.

Right guy, wrong time.

Hal sat on the chair in the corner of Maggie's room at the Inn at Sinclair's Point and watched her finish packing.

". . . want to get things settled back there, close that book, so to speak," she was saying. "I don't know why Carl left that ranch to me instead of to his boys. No wonder they resent me." She shook her head. "I have to make that right for them. I don't deserve it and I don't want it."

"Have you told them that?" he asked.

"Oh, yes. I called them on Tuesday morning and told them I'd be back before the weekend. I asked them to set up an appointment for Friday afternoon or Saturday morning with Carl's lawyer so that I could make the arrangements to put it all in their names as soon as possible. They sounded shocked—I think they were afraid I'd sell it out from under them—but by the time we finished our conversation, I think they understood." She closed her suitcase and turned to face him. "I'll be very relieved once that is done. It's been hanging over me like a dust cloud since Carl died."

"And then what?"

"Then . . ." She shrugged. "I'm not sure what I'll do then. I have a couple of options."

"Would one of them be coming back here?"

"I would like that. I'm not going to pretend that I

wouldn't. I think over time, Vanessa and I can smooth things out between us. We may never be as close as some mothers and their daughters, but I think we can do better in the future than we've done in the past. But Beck . . . I don't know that he'd ever be any happier to see my face than he was at the wedding." Maggie shook her head. "I don't know what I was thinking, putting myself in a position that would only alienate him even more. I think he hates me, Hal."

"*Hate's* a strong word," he told her. "It may not be all that bad."

"Even you don't sound as if you really believe that, but I thank you for trying to make me feel better." She grabbed the handle of the suitcase and started to slide it off the bed, but Hal got up and took it from her hands. "And that is the very least I have to thank you for. You are the most amazing man I have ever known, and I've been waiting for a long time to tell you—"

"Now, Maggie, you don't need to feel that you have to apologize."

"It's taken me forever to get up the nerve to say this, so let me have my say." She cleared her throat and fought back tears, but she might never have this chance again, and he had to hear what she had to say. "I don't understand all of what I've done in my life but that's a topic for a different time. But what I do know, what I do understand, is that I've spent my entire life trying to find you again. In every relationship I had, every man I met, I was looking for you. I don't expect you to forgive me—I can't ask that of you after almost forty years—but I want you to know that I have never loved anyone but you. I know how that must sound to you after all this time, but it's the truth. I can't make up for all those years between then and now, but if you'd be my friend, Hal, I'd be grateful until the day I die."

Hal put the suitcase down on the floor.

"Well, now," he said, "I think that's a good place to start. Relationships based on friendship are the best kind. But it's going to be very hard for us to renew our . . . friendship if you're in North Dakota and I'm here in Maryland."

"Well, we can talk on the phone, and there's email . . ."

"I was thinking maybe of something a little more personal."

She stared up at him.

"I was thinking," he continued, "that maybe you should come back to St. Dennis after you get your affairs in order out west. Your family's here, Maggie. You can't repair those relationships from far away."

"Are you sure you'd be all right with that?"

"All right?" He smiled. "I'd be . . . well, I'd be very happy to see where friendship might lead us."

Maggie could barely breathe.

"Okay, then." She nodded. "I'll do that. I'll come back."

He glanced at his watch. "We need to get you to the airport if you're going to make that plane. Sometimes the traffic builds up on that bridge over the Bay and you can sit for hours." He picked up her suitcase. "Got everything?"

"I think so." She looked around the room. "Yes, I have everything."

He opened the door and stepped aside to allow her

to pass first, and walked down the wide stairwell alongside her. He chatted with Hamilton Forbes, the Realtor who'd sold him the house on Cherry Street, who was meeting his ex-wife, the mayor, Christina Pratt, for lunch. Grace Sinclair cornered him and pried the promise of an interview later that day about the arrest of Edmund Dent. Maggie joined him on the steps of the Inn while his car was brought around, and she wondered what all his friends were thinking as she and Hal left the Inn together, her suitcase in his hand.

Don't I wish it were so. She sighed as she got into the passenger side of his car.

"What was that all about?" Hal asked as he got behind the wheel.

"Oh, I was just thinking how nice St. Dennis is."

"Good. Then you will come back."

"I said I would."

They made small talk all the way to Baltimore. When they arrived at the airport, he parked the car and walked her as far as security. As she started to thank him for the ride, he grabbed her by both shoulders and kissed her soundly.

"I've had something to say that I've waited a long time to say, too." He wrapped his arms around her and held her. "I never loved anyone else, either, Maggie. I never loved anyone but you. I ache for all the years we lost, but if we can have a few years to spend together, it might all work out all right."

"How could you even think . . . after all I've done . . ." She broke down.

"Maybe I could have tried harder to find you back then," he told her. "Maybe we both gave up too soon.

All I know is that since you've been here this week, I've felt happier than I have in a long time. Don't stay away, Maggie. Take care of your business, then come back."

"Vanessa gave me the name of a doctor she spoke with here in town. She suggested that I call her for a referral to someone in North Dakota," Maggie told him. "She thought maybe it would help me if I talked to someone."

"Don't ask for a referral. Keep the number, call her—Dr. Campbell—when you come back." He kissed the top of her head. "Maybe we could both go." Then he chuckled. "Maybe we could take Beck and get a group rate . . ."

"Oh, you." She wiped the wet from her face with a tissue. "I need to go . . ."

"You go"—he kissed her one last time—"but come back to me, Maggie. This time, I'll be the one waiting for you."

"I won't let you down, Hal." She headed toward the security checkpoint, then turned and blew him a kiss. "I promise. This time, I won't let you down . . ."

Chapter 20

GRADY sat on a flat outcrop of rock and watched the Madison River rapids swirl and churn below. On the opposite bank, three rafters prepared to put into the river in the early morning light. He hoped they were all well seasoned; not far downriver was some of Montana's most challenging water, the legendary Kitchen Sink and the Greenwave Rapids, where more than one rafter had lost his life.

He'd led this small group of hikers into Bear Trap Canyon the day before, and they'd set up camp in an area where he'd had luck in the past catching trout. So far this morning, none of his charges had ventured out of their tents, but he expected that soon all four would be up and out with their waders to cast their lines and catch their breakfast. Ordinarily, Grady would already have cast off, but today, for reasons he didn't fully understand, he just wasn't in the mood to fish. If that meant he'd have nothing more than an energy bar for breakfast, well, that's what he'd have.

The rafters set off on the river, and he silently wished them luck and safe passage through the treacherous white water.

There was frost on the grass behind him, and from his perch, he watched a curious moose calf pick its way to the shore. Grady wondered where mama was; you rarely saw one without the other this time of year. The baby waded tentatively into the calm waters in this part of the river and took a long drink, then turned and scampered up the bank and disappeared into the meadow that ran behind the rock on which Grady sat.

As the sun was now fully up, Grady returned to the campsite and set about making coffee. The others would be up and about soon enough, and his work-day would begin. He loved this stretch of wilderness and usually looked forward to spending a few days here, but this week, his heart wasn't it in. He found himself looking forward to the half-hour drive back to Bozeman at the end of the day, where he'd drop off his group, so that he could head home.

But once back at his house, Grady was as restless as he'd been while out at Bear Trap Canyon. He un-packed his gear, cleaned up what needed cleaning, and threw what needed washing into the washer. He took a shower and washed off the trail dirt, then heated some frozen soup for his dinner. He tried to get into reading a James Lee Burke novel—it was set in Montana, and featured two of Grady's favorite fic-tional characters—but the drive from Bozeman had taken longer than he'd anticipated and the hour was late, and he just couldn't keep his eyes open. But once in bed, he couldn't sleep. It took him a good hour to figure it out, but he reluctantly had to admit that he was lonely.

He'd gotten used to being alone—which he didn't

mind—but being alone and being lonely were two different things. In a very short period of time, he'd gotten used to being with someone else, and now being *alone* felt lonely.

He rose early the next morning and set out to watch the sun rise over the mountains, a sight that never failed to touch him, but that morning, a cloak of clouds wrapped around the hills and allowed only a tinge of light to edge through. The sunset that evening lit the sky with fire, but it wasn't the same as watching it set on the peaceful Bay from the dock in St. Dennis. By day's end, he had to accept that nothing in his life here felt the same since he returned from Maryland, and he wasn't so much of a fool that he couldn't figure out why.

So what, he asked himself after his third sleepless night in a row, was he doing in Montana, and after he completed the hike he'd committed to for the following week, what reason would he have to stay?

"Hal, I think you'd better start over from the beginning."

The mug Beck held in his right hand wavered, and he placed it on the table carefully. He, Mia, and Vanessa sat around Hal's dining-room table, where Hal had served coffee and brought them up-to-date on the events of the past two weeks in an oh-by-the-way sort of manner.

"This all started the night of the wedding? And no one called me? Our plane didn't take off until almost one in the morning. We could have come back—"

"And that's exactly why we didn't call you. It was your wedding night, Beck. You'd had a glorious wed-

ding and plans for an equally glorious honeymoon."
Vanessa paused. "It was a glorious two weeks, wasn't
it?"

"Oh, yes." Mia sighed. "Totally glorious."

"There you are," Vanessa said. "Besides, Hal was
here. He knew what to do. He handled it."

"Well, actually, Grady handled it, mostly." Hal
looked across the table at Beck. "I hope you don't
mind, but I temporarily made him a part-time officer.
Mostly because I wanted him to be able to carry, and
he didn't have a weapon with him. Since he was
spending so much time with Vanessa—"

"Really?" Mia turned a happy face to her new
sister-in-law. "Do tell."

Vanessa shrugged nonchalantly. "Nothing much to
tell. He was with me when the break-in was discovered, and while we were checking it out his rental car
was damaged. So he offered to stay and watch my
back."

"Is he still here?" Mia turned to Hal eagerly. "Is
Grady still working with you?"

"No, it was just for the one day," Hal explained.
"That's all it took for him to get this guy and take
him down." He smiled at Mia. "The boy is good—
took charge, no nonsense, figured out how to get into
Ness's house and create enough of a distraction that
he could get Dent to turn his back. But once we had
Dent, Grady left for home."

"The same day?" Mia frowned.

"He said he had . . ." Vanessa almost said *a job to
do* but she caught herself in time. She'd given him her
word that she wouldn't be the one to spill the beans
to Mia about his business venture, and so far, she'd

been able to keep that. "Something to do that couldn't wait."

"What, a horse to feed?" Mia made a face.

Vanessa shrugged. "You'll have to ask him."

"So what happened to the accomplice?" Beck asked. "The woman?"

"No charges were brought against her," Hal told him. "Jackie Weston wasn't involved in either the break-in or the damage to Grady's car, and if she hadn't come to me when she did, who knows what might have happened to Vanessa. It would have ended very badly for everyone. As it was, the only person who got hurt was Maggie."

"I don't understand how Maggie got involved in this whole thing in the first place," Beck said.

"She'd stopped by my house to drop off something, and Edmund Dent was already there. He forced her inside at gunpoint . . ." Vanessa told him, "and forced her to call me at the shop and tell me I had to come home, or he'd kill her. Instead, she tried to warn me, told me not to come. I could hear him smacking her around while we were on the phone, so of course, I went—"

"*You let her go?*" Beck turned to Hal.

"Beck, he couldn't have stopped me. I had to go. I didn't want her blood on my hands. Maggie was very brave." Vanessa took a deep breath and looked across the table to her brother. "I learned something really important through all this. She may not have always been much of a mom—let's face it, Maggie'd never have been a contender for Mother of the Year—but she's still my mother. And I guess I . . . I guess I love her." She paused and recalled what she'd said to

Grady. "Sometimes you just have to let go of the past for the sake of the future."

"I'm glad that she was gone before we got back. I don't know that I'm ready to let go, to tell you the truth. I don't know that I want to," Beck said. "Pulling that stunt—showing up at the wedding uninvited . . . I don't know what she was thinking."

"Well, now, I guess she was thinking that she wanted to be there on the most important day of her son's life." Hal spoke up. "Even if she hadn't been there for some others."

When Beck didn't respond, Hal added, "And I expect she'll be coming back once she concludes her business in North Dakota."

"Why would she do that?" Beck asked, his eyes narrowing.

"I suppose because I asked her to."

The room fell silent for a moment. Then Beck said, "Hal, why would you do that? After all she did . . . let's face it, Maggie's never done anything but hurt you. She's hurt all of us, everyone who ever loved her."

"I suspect that people can change if you give them the chance. I'm okay with giving her another chance. Besides, like Vanessa just said, sometimes you have to let go if you want to move on."

Beck shook his head. "She's going to hurt you again. She can't be trusted."

"Well, I guess we'll have to wait and see how it all shakes out." Hal took a sip of his coffee. "Anyone need a refill?"

He looked around the table. When no one spoke up, he turned back to Beck. "I know that this is hard for you, and I'm real sorry for that. But I'm going to ask you to give her a chance. And if you can't do that, at least keep an open mind."

Beck was clearly struggling with his feelings.

"Just keep an open mind," Hal repeated.

Finally, Beck nodded slowly. "Only because you're asking me to."

"That's a start, son." Hal smiled. "That's a start . . ."

Chapter 21

"So you don't think it's too early for the tennis whites and the cute golf clothes?" Vanessa asked Grace Sinclair over coffee at Cuppachino the following morning.

"Not at all, dear," Grace assured her. "My son tells me that the tennis courts at the Inn have been booked solid for the past two or three weeks."

"Great." Vanessa smiled, envisioning the window display she was going to start on as soon as she went into the shop. "Some of the prettiest things just came in to the shop. I can't wait to get them all unpacked and on display."

"When do you think you'll be able to reopen, Vanessa?" Nita asked.

"I'll be open on Friday at the regular time," she said proudly. "The glass has all been replaced and everything cleaned up. It's all as good as new." She paused. "Except for the clothes that had been tossed on the floor. I feel as if they're tainted and I'm having a problem thinking of those things as new merchandise. I was tempted to scrap them but my insurance company would not reimburse me because they really aren't damaged, so I'm having a sale. Everything that touched the floor will be forty percent off when I re-open. I'm calling it my red-carpet sale." She grinned. "Because, of course, the rug in the shop is red."

"Very clever," Nita told her. "And you can count on me to come in. You know I can't miss a sale."

Vanessa drained the coffee from her mug. "I can't wait to get started on those windows. I'll see you ladies later."

She handed her mug to Carlo on her way out the door and crossed the street. Standing in front of her shop, she mentally dressed her mannequins, which, right at that moment, wore white sheets and signs that said WATCH FOR OUR GRAND REOPENING!

And it will be grand, she told herself as she un-locked the door and stepped inside. The boxes of white shirts, skirts, and shorts that had been delivered the day before were piled on the newly replaced counter.

"Maybe an all-white window this time," she mur-mured. "Maybe some white geraniums in white . . . no, maybe silver pots. And something white all bunched on the floor. Not chiffon, I did that for the wedding." She stood and stared at the mannequins. "Maybe I should do Astroturf to look like a golf green . . ." She frowned. "But then the window's not all white." She paused. "Does it have to be all white?"

She sighed, and tried to feel happier at the prospect of reopening Bling. She'd missed her routine, missed the interaction with her customers.

She'd been missing a lot these days, she reminded herself.

She wasn't going to think about Grady today. She'd

decided when she got up on Monday morning that she was not going to dwell on what could have been. And she wasn't going to feel sorry for herself. It had been all right to feel sad—she'd give herself sad—but not *sorry*. And if nothing else, for the first time, she'd had a glimpse of what a good relationship—a *healthy* relationship—between two people who cared about each other could be like. How could she regret that?

That was the one thing he'd given her that no one could take away. She'd never had a relationship that hadn't required her to give more than she had and take far less than what she'd wanted. With Grady, it had all been equal, give-and-take. Him to her and back again. If she were ever to have another relationship—and she wasn't sure that she wanted one—at least she knew what she could rightfully expect.

The delivery truck pulled up in front of the shop and the driver got out, disappeared inside the body of the truck, then walked to the door with boxes piled high.

"Good morning," she called to him after she unlocked the door and held it wide open for him.

"How are you today?" He went past her into the shop. "Where would you like these?"

"How about right there, by the counter. Yes, that's fine, thanks."

"Looks like another beautiful day." He smiled and went back outside. "I have two more for you."

He brought those in and set them on the floor next to the others. "That's it for today. Good luck with your reopening if I don't see you before the end of the week."

"Thanks. I'm looking forward to it." She waved from the counter, then lifted the first of the boxes and placed it on the glass to open it. "Such cute tank tops," she murmured. "I think I'll pair them with those button-down shirts that came in last week."

She set about looking for the box with the shirts, grateful to be busy, happy to be back in her routine. These days, it seemed that Bling was all she had. Funny, she reminded herself, once upon a time—oh, not so very long ago—the shop was all she wanted, all that mattered to her.

At first, she didn't hear the knock on the glass panel of the door. When the knock came louder, she responded, thinking it was Mitch, the mailman, who'd gotten into the habit of bringing in her mail rather than stuffing it through the slot, on instructions, no doubt, from his wife, the town busybody.

"Come on in, Mitch," she called from the counter where she was going through boxes. *Where did I put those cotton shirts . . . ?*

The bell over the door jingled, and she heard it close softly.

"Sorry, Mitch. I was distracted." She turned from the window and started toward the door.

"Mitch? Who's Mitch?"

"Oh." She stopped in her tracks. "Oh."

"Mind if I come in?" Grady didn't wait for her response. "Who's Mitch?" he repeated.

"The mailman."

"Hey, it looks great in here. All cleaned up, the displays all nice and tidy again." He walked over to the repaired window. "It looks great. The glass guy did a good job."

"Thanks." She forced her hands to hold on to each other so that she wouldn't reach out for him. She wasn't sure why he was there, and didn't want to make a fool out of herself.

"When do you think you'll be able to reopen?" He strolled around to the counter.

"I'll be open on Friday."

"It looks like you could open tomorrow."

"If I had the window dressing finished, I probably could. I've gotten in most of the merchandise I ordered for the summer, so I'm pretty much ready to go."

"Good for you, Ness. I'm really happy for you. I know how much this place means to you."

"Thank you." Her head was spinning. "Ah . . . did I ever thank you for saving my life?"

"I don't remember." He leaned back against the counter. "You could thank me now."

"Thank you for everything. For saving my life and Maggie's life."

"It was my pleasure."

She nodded and tried to think of something else to say. Finally, she asked, "How was your camping thing?"

"It was all right. I took four guys up to Bear Trap Canyon for a couple of days. The weather was better than they'd forecast, so it wasn't quite as cold as it could have been."

"So did you see any of those cool things you told me about?"

"What cool things?" He frowned.

"You said that sometimes when you were hiking

alone, you'd see really cool things but didn't have anyone to share them with."

"Well, I saw a baby moose and a golden eagle," he told her, "but I didn't really have anyone to share those with."

"You just said you had four people with you."

"It's not the same as having someone to share the really good moments with, Ness. It wasn't like having you with me." He reached for her hand and pulled her to him slowly. "I missed you. I started missing you as soon as I left. I was sitting in the plane, waiting for it to take off, wishing we'd have some kind of mechanical failure so that my flight wouldn't take off until the next day, so I could come back here for just one more night." He smiled. "A three-nighter, I guess that would have been."

She looked up at him, barely able to believe what she was hearing.

"I took my group out on the trail, and I came back home and I wondered what I was doing there when everything that made me smile was here in St. Dennis. So I had to take the chance, come back, and see if you missed me, too."

"You could have called." She smiled. "I would have told you."

"The service up there isn't dependable." He pulled her closer. "And besides, if we were on the phone, I wouldn't be able to do this . . ."

He kissed her mouth and her chin and then he kissed her mouth again.

"I missed you, too," she told him. "I wasn't sure if I'd ever see you again."

"Look, I don't know what this is between us. I just

know that it's been good enough that I'm not ready to see it end. I don't know that I ever will be. I want to come back and see how it works out. That is, if you feel the same way, if you're willing to see where it goes."

She nodded. "More than willing. But what about your business?"

"I have several trips already lined up for the summer. July, August, even into September, are big hiking and camping months out there. I can continue to do that. I'll just fly back and forth. It isn't that big a deal to me. I flew all over the country when I was with the Bureau. This is actually less travel than that was."

"But your house . . ."

"I've been giving a lot of thought to that. The renovations that Missy began are finished, and that was my goal—to finish what she started. While I was home I ran into a neighbor who was telling me that his son and daughter-in-law were looking for a property to use as a camp to teach riding to kids with special needs. I'm going to meet with them before I take my next trail group out, which will be in about two weeks. If they like the facilities, they can rent from me or buy it outright, but I think that would be the best use of the property."

"Well, you know I have to ask: What about the money you found in the bookcase?"

"I'm having more of a problem with that," he admitted. "I'm going to have to talk to my old boss. Is it legally mine? As Missy's husband, I'm assuming it is. But if it was gained by illegal means, what then?"

"Are you serious?" She raised an eyebrow. "You're

seriously going to ask someone at the FBI if you can keep it?"

"Here's the thing. I don't want it." He raised a hand when she started to speak. "Yeah, I know it's a lot of money. But it's blood money, as far as I'm concerned. It's money my brother paid my wife to keep silent about the fact that she knew he killed my cousin Dylan. It's money that eventually led Luther Blue to kill her."

"When you put it in those terms . . ." She weighed what he'd said. "Still, it's almost half a million dollars."

"Enough to fund that camp for kids with special needs," he said. "Enough to start a foundation that would keep it running for a while. At least it would go to some good use."

She nodded. "Why don't you skip the part where you talk to the FBI about it? What would they do with it? Let it sit in a box somewhere? Buy information with it?"

Grady laughed. "I feel I can trust John Mancini to steer me in the right direction." He ran his hands up her arms. "So, you think you could fit in a little shopping this afternoon?"

Vanessa frowned. "Shopping? What do you need to shop for?"

"Not for me, for you." He glanced down at her feet even while he kissed her neck. "I'm guessing a size, what, seven and a half? Eight?"

"We're going to shop for shoes?" Her eyebrows rose.

"Not shoes," he corrected her. "Hiking boots . . ."

*   *   *

They were, she suspected, the ugliest things she'd ever had on her feet, but she was okay with them, because they meant that she and Grady would be spending the entire day together. It meant that he wanted to share something with her that was important to him.

She still could barely believe he'd come back. She'd pinched herself twenty times between yesterday afternoon and this morning, when he woke her at four—after a very few hours of sleep—and made her eat a real breakfast before they left the house.

"Tell me again where we're going?" she asked sleepily as they walked to his rented Jeep.

"Bull Run Mountain in Virginia," he told her. "I heard it was a nice hike. We'll start with a short walk, an easy walk, so you can see if you like it."

"I like to walk. I walk up to Charles Street and back every day," she reminded him. "And I don't have to wear ugly shoes to do it."

He laughed. "You'll be very happy to have those 'ugly shoes' when you start up the mountain."

"I don't know why I couldn't have worn my running shoes." She got into the passenger seat and closed the door.

"Because you're not running. You're hiking. And you'd have been wise to wear them around the house last night to get your feet accustomed to them."

"We didn't do much walking around the house last night. As a matter of fact, as I recall, we almost didn't have dinner."

"Good point."

"So you were saying that you read somewhere that this is a nice hike." She settled into the seat and closed her eyes. "What constitutes a 'nice' hike?"

"It's supposed to have some interesting trails. Most of the trails are relatively easy. The Battle of Thoroughfare Gap was fought there during the Civil War."

"Who won?" she asked.

"I believe the Confederates won that round."

"How far is it?"

"Maybe another hour, hour and a half from here."

"No, I meant, how long is the hike?"

"Oh, you mean, how long are the trails, start to finish?"

She nodded.

"Not long at all. I think I read that the main loop is only about four and a half miles. But there are other sights to see off the main loop. If you took all those trails, too, it runs about seven miles, I think."

"Seven miles? In one day?" She wrinkled her nose and Grady laughed again.

"We don't have to do all seven," he assured her. "We don't even have to do the entire four. We can just walk until you feel tired, but I did hear that there are spectacular views from the top of the ridge."

"Don't tell me how far it is from the car to there, okay? We'll let it be a surprise." She wiggled her toes inside her new hiking boots and hoped they'd feel as comfortable when they finished as they did right at that moment.

No such luck.

The parking lot was at the end of a road, and the trail picked up to the right and across some old railroad tracks. There was a kiosk with some liability waivers to sign and some trail maps. They signed the forms and Grady studied the map, then turned to Vanessa and asked, "Ready?"

"Sure." She looked around the area, which was nicely wooded and smelled fresh and green and didn't appear to be too bad.

They walked along the trail through peaceful woodlands. At one point, Grady stopped and said, "There's an old cemetery off that way. How about we check it out? Or would you rather do that on the way back?"

"On the way back," she answered, a bit too quickly. She wasn't sure how far four and a half miles would be and the trails appeared to be a bit rustic, with some fallen trees to walk over or around.

The trail ran along streams where there were small waterfalls, and while the man-made bridges were deteriorated, there were rocks to follow across the water. It was beautiful and quiet, but the trails were beginning to lead upward. After a particularly steep ascent, Vanessa was finding it harder and harder to catch her breath.

"Are you all right?" Grady asked from time to time, and she'd nod and say, "Yes. I'm fine. Sure."

But by the time they reached the outcrop of rocks that marked the ridge, she was panting and couldn't wait to sit.

"And my feet hurt," she told Grady.

"Well, here, sit down and rest for a few minutes and let's enjoy this spectacular view." She started to sit and he said, "Wait."

He inspected the rock and the terrain off to both sides.

"What?" She frowned.

"I just wanted to make sure there were no rattle-snakes sunning themselves where you were about to plant your butt."

He sat and held a hand up to her to help her down.

"That was your idea of a joke, I hope. Though it wasn't really very funny . . ."

"No." He shook his head and opened his back-pack. "No joke. I don't make jokes about poisonous snakes."

"You mean, there really are rattlesnakes around here?" She cast dubious glances at the ground.

"Sure. You're in the woods." He looked up and saw her uncertainty. "It's okay. I checked. It's safe."

She sat but looked uncomfortable.

"So how do you feel?" he asked.

"Seriously?" She looked up at him and he nodded. "I'm tired, I'm hungry, thirsty, and I do not like snakes."

"Other than that, what do you think of the view?"

"It's beautiful," she admitted.

She looked out across a green valley. Overhead a hawk circled, and in the trees somewhere behind them, a bird was singing. "I do understand why people like to do this. Other people, though, not neces-sarily me."

He took off his backpack, opened it, and handed her a bottle of water.

"Don't drink it too quickly," he warned. "Just sip it."

She did her best not to chug it. It was lukewarm but tasted wonderful. Amazing how good water can taste when you are truly thirsty.

"And look, Ness." He pointed off to her right and

grabbed her hand. "That's a bald eagle. Look at the wingspread . . ."

"Oh." She stared at the huge bird that had soared up from below the rocks. "I've never seen one that close. Come to think of it, I don't think I've ever seen one at all. It's . . . it's breathtaking."

They watched it rise, then glide across the valley.

"That was a moment." She smiled up at him. "One I will remember for a long time."

"Good." He squeezed her hand. "Now, are you ready for lunch?"

"Oh my God, I thought you'd never ask." She leaned back on her elbows and held her face up to the sun.

"Here you go." He put something in her hand.

She opened her eyes and looked down.

"Normally, I'd be the last person to turn down a candy bar," she told him, "but I'm starving and I need real food, so I hope you have something fabulous in that backpack of yours."

"It's not a candy bar, it's an energy bar. And it *is* lunch."

"This"—she held up the wrapped bar—"is *lunch*? I walked for two hours and this is all I get?"

He nodded calmly.

"See all the good stuff it has in it?" He turned the bar over and pointed to the list of ingredients but she appeared not to notice. He shrugged, then un-wrapped his bar, took a bite, and began to chew. "It's really good. Honest. I take them out on the trail with me all the time."

"Why don't we have real food?"

"Because it's easier, more convenient, and certainly

lighter in weight. You're getting all that your body needs between the nutrition in the bar and the water."

She continued to stare at him.

Finally she said, "Grady, do you remember when we were making cookies at my house before the wedding?"

"Sure."

"And you said that Mia didn't know you had a job and if I promised not to tell her that you'd buy my silence—your words—with anything I wanted?"

"Right."

"Well, I never told her, so the offer is still good. I mean, it's still open, right?"

"Uh-huh." He took another bite. If he was worried about where this was leading, it didn't show.

"And it was *anything* I wanted, right?"

"That was the deal."

"Here." She held out her energy bar. "You're going to need it."

"Why?" He frowned and took the last bite of his.

"Because I know what I want."

"I always pay up. Go ahead. What is it?"

"I want you to carry me down off this damned mountain and buy me a burger."

Diary—

What a week this has been! First, Harbor Fest was a rousing success! There were so many people pouring into town that Chief Beck had to set out some hastily prepared signs directing people away from the docks and down to the park. The mayor said if this keeps up all summer, we're going to need to hire more police just to direct traffic. Daniel's thinking about investing in a van to use as a shuttle between the Inn and the town so that his guests don't have to drive their cars to shop or visit the historic sites where they'd have to fight to park.

Who'd have thought that one day those old houses and churches up on the square would be considered "historic"? Heh.

I must say there are some happy merchants on Charles Street, though. Lots of visitors mean lots of shoppers and diners.

Now this is the big news, and personally gratifying to me: Grady Shields is back in St. Dennis! I saw him in Cuppachino on Friday where he was picking up lunch to take to Vanessa at Bling because she was too busy to leave the shop. Isn't that sweet? I asked him if he was just visiting for the weekend and he said he thought he'd be staying longer than that. Then he said he wanted to come down to the paper later to take out an ad for his wilderness guide services because he's thinking of offering some hiking and camping tours in the Appalachians.

Well, you can imagine what was going through my mind at that moment!

Yes, of course, I secretly rejoiced that I'd remembered the right words in the right sequence and that I did find all the proper herbs. I'd have felt simply terrible if I'd turned that handsome young man into a toad.

Of course, it's possible that this extremely promising development had nothing to do with me . . . that Vanessa and Grady would have gotten back together on their own, and that the little ritual in which I'd engaged on their behalf was really nothing, after all, but words whispered while burning some smelly old vegetation.

I, however, like to think that the old girl still has it.

—Grace

Read on for a preview of
the next novel in the Chesapeake Diaries series
by Mariah Stewart

Home Again

AT the precise moment Dallas MacGregor was picking up her son, Cody, from school, the home video starring her soon-to-be-ex-husband and two of his female production assistants had already been uploaded to the Internet. By the time she arrived at her gated Hollywood Hills home—she'd stopped once on the way from the set of her latest movie promo shoot to pick up dinner—the five-thousandth viewing had already been downloaded.

The phone was on overdrive when she walked into her kitchen.

"Miss MacGregor, you have many messages. Two from your aunt Beryl." Elena, her housekeeper, cast a wary glance at Cody and handed her employer a stack of pink slips. "Something about Mr. Emilio . . ."

"Would you mind answering that?" Dallas slid the heavy paper bag onto the counter. "And why are you still here? I thought you had to leave by four?"

"Yes, miss, I . . ." Elena lifted the receiver. "Miss MacGregor's . . . oh, hello, Miss Townsend. Yes, she's home now, she just arrived. Yes, I gave her the message but . . . of course, Miss Townsend . . ."

Elena held the phone out to Dallas.

"It's your great-aunt," she whispered.

"I figured that out." Dallas smiled and took the cordless receiver from Elena. "Hello, Aunt Berry. I was just thinking about . . ."

"Dallas." Her aunt cut her off sharply. "What the hell is going on out there?"

"Not much." Dallas paused. "What's supposed to be going on?"

"That numbskull you were married to." Berry's breath came in ragged puffs.

She was obviously in a lather over something. Not unusual, Dallas thought. At eighty-one, it didn't take much to rile her aunt these days.

"What's he done now?" Dallas began emptying the bag, lining up the contents on the counter.

"Not *what* as much as *who*." Berry was becoming increasingly agitated.

"Mommy." Cody tugged at her sleeve. "Why are all those cars out there?"

"Berry, hold on for just a moment, please." Dallas glanced out the side window. There were cars lined up on the other side of the fence, cars that had not been there five minutes ago when they pulled through the gates. It wasn't especially unusual for paparazzi to follow her home, but she hadn't noticed any cars following her today. She raised the blinds just a little, and saw more cars pulling up even as she watched.

"I don't know, Cody. Maybe the studio put out something about Mommy's new movie. Maybe we should turn on the television and see."

"No!" Elena and Berry both shouted at the same time.

"What?" Dallas frowned and turned to her housekeeper, who stood behind Cody. She pointed to the child, then raised her index finger to her lips, their silent code for *not in front of Cody*.

"Berry, why don't you tell me . . . ?"

"Are you saying you don't know? Seriously?"

"Know what?"

"That idiot ex of yours . . ."

"Not ex yet, but soon, please God . . ." Dallas muttered. "And it's long been established that he's an idiot."

". . . managed to get himself filmed doing . . . all sorts of things that you will not want Cody to see . . ." Berry was almost gasping. ". . . with more than one person. It was disgusting. Perverted."

"You mean . . ." Dallas's knees went weak and she sat in the chair that Elena wisely pulled out for her.

"Yes. A sex tape. Not one, but *two* young women. I was shocked. Appalled!"

"Wait! You actually *saw* it?"

"Three times!" Dallas could almost see Berry fanning herself. "It was vile, just vile! You know, Dallas, that I never liked that man. I told you when you first brought him home that I . . ."

"Berry, where did you see this?"

"On my computer. There was a link to a site . . ."

"Hold on for a moment, Berry." Dallas put her hand over the mouthpiece and turned to Elena. "Would you mind cutting up an apple for Cody? Cody, go wash your hands so you can have your snack."

After her son left the room, Dallas took the phone outside and sat at one of the tables around the pool.

"Dear God, Berry, let me get this straight. Emilio

made a sex tape and it was put on the Internet? Is that what you're telling me?"

"Yes, and not just any sex tape. This one had . . ."

"Wait a minute, they allowed you to download the whole thing?" ·

"No, no, not all of it, just a little bit. You had to pay if you want to see the whole thing."

"And you did? You paid to watch . . ." Dallas didn't know whether to laugh or cry. The thought of her elderly aunt watching Emilio and his latest conquests burning up the sheets was horrifying and crazy funny at the same time. "Wait—did you say *three times?*"

"Yes, and it was . . ."

"Berry, why did you watch it three times?"

"Well," Berry sniffed. "I had to make sure it was really him."

The rest of the evening went downhill from there.

Dallas made every attempt to remain calm lest Cody pick up on the fact that she was almost blind with anger at the man she'd been married to for seven years.

Seven years, she repeated to herself. Seven years out of my life, wasted on that reprobate. The only good thing to come out of those years was Cody— and Dallas had to admit that she'd have weathered a lifetime of Emilio's amorous flings and general foolishness if she'd had to in order to have her son. When she filed for divorce three months ago, following the latest in Emilio's long line of infidelities, he hadn't even bothered to beg her to reconsider: they'd done that dance so often over the years that even he was tired of it.

She managed to have a normal evening with Cody and ignored the cars that parked beyond their protective fence. They had a nice dinner and watched a video together, then Cody had his bath and Dallas read a bedtime story before she tucked him in and turned off the light.

It wasn't until she went back downstairs, alone, that she permitted herself to fall apart.

There was no love lost between her and Emilio. She'd long since accepted the fact that he'd married her strictly to further his own career. For a time, she'd bought into that, insisting that her husband be signed to direct her movies, and for a time, she'd been blind to his affairs. Lately it had occurred to her that she well might be the last person in the entire state of California to catch on to Emilio's faithlessness.

For the past five years, she and Emilio battled over the same ground, over and over until Dallas no longer cared who he slept with, as long as it wasn't her. Looking back now, she realized she should have left him the first time he'd cheated on her, when the tabloids had leaked those photos of Emilio frolicking with an up-and-coming Latino actress on a sunny, sandy beach in Guatemala when he'd told her he was going to Cannes, but it had been so much easier to stay than to leave. There was Cody to consider: Emilio may have been a cheating jerk, but he did seem to love his son. Besides, Dallas's schedule had been so hectic for the past three years that she'd barely had time to read the tabloids. She'd had the blessing—or the curse—of having had parts offered to her in several movies, wonderful parts that she'd really wanted to play, so she'd signed for all of them, and had gone from one set right onto the next, leaving her time for nothing and no one other than her son. It had only been recently that Dallas admitted to herself that she'd been deliberately overworking herself to avoid having to deal with her home situation.

Well, avoid no more, she told herself as she dialed her attorney's number. This time, Emilio had gone too far. When the call went directly to voicemail, Dallas left the message that she wanted her attorney to do whatever she had to do to speed up the divorce.

"And oh," she'd added, "we need to talk about that custody arrangement we'd worked out . . ."

While she waited for the return call, she logged onto the computer in her home office. She searched the web for what she was looking for. The link to the video appeared almost instantaneously, along with a running tally of how many times the video had been watched. Her stomach churning, she clicked on the link and was asked first to confirm that she was over eighteen, then for her credit card number.

"Great," she muttered. "For the low, low price of nineteen ninety-five, I can watch my husband . . . that is, my almost ex-husband, perform daring feats with his production assistants."

The video began abruptly—"What, no music?"—and while the lighting could have been better, there was no question who was the filling in the middle of that particular sandwich. As difficult as it was to watch, she forced herself to sit through it, commenting to herself from time to time ("Emilio, Emilio, didn't anyone ever tell you to always keep your best side to the camera? And, babe, that is decidedly *not* your best side.").

When the phone rang before it was over, Dallas turned off her computer and answered the call.

"Hey, Dallas, it's Norma."

"Thanks for getting back to me right away." Dallas leaned back in her chair and exhaled. Just hearing Norma's always cool and even voice relaxed her.

"I just got in and I was going to call you as soon as I kicked off my shoes." Norma was not only Dallas's attorney, she was also her friend.

"So you heard . . ."

"Is there anyone in this town who has not? So sorry, Dallas. We knew he was a colossal shithead, but this latest stunt even beats his own personal best." Before Dallas could respond, Norma said, "So we're going to want to see if we can move the divorce along a little faster and we'll file a motion to revise those custody arrangements we'd previously agreed to."

"You read my mind."

"I'll file first thing in the morning. If nothing else, I think we should ask for sole custody for a period of at least six months, given the circumstances, which of course we'll spell out for the judge in very specific terms."

"Would it help to know that that little forty-two minute production was filmed in his house?"

"Really?" Norma made a "huh" sound. "Are you positive?"

"I picked out that furniture," Dallas replied. "Along with the carpets and the tile in the bath and the towels that were dropped around the hot tub."

"That was really stupid on his part. Now you can say you don't want Emilio to have unsupervised custody because you don't know who will be in the house or what they'll be doing. Or who might be filming it." Norma paused. "How are you doing?"

"On the one hand, I feel devastated. Humiliated. Nauseated. On the other, I feel like calling every reporter who chastised me for being so mean and unforgiving to poor Emilio when our divorce was announced and yelling, '*See? I told you he was a jerk!*'"

"Anyone you want me to call for you?"

"No. I'm not making any statements to anyone. This is strictly a 'no comment' situation if ever there was one."

"You know you can always refer people to me."

"I may have Elena start doing that tomorrow. Thanks."

"How did Cody react?"

"He hasn't. He doesn't know what's going on."

"You didn't tell him?"

"Of course not. Why would I tell him about something like that?"

"Do you really think you can keep him from finding out? Isn't he in school?"

"He just turned six. He's only in kindergarten." Dallas frowned. "How many of the kids in his class do you think caught Emilio's act?"

"They could hear their parents talking, they could see the story on TV. It's going to make the news, Dallas."

"I don't think it's going to be a problem." Dallas bit a fingernail. "At least, I hope it won't be. But if he hears about it, I'll have to tell him . . . something."

"Well, good luck with that. In the meantime, if you

think of anything else I can do for you, give me a call." Norma's calls always ended the same way, with the same closing sentence. She never bothered to wait until Dallas said good-bye. She just hung up.

What, Dallas wondered, would she tell Cody, if he should hear something?

She didn't have long to wait to find out. When she arrived at school the following afternoon, the Cody who got into the car was a very different child from the one she'd dropped off earlier that morning.

"How was school, buddy?" she asked when he got into the car.

He looked out the window and muttered something.

"What did you say?" She turned in her seat to face him.

"I didn't say anything."

"Well, how *was* school?"

He shook his head but did not look at her.

Uh-oh, she thought as she drove from the curb. *This doesn't bode well . . .*

"So what did you do today?" she asked.

"I don't want to talk."

"Why not, baby?"

"Because I don't and I'm not a baby," he yelled. He still hadn't looked at her.

Oh, God. Her hands began to shake and she clutched the wheel in an effort to make them stop.

She did not try to engage him in conversation the rest of the way home, and once they arrived, she drove in through the service entrance at the back of the property.

"Those cars out front, they're all there because . . ." Cody said accusingly. "Because . . ."

It was then that Dallas realized he was crying. She stopped the car and turned off the ignition, then got out and opened his door. She unbuckled his seat belt but he made no move toward her.

"Cody, what happened today at school?" When he didn't respond, she asked, "Does it have something to do with your dad?"

"They said he did things . . . with other ladies. Justin said his dad saw it on the computer and he heard his dad tell his mom." Huge, fat drops ran down Cody's face and Dallas's heart began to break in half.

"Justin's daddy said my daddy was a very, very bad man."

Dallas had never felt so helpless in her life. She got into the backseat and rubbed Cody's back, then coaxed him into her arms. How could she possibly explain this to her son?

"I'm never going back to school, Mommy. Not ever. Nobody can make me." He hiccupped loudly. "Not even you."

"All right, sweetie." Silently cursing Emilio for his stupidity and his carelessness, Dallas held her son tight and let him cry it out. "It's going to be all right. . . ."

But even as she promised, Dallas wondered if, for Cody, anything would ever be right again.